3800 19 0053 ✔ **KT-151-811**

HIGH LIFE HIGHLAND

A Precious Gift

HIGHLAND
LIBRARIES

WITHDRAWN

Also by Rosie Goodwin

The Bad Apple
No One's Girl
Dancing Till Midnight
Tilly Trotter's Legacy
Moonlight and Ashes
The Mallen Secret
Forsaken
The Sand Dancer
Yesterday's Shadows
The Boy from Nowhere
A Rose Among Thorns

The Lost Soul
The Ribbon Weaver
A Band of Steel
Whispers
The Misfit
The Empty Cradle
Home Front Girls
A Mother's Shame
The Soldier's Daughter
The Mill Girl
The Maid's Courage

The Claire McMullen Series
Our Little Secret
Crying Shame

Dilly's Story Series
Dilly's Sacrifice
Dilly's Lass
Dilly's Hope

The Days of The Week Collection
Mothering Sunday
The Little Angel
A Mother's Grace
The Blessed Child
A Maiden's Voyage

Rosie GOODWIN
A Precious Gift

HIGH LIFE HIGHLAND LIBRARIES	
38001900538566	
BERTRAMS	03/02/2020
SAG	£7.99
AF	

ZAFFRE

First published in Great Britain in 2019
This edition published in 2020 by
ZAFFRE
80–81 Wimpole St, London W1G 9RE

Copyright © Rosie Goodwin, 2020

All rights reserved.
No part of this publication may be reproduced,
stored or transmitted in any form by any means, electronic,
mechanical, photocopying or otherwise, without the
prior written permission of the publisher.

The right of Rosie Goodwin to be identified as Author of this
work has been asserted by her in accordance with the
Copyright, Designs and Patents Act, 1988.

This is a work of fiction. Names, places, events and
incidents are either the products of the author's
imagination or used fictitiously. Any resemblance to
actual persons, living or dead, or actual
events is purely coincidental.

A CIP catalogue record for this book is
available from the British Library.

ISBN: 978–1–78576–760–9

Also available as an ebook

1 3 5 7 9 10 8 6 4 2

Typeset by Palimpsest Book Production Limited, Falkirk, Stirlingshire
Printed and bound in Great Britain by Clays Ltd, Elcograf S.p.A.

MIX
Paper from
responsible sources
FSC® C018072

Zaffre is an imprint of Bonnier Books UK
www.bonnierbooks.co.uk

Happy Memories
of
Pauline Lydia Wilson

18th September 1942 – 31st December 2018

A very loving wife to the late Tony,
mother, sister, aunty and friend to many.
On earth you were a little star and
now you are shining brightly in heaven.
Rest in peace beyond the open door
until we all meet again, dear friend.

Friday's child is loving and giving

Prologue

'Miss Holly, the master and the mistress said I was to tell you that you're wanted in the drawing room the second you came in.'

Holly Farthing frowned as she handed her hat and coat to Ivy, the maid. She nodded. 'Thank you, Ivy.'

After quickly tidying her hair in the mirror in the hallway and smoothing her skirt, she approached the drawing room, wondering what it could be that they wanted. Her grandfather rarely sent for her and when he did it usually meant trouble, which was why she had learned to keep out of his way as much as possible.

Taking a deep breath, she entered the room to find her mother standing at the window, wringing her hands, a sure sign that something was amiss. Her grandfather was sitting in a wing chair at the side of a roaring fire and the second he set eyes on her, his lips set in a grim line. He was a tall man with a rigid posture who, although advanced in years, was still handsome, boasting a full head of steel-grey hair, a thick beard and piercing blue eyes. Holly briefly wondered why he seemed to dislike her so. She and her mother had lived with him since her mother had been widowed when Holly was just a baby and she could never remember him

1

saying so much as one kind word to her. As a child it had troubled her greatly but now, at eighteen years old, she had become accustomed to his surly ways.

'Ivy told me you wished to see me?'

'Yes, dear. Your grandfather has something he must tell you. Won't you sit down?' Her mother gestured to a chair identical to the one her grandfather favoured on the other side of the fireplace, and Holly perched on the edge of it, folding her hands primly in her lap.

For a second the old man narrowed his piercing blue eyes and stared at her before beginning, 'The thing is, you're eighteen years old now, so I've been thinking it's high time you were married. I've kept you an' your mother for long enough.'

Holly's deep blue eyes stretched wide as she stared back at him; she was so shocked that for a moment she was speechless.

'M-married?' she stuttered eventually. 'And do you have someone in mind, Grandfather?'

'As it happens I do, an' you'll meet him tonight. He owns a big hat factory in Atherstone and he's recently widowed with three young children who need a mother. I've invited him to dinner.'

Colour flooded into Holly's cheeks as she stared steadily back at him. 'And may I know the gentleman's name?'

'Dolby, Walter Dolby. That's all you need to know for now, except that you'll be set up for life with him; he ain't short of a bob or two. So just make sure you mind your manners when he arrives and we'll take it from there.'

Holly opened her mouth to protest but clamped it shut again as her mother gave her a warning glance.

'Will that be all?' She stood up, her straight back and rigid, her stance an indication of how angry and upset she was. It wasn't lost on her grandfather and he leaned forward in his chair, his hands tightly gripping the arms.

'Don't look at me like that, girl,' he barked, making Holly's mother visibly start. 'There's many a man would have seen both you an' your mother out on the streets, but I've kept you fed and clothed with a roof over your head for all these years.'

Holly merely inclined her head and, turning, left the room, closing the door softly behind her. In the hallway she almost collided with Ivy, who had clearly been listening at the door. Quickly straightening her mop cap, which was askew, the girl gave her a guilty smile and stepped aside. Normally Holly would have found it funny but today she was so angry and upset that she couldn't even raise a smile. Life as she had known it was about to change forever, and it was completely out of her control. Brushing past her, she stalked to the stairs without giving Ivy so much as a second glance. She was halfway up when the drawing room door opened again and her mother chased after her.

'I'll talk to you in a minute,' she hissed up the stairs. 'He's going back to the mill shortly and then we'll be able to talk in private.'

Holly nodded and hurried on her way, too shocked to even answer. Once in the privacy of her room she let out a sigh and flopped down onto the side of her bed.

Married! Her grandfather wanted her to be married, and worse still to someone she had never even met. Rising, she began to pace the floor. As soon as she heard the front door

3

slam, she peeped from the window and watched her grandfather climb into the coach that the groom had fetched from the stables at the back of the house and leave for the mill he owned in Attleborough. Seconds later a tap came on her bedroom door and her mother appeared looking pale and terribly upset.

'Oh, darling, I'm so sorry,' she muttered, rushing over to Holly and wrapping her arms about her slim figure. 'I had no idea he had this in mind until he told me this morning.'

Holly wriggled free of the embrace and resumed her pacing. 'Well, you know the old saying, you can lead a horse to water but you can't make it drink,' she spat, with a toss of her head.

Her mother chewed on her lip as she watched her precious girl marching up and down as if she was trying to wear a hole in the carpet.

'P-perhaps Walter will be nice?' she suggested softly, and Holly snorted in disgust.

'Nice! Is that a good enough reason to marry someone you don't know, just because they're nice? It sounds to me like this Mr Dolby is merely looking for a replacement mother for his children, but I'll tell you now, it won't be me! When and if I ever marry it will be because I love the person, not because Grandfather has ordered it!'

'Oh, darling, I'm so sorry.' Her mother was openly crying now and Holly's mood softened slightly. She'd lost count of the times she'd seen her grandfather make her mother cry with his harsh words and often wondered why she allowed him to be so hard on her. It was as if he had some sort of a hold over her and she was afraid of him.

'Look . . . I'll go through with this farce and meet him for your sake,' Holly reluctantly agreed. 'But I warn you, if I don't like him, nothing will induce me to see him again, let alone marry him!'

Her mother nodded helplessly. 'In that case we must look in your wardrobe and decide what you should wear. You'll want to look your best.'

'I will not!' Holly disagreed with a glare. 'Why should I dress myself up like a dog's dinner for a stranger? He'll take me as I am or lump it!'

'All right, dear, whatever you say.' Afraid to say another word, her mother turned and quietly scuttled from the room like a frightened mouse. Crossing to the cheval mirror that stood to one side of the four-poster bed, Holly stared at her reflection. A serious young woman with unruly long, blonde curly hair and periwinkle-blue eyes that were fringed with thick, fair lashes stared solemnly back at her. It was almost as if she was staring at a younger version of her mother, for they had the same fair hair and eyes. Holly was trying to see herself as Walter Dolby might see her and she supposed that she was reasonably attractive, although she would never term herself as beautiful. She was slightly too tall and slender for a girl and while her complexion was clear she considered her mouth to be a little too wide and her nose too snub. Yet another tap on the door interrupted her thoughts and Ivy appeared, looking worried.

'I just thought I'd pop up and check you're all right,' she said cautiously. Holly usually enjoyed her chats with Ivy, and because she had been tutored at home and so never mixed much with people her own age, the maid was the closest thing to a friend Holly had ever had. They were complete opposites in looks for Ivy was short and inclined to be skinny with mousy straight hair and grey eyes, but what she lacked in looks she more than made up for in personality. She often had Holly roaring with laughter as she spoke of her family. She came from a large family – eleven in all – and when she had first started working at the house as a maid at the age of fourteen, she declared she felt as if she had died and gone to heaven. She was paid a pittance and was often expected to work all the hours God sent, but despite that, for the first time in her life she had a room all to herself and regular meals, so she considered herself very lucky.

'We're all crammed into a tiny cottage, two-up, two-down in the courtyards in Abbey Street,' she had once told Holly bitterly. 'Crammed in like sardines in a bloody tin, we are.' She had flushed then and apologised for swearing, much to Holly's amusement. She usually provided a breath of fresh air in her grandfather's rather formal household, but today Holly wasn't in the mood to speak to anyone.

'Why wouldn't I be?' Holly instantly felt guilty for snapping. None of this was Ivy's fault after all. She sighed. 'Sorry, Ivy, I take it you heard what was said, then?'

Ivy nodded vigorously, setting her mop cap dancing as if it had a life of its own. 'I couldn't help it, I were polishin' the hall table an' I just want to tell yer I think it's bloody awful what yer gran'- father is proposin'.'

Holly shrugged. 'Aw well, there's nothing for it but to meet the chap, I suppose, but don't get worrying. Before I've even met him I can tell you I have no intention of marrying him, whether it upsets Grandfather or not.'

Ivy gave her a smile, then, glancing at the door, she told her, 'I'd best get on. I've just been told to lay the table in the dinin' room wi' all the best silver an' china. Poor old Cook is runnin' round like a headless chicken tryin' to get everythin' ready an' the mood she's in I don't want to go upsettin' her.'

'It's all right, you get on, I'm fine,' Holly assured her, and once the girl had gone she lifted a book and tried to read. Unfortunately her head was so full of meeting Mr Dolby that all the words kept blurring into one, so eventually she gave up and went to sit by the window. It looked set to be a very long day, and an even longer night.

Early that evening the first snow began to flutter down. It was no surprise; they had been expecting it for the last week but Holly hoped that it might put Mr Dolby off.

At seven o'clock precisely she went downstairs to find her mother and grandfather in the drawing room.

'Is that the best you could find to put on?' her grandfather snapped, as he stared at the plain grey dress she was wearing. 'And couldn't you have done something a little bit more elaborate with your hair instead of scraping it back into a ribbon!'

Holly shrugged. 'I'm perfectly clean and tidy,' she answered, but she had no time to say anything else, for just then they heard the doorbell ring and Ivy hurrying along the hallway to answer it. Holly suddenly felt sick and the colour drained from her cheeks as she heard Ivy taking the man's hat and coat.

'They're waitin' for you in the drawin' room, sir,' they heard her say, and the next minute Holly's worst fears were realised when Mr Dolby appeared in the doorway and gave a polite little bow towards herself and her mother.

'Good evening, Mrs Farthing, Miss Farthing, Gilbert.'

'Come on in, Walter,' Gilbert Mason boomed in a jovial voice. 'You're just in time for a drink before we go in to dinner. Now, what will it be? Whisky, brandy or perhaps you'd like a glass of wine?'

While her grandfather was pouring the drinks, Holly had time to study Walter Dolby from the corner of her eye and her heart sank. *He must be forty at least, if he's a day*, she thought glumly; even older than her mother. And he certainly hadn't been at the front of the queue when looks were handed out, although he seemed to be kindly enough. In fact, he looked almost as uncomfortable as she felt. Mr Dolby was tall and thin with a large moustache that wobbled on his top lip. His dark hair was streaked with grey and his nose seemed to cover half his face and Holly knew instantly that she could never marry him. He was old enough to be her father at least, no matter how friendly he was.

The next twenty minutes were spent in stilted conversation, which Holly deliberately didn't participate in, unless a question was directed at her, in which case she answered to avoid appearing rude, and she breathed a sigh of relief when Ivy finally came to tell them that dinner was ready.

Mr Dolby offered her his arm, which she reluctantly took, and led her into the dining room where he pulled a chair out for her and then, to her dismay, sat down next to her.

The meal that followed was excellent. A thick, warming

pea soup was followed by a beef dinner with all the trimmings that had been cooked to perfection. For dessert, Cook had made one of her special sherry trifles, and this was followed by coffee and biscuits. Normally Holly would have thoroughly enjoyed it but tonight she hardly ate a thing. The food seemed to stick in her throat and the smell of the oil on Mr Dolby's hair made her feel nauseous.

'So, Miss Farthing, or may I call you Holly? Your grand-father tells me that you'll be starting a Red Cross course after Christmas.'

Holly nodded. 'Yes, I'm greatly looking forward to it. In fact my greatest ambition is to become a nurse.'

'Really?' He looked astounded. 'But surely a woman's place is at home, running the house and caring for her children?'

'I believe that tradition is becoming rather outdated now,' Holly informed him haughtily, dabbing at her mouth with a crisp white napkin. 'More and more women are pursuing careers, and of course there are the suffragettes who believe that women should have equality and the right to vote.'

'Don't you dare talk about those hussies at my table! They're a disgrace to their sex, chaining themselves to railings and smashing shop windows,' her grandfather growled, before giving Walter Dolby an apologetic smile. 'I do apol-ogise for my granddaughter, Walter. I'm afraid she's at that age where she is very susceptible to these silly modern ideas. But for all that, I think she'll make someone a wonderful wife. She's more than capable of running a house and she's quite a fine pianist too.'

Angry colour rose in Holly's cheeks. Her grandfather was talking about her as if she wasn't even in the room, and to make things worse she could see that her mother was becoming increasingly agitated – so much so that at that moment she tipped a glass of red wine all over the tablecloth.

'Oh dear,' Emma flustered. 'Now look what I've done.' She was dabbing ineffectively at the scarlet stain that was slowly spreading across the crisp linen cloth.

'Leave it,' her father ordered shortly, and Holly stared at him resentfully. She had always thought that her grandfather was an attractive man, with his full beard and thatch of grey hair, but it suddenly hit her that he was ageing. His back was becoming slightly stooped and for the first time she noticed the lines around his eyes. His once firm stomach had turned into a slight paunch, no doubt caused by the port he was so fond of, and suddenly she could stand it no longer.

Standing so abruptly that she almost overturned her chair, she glared at him. 'If you will excuse me, I'm afraid I have rather a bad headache so I think I'll retire.' Then, before her grandfather could object, she turned to Mr Dolby and held out her hand. 'Good evening, sir.' She swept away with her head held high, but once she had reached the safety of her room, she took a long, deep breath and flattened herself against the door as the tears finally came. Walter Dolby seemed a pleasant enough man but the thought of having to be intimate with him turned her stomach.

I shan't marry him no matter what Grandfather threatens, she silently told herself, then, throwing herself onto the bed, she sobbed.

She was still there almost an hour later when her mother tentatively tapped on the door before entering. 'Oh, Holly, your grandfather is very angry with you for charging off like that. Didn't you like Mr Dolby?'

'Like him!' Holly stared at her incredulously. 'It's nothing to do with liking – the man is old enough to be my father, older even than you, I wouldn't mind betting.'

'Even so, you were rather rude leaving so abruptly,' her mother said gently.

'Good! I hope it made him realise I'm not good wife material then,' Holly answered rebelliously.

'Unfortunately it didn't. In fact he remarked that he found you quite charming, and so your grandfather asked if he might like to call again next week to see you.'

Holly groaned aloud. 'Well in that case I shall just have to be honest with him and tell him that there's no chance of me ever marrying him.'

'B-but your grandfather . . . He's going to be very angry with you if you do that. He's even saying that if you don't go along with his wishes on this, he'll turn you out onto the streets.'

'So be it.' Holly swiped the remainder of her tears away on the sleeve of her dress. Of one thing she was sure: she would sooner be homeless and sleep in shop doorways than ever be tied to Walter Dolby!

Chapter One

'How dare you be so rude in front of our guest!' Gilbert Mason scolded at breakfast the next morning.

'I'm sure she didn't mean to be, she just had a headache and—'

'Shut up!' One glare from her father silenced Holly's mother immediately but whereas Emma was shaking with nerves, Holly appeared calm.

'I wasn't aware that I was being rude,' she answered, spreading marmalade on a slice of toast. 'I merely felt unwell and wished to retire early.'

'Hmm!' Her grandfather forked a juicy sausage and bit into it before asking, 'So what did you think of Walter? He's a good man.'

'I'm sure he is but I certainly have no intentions of marrying him,' Holly stated firmly.

Her grandfather almost choked on the mouthful of food he was eating before shouting, 'What do you mean? You haven't even given the chap a chance.'

'I don't need to.' Unlike her mother, Holly refused to be cowed. 'He's far too old for me for a start and I don't want the responsibility of a ready-made family just yet.'

Controlling his temper with an obvious effort her grandfather laid down his knife and fork and rose from his chair, towering over her. 'Well, perhaps it's a bit soon for you to make the decision just yet. He'll be coming to dinner again on Saturday and maybe this time you can make a little more of an effort.'

Holly pursed her lips and stared mutinously back at him before he turned and stormed from the room, slamming the door behind him.

'Oh dear, what are we going to do?' Her mother was crying now and dabbing at her eyes with a scrap of lace handkerchief. She knew how stubborn her daughter could be when she made up her mind about something and could see no easy solution to the situation they found themselves in.

Holly's kind heart ached for her. Her mother had always been the centre of her world and she hated to see her distressed.

'We could leave,' she said calmly and Emma's eyes stretched wide.

'And where would we go?'

'We could find a little house somewhere and I could get a job. That way we would be independent.'

Emma sighed. 'That all sounds very well but I can't just up and leave my father alone.'

'Why not? He has Cook and Ivy to take care of him, he'd be perfectly all right,' Holly pointed out. 'To be honest, I've always had the feeling that he only had us here on sufferance anyway.'

Emma's head wagged from side to side. 'It isn't as simple as that. I . . . I can't just go.'

'Then I warn you, if he persists in this stupid idea of marrying me off, I shall.' Holly stood up and quietly left the room leaving her mother to her thoughts, and as she made her way back upstairs she wondered again what hold her grandfather had over her mother.

'So I take it it didn't go too well then?' Ivy asked a short time later when she carried a coal bucket to Holly's room to make the fire up.

'No, it certainly did not!' Holly tossed the embroidery she had been trying to concentrate on onto the chair at the side of the bed. 'Did you see how old he was? Well, old to me anyway! He was nice enough, admittedly, but there are things I want to do before I settle down with anyone, let alone someone my grandfather has chosen for me.'

Ivy nodded understandingly as she raked out the fire and threw some more lumps of coal on, then sitting back on her heels she said, 'I can't say as I blame you. I don't want to get married either. I don't want to end up like me mam, God bless her, havin' one baby after another and gettin' old before me time. Half the time she can't even feed 'em cos most of me dad's wages goes over the bar of the Rose an' Crown. But what will you do if the master insists on it?'

'I shall leave,' Holly informed her quietly. 'I'm quite old enough to make my way in the world and I have a little nest egg that my grandmother left me to tide me over till I find a job.'

'But what would you do? You ain't trained to be anythin' and I can hardly see you as a maid,' Ivy pointed out.

Holly shrugged to hide her fears. 'I haven't really given it a lot of thought yet but there must be something I could do. I wish my mother would come with me if it does come to that, but she's already told me that she won't.'

'Well, try not to worry too much just yet. The master might

15

change his mind.' After poking the fire to get it blazing, Ivy stood up and ran her hands down the old hessian apron she wore for her dirty jobs. 'I'd best get on but I'll see you later.'

After she'd gone, Holly pondered on her dilemma. She had never considered leaving home before and although she was putting a brave face on things she suddenly felt very confused and vulnerable as she wondered how she was going to manage on her own out in the big wide world.

Saturday evening came around all too quickly and once again Ivy admitted a bright-eyed Mr Dolby. His eyes were kindly as he smiled a greeting and he had clearly gone to great pains with his appearance, but again Holly found herself thinking that he was old enough to be her father as she stared glumly at the blooms he was carrying. 'These are for you, Miss Farthing.' He handed her a large bouquet of flowers which she knew must have cost a fortune as they were out of season. Blushing furiously she reluctantly accepted them knowing that it would be rude not to. There followed another painful meal for Holly who spoke only when spoken to. She was aware of Mr Dolby's eyes on her throughout and also of her mother's nervousness and her grandfather's scrutiny.

'So, do you have any hobbies, my dear?' Mr Dolby probed.

'Just a few,' Holly answered miserably in a voice so low he had to lean towards her to hear it.

'And do you enjoy the outdoors? Walking?'

This time she merely nodded and eventually Mr Dolby gave up trying to make conversation and instead concentrated on his food. Once the meal was over Holly had to stop herself from sighing with relief. It was customary for the gentlemen to retire to the study for a glass of port and a cigar at this stage, but that evening Gilbert Mason had other ideas.

'Why don't you join me for coffee in my study and then we can leave these two to get to know each other a little better?' her grandfather suggested to her mother, much to Holly's horror.

Emma gulped deep in her throat, knowing how much her daughter would hate that, but knowing also that she had no choice she nodded and, excusing herself, followed her father out of the room.

Ivy arrived seconds later with the coffee and seeing the arrangement she glanced worriedly at Holly. 'Would you like me to pour, Miss Holly?'

'No thank you, Ivy.' Holly gave her a reassuring smile although her stomach felt as if it was in knots. 'I can manage.'

Ivy bobbed her knee and with one last glance at Walter Dolby she quietly left the room.

'It ain't right what he's doin' to Miss Holly,' she complained to the cook when she entered the kitchen. 'He's sellin' her like the farmers sell the beasts at the cattle market.'

'Aye well, he's never had any time for her,' the rosy-cheeked cook replied with a shake of her head. Now that dinner was over she was settled in a chair at the side of the fire with a steaming mug of tea in her hand and her swollen feet up on a stool.

Meanwhile in the dining room Holly was pouring the coffee and an awkward silence had settled between her and their guest.

'Well, this is nice, isn't it?' Walter Dolby said eventually, running his finger around the collar of his shirt. He was clearly feeling almost as uncomfortable as Holly was. They both sipped at their coffee and the silence stretched between them. Normally Holly loved to chat to people but she didn't want to give him false hope.

'So . . .' He smiled at her. 'Are you looking forward to Christmas? It's hard to believe that it's only a few weeks away. Your grandfather has invited me and my children for Christmas dinner. We thought it would be nice for you to meet them and get to know them.'

Holly felt slightly faint but forced a smile. 'I, er . . . I'm afraid I'm not very good with children,' she stuttered. 'I've never had much to do with any, you see?'

He didn't seem put off by the statement whatsoever and grinned. 'Oh, I'm sure you'll get along fine. They're all very well behaved. Marcus is the oldest at nineteen. He wants to help me run the businesses when he gets a little older – he's the studious one of the bunch. Then there's Florence who is thirteen and Katie who's eight and rather spoiled, being the youngest.'

Holly gave another weak smile, feeling like a rabbit caught in a trap but worse was to come.

'I should inform you that your grandfather has given me permission to ask you to marry me . . . but . . .' he added hastily, seeing the fleeting look of panic that crossed her face, 'I shan't do that, of course, until you have got to know the children and myself a little better.'

'As I said.' Her voice came out as a croak. 'I'm sure I would make a dreadful mother.'

'Nonsense. They have a nanny and a tutor so there really wouldn't be that much for you to do, my dear. I simply wanted to put your mind at rest and for you to know that my intentions are purely honourable. You are a very attractive young lady and who knows, sometime in the not too distant future we might even add to our brood. I'm sure that we'll suit each other admirably.' He then fumbled in his jacket pocket and produced a small velvet box which he opened to reveal a gleaming sapphire ring surrounded by a halo of diamonds.

'This was my late wife's engagement ring,' he told her quietly. 'And when you feel ready I hope you will do me the very great honour of accepting it as your engagement ring.'

'Oh . . . no . . . no I couldn't,' Holly gasped, stifling the urge to run from the room.

Misunderstanding her he snapped the box shut and returned it to his pocket. 'I quite understand. Perhaps you would prefer to choose one to your own taste. That won't be a problem.'

'No . . . you don't understand, Mr Dolby,' she gushed. She knew that she was going to be in terrible trouble with her grandfather but this awful situation couldn't be endured a moment longer. 'You see, the thing is . . . I don't wish to get married, to you or anyone else. I'm sorry . . . you're a very nice man and I sincerely hope you find a new mother for your children but I have to tell you quite categorically, it won't be me.'

'I see.' He looked so embarrassed that she almost felt sorry for him but then he rose from his seat and gave her a polite little bow. 'Then I must thank you for being so honest and wish you goodnight, Miss Farthing.' With that he turned on his heel and strode out into the hallway, where he almost bumped into Ivy who was taking a tray of coffee to the master's study.

'Would you kindly inform Mr Mason that I am leaving,' he said in a clipped tone and, sensing trouble, Ivy hurried on her way, almost tripping over her skirt in her haste.

'Mr Dolby asked me to tell yer that he's leavin', sir,' she said quickly when she swept breathlessly into the room, almost dropping the tray in the process.

'Leaving! What do you mean, girl, it's still early,' the master roared as he slammed his glass of port onto a small table and charged from the room.

He found Walter just putting his hat and coat on and asked abruptly, 'So what's to do then, Walter? The night is still young.'

'Ah, but I am not,' Walter answered regretfully. 'Which I think is one of the reasons your granddaughter has just told me quite plainly that she has no intentions of marrying me.'

'She's done what?' Gilbert roared, and as his voice echoed along the long hallway and into his study, Emma began to tremble. There would be big trouble now, if she wasn't very much mistaken.

Walter Dolby placed his hand on Gilbert's arm and smiled. 'It's all right, old chap. I quite admire the girl, actually, for having the guts to speak her mind. I certainly wouldn't want to force her, or anybody else for that matter, into a marriage they weren't happy with so I'll wish you goodnight and a very Merry Christmas. No doubt we shall meet again at the club.'

Gilbert's hands clenched into fists of rage as he watched his guest step out into the snowy night and seconds later he was charging towards the dining room where he found Holly still sitting, waiting for the row that she sensed was to come.

'You idiot girl!' he growled. 'Do you even begin to realise what you've just done? Walter Dolby is one of the richest men in Warwickshire. You could have been set for life.'

'Probably, but set for what sort of life?' Holly dared to ask. It was the first time she had ever openly stood up to her grandfather and for a moment he was struck dumb as his hands clenched into fists of rage once more.

'You will sleep on what you have done and first thing tomorrow I expect you to write a letter of apology to Walter,' he boomed.

Outwardly calm, Holly stared right back at him and shook her head. 'I'm afraid I shan't be doing that, Grandfather. I only told him the truth, hopefully in such a way as not to hurt his feelings, but I shall never marry Mr Dolby, whatever you say!'

Her mother had come to stand in the doorway now after hearing the commotion and she was as pale as a piece of lint as she ner-vously chewed on her fist.

'And is that your final word on the matter?'

Holly nodded. 'Yes, Grandfather, I'm rather afraid it is. I won't be sold off like some beast in the market.'

'Then you give me no alternative. First thing tomorrow I want you out of my house!'

'Father, no!' Emma ran forward and placed her hand on his arm as tears coursed down her cheeks, but he roughly shook her off, his eyes still fixed on Holly.

'It's all right, Mother. I'm quite old enough to look after

21

myself now,' Holly told her calmly, and without another word she walked from the room with her head held high, just in time to see Ivy and Cook peeping round the kitchen door. She had no doubt they had heard every word that had been said but she had no intention of backing down now. If her grandfather wished her to leave then she would. In fact, she decided, she would start packing immediately.

Meanwhile Gilbert Mason stormed into his study and banged the door shut behind him. Only then did he sag onto the nearest chair and bury his face in his hands. What have I done? he asked himself as he stared into the fire. Everything had got out of hand but his pride was such that he felt unable to go back on what he'd said. And now his only grand-daughter would be leaving, possibly never to return. 'May God forgive me,' he muttered to the empty room as tears spilled down his cheeks.

Up in her room, Holly dragged a suitcase from the top of her wardrobe and lay it open on the bed. Suddenly what was about to happen hit her like a blow and the tears came. Where was she to go? She hardly knew anyone beyond these four walls. It was all very well putting a brave face on things to everyone, but inside she was terrified about what might lie ahead. Minutes later her mother joined her and taking her hand she shook it up and down.

'Please go and apologise,' she implored. 'I can't bear to see you leave like this.'

'Then come with me.'

Emma's blue eyes were swimming with tears but as Holly looked at her she knew what the answer would be.

'You know I can't.' Emma was sobbing now.

'But why can't you? There is clearly something that holds you here so why don't you tell me what it is?'

Emma stared back at her for a moment and then her shoulders sagged and she dropped heavily onto the side of the bed.

'It . . . it's because I didn't always have just you to worry about,' she confessed in a small voice. 'You see . . . you once had a sister . . . a twin sister.'

Chapter Two

Holly was so shocked that her mouth gaped open.

'I may as well tell you everything now,' her mother said resignedly and lowering her eyes she began, 'I met your father when I was about the same age as you are now and it was love at first sight.' Her eyes took on a dreamy look but pulling her thoughts back to the present she went on, 'I met him in the marketplace one day. His name was Michael Farthing and he was a few years older than me. He was so handsome,' she sighed as she reached up to stroke a lock of hair from Holly's flushed cheek. 'You remind me so much of him. He was working for a local farmer because he told me that he wanted to see something of the country so was travelling about finding work where he could . . .

'Anyway, within no time I knew that he was the man for me so I told your grandfather about him. He went mad. He had brought me up single-handed since your grandmother died when I was eight and we'd been happy enough, although your grandfather never really got over her death. He and my mother were very close. Father had given me the best education that he could and I think he had hoped for a good marriage for me.

'In the end I invited Michael to dinner, but from the second they met they didn't get on at all. Michael thought your grandfather was a snob and your grandfather told me that Michael was a waster and that I'd never do any good with him. Of course, I was young and foolish and didn't want to listen and then . . .' She lowered her eyes again here and looked ashamed. 'And then I discovered I was going to have a child. I'd explained to your father early in our relationship that I would shortly be coming into an inheritance from my late grandmother and he said he didn't care, that he'd marry me without a penny. And so we ran away. I lied about my age and we were married quietly in a little church in Wales. Michael found work on a farm and we lived in a tiny cottage; it was a two-up, two-down place but I loved it, and for a while I was happy. But within weeks he started to ask when I would come into my inheritance. He started to drink too, staying out late at night and coming home drunk. One night he became aggressive and hit me, but the next day he begged me to forgive him and swore that it would never happen again.

'I wrote to your grandfather then to tell him I was married and to ask when I might get my inheritance and that was when the real trouble started. When Father wrote back he informed me that my grandmother had left a codicil in her will stating that I should receive my inheritance only when my grandfather thought I would spend it wisely and he told me that for as long as I stayed with Michael he would ensure that I never received a single penny.'

Tears were flowing freely now as the memories flooded back. 'When I showed it to your father he was like a mad thing and he slapped me so hard that I saw stars. It was then that I began to realise he'd only married me for my money and I was heartbroken. The next day he didn't come home from work. I wasn't too worried because he often went to the inn first. Eventually I went to bed and fell asleep and when I woke the next morning I found that he hadn't been home. He'd left me . . . with a baby on the way,' Emma said brokenly.

'Oh, Mother . . .' Holly's heart went out to her as she thought of how frightening that must have been for a young woman all alone and far from home. 'So what did you do?'

Emma shrugged. 'What could I do? I had no money, nothing. The next day I went to see the farmer he had worked for and he informed me that your father hadn't turned up at work for two days. I knew then that he wasn't coming back so I pawned my wedding ring and that paid for the train fare back to Nuneaton. I didn't have anywhere else to go and I couldn't work because I was almost due to have you by then. I had to throw myself on my father's mercy and thankfully he didn't turn me away, but he did make me promise to tell everyone that I had been widowed and to never have anything to do with your father again. That wasn't hard because by then any love I had ever felt for him had died.'

'So my father is still alive somewhere then?' Holly questioned and Emma nodded.

'As far as I know. He's never been in touch from that day to this, even though he must have realised that I would come home with my tail between my legs when he left me penniless. Soon after I went into labour and gave birth to you and your sister. She was older than you by ten minutes and I called her Laura but from the start she was a weak little thing. While you thrived she seemed to fade away in front of my very eyes despite your grandfather summoning the best doctors that he could find to tend her. I loved the two of you so much, you were all that was left for me, so when I lost Laura . . .' She stifled a sob as she thought back to that heart-breaking time. Even now, after all these years, she still grieved for the child she had lost. 'And so now you must see why I can't leave him? Many men would have closed the door on me when I came creeping back but he didn't and so now I owe it to him to stay here.'

Suddenly, Holly was viewing her grandfather through different eyes. It was no wonder he was so cold towards her mother and herself. It must have broken his heart when she ran away with someone who turned out to be a scoundrel. Perhaps that was why he wanted to arrange her own marriage, to try to avoid history repeating itself? Even so she knew that she couldn't marry Walter Dolby and so now she slowly continued to pack her case.

'Please don't go until the morning; your grandfather might have a change of heart,' Emma pleaded but Holly shook her head. Although she was sorely tempted, she knew that if she waited she might lose her nerve and end up staying – possibly for ever. Oh, but it was going to be so hard to walk away from her mother and the life she had known.

'I think we both know there's little chance of that happening, so it's best I go now,' she said in a wobbly voice. 'But don't worry, I shall go to Mrs Lockett. I'm sure she will put me up for the night, which will give me some time to think about where I'm going.'

Verity Lockett was the local vicar's wife and much loved by everyone in the parish and Holly was sure that she wouldn't turn her away. She had attended her Sunday school in Chilvers Coton Parish Hall for as long as she could remember and was very fond of the kindly woman.

'Well, will you at least promise to write to me when you're settled?'

Holly nodded and Emma hurried away, returning minutes later with an envelope that she pressed into her daughter's hand.

'There's enough money in there to ensure that you can find somewhere to stay for quite some time, and once I know where you are I shall send you some more,' she promised. They were interrupted then by a tap at the door and praying that it was her father with a change of heart Emma almost ran to open it, only to be disappointed when she found Ivy standing there.

Ivy glanced nervously over her shoulder before muttering, 'Please, Mrs Farthing . . . I was wondering . . . do you think Miss Holly would let me go with her? I ain't been eaves-droppin', honest I ain't. But the thing is we could all hear what the master were shoutin' all over the house.'

Both Emma and Holly looked astounded.

'B-but why would you want to come with me?' Holly questioned eventually. 'Your family are here and you have a regular job.'

'Huh! Some family, eh? They only want me fer the wages I cough up every week. An' as fer the job, I'm sure I'll be very easy to replace. So please, Miss Holly, let me come with you. We've got close since I started to work here, you've even taught me to read an' write but I'm a bit more streetwise than you an' you'd be safer wi' me taggin' along, I know it.

Surely it'd be far safer wi' two of us to look out fer each other?'

'She's right, Holly,' Emma said. Despite the fact that her heart was breaking at the thought of her daughter leaving, if Ivy was by her side, it would at least offer some semblance of reassurance.

'You wouldn't 'ave to keep me,' Ivy went on hurriedly. 'I've saved what bit o' me wages I've been allowed to keep ever since I started here so I've got some money to tide me over, an' we stand so much more of a chance if there's two of us an' we can both find a job. We might even be able to afford a little place to rent, so what do yer say?'

Holly still looked doubtful, although she had to admit that the thought of going out into the big wide world wouldn't seem quite so daunting if she wasn't alone.

'All right then, but only if you're quite sure this is what you really want to do,' Holly agreed.

Ivy beamed. 'I am sure. I've never been surer of anythin' in me life. But now I'd better go an' pack. It'll only take me a matter o' minutes.'

'No,' Holly told her hastily. 'It's better if you stay here tonight, Ivy. I'll meet you at the train station in the morning at nine o'clock and then we'll decide where we're going.'

'All right, miss.' Ivy looked slightly disappointed but nodded before quietly slipping away. Deep down she supposed that what Holly had suggested made sense. At least this way she would perhaps be able to go and say her good-byes to her own family tonight after all her jobs were done that evening.

Suddenly, to Holly, every moment was precious, for who

knew when she and her mother might see each other again? There were so many questions that Holly longed to ask, but they were trapped inside her for now. There was just too much to take in all at once and her mind was in a whirl. It was as if the parts of a jigsaw puzzle were falling into place. In the past, when Holly had asked about her father, her mother had always changed the subject. She'd assumed it was because it was too painful for her to talk about him, but now finally she understood the real reason. She could also understand why her grandfather was as he was too. It must have hurt him very much when her mother ran away and she supposed it was all credit to him that he had taken her back in when her husband had deserted her. Even so, she couldn't go along with his wish for her to marry someone she didn't love and so now there really was no alternative but to leave, as frightening as that idea was. And to think she had once had a sister she had never even known about! The thought was painful. She had always longed for a sister.

'I wish you'd told me all this earlier,' Holly said brokenly as she laid some clean underwear in the case. She was restricted to what she could take so was being very careful what she chose. Three warm outfits, underwear, nightwear and her coat would be all she could carry. She doubted she would need her prettier clothes, anyway, if and when she found a job.

'I always meant to,' her mother said in a strangled voice. 'I just never found the right moment somehow. Oh please, darling . . . I can't bear this. I feel as if my heart is being ripped out of me. You've been my whole world since Laura died. Let me talk to your grandfather and try to get him to change his mind.'

Holly looked at her sadly. 'You know you'd be wasting your time. Grandfather is as stubborn as a mule when he sets his mind to something.'

Holly continued to pack her bag then, pausing, she suddenly asked quietly, 'Where did my father come from? I mean, was he from these parts?'

Her mother shook her head. She now deeply regretted not being honest with her daughter before and didn't intend to tell her any more lies. Just look where it had led! 'No, he came from London. I believe his family lived in Whitechapel, somewhere down by the docks, although I never met them.'

'Didn't you even go to see if he was there when he left you?' Holly was surprised.

'What would have been the point? My love for him had died by that stage and all I wanted was the best for you . . . and your sister, of course.'

Holly loaded the last of the things she wanted to take with her into her bag and snapped it firmly shut before reaching for her coat. 'Are you quite sure that you won't come with me?' she asked one last time.

For a moment her mother hesitated but then she shook her head. 'I can't leave my father, darling, not after the way he stood by me. He's getting old now and I'm all he has, please try to understand.'

Holly nodded compassionately as she shrugged her coat on and fastened her hat to her thick curls with a lethal-looking hat pin. There seemed nothing left to say now.

Lifting her bag she walked slowly towards the door but suddenly her mother had her in a fierce embrace.

'Promise me that you'll let me know where you are just as soon as you can, and should you ever need me, please come back home. Your grandfather will calm down and regret his decision in no time, I'm sure.'

Holly returned the embrace, tears clamouring at her throat, staring into the eyes that were so like her own for a moment. Then she gently pushed her mother aside, threw open the door and hurried on her way, knowing that if she didn't go now her courage would fail her.

Ivy was waiting for her in the hallway.

'I'll see you in the morning then,' she whispered and Holly nodded before opening the front door and stepping out into the bitter night air. She strode away without once looking back and it wasn't until the vicarage came into sight that her steps began to falter as the enormity of what she was about to do struck home. She was leaving behind all she had ever known and stepping into the great unknown and it was a frightening thought.

At the stout oak door of the vicarage she paused and tried to compose herself as her breath hung on the frosty air like gossamer lace all around her, then lifting her hand she rapped firmly with the big brass door knocker.

Within seconds she heard footsteps approaching and the door was opened by Lily, the Locketts' young maid.

'Why, hello, Miss Holly,' she greeted her with a smile. 'What brings you out on such a cold and frosty night?'

'I . . . I'd like to see Mrs Lockett if she's in, please?'

'Oh aye, she's in all right,' Lily told her cheerily. 'She's sat at the side o' the fire wi' the vicar. Come on in out o' the cold an' I'll go an' tell her yer here.'

Holly gratefully did as she was asked and the warm air inside wrapped itself around her like a blanket, yet still she found that she couldn't stop trembling. She had so many happy memories of attending the Sunday school the kindly woman had run each week when she was younger. Mrs Lockett used to supply all the children with sweeties and the air had rung with laughter, but tonight, in her distress, it felt as if those times were a million years ago.

'Why, Holly, hello dear.' Verity Lockett appeared and looked somewhat surprised to see her at that time of night, but nevertheless she held her arms out in welcome. 'Whatever are you doing out on such a night?' she asked, much as Lily had done only seconds earlier. Her hair was piled becomingly on top of her head and her face was flushed and rosy from the warmth of the fire.

She pecked Holly on the cheek and stared at her with a question in her eyes and that was Holly's undoing. Suddenly she began to sob violently, releasing the tears she had held back.

'I . . . I've left home.'

'You've what?' Verity was sure she must be hearing things. She knew how close Holly and her mother were.

In between sobs, Holly managed to tell her all about the row with her grandfather and the way he had ordered her to leave and why. 'And so . . . I was wondering if you would let me stay here,' she ended in a strangled voice. 'It would be just for tonight. I'm meeting Ivy, our maid, at the train station in the morning and she's coming with me.'

Ivy often attended church with Holly and Verity was pleased that at least Holly wouldn't be leaving on her own although she was a little concerned about her choice of travelling companion. Ivy was a very needy girl from what Verity had seen of her and she worried that Holly could well end up looking after her as well as herself.

However, she pushed her concerns aside for the moment. 'But of course you can stay,' she told her soothingly. 'And for as long as you like. Why don't you just give it a little time to see if your grandfather has a change of heart?'

Holly shook her head. 'Thank you but no. Grandfather won't change his mind. He has his heart set on me marrying Mr Dolby, and nice a man as he is, I couldn't bear to marry someone I didn't love. Why, even his son is older than me!'

Verity quite agreed with her although she didn't voice her opinion. She and Emma were close and she could only imagine the state that poor woman must be in.

'Then come through to the drawing room and I'll get Lily to make you a nice hot cup of cocoa. You look like you need it,' she said kindly. So after removing her coat and bonnet, Holly meekly followed. There could be no going back now. Tomorrow would be the start of her new life.

Chapter Three

Once Holly was seated at the fireside and Lily had brought them a tray of hot cocoa, Reverend Lockett tactfully retired to bed to give the women a chance to talk and after Verity sent Lily off to light the fire in the spare room, she was able to give Holly her full attention.

'Perhaps if you went home and tried to reason with your grandfather he might change his mind?' she suggested gently but Holly shook her head.

'It wouldn't be any use,' she answered dully.

Verity peered at her over the rim of her cup and sighed. 'And who suggested that Ivy might come with you? Was it your mother?'

'No, it was Ivy herself actually. I think she'll be glad of a chance to get away from here. Her father turns up on the doorstep regularly to take most of her wages off her. I don't think the poor girl even knew what it was like to have regular meals and a clean bed to sleep in until she came to work for my grandfather. From what she's told me neither her mother nor her father ever showed her an ounce of love or kindness while she lived at home so I doubt she'll miss them, although I know she worries about her brothers and sisters, poor little things.'

'Hmm, I can understand that but are you quite sure that Ivy is the right one to come with you? What I mean is . . .

I would have felt easier if it was someone who could look after you. I'm afraid that Ivy might prove to be a burden and you may well end up looking after her.'

Holly shrugged. The emotions of the night were catching up with her and suddenly she was weary. 'Actually, Ivy is tougher than she looks. She's had to be to survive,' she explained. 'And I've never been away from home before without either my mother or grandfather, so at least I'll have someone I know with me.'

'There is that,' Verity admitted, although she still felt very uneasy about the whole thing. Holly had led a very sheltered life in many ways and as Verity knew from the various poor people of the parish that she visited, it could be a very hard world beyond your own four walls.

Eventually, when she was convinced that nothing she could say would make the girl change her mind about leaving, she showed Holly to her room, and once left to her thoughts Holly miserably got into bed and lay staring at the dancing shadows the flickering flames in the grate were creating on the ceiling. She was exhausted and yet sleep eluded her as she thought about the enormous step she was about to take and reflected on what she had learned that day. She had once had a sister, albeit briefly. The thought almost broke her heart as she thought how wonderful it would have been had Laura lived. And then she wondered what her mother was doing and the tears came again. They had never been apart before and she was missing her already. And on top of that, she worried about how her mother would manage without her. Their bond was strong and they had always supported each other, but now her mother would be on her own and at the mercy of her grandfather, who could be harsh when he was angry.

At that moment Ivy was creeping through the almost deserted streets to her home to say her goodbyes to her own family. Once she reached the house, which was little more than a slum, she slipped into the tiny kitchen and as usual she found her mother sitting at the side of a dying fire with a half-empty bottle of cheap gin in her hand. Her siblings were all fast asleep in bed and she rightly assumed that her father would be at the pub.

The woman looked mildly surprised to see her and greeted her with, 'What are you doin' here at this time o' night? Come to bring us some money 'ave yer?'

'No, I brought you my wages round last week,' Ivy said meekly, suddenly feeling guilty. 'I just came to tell yer that I'll be goin' away tomorrer . . . to live in London.'

'London!' Her mother's mouth gaped slackly open. 'But what about us? What'll I do wi'out yer money?'

Ivy was profoundly hurt. Here she was telling her mother that she was about to embark on a new life but all she could think about was how it would affect the family.

'Don't worry,' she said dully. 'I shall be getting a job when we get there and I'll send you some money each week.'

'That's all right then!' Her mother sniffed as Ivy went on to explain why she was going.

'Well, just so long as yer send us yer wages,' the woman said coldly and Ivy left soon after with tears in her eyes. But then, she asked herself, had she really expected any other reaction? There had been no kiss, no good luck, just concern about the lack of money.

With a heartfelt sigh she set off into the cold night and began the journey back to her employer's house.

When Holly came downstairs early the following morning, pale and with dark shadows beneath her eyes, she found Verity already up and Lily cleaning the fire grates out.

'Come along, I insist you have a good breakfast inside you before you leave,' Verity urged, nudging her towards the kitchen. 'It's not quite seven o'clock yet so you've plenty of time. Judging by the smell, Cook is already preparing it, if I'm not mistaken.'

They followed the enticing smell of frying bacon to the kitchen and soon after, the kindly cook placed the most enormous plate of food in front of her. There were juicy sausages, crispy bacon, mushrooms, fried bread and fried eggs and Holly's stomach lurched at the sight of it. The last thing she wanted to do was eat at that moment but even so she didn't wish to offend the cook so she gamely picked at it as Verity joined her at the table and watched her.

'I'm off to meet Mrs Branning – you know, Sunday Branning from Treetops? – this afternoon,' she said cheerfully in an attempt to lighten the mood. 'She really is such an angel the way she looks after all the children she takes in. She has to buy some new clothes for some of them today, so I offered to go along with her to help.' She had hoped that if she kept up a light-hearted chatter it might cheer Holly up a little, but her tactic didn't appear to be working, as Holly stared lifelessly ahead, so in the end she remained silent as she ate her breakfast.

By the time they had finished it was almost eight o'clock and Holly knew that it was time to leave so she hurried to her room to fetch her bag.

The vicar's wife became quite emotional when she said goodbye. She had known Holly since she was a little girl and was very concerned about what might become of her out in the big bad world.

'Promise me that you'll write and take good care of yourself.'

Holly nodded numbly as the kindly woman kissed her cheek. 'Thank you for the kindness you have shown me, Mrs Lockett, I shall be forever grateful.' Then she turned in the direction of the train station. She took the short cut from Coton across the Pingle Fields where a fair was in the process of setting up and memories came flooding back. She could remember her mother taking her there once when she was a little girl and she had thought it was magical. Thinking about it, she could still taste the sticky toffee apple her mother had bought her and remember the thrill of riding on the gaily painted horses of the carousel. They had gone to the hall of mirrors, where Holly had giggled at the sight of their distorted reflection, and then had a go on the hoopla stall where she had won a goldfish in a bag. She pushed the memories away and went through the tunnel that led into Riversley Park. The River Anchor ran right through the centre of it and as she walked along its banks it struck her that the leafless weeping willows that were trailing their branches in the sluggish water looked about as miserable as she felt.

Soon she was walking through the marketplace where the traders were setting up their stalls. It wouldn't be long before the stalls would be full of everything from fresh fish to ribbons and buckets and Holly had always loved to wander amongst them. It felt strange to know that she might never do so again, and as she passed through Bond Gate and Trent Valley Railway Station came into view, she was in a very sombre mood indeed. Part of her wanted to run home, but the other part of her baulked at the thought of marrying Walter Dolby, so she forced herself to move on. Seconds later she spotted Ivy standing outside the ticket office anxiously looking this way and that. As soon as the girl spotted her, her face broke into a wide smile and she raced towards her. Though she was dressed in her Sunday best, Holly couldn't help but notice that her clothes were very old and worn, no doubt purchased from the rag stall in the market.

'Was everything all right back at home when you left?' Holly questioned.

Ivy shrugged. 'Not really, miss. Yer mam an' yer gran'father had a hell of a row after yer'd gone last night. Yer could hear 'em all over the house an' it ended wi' yer poor mam goin' upstairs in tears. Yer gran'father were off out to the mill first thing this mornin' wi'out a bite o' breakfast in his belly an' when he'd gone yer mam came down to see me off. She said to tell yer she loves yer an' to take care. I told her, don't you worry now, I'll see as she's all right.'

Holly smiled in spite of the sinking feeling in the pit of her stomach as she thought of her poor mother all alone back at the house.

'So where are we goin'?' Ivy asked.

Holly's thoughts were jerked back to the present and drawing herself up to her full height she answered truthfully, 'It all depends where the first train leaving here is bound. Wherever it's going, we'll get on it.'

Ivy hopped from foot to foot in her excitement. 'Ooh, it's like goin' on an adventure, ain't it?' she chirped. 'I ain't never been on a train before.'

The man at the ticket desk smiled kindly at the girl as Holly approached. 'Where is the next train bound for?' she asked and after glancing at his timetable he scratched his whiskery chin.

'That'd be London, Euston, miss. It's due in fifteen minutes.'

'Then I'll have two tickets please. One way,' she told him pointedly.

He looked at her curiously for a moment but then gave her the tickets and told her, 'There's a fire in the waitin' room if you'd like to wait in there. It's a bit parky out here, ain't it?'

'Thank you.' She took the change he placed in front of her and with Ivy trotting along behind her like a little puppy she made her way to the platform and into the waiting room.

'Cor, it's nice an' warm in here, ain't it?' Ivy held her hands out to the cheery blaze and glanced around. Holly, meanwhile, sat sedately on one of the benches set along the wall and remained silent.

But when the train roared into the station in a hiss of steam and smoke that enveloped the platform, Ivy's excitement died abruptly.

41

'Crikey they's noisy things, ain't they?' she muttered nervously as she clutched the old carpet bag that contained the few meagre clothes she possessed tightly to her.

Holly gave her a reassuring smile as the train drew to a halt. 'You'll be all right, it's quite safe,' she assured her as the guard opened a carriage door for her.

Ivy didn't look too sure about that, but she followed her onto the train all the same and perched on the edge of the seat, her eyes looking huge in her pale face.

'So how long will it take us to get there?' she enquired nervously.

'Not more than a few hours I shouldn't think.' Holly reached out to pat her hand distractedly. She was so nervous that she could barely think straight. Luckily they had the carriage to themselves, which was just as well, for when the train set off again Ivy let out a fearful screech.

''Ere, yer didn't warn me they went this fast,' she groaned as the train pulled out of the station.

Holly ignored her and as the train picked up speed she stared at the familiar town, wondering when and if she would ever see it again. Soon the houses gave way to fields and Ivy's complaints stopped as she stared in awe at the passing scenery.

'Crikey, I never knew there were so much space.'

Holly gave her a weak smile. 'It's even nicer in the summer when the sheep and cows are grazing in the fields,' she informed her. 'But I dare say they'll all be in their barns for the winter now. It is nearly Christmas, after all.'

The thought of the festive season away from home suddenly brought a lump to her throat and she hastily turned to stare from the other window so that Ivy wouldn't see the tears in

42

her eyes. It would be a very lonely time for her mother without her there, she was sure, and guilt stabbed at her like a knife.

It was soon clear that Ivy was thinking along the same lines for she suddenly blurted out, 'I hope yer mam don't get into trouble about me comin' with yer. She were goin' to tell yer gran'father later today. I popped to see me mam last night to explain.' She sniffed loudly and withdrawing a scrap of linen that had been torn from an old sheet she noisily blew her nose. 'Not that she much cared,' she said sadly. 'The only thing she'll miss is me wages.'

Holly's soft heart melted and hotching along the seat she placed her arm about Ivy's thin shoulders. 'They'll all be fine without us. And we've got each other so we'll be all right.' She wasn't sure if she was trying to reassure Ivy or herself. Suddenly they were just two young women stepping into the unknown. It was a very daunting thought.

Chapter Four

By the time the train drew into Euston Station they were both hungry and thirsty and more than a little apprehensive about the journey they had embarked on. Neither of them had eaten much at breakfast and so Holly suggested, 'Why don't we find somewhere we can get something to eat and then we'll start to look for a place to stay? We can look for a job tomorrow.'

Ivy nodded, her face solemn as she stared at the crowds of people milling around them. She had never seen so many people all in one place before and was feeling a little over-whelmed. They followed a throng of people who all seemed to be heading for the exit and emerged into Euston Square where an old man with a grubby bandage wrapped around his eyes was sitting against a wall with a bowl in front of him. As they passed he asked pathetically, 'Spare a penny fer an old blind man?'

Holly's soft heart made her reach into her purse and drop some coins into his bowl before they tentatively went on with no idea whatsoever of where they were going. An old lady was selling little posies of dried heather and there was a cart of pies and peas. Beside this, a woman was selling tiny bags of food for the pigeons that hopped across the pavements and perched on the roofs. The streets were alive with traffic – horse-drawn cabs and carts, as well as motor cars, which were a rarity back home. The vehicles seemed to be coming from every direction, with the cars sounding their horns and the drivers of the horse-drawn vehicles shouting at their horses and any pedestrians who got in their way. It was so noisy Holly could hardly hear herself think and there was not a patch of grass to be seen. Instead, everywhere she looked, the buildings towered above them, belching thick black smoke from their chimneys. Suddenly she felt very small and vulnerable.

'We'll get something to eat here,' Holly said, gesturing to the man selling pies from a cart and feeling totally out of her depth. 'And there's a drinking fountain over there, look, so we'll have a drink of water, which should tide us over until we can find somewhere to get a cup of tea.'

Holly approached the old man and ordered their food. He stared at her curiously as he spooned peas into a bowl. 'New here, are yer, dearie?' he enquired.

Holly nodded as she fumbled in her purse for the money to pay him before dropping it carelessly back into her bag.

'Hmm, I thought as much.' He handed her the first tray. 'Well, take a bit of advice from me. Be careful wi' yer purse. The dippers, or pickpockets as you might know 'em, are rife round here an' yer don't even know they've dipped yer till yer come to get yer money out again, be it in yer bag or in yer pocket.'

'Thank you, I'll remember that.' Holly hastily did the clasp on her bag up and put it under her arm as she took the second tray and joined Ivy.

As they stood eating their pies they gazed about. Traffic was zooming past them at an alarming rate and Holly thought longingly of the much quieter streets at home. It felt a very long way away and she had to fight down the panic that was threatening to overwhelm her. Everything was so loud and large here and not at all like the pictures of the famous landmarks she had looked at in books. Those pictures had made London seem a very glamorous, adventurous place but in reality she could see now why it was called the big smoke.

The pies were surprisingly tasty and by the time they'd eaten they were both feeling a little more optimistic as they crossed to the drinking fountain and cupped their hands to take a drink.

'So what do we do now?' Ivy looked completely lost.

Crossing back to the old man who had sold them their dinner, Holly waited patiently as he served a customer before asking, 'Would you happen to know of anywhere round here where we might be able to rent a small house?'

He chuckled. 'Yer in London now, luvvie. You'll be lucky to afford a room in a shared house unless yer prepared to go close to the docks.'

'Oh, I see . . . thank you.' Feeling disappointed, Holly took Ivy's elbow and they set off with no idea where they were going whatsoever. The shops windows they passed were decorated with baubles for Christmas, which only made Holly realise again how far away from home they were, and her spirits sank still lower.

They set off and found themselves walking through a market that appeared bigger than the whole of their home town, where the stallholders competed with each other to shout their wares louder than their neighbours. Soon they veered off into an alleyway that was overshadowed by dingy, ill-kept houses where children played barefoot in the street despite the freezing weather, and old women sat on the steps smoking pipes and watching them with lifeless eyes. The stink in the alley was such that they swiftly turned to make their way back to the main thoroughfare. Eventually, they reached the Thames and were disappointed to see that it was a dull, sludgy brown colour, with houses perched along the shore that were little more than huts.

Finally, three hours later, they stopped, exhausted, to sit on a low wall outside a large house in Mayfair, which was clearly a wealthy area, and the contrast between this and the poorer places they had walked through was startling. They were both feeling totally worn out and dispirited as it dawned on them both how very different life here was going to be and they were suddenly afraid of the enormous step they had taken. Ivy had barely said a word all afternoon as they had trudged around the busy streets. But now a thick smog was settling across London and it was so cold that their noses were glowing. The pieman had been right when he told them how expensive it would be to rent somewhere to stay and now the light was fading from the afternoon.

'I don't reckon I can walk much further in these boots,' Ivy whimpered, rubbing her sore heels. 'They're too tight fer me an' I've got blisters on me heels. Me bag is gettin' heavier an' all, unless it's me gettin' weaker.'

Holly made a decision. 'Come on,' she urged encouragingly. 'We'll check into a hotel for the night and begin our search again in the morning.'

'But one o' them posh hotels we passed will cost a fortune.

Can we afford it?' Ivy queried worriedly. 'An' will they even let me in, dressed like this.' She stared down at her worn, faded clothes in dismay.

'We'll get you a new outfit tomorrow,' Holly promised. 'But come on, I'm so cold I can't feel my hands and feet any more. If we stay out here much longer we're likely to catch our death of cold.'

After a lot more tramping they finally booked in to a hotel close to Euston Station. The room was basic but clean and they were pleased to find a fire burning in there along with two single beds.

'I'm sorry we have to share but this was cheaper than two separate rooms,' Holly apologised as she sank down wearily into a chair at the side of the fire.

Ivy was feeling better already now that she had her shoes off and grinned. 'Sharin' don't bother me, miss. In fact, I prefer it.'

'Don't you think you ought to stop addressing me as miss now and call me by my name?' Holly suggested.

Ivy blinked in surprise. 'I can try,' she said cautiously. 'But it's gonna take some gettin' used to, miss . . . sorry, I mean, Holly.'

Half an hour later when they had thawed out and were feeling a little more human, Holly ordered a meal to be sent up to their room and when it arrived, Ivy looked at the various covered dishes the maid wheeled in greedily.

'Cor, look at this,' she yelped as she lifted one lid to reveal thinly cut slices of chicken. 'An' there's all these veg an' tatties to go with it.' She eagerly began to fill their plates and passed one to Holly, saying gleefully, 'I could get used to bein' waited on like this. An' there won't be no washin' up to do, neither.'

'Hmm, well don't get too used to it because I'm afraid my money won't last long if we don't find somewhere reasonable for us to stay.'

The next morning after breakfast, Holly paid the hotel bill and they set off in search of somewhere to stay again. Ivy had slept well but Holly had lain awake for much of the night. It had dawned on her in the early hours of the morning that there could be no going back now and she was terrified of what might happen to them if she couldn't find them somewhere to live, so while Ivy was in a more optimistic mood, Holly looked pale and drawn.

By mid-afternoon they were both forced to admit that what the pieman had told them was true. They were going to have to look for a room to rent rather than a house, at least until they had both found employment. As the light was fading they found themselves wandering through Soho.

'Ooh, I ain't too keen on it round here,' Ivy commented ner-vously. There seemed to be a large number of clubs with posters of women in various stages of undress outside them, and posh carriages were drawing up outside them depositing well-dressed gentlemen who hastily disappeared inside. Dotted amongst the clubs were shops with grimy windows that seemingly catered to every nationality, and grubby-looking little terraced houses.

It was in the window of one such house that they spotted a sign saying 'Rooms Vacant' and they glanced at each other.

'What do yer think?' Ivy was the first to speak. 'I know it's a bit rough round here but anythin's better than nothin', ain't it? An' it is gettin' dark,' she pointed out.

Holly frowned for a moment as she stared at the paint peeling off the window frames. How different this was to the comforts of her old home. 'I suppose it wouldn't hurt to look,' she conceded and with their minds made up she tapped on the door.

After a while they heard the shuffle of footsteps and an old woman opened the door to peer at them suspiciously. Her straggly grey hair was pulled back into an untidy bun on the back of her head and an old shawl of indistinguishable colour was wrapped about her shoulders.

'Yes?' she snapped.

Holly licked her lips nervously and explained, 'We're looking for a room to rent and saw your sign in the window.'

The woman frowned before asking, 'You ain't doxies, are you?'

Holly had no idea what a doxy was but she shook her head. 'No, we've just come to live in London and we're looking for somewhere to stay until we can rent a house.'

'Hmm!' The woman didn't sound convinced but she opened the door wider and ushered them inside all the same. Instantly the cloying smell of stale urine, boiled cabbage and rotting food assailed them and Holly felt the back of her throat burn with the putrid odours. The walls in the long hallway were painted a dull, drab brown and dirty lino, which was full of holes, covered the floor. Somewhere they could hear a baby crying and what sounded like a couple having a blazing row.

'Only room as I've got vacant is up in the attic. It'd mean yer goin' up four flights o' stairs,' the old woman informed them shortly.

Hoping to soften her up a little, Holly smiled at her politely. 'I'm sure we could manage that. Might we be allowed to look at the room?'

The old woman shuffled away into one of the downstairs rooms muttering beneath her breath and seconds later she returned with a key which she passed to Holly, warning her, 'Don't yer go thinkin' o' nickin' owt. I knows exactly what's in there!'

'I wouldn't dream of it,' Holly assured her as colour flooded into her cheeks. From what she had seen of the house so far she couldn't imagine there would be anything in the whole place worth stealing, even if she had a mind to.

'I'll wait here while yer go up an' have a look, it's the last door on the top floor,' the old woman responded and turning about Holly and Ivy began the long trek up the stairs, which creaked alarmingly in places.

They were both huffing and puffing by the time they reached the top.

'That must be it, that door there,' Ivy puffed, pointing.

Holly inserted the key and as they stepped inside she groaned with dismay. Ivy, on the other hand, had lived in far worse than this back in the courtyards in Abbey Street and wasn't put off at all.

A window that was so dirty they could barely see through it was set in one wall and a small table with two mismatched chairs stood beneath it. On the other wall was a double bed covered in grimy blankets with a large chest of drawers to

51

one side of it, and oppos-ite that was a small sink and what looked like a little cooker. The only other furniture in the room was an old easy chair that stood next to a small fireplace that was clogged with dead ashes. As Ivy ventured into the room, she coughed as a cloud of dust rose into the air but Holly hovered in the doorway chewing on her lip.

'I-it's not very nice is it?' she gulped and Ivy laughed as she walked to the window and rubbed a little circle clean with the sleeve of her old coat.

'It just needs a bloody . . . sorry, miss . . . I mean, Holly, a damned good clean. I reckon it could be quite cosy.'

'But it's so cold up here!' Holly was shivering and her breath hung on the air in front of her.

'Well it will be till we get some coal an' get a fire lit,' Ivy said practically. 'Come on, let's go back down an' ask the old lady how much a week she wants for it. It will do us till we can find somewhere better.'

Despite her misgivings, Holly followed Ivy back down the stairs with a heavy heart. After all, like Ivy said, it would only be temporary.

'So how much a week do yer want for the room then?' Ivy boldly asked the woman.

'Seven shillins,' the old dear responded instantly.

Ivy laughed. 'Seven shillins! Come off it! It ain't worth that. How about five an' a tanner?'

The old woman glared at her. 'Six an' sixpence.'

Ivy shook her head. 'Six bob an' that's me final offer. Yer won't find many as will want to tackle them stairs every day.'

The old woman sniffed, disgruntled. 'Huh! It's bloody daylight robbery! Cheatin' an old woman out of her fair dues!'

'Fine, then we'll find somewhere else.' Ivy lifted her bag and made for the door with Holly close behind her.

'All right, all right,' the old woman grumbled. 'But I wants two weeks up front!'

Ivy grinned as Holly took her purse from her bag and counted the money into the old woman's hand.

'The toilet's out in the backyard through that door there.' The old woman pointed to the end of the hallway. 'An' I don't want you bringin' men back to your room else you'll be out on your arses quicker than you can say Jack Robinson, do yer hear me?'

'We hear you,' Ivy affirmed and Holly was shocked. She'd never seen Ivy so assertive. She was usually such a nervous little thing.

'You're responsible fer buyin' yer own coal an' gettin' yer own meals,' the old woman went on. 'An' I'm Mrs Hall, by the way. That's the door to my room there. Just remember what I said, though, this is a respectable house an' I won't have no hanky-panky.'

Ivy didn't even bother to answer but turned and started to lug her bag up the stairs again.

'You did well there,' Holly told her when they finally arrived on their landing. 'I've never seen you stand up to anyone like that before.'

Ivy shrugged as she unlocked the door. 'Well, she ain't the sort o' person you're used to dealin' with, is she?' she answered. 'An' I weren't goin' to let her get away wi' more than is reasonable.'

They stared around the room silently for a moment, until Ivy eventually said, 'Right, if I go an' find a shop before they close I can get some cleanin' things an' get this place ship-shape by bedtime.'

'I'll help,' Holly said quickly but Ivy merely grinned.

'An' since when have you been used to cleanin' an' gettin' your hands dirty? No, leave it to me.'

But Holly was not to be put off so easily. 'That was in my other life. This is the start of a new one so I'll have to get used to it. You're not my maid now, Ivy, and I want to pull my weight.'

Ivy grinned as Holly handed her some money.

'While I'm gone you could unpack our things into the chest o' drawers,' she suggested as she left, leaving Holly to stare about and think ruefully of her lovely bedroom and secure, comfortable life back at home.

Chapter Five

Almost an hour later Ivy returned carrying so much stuff that Holly wondered how she had managed to get it all up the stairs. She was obviously much stronger than she looked. She had even purchased a small bag of coal and instantly set to getting the grate cleaned out and a fire lit while Holly looked on. She had no idea how to go about it, but Ivy was used to doing such chores.

Once the fire was going, Ivy hunted about and found an old kettle beneath the sink, which she filled with water and set on the fire.

'Now, while that's gettin' hot I'm goin' back out to buy us some new beddin'.' She rubbed her hands down her skirt and nodded towards the bed. 'I don't know about you but I don't fancy sleepin' under them manky things, do you? Though I've no doubt they'll be fine when they've had a good wash.'

Holly hastily handed her some more money.

'An' while I'm at it, I'll get us some groceries, an' all. Milk, tea, bread an' perhaps some cheese fer supper, eh? We'll be ready for sommat to eat by the time we've got this place clean.'

Within seconds she was gone again and, determined to do her bit, Holly went through the cleaning things Ivy had bought and soon had her very first go at cleaning a window.

Ivy and the staff back at home had always done this sort of thing and it came to her what a sheltered life she had led. Usually at this time, she'd probably be having tea with her mother and her heart hurt at the thought of her sitting alone with no one to talk to. She hoped she wasn't missing her too much.

It was pitch-dark by the time Ivy arrived back again, once more loaded down with bags.

'There's a market sells all sorts not far away,' she told Holly breathlessly. 'I got these pillows an' blankets off a second-hand stall there but they're nice an' clean, look.'

She looked approvingly at the clean window and the floor which Holly had almost finished scrubbing then said, 'By, it's lookin' better already wi'out them cobwebs in the corners an' wi'out all the dust flyin' up every time you walk across the room.'

Two hours later the room, although still very basic, was clean as a new pin.

'We could perhaps get some curtains and a rug for in front of the fire tomorrow to make the place look a bit more homely,' Holly suggested as they sat sipping a welcome cup of tea.

Ivy looked a bit concerned. 'But that'll cost yet more money,' she pointed out.

'I know, but we can take anything we buy with us when we move and I've got plenty to be going on with,' Holly assured her. 'All we need to do now is find ourselves a job.'

Ivy frowned. 'But what sort o' job will you be able to do? I mean, it's easy for me, I'll be quite happy cleanin' or some-thin' but you ain't been brought up to do jobs like that.

Perhaps you could try to get a position as a nanny or some-thin'?'

'I quite fancy doing shop work,' Holly said thoughtfully. 'Yes, perhaps in a dress shop.'

Ivy yawned and Holly felt guilty. 'Why don't we get washed and have an early night so as we can get an early start in the morning?' she suggested.

Ivy nodded in agreement. 'That ain't a bad idea, I'm filthy,' she said ruefully as she stared down at the state of her clothes. 'We'll have to find a way to wash these.'

'Oh, I already worked that out when I went to use the toilet in the yard,' Holly assured her. 'There's a wash house out there where we can rub things through. We'll have to dry them in here by the fire though. Meanwhile I can lend you an outfit for tomorrow. My clothes might be a bit big on you but at least you'll be neat and tidy for looking for a job.'

The girls made sandwiches with the bread and the ham hock that Ivy had bought and after having a thorough wash at the sink they sank into bed, exhausted. They had only been away from home for two days yet already to Holly it felt like two years and she missed her mother dreadfully. But not enough to go back with my tail between my legs and be forced to marry Mr Dolby, she told herself.

Already Ivy was snoring softly and soon after Holly fell into an exhausted sleep too.

The next morning they were up bright and early and Ivy made toast for them in front of the fire with the remaining bread. This was washed down with two strong cups of tea and then Holly sorted out an outfit for Ivy to borrow.

As Holly had thought, the skirt and blouse she lent her were a little large for her but even so, as Ivy stared at herself in the cracked mirror that hung above the fireplace, her face was so animated that she looked almost pretty.

'Why, I feel like a real toff,' she chuckled. 'Trouble is, soon as I open me mouth I'll let meself down, won't I?'

Holly smiled at her indulgently. Strangely, since they had left home, Ivy's confidence seemed to have grown and Holly wondered if it was because she didn't have to worry about visits from her violent father any more.

'Right,' Ivy said as she dragged her old coat on, wishing that she didn't need it. 'I reckon we'd be best to split up then meet again at lunchtime. We're not goin' to be lookin' for the same sorts o' jobs so we'd probably do best on our own.'

Feeling slightly nervous, Holly nodded, thinking how strange it was that since their arrival she had come to rely on Ivy rather than the other way around.

As they stepped out onto the landing together they were confronted by a small girl sitting against the wall with her arms wrapped about her knees and tears streaming down her face. She looked to be no older than four or five years old and from the door next to her they could hear the sounds of a violent argument going on. The clothes she wore were little more than rags and as Holly looked sympathetically down on her she noticed that her hair was crawling with lice.

'Are you all right, pet? she asked, stooping to the child's level.

The little girl stared solemnly up at her. 'Me ma an' pa is 'avin' a row cos she ain't got no money to give him,' the child informed her. 'But me ma's only got a few pence an' she needs that fer the baby cos she says her milk 'as dried up, so she won't give it 'im.'

Holly opened her bag and took out some coins, which she held out to the child. 'What's your name?' she asked gently.

'Sally, miss.'

'Right, Sally, I want you to take this money and go and get some bread and some milk for the baby and take it back to your mother. Do you think you could do that?'

The child stared at the money incredulously before swiping her arm across her snotty nose and scrubbing at the tears on her thin cheeks, then she snatched the money as if she was afraid Holly might change her mind. 'Yes, miss.' And she was off, haring down the stairs.

Ivy shook her head. 'Poor little sod,' she said quietly. 'She reminds me of some o' the little 'uns from the courtyards back home.'

Holly nodded in agreement. 'Did you see how thin she was? She looked as if one good puff of wind would blow her away.'

By the time they reached the street there was no sign of Sally and hugging her old coat about her, Ivy suggested, 'Why don't you go into town an' try the shops? I'm goin' to head fer the factories. We'll meet back here at two o'clock, eh? We'll be ready fer somethin' to eat by then.'

Although Holly nodded in agreement, she felt very apprehensive as Ivy turned and walked away from her, but, determined to follow through with her plan, she plastered on a smile and set off to find a job.

Holly was patiently waiting outside their lodging house at a quarter past two that afternoon when Ivy came scooting round the corner. Her nose was glowing and her hands were blue with cold but she was beaming like a Cheshire cat.

'Sorry I'm late.' She skidded to a halt blowing on her hands to try and warm them. 'But I stopped for a cup o' tea in a café earlier on an' the lady in there told me there were jobs goin' at the Bryant an' May match factory in Bow so I hopped on a tram an' went straight there.' She smiled proudly. 'I got a job an' I can start in the mornin'. The pay ain't brilliant admittedly, it's fifteen bob a week, but it's better than nothin' till somethin' better turns up, ain't it? How did you do?'

Holly hung her head and shrugged dispiritedly. 'No good at all up to now and I must have gone into almost every shop in Oxford Street asking if there were any vacancies. But well done you, although I've heard the match factories aren't very nice places to work,' she ended worriedly.

Ivy sniffed, 'Well, as I said it's only for now. Somethin' better is bound to be round the corner. But come on, it's far too cold to stand about round here. I found a little café that's cheap an' cheerful nearby.'

Linking her arm through Holly's she began to haul her along, chattering as she went. When Holly could finally get a word in edgeways she asked, 'So what job will you be doing exactly?'

Ivy chuckled. 'I shall be cuttin' pieces of wood down into match-sized pieces then dippin' the heads of 'em into red phosphorus, then they go on from me to be packed into boxes.'

'But I'm sure I read somewhere that working with phosphorus could be dangerous.'

Ivy nodded. 'White phosphorus can but apparently the red ain't so bad. One o' the girls were tellin' me that a lot o' the women who used to work wi' the white stuff developed what they call "phossy jaw" which could be fatal. It would start with severe toothache then their gums would start to swell and their bones would glow greeny white in the dark. After that their minds would go funny and everythin' would stop workin'. The women all came out on strike some years ago an' that's when they changed to red phosphorus, which ain't quite so dangerous.'

'I still don't like the thought of you working somewhere like that,' Holly said with a frown.

'Don't be daft, I'll be fine,' Ivy assured her as they came to the doorway of a small café. 'Here we are. Let's get some grub, me stomach thinks me throat's cut.'

As soon as they had eaten they set off again in search of a job for Holly and eventually they branched off Oxford Street into Cavendish Street, one of the side streets. After trying a few more shops they came to one with the sign 'Miss May's Modes' written in gilt letters on a large sign above the door. Beautiful gowns were displayed on mannequins in the window along with a small sign that read, 'Assistant needed, apply within'.

'This looks promisin',' Ivy chirped. 'Go on in and give it

a go. The worst she can say is no. I'll wait out here for yer. I don't wanna come in an' spoil yer chances.'

Holly took a deep breath and as she entered the shop a small bell above the door tinkled. Seconds later a small, immaculately dressed woman appeared through a curtain behind the counter and smiled at her. Her greying hair was styled into an elegant twist on the back of her head and she had light blue eyes. Although she was now well into middle-age she was still very attractive and Holly imagined that she must have been quite a beauty in her younger days.

'Good afternoon, miss. How may I help you?' Her voice had a musical quality to it and Holly gulped nervously.

'I, er . . . Actually I came in to enquire about the position in the window.'

'Oh, I see.' The woman looked Holly up and down. The girl was very neatly turned out and she spoke beautifully too. 'Have you had experience of shop work before?' she enquired and Holly coloured slightly as she shook her head.

'No I haven't . . . but I'd work very hard and I'm a fast learner.'

'Hmm.' The woman strummed her fingers on the counter. She had been hoping for someone who had experience of shop work but up to now the girls and women who had applied for the job had been totally unsuitable. 'I see. Are you any good with figures?'

'Oh yes,' Holly assured her. 'I had a private tutor and I've always been very good at figures.'

'Then let me show you round and tell you what the job entails,' the woman said and proceeded to show her what was in the various drawers and cupboards. There were gloves and scarves, a selection of ladies' underwear, all made of the best quality silk, and stockings and suspenders and almost anything a woman could need. At the other end of the shop were long shelves containing bolts of material in all the colours of the rainbow which would be made into gowns for Miss May's customers. Through a door at the back of the shop Holly could hear the whirr of sewing machines.

'That's the workshop,' the woman informed her. 'I employ two seamstresses full time to make or alter the gowns that are bought from here. The hours you would be expected to work are eight till five every weekday and eight till twelve on Saturday. Could you manage that?'

'Oh yes,' Holly agreed enthusiastically. Miss May, as she then introduced herself, went on to tell Holly of the wage she could expect. 'I would give you a month's trial at fifteen shillings a week and then if you proved to be satisfactory I will increase it to eighteen and sixpence.'

Again Holly nodded.

'Good. I shall expect you to serve the customers when they enter the shop and always show them respect. There will be times when I have to be out buying the items that the seamstresses don't make and in my absence you would be in charge.'

Holly looked a little disturbed at that but the woman assured her, 'Don't worry, for the first few days you will watch me. I wouldn't dream of asking you to use the till or be here alone until you felt quite confident that you could manage. Finally, I must warn you that I am a stickler for punctuality. I won't tolerate someone who comes in late.'

'Oh, I would never do that,' Holly assured her and the woman smiled.

'Then in that case I am happy to offer you the job as my assistant on a month's trial starting next Monday morning at eight o'clock sharp.' She shook Holly's hand and the girl floated out of the shop with a smile on her face that stretched from ear to ear.

'I got it!' she whooped to Ivy who was standing discreetly out of sight just along the road. 'What with both of us working we'll be able to get out of Soho and rent our own little place in no time.'

Ivy smiled at her excitedly. 'Well done, miss . . . I mean, Holly.' She herself had been working since she was fourteen years old but she knew that this was a huge step for her friend and she couldn't have been more proud of her.

Chapter Six

When Ivy arrived home from her first day in the match factory the next day, Holly stared at her hands in horror. They were sore and red and covered in splinters and tiny cuts.

'You'll need to soak them in warm water and let me get all those splinters out for you otherwise they could get infected,' she warned.

Ivy smiled bravely, although her back ached and her hands were throbbing. 'They'll harden up, no doubt,' she answered nonchalantly, taking the welcome cup of steaming tea Holly had ready for her.

'I made us a bit of dinner too,' Holly told her. 'Although I'm afraid it's not much. Just jacket potato and cheese. I think you're going to have to give me some cooking lessons.'

Hurrying to the oven she took the potatoes out but when Ivy tried to cut into hers she found it was still hard in the middle, although she didn't say anything.

It was Holly herself who commented, 'These are awful, aren't they?'

She looked so downhearted that Ivy chuckled. 'A bit chewy admittedly, but as me mam used to say, "What don't fatten'll fill". They're better than nowt an' you'll get the hang of it.'

Holly sighed despondently. She had spent the whole afternoon trying to clean the filthy oven but was sure that she hadn't made half as good a job of it as Ivy would have done.

'I don't seem to be much good at looking after myself at all,' she groaned. 'Goodness knows what would have happened to me if you hadn't come with me.'

A tear trickled down her cheek and, glad of an excuse to leave the potato, Ivy hurried over to comfort her.

'It was you who taught me to read and write enough to get by so it won't be any hardship for me to teach you a few practical housekeepin' things, will it? We'll make a good team, you just wait and see. But now is there any hot water left in that kettle? I must admit I'm worn out an' all I really want is a good wash an' an early night.'

Outside the wind was rattling the windowpanes but Holly had kept the fire going, so although the room was sparse at least it was warm and cosy.

'I'll put some in the bowl for you,' Holly offered obligingly, wishing she could have started her new job today as well. 'But then I insist on getting those splinters out for you before you go to bed and then you can soak them in salt water.'

As Holly removed the splinters with her hat pin, which was the only sharp thing she had to hand, Ivy gritted her teeth bravely. In truth, she hadn't enjoyed the first day of her new job at all but she wouldn't tell Holly that. She knew her friend wouldn't want her to go back there if she knew how hard it really was. She had found herself working in a large room full of long tables and benches where she and the other women she worked with had to chop wood down with lethally sharp little knives into match sizes. They were then dipped into dishes of horrible-smelling red phosphorus

66

that glowed even in the daylight, and left to dry before going to the packing area where they were counted and put into little boxes. It was very boring, although some of the women she worked with had cheered the place up no end by singing popular songs. They had started off with 'I'm shy, Mary Ellen, I'm shy', which had had Ivy giggling, before they began on 'Down by the Old Mill Stream'. By the end of the day she had found herself singing along with them and they had finished the afternoon with their rendition of 'Let Me Call You Sweetheart'. Most of them were hopelessly out of tune and would never get jobs on stage but at least it had helped pass the time.

When Holly was finally happy with her efforts she allowed Ivy to hop into bed and within minutes the girl was fast asleep, her gentle snores echoing around the bleak little room. Holly wasn't tired, although she had tried to keep herself busy during the day, and she lay awake for a long while listening to the wind howling outside and thinking about all the home comforts that she used to take for granted. The most pressing of these was the privy and she was grateful that they had bought a chamber pot for use late in the evening and during the night to prevent them having to go all the way downstairs to the rather disgusting toilet outside, which was shared by all the families in the house. They had agreed that they would take it in turns to empty and rinse it out each morning. It was a job that Holly wasn't looking forward to. She had never had to do any menial work before and was only now realising how pampered she had been, although she was determined to learn.

Once again she fell asleep dreaming of home and fighting

a wave of hopeless homesickness, but still she had no wish to return. Even living as she was now was preferable to living in luxury with a man she didn't love.

At eight o'clock sharp the following Monday morning, Holly was outside Miss May's Modes ready to begin her first day in her new job. She had used the wash house at her lodgings and washed all of her own and Ivy's clothes while Ivy was at work, then dried them over the back of the chair by the fire in their room before ironing them with a flatiron she had bought second-hand at one of the markets that seemed to be dotted about the capital. Ivy had taught her how to iron as well as helping her make basic meals and already Holly was feeling a little more optimistic. The day before, she had written a long letter to her mother telling her all that had happened to her and Ivy since they had arrived in London, but she had put no return address on the letter. She would only do that when she and Ivy had managed to find some-where a little more salubrious to live. She dared not tell her mother of the dwelling they were currently living in, or admit how homesick she really felt. Now she patted her hat and entered the shop to find Miss May already there putting some money into the till.

'Ah, right on time,' the woman noted approvingly, then pointing to the curtain she told her, 'You can hang your hat and coat in there. I use that room as the staff room and there is also a fitting room in there where clients may try garments on.'

Holly nodded and quickly did as she was told.

For the first couple of hours she was nervous and quietly observed the way Miss May greeted and dealt with the customers, but shortly before lunchtime, as her confidence grew, she attempted her first sale and felt proud when she managed to satisfy the customer, although she was still quite wary of the huge old-fashioned till.

'So how did it go?' Ivy enquired kindly when they arrived back at their room minutes apart that evening.

'Actually I quite enjoyed it and being the week before Christmas we were ever so busy.' Holly went to turn the heat on beneath the small pan of stew Ivy had prepared before they left for work that morning. 'There were ladies coming in and buying all manner of things as gifts: silk stockings, gloves and scarves, mainly.' She realised with a little pang then that this would be her first Christmas away from home and her mother but she quickly pulled her thoughts back to the present as she asked, 'Do you know what days you'll be given off over Christmas yet?'

Ivy was busy stirring the fire back to life before adding some more nuggets of coal. 'Yes, because Christmas Day falls on a Monday this year we have Christmas Eve and Christmas Day, but the gaffer said we'd be allowed to leave a couple of hours early on Saturday. I dare say that's to help out the women who have families so they's can get their shoppin' done. What about you?'

'The same, although I'm not allowed to finish early this Saturday. Miss May says that's one of the busiest days of the year. You know, for people buying last-minute gifts. We had one gentleman come in today and he bought a selection of real silk underwear for his wife.' She blushed as she recalled laying out the silk knickers on the counter in front of him and the glimpse of a smile she had seen on Miss May's face when she noticed her new assistant's embarrassment.

'Huh! For his fancy piece, more like,' Ivy responded with a grin. She crossed to the curtains and drew them tight against the cold night air then commented, 'Well, at least there's no sign o' snow yet. That's somethin', I suppose, although it's still damn cold! Oops sorry.' Ivy knew that Holly disapproved of swearing but she still forgot herself from time to time.

Holly grinned as she admired her handiwork. She had bought the curtains for a snip from yet another second-hand stall a couple of days before and had then spent a whole afternoon altering them to fit their window. They were a wonderful deep red velvet, a little faded along the edges admittedly, but still beautiful quality and they softened the room no end, as did the cushions she had bought for the chairs. She liked to imagine that they had once graced the drawing room of a very grand house. Very slowly, the place was beginning to feel a little more like home, although neither of the girls wanted to stay there for long.

'So what shall we do for Christmas then?' Holly asked. 'I thought we might go to a service at the church on the evening of Christmas Eve and seeing as you may get to finish early on Saturday you could perhaps buy us a chicken and some veg to cook for Christmas Day.'

'Sounds lovely to me,' Ivy agreed and they made a pact that this Christmas would be as special as they could make it.

Two days later, as Holly was serving a customer in the shop, she heard two of the ladies who were waiting to be served talking about the Red Cross course they were attending, and her ears pricked up, one of her regrets about leaving home was that she had not been able to start the course as she had planned.

'Excuse me asking, but I couldn't help overhearing you talking about a Red Cross course,' she said politely when it was their turn to be served. 'Is it anywhere around here?'

'Why yes, dear,' the plumpest of the women told her with a friendly smile. She was wearing a hat trimmed with peacock feathers that seemed to have a life of their own and Holly could barely take her eyes off them. 'It's one evening a week at the University Hospital, I'm sure you would be most welcome if you cared to go along. And now I wonder if you could show me some leather gloves, please. I'm buying them for my daughter.'

'Yes, of course.' Holly hurried to the glove drawer and soon the two ladies were pawing indecisively over the selection she had laid out before them on the counter.

'I think Susan would like this pair, Maude,' the plump woman's companion advised her, lifting a fine pair of dove-grey kid gloves. 'The colour is so pretty, she could wear them to church and for special occasions.'

'Yes, she could, but then this black pair would so much more practical,' her friend pondered. Eventually she decided to take both pairs, much to Miss May's delight.

'Well done, dear,' she praised Holly when the women left the shop with the gloves beautifully gift-wrapped. 'You certainly have a way with the customers and I think you'll be ready to start using the till when we come back after Christmas. Spending it with your family, are you?'

Holly had avoided talking about her private life and was reluctant to say too much now. 'No, my family live in the Midlands so I shall be spending it with my friend. She and I share a room.'

'Oh, I see.' Miss May looked mildly surprised. She could tell that Holly came from good stock by the way she spoke and carried herself. In actual fact, she had thought it strange that a girl who had clearly been well educated had come seeking shop work in the first place. Of course, she was very pleased that she had. Holly's manners were impeccable and already she was a great favourite with her regular customers. 'And where are you living?'

The question took Holly by surprise. She had hoped that her employer need never know what a run-down area she was living in at present but now she found that she couldn't lie.

'Actually, we hoped to rent a small flat or a house but when we arrived in London we found that they were all too expensive so we ended up renting an attic room in Soho. Just for now,' she added hastily. 'Ivy is working too now, so soon . . .' She broke off when she saw the corners of Miss May's mouth lift with amusement.

'Your friend is called Ivy?'

Holly sighed. 'Yes, I know . . . Holly and Ivy, we often get teased about it. We were both born in December and our birthdays are only two weeks apart so I think our mothers must have decided to give us a festive name.' Thankfully the conversation was stopped from going any further when the shop bell tinkled and a number of customers descended on them all at once and for the rest of the afternoon they were rushed off their feet.

Holly had forgotten all about their conversation when Miss May finally turned the sign on the door to 'Closed'. Her feet were throbbing and all she wanted was to get home to a nice hot cup of tea and put her feet up. Miss May seemed to have other ideas, however, when she asked bluntly, 'Did you run away from home, dear?'

Holly looked shocked but after a moment she sadly shook her head. 'Not exactly,' she muttered miserably, and suddenly the whole sorry story came tumbling out.

'So you're telling me that because you wouldn't marry an older widower who your grandfather had chosen for you, he ordered you to leave?' Miss May looked incredulous as Holly lowered her head.

'That's about the long and the short of it.'

Miss May sat down heavily on a chair close to the counter and studied Holly closely. She had taken a great liking to this young lady: she was kind and considerate and nothing was ever too much trouble for her, which was probably why she was so popular with everyone who entered the shop. She considered herself to be a very good judge of character and wondered if she dare voice what she was thinking. Silence stretched between them for a time until eventually she said tentatively, 'I might be able to help you regarding your accommodation.'

Holly looked bemused.

'The thing is,' Miss May went on, 'above this shop is a little flat. It's been empty for some time unfortunately so I can't say exactly what state it's in. I let it out for a while but the tenants were dreadful and eventually I gave them notice to leave. It's stood empty ever since because although I'm addressed as Miss May I'm actually a married woman and myself and my husband have a house in Mayfair, so you see I have no use for it, but it might be just the job for you and your friend. Would you like to take a look at it?'

Holly's face stretched into a radiant smile. 'Oh, yes please,' she gushed, and so Miss May hurried away to return minutes later with a key.

'The flat is accessed from a door next to the shop,' she informed Holly as she led her outside the shop and directed her through another door and up a narrow staircase. 'There's a light at the top of the stairs,' Miss May informed her. 'And when that's on you'll be able to take a look around.'

There was electric lighting in the flat as well? Holly could hardly wait. Surely anywhere would be better than where she and Ivy were living now? They were kept awake constantly by little Sally's parents having blazing rows and the sound of children crying. So much so that sometimes when it was time to get up she felt as if she hadn't been to bed.

At the top of the stairs the kindly woman opened the door and beckoned Holly into what was clearly a decent-sized living room. Cobwebs adorned the corners and it looked neglected but Holly could imagine how lovely it would be with some tender loving care. There was a large sash window overlooking the street below and a fireplace that was full of dead ashes. A settee stood in front of it and although it was dusty, Holly could just imagine it with some pretty cushions on after having a good clean. There was also a dark wood table and chairs and a long sideboard along one wall. Another door led into a small but adequate kitchen and yet two more doors led to small bedrooms, both with brass bedsteads and an assortment of drawers. There was even a wardrobe in one of them and after living in the room they were in now it appeared luxurious to Holly.

'Oh, it's beautiful,' she breathed, but then practicality kicked in and she frowned. 'But how much would the rent be? This is a much nicer area than where we live now so I'm not sure that we could afford it.'

'How much are you paying for your room now?'

'Six shillings a week.'

'Hmm, quite expensive for sharing one room, I would think,' Miss May commented. 'How about eight shillings a week?'

Holly stared at her dumbfounded. She knew this was not nearly enough from the flats that she and Ivy had viewed before taking their room, which had been all they could afford at the time. But they could comfortably manage the extra now that they were both working.

'That's very cheap for a flat,' she answered, and Miss May shrugged.

'Well, the way I look at it is it's a shame for it to stand empty. It's only going to get damp.'

Again Holly hesitated. It just seemed too good to be true. 'But why would you do this for me?' she asked softly. 'You hardly know me.'

'Let's just say that what you told me struck a chord.' Miss May sighed. 'I once found myself in a very similar position, believe it or not. My parents had high hopes of me marrying a friend of the family, but I had already fallen in love with my husband who had barely a penny to his name. Eventually they put so much pressure on me to give him up and things became so bad at home that we ran off to get married, and I don't mind telling you I've never regretted it for a single second. Unfortunately, he suffers with ill health now and needs nursing so one of the perks of you living above the shop might be that I could spend a little more time at home with him once you've learned all the ropes and feel comfortable running the shop alone. I wouldn't have to come in so early in the morning to open up and let the seamstresses in for a start, so you see you living here could be advantageous to us both. What do you think?'

It was all Holly could do to stop herself from throwing her arms about the woman but her smile said it all.

Miss May grinned. 'I think perhaps you'd better bring your friend to look at the place and then you can make your decision. Here take the key and you can tell me in the morning.' With that she turned off the light and made her way downstairs with a bright-eyed Holly following very close behind. Things were looking up. Suddenly she could hardly wait to get home to tell Ivy the wonderful news.

Chapter Seven

Later that night, Ivy stood in the little flat above the shop and stared about her in amazement. 'Are yer quite sure you heard her right?' she questioned. 'All this fer just eight bob a week? Why, we've even got us own bedrooms an' a proper little kitchen to cook in.'

'I know.' Holly gave a little twirl of excitement. 'Just think we might even dare to venture out after dark without worrying about women of the night shouting after us on street corners because they think we're after their clients. Oh, do say you like it, Ivy!'

'Like it! I bloody love it,' Ivy responded, hardly able to believe their luck. 'But when did she say we could move in?'

'We haven't spoken about that yet but I dare say as soon as we're ready. Bear in mind it will be Christmas in a few days' time and you won't want to be moving then . . . will you?'

'Not 'alf! I'd carry our stuff here tonight given half a chance.'

'In that case I'll speak to Miss May first thing in the morning then,' Holly promised and after leaving the flat they carefully locked the door behind them and made their way back to Soho.

'I don't see why you shouldn't move in just as soon as you like,' Miss May told Holly the next day, and so that very evening she and Ivy packed up some of their meagre possessions, took down the curtains that Holly had made and set off for the flat.

'We can bring the rest tomorrow after work,' Ivy said. 'Though I have a feelin' Mrs Hall ain't goin' to be none too pleased when we tell her we're leavin'.'

Holly shrugged. 'She can't complain. We've paid the rent up till the end of this week,' she pointed out, but as it turned out, Ivy was proved to be right.

'What do yer mean, yer goin' tonight?' Mrs Hall sputtered when late the next evening Holly tapped on her door to return the key. 'It's almost Christmas – what chance do I 'ave of lettin' it out again till after the 'olidays? Yer should 'ave given me some notice so I'm goin' to ask fer another week's rent fer me inconvenience.'

'Ask away but yer won't get it.' Ivy stepped forward and taking the key from Holly she firmly pressed it into the woman's hand. 'We paid fair an' square fer the time we were here an' you'll not get a penny piece more.'

'Humph! Ungrateful bitches,' Mrs Hall grumbled as she went back into her own room, slamming the door resoundingly behind her.

They had almost reached the front door when Sally, the little girl from the room next to theirs, appeared from the street, her face pinched and her poor little hands blue with cold.

'Oh, I'm glad I've seen you, I wanted to say goodbye,' Holly told her and was shocked when the little girl's face crumpled. Holly often slipped her a penny and she would miss her. Now Holly fumbled in her purse and pressed some coins into the little girl's hand.

'Go and buy yourself some sweeties,' she urged her and suddenly the little girl threw her arms about her waist and hugged her fiercely before disappearing out of the door again like a shot from a gun. She knew better than to go home with money in her hand, as her father would take it off her and she had every intention of doing exactly what Holly had suggested.

'Poor little mite. I hope she'll be all right,' Holly fretted.

Ivy gave her a sympathetic smile. She knew what a soft heart Holly had.

'Come on,' she urged. 'If we want to get our new place all set up for Christmas we need to get a move on.'

For the next few nights and every spare minute they had when they weren't working was spent scrubbing and cleaning the little flat from top to bottom and it was soon transformed into a comfortable little home that they were very proud of. Ivy had attacked the dark wood table and chairs and the old sideboard with lavender furniture wax and now it gleamed in the light from the fire. The bare floorboards had been scrubbed until they were almost white and Ivy had white-washed the walls, which had brightened the place up no end. Even the fabric on the sofa had been thoroughly washed and now looked inviting with its pretty cushions spread across it. The curtains that Holly had stitched for their old room hung at the window in the living room, although after Christmas they would have to buy some more for their bedrooms.

'There, I reckon we're all ready fer Christmas now,' Ivy said as she stood back and eyed their little home with pride. 'It's a shame we couldn't have got us a Christmas tree though.'

'Perhaps next year. At least we have a chicken to cook,' Holly pointed out. 'And tonight we'll go to the carol service at St Anne's. I'm starting my Red Cross course there after the New Year.'

They spent Christmas and the New Year quietly at home together, content in each other's company, although Holly's thoughts constantly drifted to her mother and she wondered how she would be coping with their first Christmas apart. She hoped she managed to enjoy it, because she hated to think of her mother being unhappy without her.

On the stroke of twelve on New Year's Eve, as they listened to the chimes of Big Ben, the girls toasted each other with a glass of sherry that Ivy had bought especially for the occasion, and Holly resolved to make her mother proud of her in the coming year. Neither of them had drunk alcohol before and Holly wasn't that keen on it but Ivy drank two small glasses straight off and then couldn't stop giggling.

The day after, they were back at work bright and early and Holly began to feel a little happier, though she still missed her mother dreadfully and wondered if it might be possible to visit her. She suggested it to Ivy that night as they sat eating dinner.

'I don't see why not,' Ivy answered. 'You could always meet her away from the house if you don't feel comfortable going back there. Your gran'father couldn't object to that surely? There's no reason why you couldn't let her have your address either. At least we have somewhere respectable to live now.'

And so that very evening Holly sat down and wrote to her mother.

Dear Mother,

I hope this letter finds you well and that you had a good Christmas and New Year. Both Ivy and I are well and are now living in a very nice flat above the shop where I work. My employer, Miss May, is a dear soul and Ivy and I are enjoying making the flat into a home when we are not working. We had a quiet Christmas together and I must admit that I missed you terribly and I know Ivy missed her family too. In fact, she sent a large portion of her wages home to ensure her mother had money to buy some little gifts for her siblings. I pray that some time soon I might see you, there is so much to tell. It is so different living here to being back in our sleepy little market town. Everything here is hustle and bustle and the city never seems to sleep! I found it hard to adjust at first but thankfully I am getting more used to it now. Do give my love to Cook and, of course, my regards to Grandfather. It seems so long since I last saw you . . .

She went on to talk of trivialities before adding their address and the next morning during her short break she hurried along to the post box to post it.

The girls spent the next weekend scouring the markets for things for their flat. Holly still had some of the money her mother had given her and she was eager to make their little place into a real home. They bought a roll of oil cloth, which they managed to fit in the lounge themselves and then they found a large rug to cover most of it and make the room feel warmer. She also bought some material which she sewed into curtains for their bedrooms.

'Cor, it looks quite posh now, don't it?' Ivy commented proudly. 'An' now we've got it all just about how we want it we can start to do a bit o' sightseein' on our days off.' She was longing to see some of the sights Holly had shown her in books. There was Buckingham Palace, Trafalgar Square and the Houses of Parliament, to name but a few, but up until now there had been no time.

'We'll start this very Sunday,' Holly agreed. Thankfully, although it was cold the snow had held off. 'We can use the trams to see most of the places.'

The following day, Miss May followed them upstairs to see what they had done with the place and she was clearly impressed with their efforts.

'Why, you've made it into a real little home,' she said approvingly as she looked around admiringly.

Holly hurried away to put the kettle on for tea and Miss May eyed Ivy with interest. She and Holly seemed poles apart in every way. Ivy was nowhere near as well spoken as Holly but it was clear that they were close and she wondered how they had met.

'Did you know each other back in your home town?' she asked tentatively as she took a seat on the sofa beside the fire.

'Yer could say that . . . I was Holly's maid.' Ivy chortled with laughter at the astonished look on Miss May's face. 'An' when I knew she were comin' here there was no way I could let her come on her own.'

'I see. How very unusual for two such young ladies to

choose to come and live in the capital all alone,' Miss May commented.

When Holly appeared with a tray of tea, Miss May told her, 'Ivy here was just telling me that she was your maid when you lived at home. Whatever made you both come all this way to live?'

'Oh, well, as you know I needed to get away, and we just got on the first train out, so we could have ended up anywhere, I suppose,' Holly said as she poured the tea into some dainty china cups she had found on a stall in the market. 'How is your husband?' she asked, and the woman's face clouded.

'Not well at all to be honest. He has a degenerative muscle-wasting disease and struggles to get about now. That was something I was going to talk to you about actually.' She eyed Holly thoughtfully for a moment before asking, 'Do you feel confident enough to open the shop each morning for me yet? Just so that I can have a little extra time with him before I have to come into work each day.'

'Of course,' Holly agreed eagerly. She had grown very fond of her employer and would have done anything to please her.

'In that case I'll give you the key to the shop door.' Miss May fumbled in her bag for it. 'I'll aim to be in for ten each morning. That will give me time to help Ernest get dressed and get him settled.'

'That's no problem at all,' Holly assured her. 'Make it even later than that if you need to. I know how to use the till now and I know where everything is so I'll be fine.'

'That is a weight off my mind, dear, thank you so much.' Miss May finished her tea and rose reluctantly. 'Well, I really ought to be off, my husband will be wondering where I've got to,' she told them. 'Although I must admit I could quite happily sit here by your fire all night. It's so cosy up here.'

Miss May left feeling a lot happier than when she had arrived and Holly glowed with pride at the trust she had placed in her.

'I reckon we've really dropped on us feet here,' Ivy sighed happily as she sipped at her second cup of tea. And Holly could only agree with her.

The arrangement worked well. Each day Holly made sure she had opened the shop in time for the seamstresses to arrive and then she would attend to customers who came in, or tidy up until Miss May arrived.

The two seamstresses were both London born and bred and Holly got on well with them. Dora Brindley was a huge, motherly woman who came from Whitechapel and Enid Weston was her complete opposite, tiny and birdlike who proudly informed Holly that she had been born within the sound of Bow Bells.

'My friend works in Bow,' Holly informed her one morning as Dora was setting her sewing machine up ready to start work. 'At the Bryant and May match factory.'

'Hmm, well she'd do well to look for another job,' Dora warned. 'It ain't a good place to work long-term. All that phosphorus they have to work with affects their health in the end. A very good friend o' mine died from phossy jaw from workin' there and it weren't a pretty sight, I don't mind tellin' you.'

Holly nibbled her lip anxiously as she returned to the shop

and turned the sign on the door to 'Open'. Perhaps she should have a word with Ivy about it. She couldn't bear to think of anything like that happening to her.

When she raised the subject that evening Ivy's reaction was far from what she would have expected.

'I've been thinkin' much the same meself,' Ivy admitted. 'Some o' the poor women I work with have gripin' toothache and loads of 'em suffer from abscesses an' all. Still, the job is better than nothin' for now but don't worry, when we have a bit behind us, I'll look around for some other job. There's bound to be somethin' goin'.'

The following day the bell above the shop door tinkled and a rather stout lady in a very heavily plumed hat breezed in.

'Ah, Lady Hamilton.' Miss May scooted forward to greet her, pulling out a chair, and glancing through the window Holly saw a chauffeured automobile standing at the kerb.

'Good morning.' The woman sat down and inclined her head imperiously. 'I have come to choose the material and the pattern for a new gown. It's for Ladies' Day at Ascot in June. One must look one's best for such an event. All the most elite people will be there, of course, and one wouldn't like to be outdone.'

'Of course,' Miss May agreed as Holly tried hard not to laugh. It appeared that this woman was larger than life in every way and was clearly a raging snob.

'Holly, would you lift some of the material down for me?' Miss May simpered. 'What sort of thing did you have in mind, Lady Hamilton?'

The woman waved a heavily beringed hand airily. 'Oh

something bright, don't you think? It will be summertime after all. What's that blue satin the girl has there? The colour reminds me of summer skies.'

As Miss May stared worriedly at the lady's large girth she thought that the material would be quite wrong for her. It could only accentuate her portly figure but as she had taught Holly, the customer was always right, so she fetched the material Holly had just laid on the counter and spread it across the lady's lap.

'It's a very fine quality,' she assured her. 'But perhaps we could use it for accents on something a little more discreet?'

'Nonsense,' the woman snorted, clearly used to always having her own way. 'Let me look at the pattern book.' And so for the next twenty minutes she pored through the patterns, finally settling on one that again Miss May thought was quite unsuitable. Even so she sent for one of the seamstresses who ushered her into a fitting room where she took her measurements. When the woman finally breezed out of the shop sometime later Miss May sighed. 'Aw well, it's her choice, I suppose.'

Holly giggled. 'They'll certainly see her coming,' she said wickedly. 'Especially if she has a milliner make her a hat in the same material.'

'She lost her husband a short while ago,' Miss May informed her. 'And from the rumours I've heard she's having a whale of a time and is very attracted to younger male escorts.'

They both fell about laughing and Holly realised that in actual fact Miss May had quite a wicked sense of humour despite the prim façade she presented to the public and her customers.

Chapter Eight

On Saturday morning Holly glanced at the clock on the wall in the shop. There was only an hour to go until she could leave and then she and Ivy were going shopping for some new clothes for Ivy and a new skirt and blouse for herself. Lady Hamilton, it appeared, was not the only one who wished to have a gown made for the various society events over the summer and they had had a steady stream of customers requiring new gowns all week. She was busy returning the bolts of material to the shelves when the shop bell tinkled and, plastering a smile to her face, Holly turned to greet the customer. Her mouth fell open when she saw who it was, and quite forgetting herself she whispered, 'Mother!'

'Oh, darling, I've missed you so much!' her mother answered and seconds later, quite forgetting where she was, Holly was in her arms.

'Ahem! Why don't you take your guest through to the staff room?' Miss May suggested and Holly smiled at her apologetically.

'I'm so sorry, I had no idea she was coming.'

'It's quite all right. In fact, why don't you take her upstairs to your flat? It's almost time for you to finish work now anyway.'

'Thank you, Miss May.' Holly flashed her a grateful smile then still holding fast to her mother's hand she dragged her out of the shop and up the stairs to her new home.

'I'm sorry to come unannounced,' her mother said breathlessly as Holly hauled her into the small lounge, her face alight. 'But once you sent me your address I couldn't wait to see you. I needed to know that you're all right.'

'Well, as you can see, I am,' Holly told her as she filled the kettle at the sink. 'And it's wonderful to see you. Now tell me everything that's gone on back at home.'

Emma removed her hat and after placing it on the table she told her daughter excitedly, 'That's partly why I've come to see you. You see, your grandfather has had a change of heart and he's said that you can come home.'

Holly looked astounded as she tried to digest what her mother had said. 'And what brought that about?' She was surprised that she wasn't feeling happy about it.

'Well, a few days after you'd gone Mr Dolby turned up with the most enormous bunch of flowers for me and a bottle of fine brandy for your grandfather. He said it was his way of apologising for what had happened and he's been to see us a few times since then. He as good as told me that it had actually been your grandfather's idea that he should court you and he said that as soon as he offered you the ring, he'd realised it was a terrible idea and that you were far too young to tie yourself down to a man of his age with a ready-made family. He was most distressed to hear that you had left home and begged your grandfather to let you return. He's actually a very nice man. So what do you think? Will you come back with me?'

Holly frowned as she spooned tea leaves into the pot. Part of her welcomed the chance of returning to the comfortable existence she had known at home and yet in that moment she also realised that although she missed her mother dreadfully she was actually very happy having her independence and living with Ivy. But she loved her mother dearly, so how could she tell her that without hurting her feelings?

'The thing is . . .' she began, choosing her words carefully. 'It isn't as simple as that. Ivy and I rent the flat from Miss May who owns the shop downstairs, as I told you in my letter. Her husband is very poorly and she's come to rely on me. And . . . well, to be honest, we're happy here now we have somewhere nice to live. Grandfather was always so strict with us, we had very little freedom, but here I get to meet people and me and Ivy can come and go as we please . . . and I am grown up now,' she ended softly. 'I would have flown the nest sooner or later anyway.'

Just for a second she saw the hurt flash in her mother's eyes but then Emma forced a smile. 'I suppose I can understand how you feel. I should have stood up to my father and made him give you a little more time with people of your own age.'

'It's all right. I understand how hard it was for you.' Holly gave her mother's hand a reassuring squeeze as she blinked back tears. Seeing her again had brought home to her just how much she had missed her and she couldn't bear to think she'd upset her. 'At least now we can keep in touch properly and I can even come home and visit from time to time if grandfather has no objections.'

'Yes, yes of course you can.' Emma hastily brushed away a tear and forced a smile. Glancing around the cosy room she remarked, 'You've certainly made this place very cosy. And how is Ivy?'

Holly had no time to answer for at that moment they heard footsteps clattering up the stairs and seconds later Ivy burst into the room in her work clothes looking somewhat bedraggled. She skidded to a halt when she saw Emma and then her face broke into a broad smile.

'Why, this is a nice surprise.' She dumped the bag of shopping she had bought on her way home from work on the table then glancing down at her work clothes she told her, 'Sorry about the state I'm in. I suppose Holly's told you I work at the match factory. It's quite a dirty job, unfortunately, but I'm going to start to look for something else very soon.' Then grinning at Holly she told her, 'Hurry up with that tea, will you, me mouth is like the bottom of a bird cage. An' there's a nice sponge cake to go wi' it in the bag.'

Emma smiled. She was pleased to see that Ivy hadn't changed at all in some ways, although she did seem a lot more confident now, perhaps because here in London she was in charge of her own destiny? Whatever the reason she had to admit that both girls seemed content, although she was bitterly disappointed that Holly didn't want to come home with her. She had missed her more than she could say but now she realised that it was inevitable that Holly would have become independent one day, her father had just hurried the process along.

They spent the next couple of hours munching cake and drinking tea, reminiscing about old times, and sharing their hopes for the future, until Emma glanced at the clock on the mantelpiece.

'I'm afraid I should be getting back to Euston,' she told the girls regretfully. 'My train leaves in less than an hour.'

'We'll come with you,' Holly offered. The visit had gone

far too quickly and she was eager to spend every precious moment she could with her mother. 'When we've seen you on your way we have to go shopping for some new clothes for Ivy and I could do with a new skirt and blouse for wearing in the shop myself.'

'Well, now that I know where you are I'll have your clothes sent on to you,' Emma promised. Packing them up would give her something to do and relieve some of the lonely boredom that stretched ahead of her back at home.

Once at Euston Station, Emma gave the girls a hug, bravely holding back the tears. 'Be sure to write at least once a week,' she told Holly. 'And come home for a visit whenever you find the time. Your room is just as you left it.'

'I will,' Holly promised, although she didn't know how she would manage with the hours she worked, unless it was a very fleeting visit. But she was sure Miss May would give her some time off when she had worked for her a little longer if she explained how much she missed her mother and made the time up when she got back.

They watched Emma board the train then stood and waved until it was out of sight.

Glancing at Holly, Ivy saw that there were tears in her eyes and she put her arm about her shoulders. 'Come on, let's go shopping; it'll cheer you up,' she told her friend, and arm in arm they headed for the market with Ivy clutching her pay packet. Holly was reluctant, but she went along anyway, not wanting to disappoint her friend.

Later, Ivy urged Holly to come to Whitechapel where some of Ivy's colleagues had said they would be able to find good second-hand clothes for a reasonable price. As they wandered through the streets it suddenly struck Holly that she was in the area her father came from. She had never given it much thought before but suddenly she wondered what he was like. Oh, she knew what her mother had told her and she believed every word but she suddenly wished that she could have met him herself, just once. After believing him to be dead for so many years, it had come as a shock to her to know that he was still alive out there somewhere. She might even pass him now on the street but how would she know? She suddenly remembered that Dora Brindley, one of the seamstresses who worked at the shop, came from there too. Would it be worth asking her if she knew a family by the name of Farthing?

'Penny for 'em? You've gone all quiet on me.' Ivy's voice interrupted her thoughts and Holly gave a sad smile.

'I was just thinking that this is where my father lived,' she answered and Ivy gave her a sympathetic smile. Her own father had left a lot to be desired but at least she had known him and she could only imagine how hard it must be for her friend.

'From what you've told me an' how he treated yer mam, yer better off wi'out him,' she told her.

Holly supposed she was right, but if she could just meet him once it would ease her mind.

'Let's go in this café here for a cuppa, eh?' said Ivy, hoping to lighten the mood. 'All this shoppin' is thirsty work.' She grabbed Holly's elbow and hauled her into the first café they came to.

The next day dawned bright and clear if cold and after dinner Ivy suggested, 'Let's go for a stroll in Hyde Park. A bit o' fresh air will do us good.'

Holly had seemed very preoccupied since her mother had gone back to the Midlands, and even the shopping trip hadn't helped. Ivy hoped that a walk in the park, surrounded by beauty, might cheer her up a little.

When they got there, they were surprised to find that many women were milling about bearing placards, which said 'Votes for Women'.

'These must be them suffragettes they're always on about in the newspapers,' Ivy said intrigued. 'Look.' She pointed ahead to where one woman was standing on a raised platform addressing a crowd. 'Let's go an' listen to what she has to say.'

Holly wasn't too sure about it but Ivy wasn't taking no for an answer so she followed her to where a large crowd of women had assembled to listen to the speaker. They had been there no more than a few minutes when suddenly a large number of policemen with truncheons appeared from nowhere and all hell seemed to break out as they tried to disperse the crowd. Women began to scream as the police manhandled them and now it was Holly who urged, 'Come on, I think we should get out of here, there's going to be big trouble.'

Some of the women clearly had the same idea but others were openly fighting the police and screaming abuse at them.

By the time they reached the road again and began to hurriedly walk along it, Holly's nerves were in shreds but Ivy was buzzing with excitement and indignation.

'Can't see what the women were doin' wrong!' she said. 'It were a peaceful enough talk so why did the coppers have to come an' interfere! From what I heard that woman was talkin' a lot o' sense. Why shouldn't we women be allowed to vote an' have the same rights as men?'

Holly shrugged. She hated trouble of any sort and had no intention of getting mixed up in it but Ivy was well and truly riled.

'I shall be comin' again to hear what the women have to say,' she declared as they hurried home arm in arm, and Holly had no doubt she would. She, on the other hand, was eager to pursue her Red Cross training and intended to do something about it that very week now that they were settled. She would make her mother, even her grandfather, proud.

Chapter Nine

'I've enrolled at the University College Hospital on Florence Nightingale's Red Cross course,' Holly excitedly told Ivy later that week when they had both finished work.

'Funny you should say that. I've enrolled on an evening course too to improve my English. I was thinkin' if I want to get out o' the match factory I might fancy doin' office work.'

'Oh, that's wonderful.' Holly was really proud of her. Until she had begun to teach her to read and write Ivy had been totally uneducated but Holly had been amazed at the speed she had picked everything up. She had learned her alphabet in a week and by the end of the first month had been able to write short sentences and read anything Holly had put before her. In no time at all she had been better with figures than Holly was herself and had turned into a sponge for learning. She was very intelligent and Holly was thrilled that she wanted to learn more.

'So when are your classes then?' Ivy asked as she began to fry them up some bacon and eggs.

'Two nights a week, Tuesdays and Thursdays. They do a more in-depth one but that is all day on Wednesdays and I have to work,' Holly said regretfully.

'So why don't you ask Miss May if you can work Saturday afternoons and a bit extra each night to make up the time?'

Ivy suggested. 'I'm sure she wouldn't mind if you really wanted to do it.'

The same thought had occurred to Holly but she wasn't sure if she was brave enough to suggest it to her employer; Miss May was very good to them and Holly didn't want her to think that she was taking advantage.

'I'll think about it,' she said as they sat down to eat their meal. When they'd finished Ivy scuttled away to get changed from her work clothes into one of the second-hand dresses they had bought on the market the weekend before. Dora Brindley had kindly volunteered to alter it for her and when she came out of the bedroom Holly let out a low whistle of approval. Dora had done a wonderful job of the alterations and suddenly Ivy looked like quite a lady. The dress was in a soft green heavy cotton with a tailored straight skirt. The top was high necked with a close-fitting bodice and long fitted sleeves, and with her hair piled high on top of her head she was transformed.

'Crikey . . . you look amazing,' Holly gasped and Ivy blushed, making her plain little face look almost pretty.

'Thanks.' She self-consciously smoothed her skirt and patted her hair. 'One o' the girls at work showed me how to do my hair. I could do yours for you, if you like, but not tonight. There's a suffragette meetin' I don't want to miss. Did you know they have Sylvia Pankhurst, one of the leaders of the movement, in Holloway prison? They've been force-feedin' the poor woman. An' all because she stands up for a woman's rights an' what she believes in.'

'Umm . . . I don't think it's quite like that. Didn't the suffragettes go on the rampage smashing shop windows and waving placards recently? That's probably why she was arrested,' Holly pointed out quietly.

Ivy shrugged as she lifted her old coat. Unfortunately she hadn't come across a decent second-hand one yet so this would have to do for now, although she hated having to cover her lovely new dress up with it.

'Far as I'm concerned, even that ain't reason enough for lockin' her up,' she grumbled as she did the buttons on her coat up. Then she headed purposefully for the door. 'Ta-ra for now,' she chirped and with a cheery wave she was gone, leaving Holly to wonder again at the change in her. Ivy was like a different person from the nervous little thing who used to jump at her own shadow when she first went to work for her grandfather. And she supposed that was no bad thing. Ivy had gained so much confidence since they'd moved to London, although she hoped that she wouldn't get overly involved with the suffragettes and end up in Holloway Prison.

The next day as they were tidying the shop during a lull in customers, Holly told Miss May about the courses she had signed up to, watching for the woman's reaction.

'Why, what a grand thing to do,' Miss May said approvingly and that gave Holly the opportunity she had been hoping for.

'Actually,' she began tentatively while she had the courage. 'The best course is one that's run at the University College Hospital all day every Wednesday so I was wondering if . . .' She licked her dry lips, suddenly nervous and hurried on, 'I was wondering if we might juggle my hours about so that I could attend that one too? I thought I could work all day on Saturdays instead of finishing at dinner time and make the rest of the hours up during the week by opening the shop an hour earlier? Even if it was too early for customers I could make sure that everywhere was thoroughly clean and tidy before they came in instead of us trying to do the cleaning in between clients. What do you think? I'll quite understand if you're not happy with the idea.'

Miss May was staring at her thoughtfully through narrowed eyes and Holly's heart sank. But then the woman surprised her when she said, 'I think it's an excellent idea. I was never fortunate enough to have a daughter of my own but if I had I would have encouraged her to do something like that. You can certainly sign up for the course and start as soon as you like. I might just decide to close on Wednesdays. I've been thinking of having a closing day for some time. It would give me a little more time to spend with my husband and the shop is doing so well I can certainly afford to.'

'Oh, thank you.' Holly was so delighted that she rushed forward and pecked the woman on the cheek then flushed and hastily stepped back. However, rather than be annoyed Miss May seemed to like the gesture and smiled at her.

'You're a good girl, Holly,' she said gently, then becoming business like again she asked, 'Could you go through to the sewing room and ask Dora how Lady Hamilton's gown is coming along. She'll be in for a first fitting later on.'

Only too happy to oblige, Holly scooted away.

By the end of January both girls were settled in their courses and were enjoying them immensely. On Sundays, when Ivy wasn't attending a suffragette meeting, they would have a lie-in and a leisurely lunch, then go for a stroll to visit places of interest. They also visited a music hall and some of the museums. Holly wrote regularly to her mother who always replied by return of post. Much as she loved to hear from her, the letters always made her feel homesick, although for most of the time now she was enjoying living in London. She was surprised to notice that Walter Dolby was often mentioned in her letters.

'You don't think she's growing fond of him, do you?' Holly asked Ivy one day.

'Would it be such a bad thing if she was?' Ivy paused. She was washing the dinner pots at the sink. They took it in turns now. 'She is still quite young, after all. She's not quite forty yet, is she? Still young enough to meet someone else, I should think.'

'But it's not that simple, is it?' Holly sighed, her face creased with worry. 'My father is probably still alive somewhere, so even if she did fall in love again she could never remarry while she's still legally wed to my father.'

'Hmm, I see what you mean.' Ivy shrugged. 'But don't go worryin' over it. Her an' Mr Dolby are probably just friends.'

Holly remained silent, hoping she was right. It hurt her though, to think of her mother stuck at home with only her grandfather and the staff for company. Now that she was living independently she had realised how much her mother had sacrificed for her to ensure that she had a stable childhood. She hoped she would one day find the happiness she truly deserved.

On the first of March the suffragettes deployed new militant tactics as they stepped up their campaign for the vote. Led by their leader Mrs Emmeline Pankhurst, many of them attacked shops in the West End with stones and hammers, which they had hidden in their muffs, causing thousands of pounds worth of damage. Two of them even hurled stones at 10 Downing Street, and within twenty minutes they had left a trail of devastation in their wake from Oxford Street to the Strand. Swan and Edgar's store in Piccadilly was only one of the most well-known stores to be attacked and it resulted in 120 women being arrested.

Thankfully, Ivy had a heavy cold and hadn't attended this particular march but Holly was horrified.

'Just think what might have happened if you had gone,' she said to Ivy as she read the newspaper. 'You could have been arrested too!' She still wasn't at all happy about her being involved with the suffragettes but Ivy wouldn't budge on her decision to be part of them and believed wholeheartedly in what the movement was striving for.

'The government have brought it on themselves,' Ivy replied shortly. 'They've granted concessions to the miners and the railwaymen after they went on strike but they still won't listen to women.'

Holly could only sigh. It seemed that Ivy had made her mind up to support the movement no matter what she said.

Then only four days later Ivy was late home from work.

It was most unlike her and as Holly prepared their evening meal she started to worry.

At nine o'clock she finally decided to go and look for her. What if she had been attacked on her way home from work? She might be lying in an alley injured somewhere. She had got no further than the shop door when she saw a rather bedraggled Ivy further along the street heading towards her. Her hat was askew and there was a tear in her new coat.

'Oh, where have you been? I've been so worried. I was just setting off to look for you.' Holly scolded, feeling like her mother.

'I, er . . . I was at the police station,' Ivy told her, shuffling from foot to foot.

'The police station!' Holly looked shocked. 'But why?'

'The suffragettes stormed into the House of Commons today and ninety-six of us got arrested.'

'You what?' Holly was appalled.

'It's all right,' Ivy assured her. 'They had us all up in front o' the magistrates a couple of hours ago and because it was my first offence I got off wi' a caution and a hand slap.'

Holly's lips pressed into a disapproving line as she shook her head.

'Oh, Ivy, where is this going to end? Can't you see the danger you're putting yourself in?'

Ivy grinned. 'It'll end when us women get the vote an' equal rights to men,' she replied and Holly knew it was pointless to argue with her further.

Chapter Ten

In April the papers were full of the tragedy that had occurred on the *Titanic*, reputably an unsinkable ship, that had sunk after hitting an iceberg on its maiden voyage from Southampton to New York killing hundreds of people in the icy seas.

'Eeh, yer can't begin to imagine how terrifyin' it must have been fer all them poor souls, can you?' Ivy said as she read the report aloud to Holly.

Holly shook her head as tears filled her eyes, grateful that no one she loved had been aboard. It just went to show how fragile life was. Suddenly she had the overwhelming urge to see her mother and decided there and then that she would visit her the very next Sunday. She would even bear the brunt of her grandfather's bad temper if need be. Her mother was all she had.

She received a rapturous welcome when she got back home from her mother and the cook.

'Why didn't yer tell us yer were comin'? I'd have cooked yer favourite,' the cook scolded her but Holly only smiled.

'To be honest it was a last-minute decision,' she admitted. 'And I can only stay for a couple of hours because the trains to Euston don't run as regularly on Sundays.'

Her mother's smile faltered for a second but then deciding to make the most of every precious second they had together she whipped her daughter off to the drawing room.

'Father, look who's come to see us,' she said happily and for the first time since he had ordered her from his house she and her grandfather found themselves face to face.

'Hello, Grandfather.' Holly wasn't at all sure of what sort of a welcome, if any, she might get from him but to her surprise he smiled at her.

Folding the newspaper he had been reading he laid it aside before saying, 'Hello, Holly. You're looking very well.'

'Thank you, and so are you,' she replied primly but she was lying. He seemed to have shrunk in size and looked so much older than the last time she had seen him.

'Will you be staying for a while?'

She shook her head. 'No, I have to return today for work tomorrow but I can stay for dinner . . . if that's all right?'

'Of course it is,' he answered then rising from his chair he said, 'I'll leave you and your mother to it then. I'm sure you have a lot to catch up on.'

She inclined her head and when he had left the room, closing the door softly behind him, she let out a deep breath.

'He's changed,' she remarked to her mother and Emma nodded.

'Yes, he has, I think he's softening in his old age,' she agreed. 'I also think he deeply regrets trying to force you into a marriage with Walter . . . I mean, Mr Dolby.'

'You two seem to be getting on very well,' Holly commented, and her suspicions were confirmed when she saw a flush creep into her mother's cheeks.

'We do get on well,' she admitted. 'Walter has become a good friend and his children are lovely too. I've met them a couple of times now.' Seeing the grin on her daughter's face she then added hastily, 'As I said, we're nothing more than friends. How could we ever be more when your father is still probably out there somewhere?' she ended bitterly. Then hoping to change what was for her a very painful subject she said, 'But now that's enough about me. Tell me all about what you and Ivy have been up to.'

And so for the next hour Holly told her all about her nursing course and Ivy's involvement with the suffragettes. 'Thankfully she doesn't spend all her spare time with them though,' she told her mother. 'She's enrolled in evening classes and she's doing really well. My course is going well too, in fact the sister who trains us thinks I should be ready to go onto the wards soon and I can hardly wait.'

Emma experienced a mixture of emotions as she saw how animated Holly became as she spoke of her nursing and, much as she hated to admit it, she was forced to acknowledge that the girl had blossomed into a confident young woman since leaving home.

'And what about romance? The young men must be queuing up to take you out,' she teased.

'Huh! I don't have time for that sort of thing,' Holly scoffed. 'What with working in the shop and my nursing training I'm too busy for anything else.'

'All that will change when you fall in love,' her mother told her but Holly didn't believe it. She was quite happy with her life as it was without the complications of a romance.

Cook came to the door then. 'Dinner will be served in five minutes, can you go through to the dinin' room?'

It was Cook herself who served it when they were seated

and when she had gone Holly whispered to her mother, 'Didn't you get a maid to replace Ivy?'

Emma shook her head. 'We have a woman come in to see to the fires and do the laundry but I see to the rest myself now. It gives me something to do.'

In that moment Holly sensed her mother's loneliness and she felt terribly guilty, but she knew that she could never come home again to live. She had her independence and although she worked hard she was enjoying it. Her grandfather joined them then and throughout dinner he was surprisingly civil asking her all about where she lived and what she was doing. Holly even thought at one moment that he was about to apologise for his behaviour.

All too soon it was time for her to leave and her grandfather even came into the hall to say goodbye.

'Just remember . . .' He looked decidedly uncomfortable. 'If you ever need anything, or you want to come home, we're always here for you.' He paused then, his voice shaky, as if there was something else he wanted to say, but then clearly thinking better of it he turned and disappeared into the drawing room as Holly's mouth dropped open with shock.

'I told you he regretted what he'd done, didn't I?' Emma whispered and Holly nodded, but it was time to go. She hovered uncertainly, torn between the new life she was building in London with Ivy, and leaving her home again. The partings were still extremely difficult for her but Ivy was relying on her so after giving herself a mental shake she embraced her mother and gave her one last kiss before setting off for the station with tears in her eyes.

105

It was early in May and Ivy was returning from her evening course when she suddenly tripped and sprawled in a most unladylike manner across the pavement. The paperwork she had been carrying in a folder spewed out and she had to crawl on her hands and knees to try to grab it before the wind blew it away. Suddenly someone was helping her and glancing up she stared into the eyes of a handsome young man who was scooping up the papers. When they were all collected together he offered her his hand and helped her to her feet asking, 'Are you all right? You had quite a tumble there.'

Ivy flushed as she looked down at the stains on the knees of her skirt, wishing that the ground would just open up and swallow her.

'Yes, thanks . . . I wasn't lookin' where I was goin', Serves meself right, don't it?'

She glanced at the palms of her hands but managed to keep her smile in place as he took her folder and carefully placed the paperwork inside it before handing it back to her.

'You look a bit shaken up,' he said, clearly concerned. 'Look, there's a café just along here. Let me buy you a cup of tea.'

Ivy opened her mouth to refuse but there was something about him that made her think again and so she nodded. 'That would be nice, thank you.'

He took her elbow and steered her along the pavement as if he was afraid she might fall again and Ivy felt a tingle run up her arm, it was nice to feel protected.

Once in the café he found them a table and when he went up to the counter to order their drinks she took the opportunity to have a good look at him. She had already noticed that he was very well spoken and now she saw that he stood a head above her and his clothes were of good quality, although they looked a little worn. He had a thatch of springy dark hair and his eyes were a wonderful tawny colour. He was lean but well muscled and Ivy felt her heart do a little flip. She had never felt like this about any man before and couldn't quite understand her feelings. But she had no time to ponder because seconds later he was back bearing two steaming mugs, one of which he placed in front of her.

'My mother always said that hot, sweet tea is good for shock.' His eyes were smiling as he measured two heaped teaspoonfuls of sugar into hers and gave it a good stir.

'Thank you.' Ivy did feel a little shaken, but after taking a few sips she began to feel a better.

'So are you from round here?' he asked, seemingly genuinely interested and again Ivy felt herself flush.

'Y-yes, I live above a clothes shop with my friend in Cavendish Street. We share a little flat. I . . . I'm Ivy, by the way. Ivy Massey.'

'I'm very pleased to meet you, Miss Massey,' he answered, holding out his hand. 'Although I would rather it could have been under less distressing circumstances. I'm Jeremy Pilkington-Hughes. I live here too, or what I should say is I lodge here, my parents have a country estate in Berkshire but my work keeps me in the capital. I'm a journalist.'

'Oh!' Ivy gulped. A country estate, she had thought he was posh and now he had confirmed it.

'And may I ask what you do for a living?'

Somehow Ivy didn't want him to know that she worked

in a match factory so she merely skirted around the truth and said, 'Actually I'm training for an office job. That's where I was coming from when I fell, one of my evening courses.'

'Excellent.' He smiled showing off his straight white teeth to perfection and again Ivy's heart did a little flutter. Completely unused to such feelings she took a long gulp of her tea, almost choking herself in the process and then blushed crimson. What must he think of her? They were clearly poles apart in class yet for all that he was talking to her on a level and she was sure she had never seen such a handsome young man in her life. They talked of the happenings in the city for a short time then and Ivy felt herself beginning to relax a little, until she caught sight of the clock on the café wall and told him apologetically, 'I really ought to be going now. My friend will be worried if I'm late. But thank you for helping me and for the tea. I feel much better now.'

He rose from the table with her. 'It was my pleasure, but please let me see you home. I'm sure it isn't safe for attractive young ladies like yourself to be walking the streets all alone at night.'

'Th-thank you.'

Back out on the pavement, he took her elbow again and Ivy felt as if her heart was going to burst out of her chest with joy. By the time they reached the shop she was smiling from ear to ear.

'This is it then. Thank you again.'

He doffed his hat and gave her a little bow. 'As I said, it was my pleasure entirely. Goodnight, Miss Massey.' And turning on his heel he strode away while Ivy stood watching him, mesmerised, until he turned a corner and was out of sight.

Her fingers were shaking so much that she could barely get the key in the lock and when she finally managed it she thundered up the stairs. Holly was sewing when she burst into the living room and she looked up. 'Oh, here you are,' she greeted her. 'I was just beginning to get a little worried. Did your course run over?'

'No.' Ivy took her hat off and flung it on the table along with her folder, then, grinning from ear to ear, she told Holly about her fall and the way Jeremy had helped her.

Holly tutted when she saw the state of Ivy's palms and hurried away to get a bowl of warm water and a cloth to bathe them. She had never seen Ivy in such a high state of excitement before. Despite the fall, there was a glow about her and her eyes were sparkling and she wondered if it might just have something to do with Jeremy Pilkington-Hughes.

'This young man sounds very nice,' she commented as she gently bathed Ivy's hands and her friend stared dreamily off into space. 'Oh . . . he is, and he's so handsome!'

'Hmm.' Holly looked up from what she was doing and eyed her friend thoughtfully. If she wasn't very much mistaken Ivy was smitten!

Chapter Eleven

It was mid-morning the next day when the bell above the shop door sounded and a young delivery boy entered bearing the most beautiful bouquet Holly had ever seen.

'Miss Ivy Massey?' he enquired as Holly approached him.

'No, she's at work at present, I'm afraid, but you can leave them with me and I'll make sure she gets them.'

The young man departed and as Holly carried the blooms into the back room Miss May raised her eyebrows. 'It seems young Ivy has an admirer.'

'It does, doesn't it.' Holly grinned and quickly told the woman what had happened the night before. 'The trouble is, she just went on and on about him for hours and then suddenly realised that she didn't even know where he lived so then she went into the depths of despair and convinced herself she was never going to see him again. I've no doubt these will cheer her up no end if they're from him.'

'I can't think of anyone else she knows well enough to send her flowers.'

Holly eyed the little envelope nestling amongst the blooms. 'Neither can I but we'll know soon enough. I hope they are, actually. I don't think I can stand any more of her moping about with a miserable face.'

Later, once the shop was closed, Holly carried the flowers up to the flat and stood them in water in the little sink. They were the first thing Ivy saw when she came in a short time later and her face lit up.

'Are they for me?' she gasped and when Holly nodded she rushed over and plucked the little envelope out and read the message.

Dear Miss Massey,
It was so nice to meet you last night. I shall call around this evening to ensure that you are fully recovered, with love, Jeremy Pilkington-Hughes xx

'Oh my goodness!' Ivy flew into a panic as she stared down at her work clothes. 'What shall I wear . . . and what shall I say to him?'

Holly giggled. 'Put your new dress on,' she advised. 'And just be yourself.'

Ivy fled into the bedroom leaving Holly smiling as she finished preparing their evening meal; it was nice to see her friend so happy.

When they had eaten, Holly left for her Red Cross training, while Ivy paced the flat like a caged animal. When she returned later that evening she found Ivy tucking into a large box of chocolates.

'Jeremy bought them for me,' she told Holly. 'And don't worry, I've saved you some.' She sighed happily then as she went on, 'We had such a wonderful evening, though what he sees in me I don't know. He's so handsome he could have any girl he wanted. He's calling for me after dinner on Sunday and we're going for a walk in the park.'

'How lovely,' Holly said, genuinely pleased for her. 'You

deserve to meet someone nice, though personally I think Jeremy is the lucky one.'

For the rest of the week Ivy floated about as if she were on a cloud and when the knock on the door came after lunch on Sunday she flew down the stairs to meet him while Holly peeped through the curtains to get a glimpse of him. As Ivy had said, he was very good-looking and he certainly seemed keen, but she couldn't help thinking that things seemed to be happening a little too fast. Still, what do I know about love? she asked herself and prepared to settle down to a lonely afternoon. At least while Ivy was out with Jeremy she wasn't risking getting arrested again with the suffragettes.

After that day, Ivy saw Jeremy a couple of times a week and she spoke of him constantly; Jeremy does this and Jeremy says that, she would chatter and eventually Holly taught herself to listen with half an ear. She did notice, though, that wherever they went Ivy tended to pay for him, which she found quite strange considering he was supposed to be a journalist. Surely he must earn much more than Ivy?

She tactfully broached the subject one day when they were having a rare evening in together and Ivy instantly rushed to his defence.

'It's because he's between jobs,' she told her.

'But surely if his family are so well off he would receive a monthly allowance?' Holly pressed.

'Ah well, he and his father have had a little fall-out,' Ivy explained. 'His father doesn't want him to work. He wants him to learn how to run their estate ready for when he retires but Jeremy doesn't want to do that just yet. It would mean wasting all the years he spent at university to qualify as a journalist.'

'Oh.' Holly thought the whole story rather strange but didn't want to upset Ivy so kept her concerns to herself.

The following week the nursing sister who ran the Red Cross course she had been attending pulled Holly to one side. 'I really don't think there's much more I can teach you now. I think you're ready to go on the wards. I've already spoken to the matron and she's happy to take you on as from this Wednesday. The pay will be minimal of course, but you will be supplied with a uniform so good luck. It's been a pleasure to teach you and I have no doubt you will make an excellent nurse. Report to the matron's office at seven o'clock sharp on Wednesday morning.'

'Oh, thank you, Sister,' Holly breathed, her eyes shining with excitement. At last she was going to put all her training to real use on real people instead of dummies.

She was there on the dot along with two other girls who looked as nervous as she felt. Matron Lewis eventually admitted them to her room and eyed them up and down before telling them, 'Right, nurses, the first thing we need to do is get you your uniforms. Nurse Blythe there will take you along for them when we've spoken but understand you are still only trainees. Many of the dirty jobs will fall to you until you've had further training. Patients' bed baths, washing the bedpans, rolling bandages, etc, do you think you can handle that?'

'Yes, Matron,' the girls all breathed together, although

Holly did think the little brunette on her right didn't look too sure about it.

'Whichever ward you are allocated to, you will do exactly as the ward sister tells you. I will stand for no fraternising or over-familiarity with the patients and I expect you to be spotless at all times. A large work apron will be supplied along with your uniform for you to wear when doing dirty jobs.' She continued reeling off rules and regulations until Holly felt quite dizzy but at last they were sent on their way with Nurse Blythe. She was a plump, middle-aged woman who appeared to be almost as strict as Matron. She led them through the hospital to the supply room and, gauging their sizes, she began to issue them with their uniforms. They were given two navy-blue dresses with white pinstripes, each with crisp white collars and detachable white cuffs. Then came a large white apron with a red cross on the bodice. There was a white triangular headdress, which Holly had no idea how to fasten, and the work apron. Finally came a royal-blue cape lined in red.

'You will be responsible for supplying your own stockings and sensible flat, black shoes,' the nurse informed them. 'And now I shall show you just one time how to fasten your headdress and then I expect you all to be changed and ready for duty in ten minutes. You may leave your day clothes in here until you go home just this once, they will be quite safe. Any questions?'

All three of them shook their heads, so approaching the little brunette, the nurse expertly showed them how to fasten their headdress before leaving them with the warning, 'I shall be back in ten minutes exactly. Make sure you are all ready.'

'Phew,' the brunette breathed when the door closed behind her. 'She's a bit of a tartar, ain't she? I hope all the nurses ain't like that else I won't last long.' They all hurriedly turned their backs on each other while they got changed and just managed to be ready for when Nurse Blythe reappeared.

She tutted when she saw the state of the third girl's head-dress, which looked as if it had been fastened while drunk. She was a skinny, mousy-haired girl who looked like she wouldn't say boo to a goose and Holly wondered how she would fare with such strict rules.

'I'll show you how to fasten it again just one more time,' Nurse Blythe scolded. 'But don't make me have to show you again.'

At last they were all lined up regimentally in front of her and she eyed them critically. 'I dare say you'll have to do,' she muttered as she stared down at the clipboard she was holding.

'You, Worthing' – she pointed to the brunette – 'have been assigned to the children's ward. Miller, you are on women's surgical.' This was the mousy-haired girl. 'And you, Farthing, are on men's surgical. Now follow me, all of you.'

They trooped through the hospital until Holly was completely lost. It was a huge place full of winding corridors that all looked the same and she wondered how she would ever find her way about.

Nurse Blythe showed the other two girls to their wards first before escorting Holly to men's surgical where she handed her over to a sister in a navy-blue uniform.

'Ah, Nurse Farthing, you're just in time to help out with

the patients' bed baths,' she told her. 'I'm Sister Trent and any concerns you have, you address to me.'

'Yes, Sister,' Holly replied meekly as her stomach turned over. Suddenly the thought of washing semi-naked men was daunting, but then she knew that someone had to do it. The curtains were drawn around the second bed on the left of the ward and opening them just enough for Holly to squeeze through, she told the nurse within, 'Nurse Farthing will help you now, Nurse King.'

'Yes, Sister.' The young nurse gave Holly a welcoming smile as Holly quickly tied her work apron over her uniform to protect it, and rolled up the sleeves of her dress.

Her first day at the hospital passed in a blur of washing bedpans, not a job for the faint-hearted as Holly soon discovered, giving patients bed baths, accompanying Nurse King to the various operating theatres with the patients due for operations, and mopping floors.

'Ooh, yer don't half look posh in yer uniform,' Ivy cooed that evening when Holly arrived home and flopped into a chair exhausted. 'How did it go?'

'All right, I suppose,' Holly answered half-heartedly. 'But I stink of disinfectant and my arms ache from turning patients and mopping floors.'

Ivy giggled. 'Well, you have to start somewhere. As you gain more qualifications at your evening classes you'll be given more responsibility. I take my hat off to you, I don't think I could do it. In fact, I can't think of anything worse than being around sick people all day but then you're much more loving and giving than me. Anyway, your dinner is in the oven keeping warm. I have to shoot off now to meet

Jeremy but you can tell me more about it when I get back. Ta-ra fer now.'

With that she went charging off down the stairs while Holly dragged herself over to the oven to see what there was to eat. It looked like cottage pie but she was so tired she decided she'd turn the oven off and have it later. She went and settled back down in the chair and within minutes she was fast asleep.

She was still there when Ivy returned later that evening and smiling she hurried away to fetch a blanket from the bed and draped it gently across Holly's sleeping form before creeping away to her own room.

Towards the end of May, the weather took a turn for the better and suddenly women with bright parasols and gaily coloured dresses together with smartly dressed gentlemen were seen parading the streets. The smog that so often shrouded London seemed to disappear as if by magic and the street vendors appeared again, selling everything from posies of violets to jellied eels and pea soup. Once again the city was vibrant with sound and a million different smells and both girls tried to spend as much time as they possibly could outdoors enjoying the warm spring sunshine.

'Ain't it just grand?' Ivy commented one Sunday afternoon as she was getting ready to meet Jeremy.

'It certainly is . . . Oh, and by the way the rent is due this week,' Holly reminded her.

Just for an instant she saw a frown flit across Ivy's face but then she was smiling again. 'Of course it is but I ain't had time to go to the bank, will you pay my half for me till I get paid on Friday?'

Holly thought this very strange. Ivy had always been very punctual at paying her half of the bills. In fact, she had even managed to save a tidy sum from her wages but she nodded anyway.

'Of course I will. Have a good time.'

Once again she watched from the window as Ivy went off on Jeremy's arm. She had to admit he was very handsome and she could understand why Ivy was so besotted with him. He was tall and upright with thick dark hair, and he towered over Ivy making her appear very small and dainty. A thought occurred to her. Since the day he had sent Ivy flowers there had been no more and suddenly Ivy seemed short of money, and she'd noticed that she hadn't sent any money home to her mother for a while either. What if he was taking money from her? Ivy had told her that he still hadn't found a job, but she was usually so sensible. I'm probably worrying about nothing, Ivy is no fool, Holly assured herself and settled down to a quiet afternoon.

The following morning when Miss May arrived at the shop, Holly thought she looked troubled and this was borne out when the woman confided over a mid-morning cup of tea, 'My husband isn't at all well. I almost didn't come in this morning as I didn't want to leave him alone.'

'I could have managed,' Holly told her sympathetically.

'I'm sure you could but between you and me I'm wondering how much longer I'm going to be able to keep the shop open,' her employer informed her. 'I was thinking of perhaps closing for two days a week instead of one. There would still be more than enough work to keep the seamstresses employed full-time, but what about you?'

'Oh, I could manage. I'd just do two days a week instead of one at the hospital, and I'd get paid for that so I wouldn't be any worse off,' Holly assured her.

'In that case I might close on Mondays too,' Miss May answered thoughtfully, as Holly turned to serve a customer who had just walked in.

Two weeks later Miss May put the new shop hours into operation and Holly began to work at the hospital two days a week.

'I shan't be any worse off,' she told Ivy over dinner one evening. 'And I'll be getting a lot more nursing experience in, so all in all it's worked out well . . . Did you hear what I said, Ivy?'

'What . . .? Sorry, what did you say?'

Holly sighed. Ivy seemed to be very preoccupied these days. She repeated what she'd said and Ivy nodded.

'Hmm, that's good then.' She wandered away to get ready to see Jeremy. There was clearly something bothering her friend but until she chose to tell her what it was there wasn't much she could do about it. It didn't stop her being concerned though.

Chapter Twelve

Sister was inspecting the ward before the doctors did their morning rounds one morning in June when she told them, 'There will be a new doctor on the ward this morning, nurses. His name is Doctor Parkin and he has just transferred here from Guy's Hospital so I shall expect you all to show him how efficient we are.'

'Yes, Sister,' the nurses chorused as she walked along the line they had formed, inspecting their uniforms. Woe betide any of them if she found so much as a button out of place. It was the same for the patients before the morning visit. The nurses had to truss them up so tightly in their sheets that the poor souls could barely move, but rather that than risk a crease in their bedspreads. It was even worse on the days when the matron accompanied the doctors.

Unfortunately for Holly one of the patients who was allocated to her care suddenly needed the toilet just as the doctors arrived, so she had to quickly pull the curtains about the woman's bed and hurry off to the sluice room to fetch a bedpan. By the time the woman had finished, the doctors had almost completed their round and as she flicked the curtains aside again she found them standing at the foot of the patient's bed and Sister looked none too pleased.

'Couldn't you have waited, Mrs Batty?' she asked crossly and the old woman gave her a gummy grin.

''Fraid not, luvvy. Yer know the old sayin', "When yer've got to go yer've got to go," an' ooh I don't 'alf feel better now.'

Holly hurried past the doctors with the covered bedpan in her hand and caught the eye of a young doctor who was doing his best not to smile. This, she assumed, was Dr Parkin.

'So, Mrs Batty,' she heard him say as he unhooked her notes from the bottom of her bed and quickly read through them. 'You've had your appendix removed, I see. How are you feeling now?'

'Ooh, ever so much better, luvvy,' the old woman told him cheerily. 'But I ain't ready to go 'ome just yet. It won't 'urt me old man to see to 'isself for a while. 'Appen he'll appreciate me a bit more when I do go back. An' why would I wanna rush away anyway when I 'ave a handsome young man like you lookin' after me?' She gave the young doctor a suggestive wink which brought colour flooding into his cheeks.

Holly grinned to herself as she disappeared into the sluice. Mrs Batty was a card, there was no mistake about it, but thankfully the young man appeared to have a good sense of humour, unlike some of the other doctors.

To her surprise she found him waiting for her when she came out of the sluice.

'Ah, Nurse Farthing, isn't it?' He held out his hand and she shook it awkwardly. 'I'm Dr Parkin and I believe you are caring for Mrs Batty?'

'Yes, doctor.'

'Well, the good news is I've examined her and she's coming along nicely. I think she could go home the day after tomorrow when she's had her stitches out if she continues as she is. I shall come to the ward to remove them myself late tomorrow afternoon.'

'Very well, doctor.' He was very good-looking: tall and broad-shouldered with thick, dark hair that had a tendency to curl, and deep brown eyes, fringed with thick lashes that most girls would envy. But it was his attitude that Holly found the most appealing. He spoke to her as an equal whereas most of the doctors tended to talk down to the nurses, especially the Red Cross ones who weren't yet fully qualified. Suddenly she found herself looking forward to seeing him again but at that moment the sister bore down on her with a list of jobs as long as her arm and for the rest of the morning Holly was too busy to think about anything else.

Her lunch hour was delayed by almost an hour that day because of an emergency arriving on the ward and as she headed for the hospital canteen she was looking forward to a nice hot cup of tea and a sandwich to tide her over until she and Ivy had their evening meal. Laden with a tray she glanced around for an empty table and when she found one she sat down and began to eat her meal. Seconds later a male voice asked, 'Would you mind very much if I join you?'

Holly felt hot colour flood into her cheeks as she glanced up into the handsome face of the young doctor who had visited the ward earlier.

'I, er . . . I don't mind,' she said. 'But the doctors aren't encouraged to mix with the nurses.'

He laughed. 'Not during work hours perhaps but we're on our lunch break, aren't we? Who could object to that?' He slid onto the chair opposite her and suddenly Holly felt tongue-tied. What did one say to a qualified doctor? He was almost like a god in her eyes – and in the eyes of most of the other nurses if the way they were glancing enviously across at her was anything to go by.

He took a huge bite out of his sandwich and a gulp of tea before asking, 'So, do you have a first name, Nurse Farthing?'

She gulped. 'Yes . . . it's Holly.'

He held his hand out and she felt she had no choice but to shake it though she was very aware of people watching them.

'I'm Richard. It's nice to meet you, Holly. Have you been here long?'

She hastily explained that she merely worked part-time as she also had another job.

'It seems you're a young woman of many talents,' he commented admiringly after Holly had told him all about the work she did in Miss May's shop, and she blushed becomingly.

'Are you from around these parts?'

'Actually I came here from my home in Nuneaton in Warwickshire.'

'Ah, the home of George Eliot, the novelist,' he remarked. He seemed so genuinely interested in everything she had to say and was so remarkably easy to talk to that the time seemed to pass in the blink of an eye.

Sadly, however, much as Holly would have liked to sit talking to him all day, she had to get back to the ward. 'I really ought to go,' she told him eventually after glancing at the large clock on the wall. 'Sister is a stickler for timekeeping.'

'From what I saw of her she's a stickler for everything.' He grinned, revealing a lovely set of white teeth. 'Goodbye for now, Holly. I'll see you tomorrow when I come to take Mrs Batty's stitches out.'

'I don't work on Thursdays so I won't be here,' she told him, crestfallen, wishing that she was going to be there.

Ivy was already in the flat when she got home that evening and she seemed to be rather down in the dumps.

'Is anything wrong?' Holly asked as they sat down to their meal of sausage and mash some time later.

Ivy shrugged. 'Not really, Jeremy is busy again tonight so I'm going to a suffragette meeting. He's started working for the *Daily Telegraph* now, it pays slightly more than the *Daily News* did.'

Holly casually mentioned the new doctor she had met that day then and for the first time that evening, Ivy grinned.

'Do I detect a hint of romance in the air?' she teased.

'Of course not. I was merely commenting on how pleasant he was,' Holly retorted and quickly changed the subject.

'Actually, I was thinkin' of leavin' my job,' Ivy informed her. 'I've almost finished my evening course now and Emmeline Pankhurst has offered me a job in Poplar at their headquarters. I'd be seein' to the printin' of the magazines and doing the clerical work. What do you think?'

'I think it would be much safer for you than working in the match factory,' Holly said enthusiastically. She'd noticed that Ivy's skin had taken on a yellowish tinge lately and she was sure it was because of the job she did. She couldn't help but worry about her. 'Will it be more money?'

'Not an awful lot more,' Ivy admitted. 'But I think I'd enjoy it.'

'Then if you get the chance do it,' Holly advised and Ivy

nodded. 'Er . . . where did you say Jeremy was this evening?' she asked.

Ivy shrugged. 'Off chasing some story or other for the newspaper,' she grumbled. 'That's the trouble with a journalist's job, they have to chase stories no matter what time of the day or night it is.'

Seeing how disgruntled Ivy was, Holly let the subject drop but she couldn't help wondering if perhaps Jeremy and Ivy were drifting apart. That would surely explain Ivy's sudden mood swings.

Ivy didn't see Jeremy again until early the following week and she was none too pleased about it.

'So exactly when are you plannin' on takin' me to meet your family?' she queried. 'You keep saying you will but every time I mention it you always come up with some excuse.'

'There's nothing I'd like more than for them to meet you,' he told her silkily as he traced his finger tenderly down her cheek and Ivy felt herself melting. Just one glance at his handsome face and she was like putty in his hands and he knew it. 'But I daren't take time off from my new job just yet. Look what I bought with my wages.' He stared down at his new suit and smart shoes and Ivy had to admit he did look very grand.

'Well, now you've got some money again you can perhaps take me out somewhere nice instead of to your poky little room all the time,' she said churlishly. She wasn't going to forgive him that easily. In actual fact, the first time he had taken her to his lodgings she had been appalled and rather shocked. After all, Jeremy came from a very well-to-do family so she would never have imagined him living in such a hovel.

He rented two rooms in a large terraced house in Whitechapel and to say they left a lot to be desired would have been putting it mildly, as she'd told him.

'Ah, but there's a reason for it,' he'd told her. 'I am a journalist after all and these lower class areas tend to be where I get most of my stories from. Whitechapel is full of thieves and villains, what better place is there for me to be? But only for now, of course. I don't intend to stay here for long, I assure you.'

And Ivy believed him, just as she believed everything he told her.

'I tell you what,' he said with the smile that could always melt her heart. 'We'll go to the picture house. I don't know what's showing but there's bound to be something on we fancy. What do you say?'

Ivy immediately perked up and linking her arm with his she followed him through the streets adoringly. He had told her that he was planning to buy a motor car soon and then they would travel in style.

They had reached the door of the theatre when Jeremy reached into his pocket and softly swore under his breath.

'I don't believe it,' he muttered grimly. 'I've only gone and left my wallet in the pocket of my old suit . . . you couldn't lend me a few bob, could you, sweetheart?'

Ivy's face fell. 'B-but you haven't given me back what you borrowed last week . . . or the week before,' she pointed out. 'And I've had to pay my share of the rent and the bills this week so I'm a bit short.'

He shrugged. 'It's back to my room then or we could go for a nice walk.'

Ivy sighed as they turned in the direction of Whitechapel. She'd been on her feet at work since early that morning and hardly felt up to tramping the streets.

As they let themselves into the house where Jeremy lived a host of smells assaulted her and she wrinkled her nose. It reminded her very much of the nasty flat in Soho she and Holly had lived in: boiled cabbage, stale urine and other things that she couldn't name made her want to gag. A baby was crying somewhere and as they climbed the stairs she couldn't help but wonder where the attentive man she had met a short while ago had gone.

Once in his rooms she stared about in dismay. A small sink in the corner of the room was full of dirty pots, and discarded clothes were strewn everywhere. Jeremy would certainly never win any prizes for housekeeping. But then she supposed if he had been used to having servants wait on him he wouldn't know how to look after himself.

'Put the kettle on while I have a tidy up,' she told him resignedly as she began to lift clothes and sort them into piles but it soon became clear that Jeremy had other things on his mind.

'Never mind that, give us a kiss,' he said, snatching her to him and placing his mouth over hers. As always she felt herself melt against him but when a few minutes later his hand strayed to her breast she gently began to push him away.

'No, Jeremy, I've told you, I'm not prepared to do that sort o' thing till I've got a ring on me finger,' she told him breathlessly. This happened every time they met now and each time it became that little bit harder to say no.

He instantly turned away from her with an aggrieved

expression on his face and lit a cigarette, which made her feel guilty.

'Haven't I told you we'll be married one day,' he said miserably. 'I just need to get established in my new job first. But I'm only flesh and blood, you know, and a man has needs! If you really loved me you wouldn't push me away all the time. I haven't even got any money because I had to spend my wages on new clothes. It wouldn't look good if a journalist turned up looking like a tramp, would it?'

Ivy immediately fumbled in her bag and emptied the entire contents of her purse onto the table.

'Have it all, I can manage until I get paid again. And I do love you,' she gushed, terrified that she was going to lose him. He was so handsome that she was sure he could have had any girl he wanted. She hurried over to him and clung to his arm like a limpet. 'I'm just frightened that's all. What if . . . you know? I found out I was having a baby?'

'That wouldn't happen because I'd be careful,' he snapped, shrugging her hand from his arm and now she was really afraid. He was the first person she thought of every morning and the last one she thought of at night and the prospect of living without him was unbearable.

'Please . . . don't be angry with me.' She flung her arms about his neck and for a moment he held himself stiffly. But then dropping his cigarette butt onto the floor he ground it out on the bare floorboards with the heel of his shiny new shoe and took her into his arms again, and this time when his hand once more found her breast she didn't stop him.

Chapter Thirteen

'Well you certainly look happier than when you went out,' Holly commented when Ivy got in late that evening. The sparkle was back in her eyes and she couldn't seem to stop smiling. Holly had been sewing a button onto the dress of her uniform but she laid it aside to go and put some milk on the stove to warm for their cocoa.

'Oh, don't bother doing me a hot drink tonight,' Ivy told her. 'It's been a long day so I think I'll get an early night, if you don't mind. G'night, Holly.' And with that she went tripping into her bedroom leaving Holly to stare after her with a concerned frown on her face. She so wanted Ivy to be happy but there was something about Jeremy that didn't feel right, although as yet she couldn't quite put her finger on what it was. Feeling restless she decided to write to her mother, maybe writing about her concerns would help her make sense of them, and considering what her mother had been through with her father, she might have some useful advice. So settling down at the small table she began.

Dear Mother,

I hope this letter finds you and Grandfather well and keeping good health. The weather here is marvellous, it's so nice to see the sun but it does make me miss the lovely walks you and I used to take in the wide open spaces on glorious Sunday afternoons. Of course there are parks here but it isn't the same as being surrounded by fields as we are back at home.

Ivy and I are well, although I must admit that I have a niggling concern about the young man she is seeing. He's a journalist from a very well-to-do family by all accounts, but the strange thing is he never seems to have any money, nor does Ivy and I'm growing a little concerned that she might be giving her wages to him. I'm probably worrying over nothing but as you know, Ivy is a very kind, generous person and she is so besotted with him. I would hate to think that she was being exploited. But that's enough of my concerns . . .

She went on to tell her mother all about her work at the hospital and in the shop and when she'd finished, she popped it in an envelope and placed it on the mantelpiece ready to be posted the next morning. She always felt better after writing to her mother, it somehow seemed to bring her closer and, smiling again, she gave a wide yawn and went to bed.

The following week, her mother sent her a reply, in which she suggested that people in love rarely listened to reason, as she knew all too well, so all Holly could do was wait and make sure she was there for her friend should her concerns prove to be well founded.

Holly knew she was speaking sense, so she resolved to try to set her worries aside, but remain vigilant, just in case Ivy needed her.

Over the next weeks London seemed to be teeming with people who were coming to see the sights. The weather was unbearably hot and humid and Ivy arrived home from the factory each night feeling like a wet rag.

'Phew, it feels as if the streets are full o' people,' she complained as she walked through the door one July evening, just as Holly was putting their supper on the table – she had called in at the greengrocer's on the way home from the hospital and bought a selection of salad and cold meat as it was far too hot to attempt to cook.

'I know what you mean,' Holly agreed. 'The shop has been really busy with people of all nationalities all out to buy souvenirs to take home. We've just about sold out of gloves and scarves. I shall be quite glad when things quieten down a bit. There is no escaping the tourists, especially the Americans. There seem to be droves of them.'

'I shall just be glad when I start at the suffragettes' head-quarters,' Ivy wheezed, pushing the window of the flat as far open as it would go. 'I swear I shall melt clean away if I have to stay in that match factory for much longer.'

'It's not much better at the hospital,' Holly agreed. 'Though it's not so bad down in the shop. Miss May has taken to leaving the door wedged open to let a little air in. The only trouble is that one of us has to be in there every minute in case someone comes in and decides to help themselves to the stock.' She placed a plate in front of her friend. 'I got us a nice bit of ham to go with the salad.'

Ivy pushed it away. 'It looks lovely but I'm too hot to even attempt that at the minute,' she said, fanning herself with the newspaper. 'Ooh, what I wouldn't give to be back home swimming in the blue lagoon now.' She giggled as she confided, 'I used to go there sometimes in the summer wi' me brothers an' sisters an' we'd strip off down to us underwear an' dive in. Me mam would have skinned us alive had she known.' In her mind's eye she could see them all now splashing about in the cool water and she felt a pang of conscience. 'I just hope they're all right,' she muttered. It had been some time since she had posted any money home but she decided that as soon as she got paid she would send some again.

Holly too was feeling guilty as it was some time since she had visited her mother. The problem was with her nursing and her job in the shop she had very little free time. Her mother had been very understanding about it and had promised that she would visit Holly. But not until the weather cooled down, she had written. After being accustomed to living in a sleepy market town in the Midlands she always found the capital too busy for her liking and had rightly guessed that it would be even busier while the weather was so hot. She felt guilty for not coming, though, considering how much time she had on her hands, so she had started to write to her daughter even more frequently.

In one of her replies, Holly wrote:

Dear Mother,

I don't blame you for not wanting to be here at present. It feels as if you are walking shoulder to shoulder everywhere you go with all the visitors that have come into the city. They seem to have come from every corner of the globe and it makes me miss the tranquillity of home

*and you more than ever. Still, summer will be over soon
and hopefully things will quieten down again*

*Ivy is very much looking forward to starting her new
job in the suffragette offices and she is still seeing Jeremy
and seems as smitten with him as ever. I know that she
misses home too, though, and she often speaks of her
siblings and her mother, although I don't think she misses
her father very much. I think of you every day and pray
that you and Grandfather are keeping well. I can hardly
wait to see you again.*

Until then I remain your ever loving daughter,
Holly xxxxx

In August, when she had passed all the exams on her course
with flying colours, Ivy left the match factory and went to
work in the suffragette office and she seemed to love it. Now
she could go to work respectably dressed each day, and the
work was much less physically demanding, as well, she felt,
as not being very difficult. She did any typing that needed
doing as well as seeing to the printing of the magazines and
sometimes Holly felt so proud of her she felt she could burst.
The timid, skinny girl who had accompanied her to London
was gone and in her place was a confident, capable young
lady. Ivy's figure had filled out slightly and now with her hair
shining and dressed in respectable clothes she was quite
attractive. The only thing that did still concern Holly, though,
was Ivy's relationship with Jeremy. She still saw him at every
opportunity although it was clear that this was nowhere near
as often as she would have liked, and Holly had formed the

opinion that he was taking advantage of her, not that she would have dared voice her fears to Ivy. Her mother's advice was right, for Ivy would have defended him to the death.

'So when am I finally going to meet him?' she asked Ivy one evening. Every time she'd suggested it before Jeremy always seemed to be busy, and gave Ivy one reason after another why he couldn't come.

'Oh, not that again.' Ivy sighed and raised her eyebrows. She was getting ready to meet him. 'You sound worse than me mother when you start.'

'I don't mean to,' Holly defended herself. 'But you've been seeing him for some time now. I just thought it might be nice if I got to know him.'

'All right then, what if I invite him round to tea on Sunday?'

Holly grinned. 'That's a good idea. I'll make us a cake.'

'You make a cake?' Ivy snorted with laughter. 'Your cookin' might have improved but I don't reckon you're up to that yet.'

'Well, we'll see shall we!' Holly said peevishly. 'A sponge can't be all that hard to make. Come Sunday you'll be eating your words and asking for an extra slice you'll see!'

Ivy grinned as she gave her a wave and sped off down the stairs leaving Holly to start searching for the second-hand copy of *Mrs Beeton's Cookery Book* she had bought some time ago from the market.

Unknown to Ivy it took three attempts before Holly managed to produce a cake that was edible but on Sunday afternoon she laid out a little feast fit for a king. There were thinly sliced cucumber sandwiches, cheese and ham sandwiches, as well as a variety of pickles and some sausage rolls that Holly had bought from the butcher. And in the centre of the table the cake she had gone to such trouble over took pride of place.

'How does it look?' she asked Ivy as she came out of her bedroom shortly before Jeremy was due to arrive.

'I have to say you've done a grand job,' Ivy admitted, giving her friend a quick hug. 'It's really nice of you to go to so much trouble.'

'It's worth it if Jeremy is going to be a part of our lives. The least I can do is get to know him,' Holly pointed out. They glanced at the clock together then.

'Another half an hour and he should be here. I told him four o'clock.' Ivy was actually quite excited about the visit and could hardly wait to show him off. Up to now he hadn't introduced her to any of his friends but when she'd remarked on it he'd kissed her tenderly. 'That's because I don't get to see anywhere near as much of you as I'd like and when I do I want you all to myself,' he'd assured her. Perhaps that will change after he's met Holly, Ivy thought as she straightened the cushions on the small sofa and they sat down to wait.

Four o'clock came and went. For the first half an hour Ivy wasn't too worried. Jeremy had never been the best timekeeper. But by five o'clock she was pacing the floor and repeatedly crossing to the window to peer up and down the street.

'I can't think what's keeping him. The sandwiches are starting to curl at the edges. They'll be ruined soon,' she fretted, feeling humiliated. Holly had gone to so much trouble and now it was beginning to look like he wasn't even going to bother to come.

'Look, why don't we tuck in?' Holly suggested at six o'clock. 'Jeremy obviously couldn't make it and it's a shame to let all this good food go to waste.'

With a sigh, Ivy nodded, finally accepting that Jeremy wasn't going to come. 'The paper must have sent him out on a story,' she excused him but inside she was seething. I'll give him a right tongue-lashing when I next see him, she promised herself.

But it was three days before she finally saw him again after work and by then she had worked herself up into a rage. 'What the hell did you think you were doing not turning up like that?' she spat at him as he tried to take her hand. 'Holly had laid you a lovely tea out and you couldn't even be bothered to come and eat it. I don't think I've ever felt so embarrassed.'

'I'm so sorry,' he said with the smile that could usually melt her. 'I'm sure you've guessed what happened. A story broke and the paper wanted me out to cover it at the last minute. I was literally setting off to come to you when I got word and there was nothing I could do. You must know I wouldn't have let you down if I could possibly help it.'

He looked so repentant that she wavered. His tawny eyes were moist and he looked at her with such a regretful expression that she couldn't help softening. She supposed that journalists were a little like doctors and could be called on at any hour of the day or night, so was she being too hard on him? His arm had snaked about her waist by then and she knew she was lost. There would be other times, after all, and Holly had been very good about it.

The week after the tea, Holly arrived on the women's surgical ward to find the ward sister waiting for her.

'Nurse Farthing, Matron would like a word with you in her office. Immediately, if you please.'

Holly's heart sank as she tried to think of what she might have done wrong, but she nodded and was on her way in seconds. Whatever it was she may as well face the music and get it over with.

'Come in,' the matron called when Holly tapped on her door and after taking a deep breath Holly straightened her back, smoothed her apron and entered the room.

Matron was seated at her desk with a mountain of paperwork teetering in front of her but at the sight of Holly she smiled.

'Ah, Nurse Farthing. Do take a seat.'

Holly perched awkwardly on the edge of a hard-backed chair.

'We have a new influx of Red Cross nurses joining the staff this morning,' the matron informed her. 'And I was wondering if I might put you in charge of them to show them the ropes. I've been extremely pleased with you since you started here and so have the sisters on the wards where you have worked so I can't think of anyone I would rather entrust the new recruits to. What do you think? Could you do it?'

'Well, I . . .' Holly gulped. 'I dare say I could.' She was delighted to have such a glowing report from the matron herself, although it had come as something of a shock. 'But as you know I only nurse for two days a week so am I really the right person for the job?'

Matron waved her hand. 'Absolutely. I want you to show them around, explain what we expect of them and allow them to come to you with any concerns they have. If the concerns are anything that you can't deal with you can ask me for advice, of course, but it will save me a lot of valuable time that can be better spent elsewhere if you will take on the responsibility.'

'In that case I'd be delighted to,' Holly told her with a smile.

'Right, I shall want you to keep a close eye on them.' The woman peered at her over the top of her glasses. 'We can usually sort the wheat from the chaff within days so I'd like you to report their progress back to me on a weekly basis. And now, nurse, if you'd like to go along to reception they should be here any minute . . . and thank you.'

Feeling proud, Holly found the new recruits all nervously waiting on a bench and she quickly introduced herself and showed them the small clipboard Matron had given her telling them where they would each be working.

'Nurse Jenkins, we'll get you settled in the maternity ward first,' she addressed a small, fair-haired girl who barely looked old enough to be there. They all set off and just before lunchtime when she had shown the last girl to her ward, she almost bumped into Dr Parkin in the corridor leading to the men's geriatric ward.

'Ah, Nurse Farthing, word is about that you've had a promotion,' he said with a teasing smile.

She flushed as she stared up into his face. She supposed that he wasn't handsome in the traditional sense: his mouth was a little too wide to be termed as perfect and his thick hair always seemed to be in need of a good brush, but every time she looked into his twinkling brown eyes she felt her heart give a little leap. 'I'm not sure that you'd call it a promotion. Matron just asked me to help settle the latest batch of Red Cross nurses in,' she explained primly.

'Hmm, which suggests she must think very highly of you, don't you think? But now you'll have to excuse me, I'm wanted in the ward and you know what Sister Barraclough is like if anyone isn't on time. I'll try and find you in the canteen at lunchtime and then you can tell me all about it.' She stared after him bemused as he raced off to the ward. Why is it I never get tongue-tied or embarrassed in front of any of the other doctors? she wondered.

As it happened another emergency was admitted to the ward she was working on shortly before she was due to go on her lunch break, so it was almost an hour later before she was able to escape to the canteen to snatch a hasty snack. A quick glance around showed her that Dr Parkin must have come and gone. But after all he was probably just being friendly and I hardly know him, she silently scolded herself as she stood in a queue waiting to be served. But in truth she was disappointed and she found herself looking out for him as she ate her meal alone.

Chapter Fourteen

'Oh, stand by your bed. Lady Hamilton's car has just pulled up outside,' Miss May hissed to Holly as they stood behind the counter in the shop sorting out the glove drawer.

Minutes later the woman breezed in on a waft of expensive French perfume. 'Ah, Miss May. First I must congratulate you on the gown you had delivered to me last week. It was a complete triumph and absolutely everyone commented on it when I wore it to the opera at the weekend.'

I bet they did, Miss May thought as she pictured the monstrosity. She could only imagine that the portly lady must have looked like a giant blancmange in the pink frothy concoction, but she kept her smile firmly in place. 'I'm so happy you were pleased with it, Lady Hamilton,' she simpered. 'And what might I do for you today?'

'As it happens, I've been invited to a ball in four weeks' time. Now, I know that doesn't give your seamstresses long to make it but I simply must have a new gown. Do you think they can manage it?'

'Oh, I'm quite sure there'll be no problem at all.' Miss May hauled the pattern book from beneath the counter and soon both she and Lady Hamilton were poring over it.

'I think this might be very flattering on you,' Miss May suggested, pointing out quite a subtle style with plain, simple lines but Lady Hamilton shook her head.

'Oh no, dear, that's far too ordinary. I want something a little more . . . flamboyant! Ah, now this is more like it!' She stabbed her finger at a particularly full-skirted affair that dripped with frills and it was all Miss May could do to stop herself shuddering as she tried to picture her customer in the end result. Even so, as she had drummed into Holly, the customer was always right so she merely nodded.

'Then perhaps we should look at fabric now. Did you have a particular colour in mind?'

Lady Hamilton glanced along the shelves tapping her lip with a heavily ringed plump finger. 'Oh, that one there is just divine,' she sighed dramatically pointing to a roll of bright yellow satin.

Holly had to keep her eyes firmly on the job she was doing to stop herself from laughing aloud as she glimpsed the look of horror on Miss May's face.

'My, er . . . escort loves me in bright colours,' she gushed, glancing surreptitiously towards the car parked outside where they could see a young man sitting in the back seat.

'It is indeed a very fine fabric,' Miss May agreed as Lady Hamilton stroked it. 'And we still have all your measurements so there is no need for you to be measured again. Could you perhaps call in for your first fitting towards the end of next week? Shall we say Thursday afternoon about three o'clock?'

'Perfect, my dear Miss May. Good day, ladies.'

They stood primly side by side as Lady Hamilton waddled from the shop and watched until the chauffeur pulled the car away from the kerb then, unable to hold it back any longer, Holly broke into a fit of the giggles. 'Oh dear, she's going to look like a big daffodil in that,' she commented.

'A giant dandelion more like,' Miss May sighed. 'And did you see the young man in the car? He was young enough to be her son at least!' But then seeing the funny side of it she too started to laugh until the tears ran down her cheeks.

Holly told Ivy about the incident that evening when she got back from the office but Ivy was in no mood for light-heartedness. She hadn't seen hide nor hair of Jeremy for almost a week now and she was missing him dreadfully.

'Look, you know where he lives, why don't you just go round there and see what's going on?' Holly suggested.

'I suppose I could.' Ivy pushed her food half-heartedly round her plate but then making a decision she suddenly scraped her chair back from the table and said, 'In fact, I reckon I'll go round there right now. There ain't no time like the present, is there? An' he'd better have a good excuse fer staying away an' all, else he'll feel the length o' me tongue!'

Holly grinned as her friend hurried away to fetch her hat and coat. Ivy never failed to make her smile.

When Ivy arrived at the house where Jeremy lived she had to step past a gaggle of snotty-nosed children who were playing with some glass marbles in the dusty gutter. They were all painfully thin, their clothes little more than rags and Ivy's heart went out to them. Fumbling in her purse she extracted some coins and tossed them onto the cobbles and there was a mad scramble to claim them. 'Go and treat yourselves to some sweeties,' she told them and smiled as they raced away, their faces glowing with anticipation at the treat ahead. Once she had reached the top of the house she tapped on Jeremy's door but there was no reply. She was just about to tap again when another door opened further along the narrow passageway and a thin woman swathed in a threadbare shawl with a howling baby in her arms appeared.

''Tain't no use you knockin', luvvie,' she told her. 'Ain't seen 'im fer the last few days.'

'Oh, I see . . . thank you,' Ivy stuttered as colour flooded into her cheeks, and turning about she made a hasty exit down the stairs. So where could he be? she asked herself as she stepped across a large pile of dog faeces. Perhaps he was away working on a story and hadn't had the chance to get word to her? It was the only thing she could think of and knowing there was no more she could do she made her way home, swallowing back tears.

At that moment, could Ivy have known it, Jeremy Pilkington-Hughes was reclining on a velvet chaise longue feeding grapes into the mouth of his latest lover.

'So do you think you could see your way clear to lending me a few shillings, Lavinia darling?' he purred encouragingly.

She turned towards him and the heavy perfume she was wearing was so overpowering that it made his eyes water.

'Now, Jeremy, don't be so naughty,' she scolded with a girlish giggle. 'I only gave you some pocket money two days ago. Whatever have you spent it on?'

He tried to keep the revulsion he felt at the sight of her heaving breasts from showing on his face as he ran a finger tenderly down her plump cheek. 'I had a few bills that were outstanding.'

'Oh, well perhaps if you were to be ever so nice to me I might manage to give you a little bit more,' she said suggestively.

He knew exactly what she meant and his hand instantly strayed to her breast which was constrained by heavy corsets. 'That would be my pleasure entirely,' he answered with a sickly smile as he grappled with the buttons on her dress, although his stomach revolted at the thought of what she wanted. This wasn't going at all as he had hoped it would, he thought to himself. Oh, Lavinia was generous with gifts admittedly but nowhere near generous enough with her cash. At this rate he would have to ask Ivy for another loan, not that she'd ever see a penny of it back. He turned his attention to the task at hand then, eager to get it over with as Lavinia lay back ready to enjoy him.

The next day found Holly working on the women's geriatric ward, never her favourite place to work. She had already checked on the new influx of Red Cross nurses and reported back to the matron and now the ward sister told her, 'Best sit with old Mrs Green, Nurse Farthing. She was admitted last night, poor old thing. The neighbours hadn't seen her about for some time so they broke into her room and found her in a rare old state. Goodness knows how long it had been since she'd eaten anything. The doctor will be round to check on her presently but I doubt there will be much he can do for her. Still, at least we can make sure her final days or hours are as comfortable as we can make them. According to the neighbours she has no family to call on.'

Holly nodded and after flicking aside the curtains the sister had pointed to, she approached the bed. A very old lady lay there, her wispy grey hair spread out across the pillow. She was so painfully thin that her body hardly showed beneath the sheets and the hands that lay on the bedspread were knotted and gnarled.

Thinking that she was asleep, Holly quietly sat down only to find that the old lady had opened her eyes and was staring at her silently. One of her hands snaked out then and she clasped Holly's as a smile spread across her face.

'Oh, Dotty, me darlin', I knew you'd come an' not desert yer old mam,' she said in a voice little above a whisper.

Before Holly could answer the curtains parted again and Dr Parkin joined her.

'How is she?'

'She seems to think I'm someone called Dotty,' Holly whispered gently.

'Ah, apparently Dotty was her daughter. She died of scarlet fever many years ago according to the neighbours and her husband died last year. Since then she's been living like a recluse, barely venturing out of her rented room, the poor old soul.'

Tears sprang to Holly's eyes at the sad tale and she gently squeezed the old woman's hand. 'Then if it gives her comfort I shall be Dotty,' she told him solemnly and he stared at her for a moment thinking what a truly compassionate young woman she was. She was pretty too, which was another thing that attracted him to her.

He leaned over her and checked the old woman's pulse before shaking his head and telling her in a low voice, 'I don't think she's long for this world now.'

Holly smiled up at him. 'I'll stay with her,' she assured him and as he slipped away he had a picture of Holly's face fixed firmly in his mind.

The old woman slept for the next half an hour and Holly sat on through her break, reluctant to leave her. What the doctor had told her had touched her deeply. No one deserved to die alone and she intended to be there for the poor lady. Eventually the old woman's eyes fluttered open again and instantly found Holly's who stood up to lean over her and smooth the thinning hair from her forehead.

'How are you feeling?'

'Better now you're here, me darlin',' the old woman croaked, her every breath laboured. 'But I wish yer dad would come. He's late home from work this evenin' an' his dinner will be ruined.'

'Don't worry, he'll be here soon,' Holly comforted her. 'And his dinner is keeping warm. It will be fine.' Again the old woman drifted off to sleep and Holly sat on feeling stiff and uncomfortable on the hard chair. But nothing would have induced her to move. She had promised she would stay and she would do just that even if it meant sitting there all night.

The afternoon wore on and eventually the sister appeared to tell her that her shift had ended but Holly shook her head. 'It's all right. She's holding my hand and I don't want to disturb her by moving it,' she whispered. 'I'll stay.'

'But she could hang on all night,' the sister pointed out.

'Then I'll stay all night if need be,' Holly answered and when the sister moved back onto the ward she was smiling. If only all her nurses were as loving and caring as Nurse Farthing her job would be so much easier.

As the light faded from the day, Holly had to blink to stay awake while poor Mrs Green slept on. At one point the night sister, who had just come on duty, brought her a sandwich and a cup of tea. Holly was concerned that Ivy would worry where she was but she was still determined to stay and was just yawning when the curtain twitched aside and Dr Parkin appeared again.

He looked surprised to see her. 'Surely you should have gone home hours ago?'

She grinned. 'Yes, I should but I don't like to leave her. She hasn't let go of my hand once. And I could say the same for you!'

He again took the old lady's pulse and listened to her heart before frowning and saying sadly, 'I don't think it will be long now. Her heart rate is very erratic.'

At that very moment the old lady's eyes blinked open and her grip on Holly's hand tightened.

'Dotty, is that you? Are you still here,' she wheezed.

'Yes, I'm here,' Holly said, leaning over her to stroke her brow tenderly.

'An' is yer dad still not home from work?' Before Holly could answer the old woman stared towards the end of the bed and suddenly a beautiful smile lit her face. 'Ah, there you are, Bertie,' she croaked, holding her hand out towards some unseen person. 'I knew you'd come eventually. That's it, luv, hold me hand now nice an' tight, eh?'

And then with a contented sigh she became still, looking so peaceful that it brought tears to Holly's eyes.

Dr Parkin leaned over her and took her pulse again before saying sadly, 'She's gone, I'm afraid.'

Holly nodded as she closed the woman's eyes and gently kissed her brow before drawing the sheet up over her face. 'Sleep tight, Mrs Green,' she whispered as a tear slid down her face.

'Come on, I reckon we both need a good strong cup of sweet tea,' Dr Parkin said softly, deeply touched by what he had just seen. Holly really was a special girl. 'I'll get the night nurse to come and lay her out.'

Holly wearily followed him to the canteen. She should really be getting home but she was too tired to argue.

Minutes later she was sipping at a steaming cup of tea as the young doctor sat opposite her.

'You were wonderful with that old lady,' he said approvingly.

Holly shrugged. 'No more than she deserved,' she answered quietly. 'No one deserves to die all alone.'

'Even so, most nurses would have been off like a shot when their shift was over.'

'Well, I'm not most nurses,' Holly told him with a little smile.

'No, you're most definitely not,' he agreed and in that moment he began to fall a little in love with her. 'Now drink your tea and then I'm going to see you home. You must be worn out.'

Holly knew that she should refuse but she quite liked the idea so she simply smiled and nodded.

Chapter Fifteen

'Eeh! I've been worried sick about you, where have yer been till this time?' Ivy asked the second Holly set foot through the door. 'An' who were that man who yer were with? I saw yer both comin' down the street.'

'If you'll let me get a word in I'll tell you,' Holly told her wearily and once she had Ivy grinned.

'Well, it's sad about the old lady that died but I have to say that young doctor looked a bit of all right! Got a soft spot for yer, has he?'

Holly blushed to the roots of her hair. 'Of course he hasn't,' she said rather too quickly as she fiddled with her nurse's cap. 'He was just being gentlemanly by walking me home. There are strict rules at the hospital saying that nurses and doctors are not allowed to walk out together.'

'Huh! That's as may be but rules are made to be broken,' Ivy retorted. She crossed to the oven and grimaced. 'I've been keepin' yer dinner warm but it looks like a burnt offerin' now. Shall I get yer some bread an' cheese instead? Or I could do you a slice o' cake?'

Holly yawned as she shook her head. 'Thanks, but I reckon I'll get off to bed, if you don't mind. Sister gave me a sandwich earlier on so I'm not that hungry really, just tired.'

Once in the privacy of her room she took off her uniform and folded it neatly across the back of a chair before pulling her nightdress on. She was too tired to even wash or brush her hair. Once between the sheets she began to think of the walk home with Dr Parkin. He'd asked her to address him as Richard but she doubted she would ever be able to do that, it was just too disrespectful. Even so they'd chatted away as if they'd known each other for years and she'd been surprised to learn that far from coming from a well-to-do family he had actually been brought up in Spitalfields by his mother.

'My family were as poor as church mice,' he'd said with a grin. 'But I wouldn't swap them for the world. I got through medical school by working every minute when I wasn't studying and my mother was tickled pink when I became a doctor. Our father left us when I was quite young, and somehow she brought us all up on her own. I don't know how she did it really, sometimes she had three jobs on the go, as well as looking after us. But what about you?'

So Holly had told him about her mother and grandfather but had been careful not to explain why she had left home. 'I just felt it was time to spread my wings,' she'd told him instead and he seemed to accept that.

'And what happened to your father?'

Holly dithered for a second before saying, 'Oh, he died when I was a baby.' She knew she should have told him the truth, for he would surely have understood seeing as his own father had left him too, but she was too embarrassed to. When they arrived back at the shop he had paused before asking, 'Do you fancy going for a walk or something on Sunday, or perhaps we could get a river boat ride along the Thames? It's my day off, unless there are any emergencies that is.'

She had been sorely tempted to accept but instead she'd told him, 'Actually, I've already made arrangements for Sunday but thank you for the offer.'

And then after they'd said goodbye she'd watched him walk away and cursed herself for a fool. Why had she turned him down? What harm could going for a walk with him have done? But in her heart she knew why she'd turned him down: it was because she was afraid of the unfamiliar feelings he aroused in her. She had never felt like this about a young man before. And now it was too late because he was highly unlikely to ever ask her out again. With a sigh she turned over and tried to sleep but strangely she didn't feel tired any more.

As Ivy left the suffragettes' office on Friday after work she found Jeremy standing outside waiting for her with a guilty smile on his face. He was dressed immaculately as usual and Ivy saw that he was attracting more than a few admiring glances from the young ladies sauntering past. Even so she managed to keep her face straight as she stood in front of him.

'Oh, so you're back from your jaunts, are you?' she said, her voice dripping with sarcasm. 'I was beginning to think you'd fallen off the face of the earth.'

'Oh sweetheart, I'm so very sorry.' He fell into step with her and attempted to take her elbow but she shrugged away from him and walked on with her eyes straight ahead. 'The thing is my mother was taken ill and I had to rush home to see her,' he told her breathlessly as he tried to keep up with her. 'I was mortified when I got home and realised I hadn't let you know but I was in such a panic because I didn't know how ill she was.'

Ivy's steps slowed. She had to admit his excuse did sound very plausible. 'And how bad was she?'

'It was a stroke.' He looked so sad that now it was her taking his arm.

'Oh, I'm so sorry. Is it serious?'

'Thankfully the doctor doesn't seem to think there will be any long-term effects as it was only a mild one. She was very lucky this time, but once again I'm so sorry that I didn't let you know. I've already told Mother that as soon as she's properly recovered I'm going to take you home for a weekend to meet her and she's really looking forward to it.'

Suddenly Ivy was putty in his hands again and hating herself for ever having doubted him.

'Well, you're back now so how about I go home and get changed and then we can go out for a bit of supper?' she suggested brightly.

His face became solemn as he shook his head. 'I'd absolutely love to,' he told her. 'But the boss has just got word to me about a story breaking in Brighton and the thing is . . .' He hung his head and looked embarrassed. 'When I arrived home I realised that I'd left my wallet back at Mother's so do you think you could see your way clear to lending me a few bob?'

Ivy pursed her lips as she thought of the pay packet she had just collected. She had intended to use it to settle up her half of the month's bills with Holly. She already owed her some because Jeremy hadn't paid back the last amount he'd borrowed from her. But then when he looked at her so beseechingly like that, with the smile that made him look like a little boy desperate to please, she felt her resolve not to give him any more money begin to waver. How could she refuse him under the circumstances? He must have been so afraid when his mother took ill.

She withdrew her wage packet asking resignedly, 'So how much do you need this time?'

Taking it from her he tipped most of it into his hand before handing a measly amount of coins left back to her.

'That should keep me ticking over nicely. And don't worry, sweetheart. I'll pay you back just as soon as ever I can. But now I really must be off if I'm going to get the train to Brighton. I'll see you as soon as I get back, have a good weekend.' And then he was off, without even a goodbye kiss, striding through the crowds and she sighed as she watched him go. Ivy was falling more and more in love with Jeremy by the day, but every so often she couldn't help thinking that he didn't feel the same. She shook the thought away. Of course he loved her, but he was going through a difficult time at the moment so wasn't able to pay her as much attention as she would have liked. She just needed to be patient.

Jeremy meanwhile had a spring in his step as he headed to a gentlemen's club in Soho. There was going to be a big card game there tonight and now that he had money in his pocket he intended to be a part of it. His latest lover, unfortunately, wasn't as generous as some he'd had before but thankfully Ivy never let him down. He was fully aware that she'd give him her last penny if he asked so he was more than happy to keep her dangling, the silly little cow!

153

'What's wrong with you?' Holly questioned when Ivy came in a short time later. 'You look like you've lost a shilling and found a penny?'

Ivy sighed as she threw her bag onto the table. 'Jeremy met me out of work. His mother has been ill so that's where he's been. And now when he gets home his editor has sent him straight off to Brighton on another story,' she said gloomily. But she didn't mention that it would be her wages paying for his train fare. She had an idea that Holly wouldn't approve.

'Oh, that's a shame.' Holly peeped at her out of the corner of her eye. 'But never mind, no doubt he'll be back in the blink of an eye. But now come and have your dinner. I've done us a nice lamb chop each.'

'I wish we could have a bit more time off to enjoy the city,' Ivy said ruefully one Sunday in September. The trouble was they were always so very busy they barely had any free time and when they did Ivy was always keen to see Jeremy, if he wasn't off reporting somewhere that was. She slipped her foot out of her shoe then and rubbed gingerly at the blister on the back of her heel.

'Looks like it's time you treated yourself to a new pair of shoes,' Holly remarked and Ivy quickly lowered her eyes.

'It's just findin' the time to go shoppin',' she excused but Holly didn't entirely believe her.

She'd noticed that Ivy still always seemed to be short of money, which was strange because the wages she earned working in the suffragette office was a little more than she'd earned in the match factory. Most months now Ivy seemed to struggle to even pay a fraction of her share of the household bills and now Holly was certain that Jeremy was taking her money. But why? If he was an aspiring journalist surely he should have been earning a good wage? She wanted to broach the subject with Ivy, but she was well aware that it was none of her business and, mindful of her mother's advice, she knew that Ivy wouldn't like her asking questions, so she wisely kept her concerns to herself. No doubt Ivy would confide in her eventually, but it was worrying all the same.

October brought an unexpected visit from Emma and Holly was thrilled to see her. It was just before lunch on a Sunday when she arrived and after giving her a rapturous welcome and telling her at least ten times how much she had missed her, Holly instantly flew into a panic.

'Oh, but why didn't you let me know you were coming? I didn't bother getting anything special in for dinner as Ivy is off on some protest march somewhere with the suffragettes. I just hope she doesn't go and get herself arrested again,' she told her mother worriedly. 'Did you know the last lot that were arrested went on hunger strike when the police locked them up for throwing bricks through shop windows and now they're being force-fed in prison? Ivy was with them at the time but she managed to get away – this time,' she ended ruefully.

Emma smiled as she took the hat pin from her hat and laid it on the table. 'I did read about that in the newspapers,' she admitted, secretly pleased that Holly hadn't gone down that path. 'But I'm sure Ivy is more than capable of looking after herself. As for dinner I was thinking it might be nice if you let me treat you. You must know of places around here where we could get a nice lunch?'

Holly nodded. Another lonely Sunday afternoon had been stretching before her so it was lovely to have company, especially her mother's.

'There's a lovely little restaurant in the next street,' she told her. 'We could go there. But first let me get you a cup of tea, you must be thirsty after your journey. How long are you staying? I could sleep on the sofa this evening if you wanted to stay over?'

Emma shook her head regretfully. 'No, darling, thank you but I have a return train ticket for late this afternoon. But that still leaves us a few hours together so let's make the most of them, eh?'

And that was exactly what they did. They had a delicious meal at the restaurant and then she walked her mother back to Euston Station.

'You're looking very well,' Holly commented as they strolled along arm in arm. Her mother had gained a little weight and it suited her and with her hair shining and a twinkle in her eye she looked very pretty.

Emma grinned. 'Thank you. I'm feeling well. It's probably because I'm getting out and about a little more now. Walter took me to the theatre in Coventry last week and we had a most enjoyable evening.'

There was mention of Walter Dolby again, Holly thought. His name had come up a few times in their conversation that afternoon.

'So . . .' she said tentatively. 'Are you and Mr Dolby getting, er . . . close?'

The smile slipped momentarily from Emma's face. 'I must admit I'm very fond of him,' she admitted. 'But only as a friend, of course. He could never be more than that while your father is probably still alive out there somewhere.'

Holly realised then that despite her words, her mother had genuine feelings for the man – she had always been able to read her like a book – and it made her sad. Holly's father had treated them shamefully, abandoning them as he had, and now her mother could never be truly happy again because she was still legally tied to him. It was so unfair.

'Why don't you try to find him?' she suggested as they turned the corner into Euston Square.

'Huh! I imagine it would be like trying to find a needle in a haystack,' her mother retorted with a sigh. 'He could be absolutely anywhere. But anyway, don't you get worrying about it. I'm quite content as I am.'

Following a tearful goodbye, Holly walked back to the flat in a thoughtful mood. She wanted her mother to find the happiness she deserved. Perhaps she could put the word around that she was looking for someone called Michael Farthing who had origin-ated from Whitechapel? It wasn't a particularly common name so it shouldn't be that hard and perhaps she could start with Dora, the seamstress who worked at the shop; she lived in Whitechapel. I'll ask her first thing in the morning, she promised herself and then hurried back to the flat to wait for Ivy to come home.

Chapter Sixteen

It was mid-morning on Tuesday before Holly was able to have a word with Dora. Although it was only October women were already coming into the shop to order gowns for Christmas so she and Miss May had been rushed off their feet.

During a welcome lull, Holly hurried into the staff room and made them all a cup of tea then carried Dora's through to the sewing room for her.

'Eeh, that's a welcome sight, luvvie.' Dora took her foot from the treadle of the sewing machine and smiled at her as she reached for her drink then glanced at her curiously as she hovered. 'Is there somethin' you were wantin'?'

'Actually, there was something I wanted to ask you,' Holly said. 'I was just wondering if you happened to know a family by the name of Farthing in Whitechapel?'

'Farthing – but that's your name, ain't it?' Dora said curiously as she took a slurp of her tea.

Holly nodded. 'Yes it is, and my father came from there origin-ally so I'm trying to find out if there's any of the family left there.'

'Hmm!' Dora tapped her lip thoughtfully. 'Well, I can't say as I can recall anyone o' that name close to us but then it's a fair-sized place. I could ask about for you, if you like?'

'Oh, yes please,' Holly said fervently and she scuttled back into the shop. All she could do now was wait.

The following week Ivy had to take a day off work sick, which was most unusual for her and Holly was worried.

'Shall I get a doctor to come in and look at you?' she offered as she got ready to go to her shift at the hospital.

Ivy was curled up in the chair at the side of the fire, her face the colour of putty.

'No, I'll be fine, I've probably just eaten sommat what's disagreed wi' me. I'll most likely be right as rain again tomorrer.'

'Then is there anything I can get you before I leave? Some toast, perhaps, and a cup of tea. It might settle your stomach.'

'No, really.' Just the thought of food made Ivy feel sick again. 'You get off. I'll probably go into work later on if I feel a bit better.'

Holly reluctantly left her and made her way through the blustery streets to the hospital. Red and russet leaves were blowing across the pavements and suddenly the day had turned chilly although after the intense heat of the summer the cooler air was welcome. She'd noticed that the air in the city was much more humid than back at home, probably because everywhere was so built up, she supposed.

She was approaching the hospital entrance when she saw Dr Parkin just ahead of her and her heart did a little flutter, as it always did at sight of him. As usual his hair was in need of a brush and his white coat was crumpled but to her he looked prefect. They'd shared a few of their breaks together since the night he had walked her home after dear old Mrs

Green had died but he had never asked her out again. She wished that she had taken him up on his offer but it was too late to do anything about it now. Even so she knew that if he asked her again she would go. He was now busily studying to further his career to become a surgeon and so he wasn't on the wards as often as he used to be and she found that she missed him.

'Ah, Nurse Farthing.' He paused when he spotted her and they entered the hospital together. 'How are your new recruits doing?' He always seemed so interested which made her feel special.

She was now in charge of each new batch of Red Cross nurses that started at the hospital and she enjoyed helping them settle in, although not all of them came up to scratch.

She grinned up at him thinking how handsome he looked. 'Unfortunately one of the first lot didn't last a day. She was asked to wheel a body to the morgue with one of the porters and she passed out.'

'Oh dear!' He grinned. 'It's not a job for the faint-hearted is it? And how are things at the shop?'

'Busy as usual.' She felt herself beginning to relax and wished that they could have stood there all day chatting. 'And what about you? How are your studies going?'

'I love it. I'm tired, but it's so fascinating, and I've been getting quite a lot of practical experience.' His eyes lit up as he spoke about his work, and Holly couldn't help smiling back at him. She loved how dedicated and enthusiastic he was about his job. It was what made him such a good doctor. He paused for a moment when he saw her grin. 'Sorry,' he said. 'I do tend to go on a bit. My mum usually tells me to shut up if

I'm boring her, and I give you permission to do the same.'

'I don't find it boring at all. In fact, I—'

A young nurse came hurtling towards them then, cutting her off before she could finish the sentence.

'Dr Parkin, Mr McKenna says you're to go and assist him in theatre as soon as ever you arrive. There's been a traffic accident an' he needs your assistance.'

He gave Holly an apologetic glance then he was gone like the wind and she sighed feeling suddenly miserable as she walked towards the children's ward. This was another of her least favourite wards. She hated to see all the poorly children, although it was nice when she saw them go home.

When she got back to the flat that evening Ivy was out and Holly took that as a good sign. She must be feeling better, she thought as she started to prepare the evening meal.

Ivy meanwhile was striding purposefully towards Jeremy's rooms, her face set in a grim line. She hadn't seen him since the Friday before when he had again borrowed most of her wages. He had promised faithfully that he would see her last night but once more he hadn't shown up at the café where they had agreed to meet to pay her back some of what he owed her. Well, he will tonight when I tell him me news, she thought to herself, her heart in her throat. Half of her wanted to turn and run back to Holly to tell her what a bloody little fool she'd been. But she'd got herself into this mess and now she would have to get herself out of it.

She was breathless by the time she'd climbed the stairs leading to Jeremy's rooms but even so she didn't pause before raising her small hand and rapping at his door. She knew he was in, she could hear movement in there.

Seconds later the door opened and there he stood, all dressed up and clearly ready to go out.

He looked momentarily shocked, but smiling quickly he told her, 'Oh, Ivy, what a shame. I was just about to go out. Another story to report, you know how it is.'

Ignoring his words she pushed past him and once inside she turned to face him.

'If you've come to tell me off about not meeting you last night I can explain I—'

'I haven't come about that,' she told him, her eyes never leaving his face. 'Well . . . not entirely.' She faltered then but after taking a deep breath she rushed on, 'I want us to get married, Jeremy.'

He blinked and ran his finger around the neck of his starched shirt collar. 'Of course you do, my darling, and so do I but first I must—'

'We can't dilly-dally any longer. You see . . . the thing is . . . I'm having a baby . . . your baby!'

Jeremy clutched at the back of the nearest chair as the colour drained from his face.

'I . . . I'm sorry to tell you like this but there didn't seem an easy way so I thought I may as well just come out with it.' She was blinking away tears now. She hadn't expected him to be pleased at the news but she'd hoped he would take it better than this.

He stood there as if he had been turned to stone for what seemed an eternity then asked in a croaky voice, 'Are you quite sure?'

'Well, I ain't had it confirmed by a doctor as yet, if that's what yer mean but I've seen me mam have enough little 'uns to know the signs. I ain't been right fer the last couple o' weeks an' then this mornin' I were really sick.'

'I see.' He sat down heavily.

'So? What are we goin' to do about it?' Ivy demanded. 'I dare say you'll want yer family at the weddin'. They'll probably be surprised at the speed we're doin' it seein' as I ain't even met 'em yet but it can't be helped.'

'Now just hold on,' he suddenly barked as panic set in. Oh why couldn't I have been more bloody careful? he thought. Ivy's face fell then and softening his voice he said, 'It isn't something that can be arranged overnight. I think perhaps you should visit a doctor first and get it confirmed then we'll go from there.'

Ivy's tears spilled over and rolled down her cheeks then. 'All right, I will soonest ever I can but meantime I'm movin' in here wi' you.'

He opened his mouth to protest but she silenced him by placing her hand gently across his mouth.

'I've made me mind up on this so there's no use arguin',' she told him. 'I'll tell Holly we're arrangin' the weddin'. There's no need to tell anyone yet about the baby an' by the time I'm showin' we'll be wed. We can say the baby came early when it's born.'

He gulped, feeling like a rat caught in a trap. 'But look at this place, it's a pit.' He spread his hands as if to prove his point. 'At least wait while I find somewhere nicer for us to live.'

Ivy shook her head. 'I don't care about that, I'd live in a

163

shed wi' you, if need be,' she said as she tried to snuggle into him, but he held her at arm's length.

'Look, Ivy, I have to go out. We'll talk about this another time,' he said desperately. 'Tomorrow, I'll meet you out of work and we'll go for something to eat.'

Her shoulders sagged but she turned slowly and headed for the door all the same. 'All right, tomorrer then, just be sure you're there.' And with a heavy heart she left the room and slowly began the steep descent to the ground floor.

Luckily Holly had gone to bed by the time she got home and Ivy sat staring into the flames of the fire long into the night. Of course she'd expected Jeremy to be shocked when she told him the news but she hadn't expected him to be quite as horrified as he had been. This was his baby she was carrying, his own flesh and blood, after all. Her hand dropped protectively to her stomach as the tears started again. And now she would have to tell Holly that she was leaving. How would she take it?

The next day Holly received two surprises. The first was when Miss May entered the shop. Holly had already opened up and was tidying away the underwear she had just shown to a customer.

She glanced up to see Miss May looking very flustered.

'Oh my dear, I've had some very bad news,' she told Holly, removing a handkerchief from her pocket and dabbing at her eyes. 'My dear brother-in-law passed away over the weekend so I need to take a few days off to go to my sister. Do you think you can manage here on your own? I've arranged for someone to care for my husband and I shouldn't be gone for more than a couple of days.'

'Of course I can manage,' Holly told her sympathetically. 'You can go straight away if you wish to.'

'Well, I would like to, if you're quite sure,' Miss May sniffed. 'He was such a dear man and they were very happy together but they were never blessed with children so I'm all she has left. They lived in Whitby so she's going to feel very isolated now that Frederick has gone. I'll probably bring her to live with me and my husband after the funeral, if she wants to, of course.'

She hurried away to give instructions to the seamstresses and finally she went through the diary with Holly.

'Lady Hamilton will be in to try on her latest gown tomorrow and Mrs Bracken will be in this afternoon to be measured. Oh, and there's a new delivery of gloves and stockings coming this afternoon too. Do you think you could see to putting them all away and checking that they're all there for me?'

'I shall be fine,' Holly assured her and soon after Miss May left to catch the train north.

The second surprise came when she closed the shop that evening and made her way up to the flat where she found Ivy packing a large carpet bag with tears streaming down her cheeks.

'What's going on, Ivy?' Holly asked in a small voice.

'Oh, Holly, I'm ever so sorry but I'm movin' out,' Ivy told her tearfully.

'Moving out!' Holly was so shocked her mouth dropped open. 'But why?'

'Me an' Jeremy are gettin' wed.'

Holly's eyes almost popped out of her head. 'But this is a bit sudden, isn't it?' As Ivy dropped her eyes guiltily, realisation dawned and Holly gasped. 'Y-you're going to have a baby?'

'Yes.' Ivy looked so miserable that Holly raced across and put her arms around her.

'Well at least he's doing the right thing by you, and it's not the end of the world,' she said comfortingly. 'You're not the first and I'm sure you won't be the last. But when is the wedding to be?'

'We ain't set a date yet but it'll be very soon,' Ivy answered. 'An' of course I'll want you there.'

'Wild horses wouldn't keep me away,' Holly assured her with a smile. 'We could perhaps get one of the seamstresses to run you up a wedding dress.'

'Oh no, it ain't goin' to be a posh affair,' Ivy told her quickly. 'We'll probably just go to the registry office.'

'And will Jeremy's family be attending?' It was all starting to sound rather vague to Holly now and she was concerned. Jeremy certainly hadn't been the most reliable of men up to now so she could only hope that he was going to do the right thing by Ivy.

Ivy shrugged. 'I don't know yet. But . . . well, will you manage here all right on yer own, wi' the bills I mean?'

'I shall be fine, don't you get worrying about me,' her friend assured her. 'If needs be I'm sure one of the nurses at the hospital will want to move in. Some of them live a way away and they're always looking for lodgings closer to the hospital. But I-I'll miss you,' she said softly, suddenly getting tearful herself.

166

'Don't worry, you'll still see plenty o' me.' Ivy squeezed her hand.

'So couldn't you wait till the day of the wedding before you move out?' Holly suggested then but Ivy shook her head and turned back to her bag, ramming the rest of her things in.

'I reckon it's better I move in wi' him now,' she answered quietly. 'He's a bit of a slippery bugger, as yer know, always standin' me up, so I just wanna be where I can keep a check on him.'

Holly certainly didn't think this boded well for Ivy's future but she kept silent. Ivy clearly loved him with all his faults and he was her choice, so what could she do?

'Right, I reckon that's it,' Ivy said eventually as she reached for her coat. The moment to leave had come and it suddenly hit her just how much she was going to miss living there. She and Holly had made it into a cosy little home and were as close as sisters.

They walked down the stairs together and after a final hug Ivy set off down the street clutching her bag. Holly watched her go with a sinking feeling in her heart. For the first time since coming to the big city she was truly alone and it was a frightening thought.

Chapter Seventeen

Miss May returned to the shop three days later to find everything running smoothly, which made what she had to say to Holly all the harder.

'How is your sister?' Holly enquired and Miss May fidgeted nervously with her glove.

'As you would expect. Very upset, of course. We have decided that as soon as the funeral is over early next week, Martha will come to live with myself and my husband. She is packing up all the belongings she wishes to bring with her even as we speak. And that leads me to something that I have to talk to you about, my dear.'

'Oh yes?' Holly cocked a curious eyebrow wondering what it might be. Miss May seemed to be all of a fluster about something.

'The thing is . . .' Miss May paused to clear her throat. 'Now that my brother-in-law has passed away my sister has no income. She has some savings, of course, but unfortunately they won't last forever so I thought that perhaps she could come and work with me in the shop . . . The trouble is I can't run to another wage so—'

'So you thought she could have my job?' Holly finished for her. She plastered on a smile, but inside her stomach was churning. She had loved working in the shop and now she was going to have to adapt to yet another change in her life. 'It won't be a problem at all,' she assured the woman. 'If I'm not working in the shop I can work at the hospital full-time. I know Matron would love it but . . . what about the flat?' Holly was terrified that she was about to lose her home as well as her job.

Miss May was so relieved that Holly didn't appear to be upset about losing the job that she rushed to reassure her. 'Oh, things can stay just as they are. And please don't think this is happening because I haven't been pleased with your work. It's quite the contrary, you've been a true help and can run the place now as well as I can. I don't mind admitting I shall miss you terribly. But you and Ivy can stay on upstairs for just as long as you want.'

'Actually, I have something to tell you as well,' Holly said. 'Ivy left on the evening you went to your sister's. She's going to be married shortly.'

'Really? Well, how wonderful. I had no idea she and her young man were so serious. But can you manage on your own?'

Holly nodded. 'I think so but if need be I thought I might offer one of the nurses at the hospital Ivy's room, if you have no objection, that is.'

'I'd have no objection whatsoever. I trust your judgement implicitly,' Miss May assured her. And so it was decided and once again it felt to Holly like her life was about to change.

Just as Holly had hoped, the matron was only too happy to offer her full-time employment and, relieved, Holly felt that things had worked out well. It was agreed that she would start in two weeks' time, which would give Miss May time to settle her sister in and let her take over Holly's job in the shop. But she missed Ivy terribly. The evenings were the worst. They had usually prepared their evening meal together and chatted about what they had been up to during the day but now when she got home only silence greeted her. Ivy had already popped round once to drop off Jeremy's address for her and one evening Holly decided she would visit her. She had asked Dora for directions as she lived in that area, although she had still had no luck in tracing anyone by the name of Farthing as yet.

It was a brisk autumn evening and as Holly walked along she was glad of the warm scarf and gloves she had treated herself to the week before. As she neared the address that Ivy had given her she found that it was as dismal an area as the one she and Ivy had rented when they had first arrived in London. Buck's Row, where Ivy lived, proved to be just as depressing and as she strolled along she glanced worriedly from side to side. This place was a breeding ground for thieves and vagabonds and she felt nervous being there after dark. At last she arrived at number 38. It was a tall, terraced house the same as all the others in the row and equally as depressing from the outside. The stench as she stepped into the hallway made her screw her nose up and she had to step past a gaggle of children playing on the floor there to reach the stairs. Ivy had told her that Jeremy lodged in the top two rooms so she began to climb. The higher she went and the more she saw of the state of the place, the stranger it seemed that someone from Jeremy's background should lodge there. At the top of the house she paused as she looked at a number of doors. What number had Ivy said? Ah, room 12, that was it. She tapped on the door tentatively and seconds later she heard footsteps inside and the door slowly inched open. Ivy stood there but this was not the Ivy that Holly knew. Her hair was straggling on her shoulders and she had a thin shawl wrapped about her. But it wasn't that that Holly was focusing on, it was Ivy's eye, which was swollen and almost shut.

'Crikey, Ivy, that's some shiner you've got there. Whatever have you done?' Holly asked with concern as she squeezed past her into the room. She had the impression that Ivy was none too pleased to see her for some reason.

'I, er . . . walked into a door when I got up to go to the toilet in the night,' Ivy told her but somehow the words didn't ring true and Holly gazed at the girl's bruised face suspiciously.

Glancing around the room Holly saw that Ivy was alone and asked, 'Jeremy out, is he?'

Ivy nodded. 'Yes, he's working. Would you like a cup of tea? I'm afraid I ain't got no milk. I forgot to get some on the way home from work.'

'That's all right. I can drink it without,' Holly said pleasantly as she settled into a rather worn armchair. There was something not right here, every instinct told her so but she kept the smile on her face. 'So you're still working then?'

Ivy nodded as she filled the kettle at the sink. 'Yes, just for the time bein' till I start to show. But how are you managin'?'

'Fine, although I'm missing you terribly, Ivy.' Holly smiled at her affectionately. She then went on to tell her about Miss May's sister and that she would soon be nursing full-time and Ivy looked pleased for her.

They sat with their tea in front of them and as Holly sipped at the scalding liquid she asked casually, 'Have you set the date for the wedding yet?'

'Er . . . no, not yet. Jeremy's always so busy, you see? We will very soon. But how do yer feel about workin' full-time at nursin'?'

Ivy was clearly keen to get off the subject of Jeremy and marriage, which only added to Holly's worries about her.

'Oh, I quite like the idea now that I've got used to it,' Holly answered, glancing around the shabby room. 'And I had a letter from my mother yesterday. Everything seems to be all right at home, thank goodness. Perhaps the next time I go for a visit you could come with me and go to see your mum too?'

'We'll see,' Ivy said cagily and they went on to talk of inconsequential things for a time. But Holly could sense that Ivy was on edge, and the conversation was stilted, so she gathered her things together, but before she left, she took Ivy's hand and stared earnestly into her eyes. 'Please, Ivy, promise me you'll come to me if ever you need me. I miss you and you know I'd do anything to help you.'

She hoped her words would encourage Ivy to confide in her, but although Ivy squeezed her hand and tears came to her eyes, she remained silent, so, with a sigh, Holly left and made her way back home through the rancid-smelling streets, feeling more than a little concerned.

She could understand why Ivy wouldn't be thrilled for her to visit. She probably didn't want her to see the state of the place they were living in, but it was the black eye that was giving Holly the most cause for concern. Walked into a door indeed! And yet she would rather believe that than the alternative, she didn't think she would be able to bear it if she found out that Jeremy was ill-treating her friend.

172

She had just turned into Oxford Street when someone calling her name made her glance nervously over her shoulder, and there hurrying towards her was Dr Parkin. Her heart did its customary little leap at the sight of him and she was suddenly glad of the darkness that would hide her blushes. She stopped and when he caught up with her he smiled.

'Hello, what are you doing out and about on such a chilly night?'

'I've just been to see a friend,' she explained.

'And are you in a rush to get home?'

She shook her head.

'Good, then perhaps you'd join me for a bit of supper? I haven't eaten since early this morning and I'm starving. There's a rather nice little restaurant just a little further up the road, what do you think?'

Holly hadn't had her evening meal yet either so she nodded shyly and taking her elbow he led her along chattering all the time. Soon he ushered her into a cosy-looking restaurant with tables covered in crisp, white tablecloths and tiny vases of flowers on each one; the waitresses were all dressed in smart black dresses and frilly white aprons. They were seated at a table by the window where they could watch the world going by, and as Dr Parkin handed her the menu, their hands brushed and Holly felt a little tingle run up her arm and she blushed. He looked so handsome sitting there that he almost took her breath away and she had to force herself to concentrate on choosing what she wanted to eat. When they'd placed their order he asked the waiter for a bottle of wine and Holly sipped hers cautiously.

'So, was it Ivy you were going to see?' he asked as they

waited for their food to be served and she nodded. She had told him about her friend moving out during her lunch break at the hospital a couple of days before.

'And how is she?'

'Oh fine,' she answered airily, reluctant to share her concerns with him. She hadn't told him, or anyone else for that matter, about the baby either, considering it to be no one else's business but Ivy's. The way she saw it the gossip would spread quickly enough when Ivy began to show.

He went on to speak of his mother and his family then and she warmed to him even more. He was clearly very fond and proud of his mother, which Holly found endearing.

'I've tried to get her to move out of Spitalfields and into a better area now that we're all grown up,' he grumbled. 'But she won't even consider it. She can be a stubborn old devil when she makes her mind up to be.' He chuckled as he topped Holly's glass up. 'She says she's always been happy enough where she is so why move now? Some of her neighbours have been her friends for years and she doesn't want to leave them.'

'I can understand that.' Holly was feeling decidedly light-headed and was smiling like a Cheshire cat. 'I don't think I'd better have any more wine, I'm not really used to it,' she admitted and he grinned.

'In that case I'll order us some coffee.' He patted his stomach contentedly. 'And I have to say that meal was delicious.'

'Yes, it was.'

It was almost an hour later when they finally left the restaurant. Holly thanked him profusely for such a treat, but he waved her thanks away, saying she was doing him a favour by keeping him company. He insisted on walking her home

174

and it seemed the most natural thing in the world to link her arm through his as they strolled along. When they reached the shop she looked up at him in the glow of the street lamp and was sure that she had never seen a more handsome man in the whole of her life.

'Thank you so much for a lovely evening,' she said shyly and he smiled down at her.

'Thank you for keeping me company. I can assure you the pleasure was all mine.' He hesitated for a moment, then said, 'I would love to do this again, but it may not be possible for a while. I didn't tell you before, but I will be transferring to another hospital next week to continue my training.'

Holly felt her stomach drop in disappointment.

'But, I would be honoured if you would allow me to write to you?'

'I'd like that. And I will write to you too.' She smiled happily, thought it wouldn't be as good as seeing him, but at least he wanted to stay in touch.

'Nothing would make me happier.' He smiled into her eyes, and lifted her gloved hand to his lips, kissing it gently.

After he'd left, Holly felt as if she were walking on air, although this feeling was tempered with the knowledge that just as she would be starting to work at the hospital full-time, he would be leaving. But he wanted to write to her, which must mean he liked her. Unable to stop smiling, as she climbed the stairs to her little flat, she wondered if she was falling just a little in love with him. Never having been in love before she couldn't be sure, she only knew that she liked the feeling and wanted it to continue.

Chapter Eighteen

November arrived bringing gusty winds and frosty nights. Holly was working six days a week at the hospital now and although it was hard work, she enjoyed it. The one disappointment was that Richard wasn't there. She missed seeing his cheerful face, but at least she had his letters to look forward to, as they were writing to each other on a weekly basis.

However, although Holly found she could cope during the week when she was busy, Sundays were proving to be very lonely indeed now. She knew that she could have gone to visit Ivy but didn't like to intrude on her and Jeremy's privacy, even though she was so worried about her dear friend, so most Sundays were spent visiting markets and writing letters home to her mother and Richard.

One Sunday she decided to visit Covent Garden market. She always loved the atmosphere there and enjoyed wondering amongst the flower stalls enjoying all the different scents. There were blooms in all the colours of the rainbow and many flowers that she had never even seen before. So early in the morning, she put on her warmest coat and a thick scarf and gloves and set off, walking briskly to try to keep warm. On the outskirts of the market were a number of stalls selling every sort of vegetable you could think of. She was just passing one such stall when someone caught her eye. The young woman was wearing a shabby coat and hat but when she turned after paying for a cabbage she realised with a little shock that it was Ivy. Her lip was split and swollen and when she saw Holly she blushed, quickly raising her hand to try and cover her lip.

'Whatever have you done now?' Holly gasped without even saying hello as she raced across to her.

'I tripped goin' up the stairs an' smashed me mouth up the banister,' Ivy muttered, looking uncomfortable.

'You must be getting accident-prone,' Holly teased, hoping to lighten the mood, but inwardly she felt sick to the core. Ivy looked upset and very down-at-heel. 'Come on, we'll find a café and go and get a cup of tea. That is if Jeremy isn't waiting for you at home?'

'No, he, er . . . he's out on a job.'

Holly steered her through the market stalls and when they found a little café they hurried inside out of the cold.

As they sat down Holly thought that Ivy had lost weight, but surely if she was having a baby she should be putting it on?

She ordered sandwiches and a pot of tea and when she put the food in front of her, Ivy ate it as if she was afraid someone might snatch it away, which worried Holly even more. Something was clearly not right here and one way or another she was determined to find out what it was.

'So how are the wedding plans coming along?'

Ivy almost choked on the food in her mouth and after hastily swallowing it she shrugged. 'We ain't really got round to plannin' it yet, what wi' Jeremy bein' so busy all the time.'

'Hmm, well, you'd best get a move on,' Holly urged. 'It's only six months until the baby is due now, isn't it?'

Ivy nodded, attacking the sandwich again. 'Yes. The end of April to the beginnin' o' May it's due to my reckonin'.'

'And where is your warm coat?' Holly asked and once again Ivy lowered her eyes.

'Oh, I like to keep that fer best.'

Holly didn't believe her for a minute. Since coming to live in London Ivy had started to take a pride in her appearance and her confidence had grown. But now she seemed to be going backwards and it troubled her. She was jumpy and there were dark shadows beneath her eyes. But what can I do to help her if she won't admit something's wrong? Holly thought desperately.

'And have you had any luck finding a new house yet?'

Colour flared in Ivy's cheeks. 'What's wi' all these questions? When's the weddin? Where's yer warm coat? Have yer found a new house?' she mimicked, then she stood so abruptly that she almost overturned her chair. 'Why don't yer just mind yer own bloody business and leave me to mind mine!' she snapped and stormed away clutching her cabbage, leaving Holly sitting there feeling totally bereft. People were openly staring now so after hastily settling the bill she scuttled out of there. She looked this way and that but Ivy had already disappeared into the crowds and her heart sank. She hadn't meant to upset her but she clearly had and now she didn't know what to do about it. Should she go and find her? She decided that it might be best if she left her to cool down a little but the afternoon was ruined now so she turned miserably in the direction of home. Ivy was her best friend and she hated them not being on good terms.

I'll go and see her on my way home from work tomorrow

178

and apologise, she promised herself. She didn't know what else she could do.

It was actually Ivy who was the first to apologise when Holly arrived the next day.

'I'm sorry I blew me top at yer yesterday,' she said the instant Holly stepped into the room. 'I reckon it's bein' pregnant. Me moods are all over the place.'

Jeremy wasn't in again and Holly was beginning to wonder if she was ever going to meet the elusive bridegroom-to-be.

'I'm sorry too, I didn't mean to sound like I was quizzing you,' she apologised, giving Ivy a hug. 'And look – I brought some milk in case you didn't have any.'

Ivy grinned. 'I don't, as it happens, an' you'll have to excuse the room bein' cold. I only just got in from the office an' I ain't had time to light the fire yet.'

'Oh, you're still working then?' Holly glanced towards the empty coal scuttle and the pile of dead ashes in the grate wondering if Ivy actually had any coal, but she daren't ask for fear of upsetting her again.

'Hmm, I thought I'd stay on fer another couple o' months until I start to show.' Ivy put the kettle on the gas ring and struck a match to light it. 'Though I'm not goin' on the suffragette rallies any more. I've got to think o' the little 'un here.' Her hand dropped to her stomach and Holly nodded understandingly. At least that's one good thing to come of all this, she thought. She had always feared Ivy would end up being arrested again and thrown into prison. Only the week before she had read in the newspaper of some of the suffragettes chaining themselves to railings and the thought of Ivy doing that terrified her.

She was about to say something else when the sound of footsteps sounded on the landing outside and the next minute the door opened and a tall, dark man appeared. This, then, is the elusive Jeremy, Holly thought. She had only ever glimpsed him through the window of the flat before and she had to admit that he was even more handsome up close and she could understand why Ivy was so taken with him.

His face was grim and he looked to be in a bad temper, and, Holly noticed, he was wearing a warm overcoat and smart suit, in marked contrast to Ivy's threadbare clothes. When he caught sight of Holly in her Red Cross uniform, he guessed immediately who she was and suddenly he smiled and was all charm.

'You must be Holly. I've heard so much about you from Ivy. It's nice to meet you at last,' he purred as he shook her hand.

In that instant, Holly's dislike of him began. His smile didn't seem to reach his eyes and although he was indeed very handsome, she thought he was smarmy but she forced a smile and inclined her head.

'So, come to see Ivy have you?' he boomed as he crossed to her and placed his arm possessively about her waist. 'She's looking well, isn't she?'

Holly could have said that, in fact, she thought Ivy looked dreadful but again she held her tongue and merely nodded.

'Actually I popped in to see if there was anything I could do to help with the wedding preparations,' she said and watched as anger flickered momentarily across his face.

'Ah, we haven't quite got round to planning that yet,' he simpered with a false smile. Holly noticed that Ivy never once took her eyes from his face. It was as if she was gauging his mood and Holly wondered if she was afraid of him.

'Really?' Holly raised her eyebrow and stared at him boldly. 'I would have thought getting that organised was a priority with a baby on the way.' She had the satisfaction of seeing Richard momentarily look uncomfortable, but she also saw the look of alarm that flitted across Ivy's face and clamped her mouth shut. The last thing she wanted to do was make things worse for her friend. Ivy seemed to be a bag of nerves as it was.

'Well, I really should be going.' Suddenly she felt in the way so she rose from her seat and after giving Ivy another hug she nodded towards Jeremy and headed for the door. 'Do pop round to see me when you have a spare minute,' she told Ivy and left, closing the door quietly behind her.

'So what did that nosy cow want?' she heard Jeremy snap as she neared the top of the stairs. Didn't he realise that the walls were paper-thin and she could hear every word? 'I thought I'd told you to cut ties with her!'

Even more concerned for her friend now, she set off down the stairs as fast as her legs would take her and all the way home she worried. But what can I do? she asked herself. If Ivy was intent on staying with him she would have to accept that it was her choice. It wouldn't stop her fretting about her though and she determined to try and see more of her, even if it meant risking upsetting Jeremy. She would have preferred Ivy to move back in with her, and she wondered if she could persuade her to leave Jeremy, but she rejected the idea. She doubted her friend would ever agree.

Unfortunately Holly didn't see Ivy again for almost two weeks. There had been a sudden influx of patients at the hospital which meant that Holly had to work longer shifts and it was far too late to visit by the time she was finished each night. One cold evening in late November, she was just warming up some soup after another long shift – she was far too tired to cook – when there was a tap on the door. When she saw who it was, her face lit up.

'Why, Ivy, this is a nice surprise. Why didn't you just let yourself in with your key?' Although Ivy no longer lived there she had insisted that she should keep her key in case she ever wished to pop round.

'I didn't like to,' Ivy answered in a small voice and as Holly drew her into the light she gasped. The whole of one side of her poor face was covered in a purple bruise and her eye was closed again.

Something in Holly snapped. 'Who did this to you?' she growled. 'And don't tell me that you tripped into a door or fell over this time because I'm not an idiot!'

Ivy stared at her and suddenly burst into tears. 'Me an' Jeremy had a big fight,' she admitted in a wobbly voice. 'It were about the weddin' an' he lost his temper. He didn't mean it though an' he's ever so sorry now. It were my fault for keepin' on about it.'

'Your fault!' Holly was appalled. 'But there is nothing in the world that should make a man hit a woman! One of the reasons you left home was because you couldn't bear to see your father hitting your mother. And why shouldn't you ask him about the wedding? You have a baby due in a few months' time for goodness' sake and it's only natural that you should want a ring on your finger!'

'Ah, but Jeremy's so busy, you see.'

Holly couldn't believe her friend was still rushing to his defence and sighed. She was clearly upset enough without her going on at her so gently she asked, 'Where is he now?'

'H-he's away for a few days, followin' a story.'

'Hmm, and do you ever get to glimpse these stories in his notes or see his name in the newspaper?'

Ivy frowned. Now that she came to think of it, Holly had a point. She had never found any paperwork in their rooms but then perhaps he kept them at the newspaper office?

She swayed and Holly quickly pressed her into the nearest fireside chair. 'Have you eaten?'

When Ivy shook her head she hurried across to the pan on the stove and ladled some of the soup into a dish then sawed off a thick wedge of bread from the loaf in the bread bin and placed them on a tray, which she carried over to Ivy.

She then went and fetched a bowl for herself but by the time she sat down Ivy had wolfed everything on the tray. Holly handed her her own portion and when Ivy went to protest she smiled. 'Please eat it, I'm really not that hungry and I can have some bread and cheese.' Within seconds that dish was empty too, so Holly cut her a large wedge of fruit cake. Ivy then swallowed two cups of steaming hot tea one after the other and when she had finished she rubbed her stomach and leaned back in the chair contentedly.

'Cor, that hit the spot, all right.' She grinned and added

hurriedly, 'I ain't had time to have anythin' yet today. I didn't bother cookin' fer meself seein' as Jeremy's away.'

'Why don't you stay here tonight?' Holly suggested and when Ivy looked concerned she rushed on, 'Just for tonight. You could have a nice bath and if Jeremy isn't there he isn't going to miss you, is he?'

'I suppose not.' Ivy had to admit to herself that the thought of sleeping in her comfy bed with crisp clean sheets was very tempting. 'All right,' she agreed. 'But I'll be getting meself back off home first thing in the mornin'.'

'Well, there's no rush. Tomorrow is Sunday so I'm not at work,' Holly pointed out. 'We could spend a leisurely day together and I could cook us a nice lunch. I got a small joint of beef from the butcher's, your favourite, and I could do some crispy roast potatoes with it just the way you like them.'

Ivy grinned, making her wince. It was obvious that her swollen face was causing her pain.

'All right,' she agreed. 'But I'll have to go back tomorrow evenin', just in case Jeremy comes home sooner than expected. I wouldn't want him to think I'd left him.'

Holly sighed with relief. At least for that short time she would know Ivy was safe.

Chapter Nineteen

A few days later after finishing her shift at the hospital Holly was letting herself into the flat when Dora Brindley appeared from the shop.

'Ah, Holly, luvvie, I was wonderin' how I was goin' to catch you now you don't work here any more. I'm needin' a word.'

'Of course, come up and I'll make you a cup of tea while we have a chat,' Holly told her, wondering what might be wrong. Dora looked concerned about something. Perhaps she'd discovered the whereabouts of her elusive father? The woman followed her up the stairs and once Holly had livened the fire up and thrown some coal onto it she went to put the kettle on, asking, 'What's wrong then, Dora?'

Dora sighed and looked uncomfortable as she sank into one of the comfy chairs. 'Well, I don't quite know how to say this cos yer might say it's none o' my business but I've been worryin' about it all day.'

'So tell me what it is,' Holly urged softly.

'Right then, but you ain't goin' to like it,' Dora warned. 'The thing is, Lady Hamilton came into the shop today to try on her latest weird and wonderful creation an' as she left I happened to spot her latest young beau in the back of her automobile, an' it were . . .'

'Go on.' Holly was impatient to hear what was wrong now.

'It were that young man who young Ivy is supposed to be marryin'. I know cos I've seen Ivy out an' about with him a few times.'

'You mean it was Jeremy Pilkington-Hughes!' Holly felt as if the air had been knocked out of her.

'Jeremy Pilkington-Hughes, my arse!' Dora snorted. 'His name's Jimmy Sullivan. He grew up near me an' a right little waster he turned out to be. He preys on women, older ones usually. He bleeds 'em of all their money then dumps 'em. Ain't never done a day's work in his whole life, he ain't. I wanted to warn Ivy when I first saw her with him but I thought perhaps he'd turned over a new leaf. But then when I saw him with her ladyship today it gave me a rare old gliff, I don't mind tellin' you.'

'Oh no, poor Ivy,' Holly gasped. 'But what do we do now? This is going to break her heart.'

Dora shrugged. 'That's entirely up to you, luvvie. I just thought as you should know.' She accepted a cup of tea then before heading for home, leaving Holly in shock. Her head was in a whirl as she thought of the mess poor Ivy had inadvertently landed herself in, but would she appreciate being told the truth about the man she loved? And she did love him; adored him, in fact, Holly was in no doubt about that.

Sleep evaded her that night as she tossed and turned trying to decide what she should do, and then it came to her. Her mother was coming to visit her shortly, she would ask her advice. Until then she would hold her tongue.

It was the middle of December and as Holly glanced around the flat she smiled with satisfaction. Her mother would be arriving shortly so she had polished every stick of furniture until she could see her face in it and a delicious roast dinner was cooking in the oven, making her stomach rumble with anticipation. At least this Sunday she would not be sitting on her own thinking about Richard, which she tended to do far too often. It felt as if he'd been away forever, and though they were still writing to each other every week, it wasn't the same as spending time together and she missed him more than she had imagined she would.

For at least the tenth time in as many minutes, she hurried to the window to look down the street for a sign of her mother and sure enough there she was striding along with a smile on her face and laden down with bags. Christmas presents, no doubt, Holly surmised as she dashed down the stairs to open the door. And then they were in each other's arms and Holly realised once more just how much she missed her, although she had no intention of ever living back at home again. She was enjoying her independence and her career too much now.

'Why, everywhere looks neat as a new pin, darling,' Emma said approvingly as she sniffed the air. It was heavy with the delicious smell of cooking and lavender polish.

'And how is Ivy?' she asked next. Holly had told her that she had left home to live with her fiancé prior to them getting married but she hadn't told her about the baby. But she would have to now.

'Oh, she was all right when I saw her last week,' Holly answered carefully. In actual fact she hadn't been all right at all and Holly was growing more and more concerned about her. She had taken a bag of groceries round to her hoping that Jeremy wouldn't be in and although Ivy had strongly protested Holly had got the impression that she was actually very grateful for them. It was clear now that he was bleeding her of every penny she had, but what could she do about it?

'Actually, I need to ask your advice about something to do with Ivy,' she said as she helped her mother off with her coat. 'But not until after lunch. I want to hear all about what's going on at home first.'

For the next hour Holly told her about her work at the hospital and her mother told her the news from home.

'Your grandfather is mellowing in his old age,' she informed her daughter. 'Walter has started to bring his children round occasionally for lunch on Sunday and believe it or not your grandfather is wonderful with them. I think he's started to bitterly regret not spending more time with you while you were growing up. In fact, he asked me to give you this envelope. He didn't know what to get you for Christmas so I think he's sent some money for you to spend as you will, although I think he's still secretly hoping that you'll be able to come home and spend some of the holiday with us.'

Holly took the envelope and placed it behind the clock on the shelf to open later. 'Of course I'll come home for a visit if I'm able to. Thank him for the gift. I have yours all wrapped up for you to take back with you, just in case I can't get home. It will all depend on how busy we are at the hospital, but I promise I'll do my best.'

They sat down to dinner and Emma praised Holly for her cooking. 'You've certainly become very self-sufficient,' she said proudly. 'Seeing as you wouldn't have known how to peel a potato not so long ago.'

When they'd finished eating Holly ignored the dirty pots for the time being and made them both another pot of tea. There would be plenty of time for washing up when her mother had gone home and she didn't want to waste one precious moment of their time together.

'Now, what was it you wanted to talk to me about?' Emma enquired as she spooned sugar into her tea. 'Something about Ivy, wasn't it?'

'Yes, it was.' Holly's smile vanished. 'The thing is I've been given some information about the man she wants to marry and I don't quite know what to do about it.'

She started to tell her mother about what had happened since Ivy met Jeremy, or Jimmy as she now knew he was, but she had barely begun the story when suddenly there was a hammering on the door downstairs.

Emma jumped and slopped some tea into her saucer. 'Goodness me, someone wants to get your attention,' she declared.

Holly hurried down the stairs to see who it was and as she opened the door someone fell through it, landing heavily on the floor.

'Ivy, whatever has happened to you?' Holly's heart began to bang against her ribcage as she realised her friend looked in a very bad way. Her poor face was black and blue and when she opened her bleeding mouth to try and talk she spat out a tooth.

'I-it was Jeremy,' Ivy gulped, clutching her chest. 'We . . . had an argument and h-he beat me.' She seemed to be having trouble breathing. At that moment Emma came clattering down the stairs and when she saw the state Ivy was in she gasped with dismay.

'We need to get her upstairs,' she told Holly and somehow between them they managed it. Holly hurried away to fetch a bowl of hot water to bathe her face, as Emma asked gently, 'Where does it hurt, darling, apart from your poor face that is?'

'I . . . I can't breathe properly,' Emma croaked painfully. 'I think he might have broken one of me ribs. A-and this arm hurts too.'

Emma gently took the arm that was dangling uselessly at the girl's side but when she tried to carefully raise it, Ivy screamed with pain and tears spurted from her eyes.

'She's going to have to go to hospital, I think this arm is broken,' Emma told Holly solemnly. 'We need to ring for an ambulance. Where is the nearest telephone?'

'It's down in the shop and I'm sure Miss May wouldn't mind me using it. I'll go and do it right now.' Holly left like a shot from a gun leaving her mother to do what little she could for Ivy.

'The ambulance is on its way,' Holly panted minutes later and all they could do then was whisper soothing words to Ivy as they waited for it to arrive.

When it came the ambulance men lifted Ivy carefully onto a stretcher making her cry out with pain.

'I'm coming with her,' Holly said determinedly.

'So am I,' Emma replied but Holly frowned.

'But I could be gone for hours. You'll miss your train if you come too,' Holly pointed out.

'As if I'd go home and leave you to deal with this all on your own,' Emma retorted indignantly. She was very fond of Ivy and there was no way she was going to leave until she at least knew the extent of her injuries. 'I'll telephone your grandfather from the hospital and explain what's happened and tell him I might not be back for a couple of days. He'll quite understand.'

And so they both squashed into the back of the ambulance with Ivy and before they knew it they were racing towards the hospital where they were shown into a waiting room while Ivy was whipped away to be examined.

'The doctor will be through to see you as soon as he's examined her,' a fresh-faced young nurse informed them.

Thankfully Ivy had been taken to University College Hospital so Holly knew the procedure. 'I'll give it a few minutes then I'll go through to see what's happening,' she told her mother. 'Most of the doctors here know me by now so I'm sure they won't mind.'

The minutes ticked away as Emma and Holly paced the room like caged animals.

'She'll be fine,' Emma told her daughter, who was clearly upset. 'She's young and strong.'

'Yes . . . but she's also pregnant,' Holly exclaimed and promptly burst into tears. 'That's what I was about to tell you when she arrived at the flat.'

Emma's hand flew to her mouth and for a moment she was so shocked that she was speechless but then pulling herself together she placed her arm about her daughter.

'Well, at least you won't have to worry now about telling her what you've discovered,' she said. 'There's no way she's going to want to go back to him after this.'

'I wouldn't be too sure about that,' Holly told her between sobs. 'I don't think this is the first time he's hurt her, in fact I know it isn't. But she's so besotted with him she always forgives him.'

A nurse appeared in the doorway then. 'The doctor will see you now, if you'd like to come this way.'

Sniffing back her tears, Holly swiped her eyes and followed the girl to the doctor's office. As they entered Holly was shocked to see that it was Richard.

'B-but I thought you were still away,' she gasped before she could stop herself.

Richard's face had lit up at the sight of her and he smiled. 'I was but there are three doctors off here with the flu at the moment so they asked for volunteers to come and help out. I was going to track you down tomorrow to tell you.' And then seeing that she wasn't alone he smiled apologetically at Emma. 'I'm so sorry. Holly and I are . . . friends. But let me tell you about Miss Massey.' His professional head was back on now as he steepled his fingers and rested his elbows on the desk before asking cautiously, 'Were you aware that Miss Massey is pregnant?'

Holly nodded. 'Is the baby . . . I mean, has she lost—?'

'No,' he assured her quickly. 'At present the baby seems fine. She does, however, have a broken arm and also two broken ribs so she's going to be in considerable pain and we'll have to monitor her closely for a few days. Unfortunately a shock like this could cause her to miscarry but hopefully that won't happen.'

Holly breathed a huge sigh of relief. It wasn't the baby's fault who its father was, after all.

'So what can we do?'

He shrugged. 'Apart from visit and bring in anything she might need from home not a lot at present, but she'll need someone to keep an eye on her when she comes home until the ribs have healed. She's gone to have her arm set at present and that could take some time so I suggest you go home and get some rest and come back tomorrow. But then, of course you will.' He grinned. 'You might even find yourself working on her ward. Do you think she might wish to press charges against whoever did this to her?'

'I think there's very little chance of her doing that,' Holly said in disgust. Then she managed a weak smile. 'Thank you, Richa— Dr Parkin. Goodnight.'

'Goodnight, Holly. Sleep well.'

Chapter Twenty

Once they were outside, Emma stepped to the kerb and hailed a cab. They were both far too tired to consider walking home.

'It's been quite a day, hasn't it?' Emma remarked, and then with a sly little grin, 'And who was that rather handsome young doctor you seem to be on such good terms with?'

'He's just a friend,' Holly answered rather too quickly and Emma changed the subject, sensing that now wasn't the right time to pry, although she could have sworn she could sense romance in the air. If she was right then she had no doubt that Holly would tell her about him in her own good time. She was clearly far too upset about what had happened to Ivy to concentrate on anything else at the moment.

Settling back in her seat she squeezed Holly's hand. 'Try not to worry about her, darling. You heard what the doctor said, it's just going to take a little time before she's right again.'

'That's the problem.' Holly chewed on her lip as she stared from the window. 'What if she goes back to him? And if she doesn't, who is going to look after her? I have to work and she's not going to be fit to be left on her own for a while.'

'We'll cross that bridge when we come to it,' Emma said wisely. 'For now we just have to keep her spirits up, and don't worry, I shan't be going anywhere until I'm quite sure she's properly on the mend.'

Holly gave her mother's hand a grateful little squeeze and they fell silent for the rest of the journey. She was so thankful that her mother had been there to help her through Ivy's crisis. She wasn't sure she could have coped with it half as well without her.

She slept fitfully that night and finally fell into a deep sleep just as dawn was streaking the sky. The next thing she knew someone was gently shaking her arm and, blinking, she looked up to see her mother standing at the side of the bed with a cup of tea in her hand.

'I'm sorry to wake you, darling, but I didn't think you'd want to be late for work.'

Holly glanced at the little clock on her bedside table and, instantly wide awake, she swung her legs out of the bed.

'Oh, goodness. Thank you, Mother, I would have overslept if you hadn't woken me. But what are you going to do all day while I'm at work?'

Emma crossed to the window and swished the curtains aside revealing the smoggy street outside. 'I shall be perfectly fine. I'll come in to visit Ivy later.'

'Don't come before four o'clock,' Holly warned as she swallowed some tea and reached for the uniform she had laid out the night before. 'Matron's a stickler for visiting times. No one is allowed into the wards one minute before four or one minute after five.'

When Holly entered the lounge some minutes later, looking very smart in her blue uniform and crisp white apron with a large red cross emblazoned upon it, she found her mother toasting bread on the fire. Looking at her, Emma couldn't help but feel proud of her daughter.

'Come on,' Emma said sternly. 'You're not leaving here until you've got at least one slice of toast inside you.'

Knowing it would be useless to argue Holly quickly took the slice she was offered and after kissing her mother shot away nibbling at it. 'I'll be back just after six,' she shouted over her shoulder before racing downstairs and slamming the door shut behind her.

The first thing Holly did when she got to the hospital was to gain the ward sister's permission to visit Ivy. She was granted five minutes only.

Ivy was sitting up in bed with her arm strapped in a sling looking as if she had been in a war. There was barely an inch of her face that wasn't covered in bruises and her lips looked swollen and sore. Even so she attempted a smile as Holly approached the bed and instantly became tearful.

'How are you feeling?' Holly immediately felt foolish for even asking such a question. It was obvious how bad Ivy must feel just by looking at her. She placed the bag she had packed with one of her own nightdresses, a hairbrush and any toiletries that Ivy might need for her stay on the bed.

'Like I've done twenty rounds in a boxing ring with someone twice as big as me,' Ivy answered sheepishly. 'I'm so sorry, Holly.'

'Don't be silly, this wasn't your fault,' Holly answered as she gently stroked Ivy's uninjured hand. 'At least the baby is all right and when you're well enough you'll come home to stay with me for a few days.'

'We'll see,' Ivy answered evasively and Holly's heart sank.

Surely she couldn't be thinking of going back to Jeremy after this?

Her worst fears were confirmed then when Ivy told her, 'I've no doubt Jeremy will come lookin' for me today when he's sobered up.'

Holly shook her head. 'But surely you won't forgive him this time? He could have killed you and the baby. I hate to say this because I know you love him, but he's no good. You must see that now.'

Ivy shrugged, making her wince with pain. 'He's not violent all the time,' she defended him. 'An' he can be very lovin'. I bet he's feelin' awful today.'

Holly was tempted more than ever to tell her friend what she knew about him but she clamped her mouth shut. Now was not the time. When Ivy had had a few days rest and time to think about it she might see sense, and then she could broach the subject.

She saw the ward sister striding towards the bed then and bent to give Ivy a gentle peck on the cheek. 'It looks like I'm going to be evicted,' she whispered. 'But I'll try to pop back in my break.' She hurried away with a heavy heart. It appeared that even now Ivy could see no wrong in Jeremy.

Unfortunately Holly was rushed off her feet that day and it wasn't until the end of her shift in the evening before she was able to see Ivy again.

She was lying in bed looking towards the door hoping for a glimpse of Jeremy.

'He mustn't realise that I'm here,' she told Holly. 'He'd come if he did so he'll probably come round to yours thinking I'm there.'

Holly hoped he would. There was nothing she would have liked more than to be able to tell him what she thought of him and give him a piece of her mind!

'Your mam came earlier,' Ivy informed her. 'But he hadn't been round by then.'

'Well, don't worry about it for now. Things will sort themselves out,' Holly told her. 'But now if there's nothing you need I'll get off. Mother will be worried if I'm any later. And, Ivy . . . please take care of yourself. I don't know how I'd cope if anything were to happen to you, I care about you very much.'

Ivy gave her a weak smile. 'And I care about you too,' she said softly.

As she left the ward, Holly bent her head to hide the tears that she'd been holding back while she was with Ivy, but which were now sliding down her cheeks. She was wiping her face with her sleeve so didn't see Richard, who'd stopped right in front of her. She gasped as she nearly bumped into him, but he grasped her arms gently, looking down at her with a concerned expression.

'Is your friend all right?' he asked.

'Yes, yes, she's fine,' she sniffed. 'But I just hate to see her like this. And that man . . . How I wish I could set the police on him.'

Richard looked grim. 'Yes, I know what you mean. I see so many women in her situation, and it makes my blood boil. Any man who would beat up a woman like that, especially when she's carrying his child . . .'

His fury and indignation comforted Holly more than sympathy would have done. It was nice to know that there was someone on Ivy's side.

'Listen, I can't stop now, but perhaps we could meet another day? And you can come and talk to me about this whenever you need.'

She nodded and smiled gratefully. 'Thank you so much, Richard. And it would be lovely to meet when you have a moment.'

He touched her cheek very briefly, but then realising where he was, he snatched his hand away, nodded at her and walked off.

Holly arrived home, still buoyed by Richard's words and the tender way he had touched her cheek, to find Emma had cooked a lovely meal for them and it reminded her of the evenings she used to share with Ivy.

'I've done you some nice lean pork chops and I've made some apple sauce, I know it's one of your favourites,' her mother told her. 'And there's some lovely buttered winter cabbage and mashed potatoes to go with them. That should warm you up.'

They sat down together and tucked in, chatting easily and very soon the conversation turned to Jeremy.

'I don't think even now she's ready to leave him,' she told her mother over dinner and Emma nodded in agreement.

'I know. When I went to see her she barely took her eyes off the door to the ward watching for him. It's as if he's put a spell on her. But then love is a funny thing. I should know; I once felt that way about your father,' she confided sadly. 'Even when he left me I was convinced he'd come back, but he never did and eventually I had to face up to the fact that he wasn't the man I'd thought he was.'

'So what do you think we should do?'

Emma shrugged. 'I suppose we could give it one more day, then if he doesn't come here we'll have to go round to his place and tell him where she is if that's what she wants. But if it comes to that we'll go together. I'm not letting you go round there on your own.'

Jeremy didn't arrive and so on Tuesday evening after dinner, Emma and Holly set off for Whitechapel. A thick smog had settled over London making the drab streets they passed through look even more sinister.

The gas lights they passed cast yellow pools of light into the swirling mist and Emma was clearly nervous. 'I can barely see a hand in front of me,' she commented. 'I hope you know where you're going. Perhaps we should leave it for tonight and try again tomorrow?'

'It's all right, we're almost there now,' Holly assured her and, sure enough, minutes later they arrived at the house where Ivy had been living.

Once inside they began the long climb to the attic rooms and as they reached the landing a small boy who was crouched there with his arms wrapped about his knees watched them curiously from eyes that had deep, dark circles beneath them.

'If you're lookin' fer the mister what lived there yer wastin' yer time,' he informed them. 'He scarpered an' took all his stuff wi' him a couple o' nights ago. There were a big to-do an' his missus come runnin' out all covered in blood. Don't know where she went though. He left the next day, probably scared that the coppers were after him.'

'I see, thank you.' Holly tried the handle of the door and it opened. The sight that met her eyes made her gasp with dismay. The room had been emptied of every stick of furniture and it looked as if a pack of scavengers had rampaged through it. It hadn't been up to much before, but now with every stick of furniture and home comfort removed it looked even worse; no doubt the people who had robbed it had sold the lot by now. Unfortunately a quick glance into the bedroom showed that everything Ivy had possessed was gone too, even her clothes.

'Now what shall we do?' she asked her mother. 'Poor Ivy only has the clothes she had on when this happened. They've taken absolutely everything she owned.'

'So we'll buy her new ones!' Emma replied stoically. 'If the ones she was wearing the other night were anything to go by they weren't up to much anyway.'

They left and slowly made their way home through the fog. As soon as they were safely indoors Emma filled the kettle. 'We'll have to tell her that he's gone now. We have no choice,' she said.

'But what will happen to her and the baby? I'd be more than happy to have her back here but Ivy is fiercely independent. And I should let her work know where she is too. They'll be worried that she hasn't turned up. I'll push a note through the suffragettes' office door on my way to work first thing in the morning.'

Holly did just that the next day and when she popped into the ward later that afternoon to see Ivy she found two of her suffragette friends at her bedside, highly indignant at what had happened.

'It's appalling that a man should be allowed to do this to a woman,' a tall, plump, red-haired woman declared angrily.

201

'It just goes to show that we're right to fight for rights for women and when you're well enough to come back your job will be waiting for you, Ivy.'

Deeply humiliated, Ivy nodded. She would rather they hadn't found out what had happened but supposed that this wasn't something she could hide as she told Holly when the women left.

'I thought you'd want them to know why you weren't in work,' Holly apologised.

Ivy sighed. 'You did right,' she admitted grudgingly. 'They were bound to find out one way or another. But Jeremy still hasn't been,' she ended fretfully.

Holly took a deep breath. It was time to tell Ivy the truth, much as she hated to do it.

'Ah, well . . . actually me and Mother went round to see him last night to tell him where you were,' she began and her heart broke at the hope that flared in Ivy's eyes.

'An' what did he say? Is he comin' to see me?' Ivy interrupted before Holly could get another word out.

'Er . . . I'm afraid not . . . You see he's gone.'

'What do you mean gone!' Ivy was struggling to sit up and Holly gently pressed her back against the pillows. She knew that she had to be cruel to be kind now.

'Just what I say, he's gone. Apparently he left the morning after you were brought in here and no one has seen him since. Your rooms are empty. And that's not the worst of it, you see . . .' She gulped deep in her throat, hating what she was having to tell her. 'Dora told me some time ago that Jeremy Pilkington-Hughes isn't his real name. He comes from Whitechapel and his real name is Jimmy Sullivan. He

202

preys on vulnerable women, wealthy ones usually. Lady Hamilton, one of the clients from Miss May's shop, is the latest one apparently.'

Ivy looked as if someone had thumped her in the stomach as she stared up at Holly disbelievingly. The colour had drained from her face making the bruises stand out in stark relief. She didn't want to accept what she was hearing and yet deep down she knew Holly would never lie to her.

'Y-you mean he only ever wanted me fer the money I gave him?' Her voice was so low that Holly had to lean towards her to hear it.

'An' . . . what about the baby? We was goin' to get married.' Slowly her face crumpled as she realised the depth of his deception. 'He never did intend to marry me, did he?' she breathed. 'He were just usin' me. No wonder he were so angry when I told him about the baby.' And then she began to sob, great tearing sobs that shook her body and all Holly could do was hold her close and whisper soothing words as tears streamed from her own eyes.

Chapter Twenty-One

On learning the circumstances of Ivy's admittance Matron kindly gave Holly permission to pop in to see Ivy on the ward during any spare minute she had so the next few days passed in a blur. Holly would finish her shift, then sit with Ivy for an hour before dashing home to have supper with her mother.

Since their conversation outside Ivy's ward, she had bumped into Richard on a few occasions and even managed to have a quick lunch with him in the hospital canteen one day, but unfortunately, with everyone looking at them curiously, it was difficult to talk about anything too personal. Even so, they had managed to touch hands briefly as they parted, and as always, the contact warmed and thrilled Holly.

Then finally after a week he sought her out to tell her, 'I think Ivy could be discharged now. Her cuts and bruises are healing nicely although her arm and her ribs will take longer, of course. I shall speak to her about leaving tomorrow after my rounds but does the poor girl have anywhere to go?'

Holly had told him about what had happened, it was pointless trying to hide it now.

'She'll come to me,' she told him. 'And then we'll go from there. My mother is at the flat so she can look after her for a few days but I think she'll want to get home for Christmas. She only came to visit for the day initially.'

Dr Parkin tapped his chin thoughtfully before suggesting, 'Why don't you ask Matron Lewis if it would be possible to take some time off? You've been running yourself into the ground here ever since Ivy was admitted and I don't want you ill as well.'

'I suppose I could do,' she answered, deeply touched that he cared, and as soon as she had the chance she went to see the matron.

'I wouldn't normally allow this, especially over the Christmas period,' Matron told her after Holly had made her request. 'But you have been working exceptionally hard and have even stayed long past your shifts on a number of occasions so just this once I'll agree to it. I want you back here the day after Boxing Day however.'

Holly thanked her profusely and rushed home to tell her mother the good news that evening.

'Excellent.' Her mother was pleased. 'And I've been thinking too and I have a suggestion to put to you. I'm going to ask Ivy if she'd like to come home with me. I've already spoken to your grandfather on the telephone and put the idea to him and he's agreeable. We thought that once Ivy is recovered she could resume her old job for a few months and then take time off until after the baby is born. What do you think?'

'It would solve a lot of problems,' Holly agreed. 'Now that Matron has given me time off I could come home with you for a few days and get her settled back in. If you'll have me, of course,' she said with a grin.

Emma was delighted with the idea and now all they had to do was persuade Ivy.

The next day they both arrived at the hospital with some of the new clothes Emma had bought for Ivy. She had packed underwear, a new skirt and blouse, a warm coat, and even shoes into a bag and when she unloaded them onto Ivy's bed the girl gasped.

'B-but I can't pay you back for them,' she protested feebly.

'You don't need to.' Emma swished the curtains about the bed so Ivy could get changed in privacy. 'They're my Christmas present to you and when we get back to the flat I have a proposition to put to you.'

They helped her to get changed, both shocked at how weak she still was, and then once Richard had signed her discharge papers, they led her to the end of the ward. 'I'll get us a cab,' Emma said, clinging on to Ivy's elbow for dear life. She was still very wobbly on her feet.

Richard emerged from the sister's office and drew Holly aside while Emma discreetly moved on.

'I was going to give you this nearer to Christmas Day,' he told her, looking slightly embarrassed. 'But now that you're going home for the holidays I thought I'd best give it to you now.' He pressed a small box into her hand and when she flipped the lid she gasped. A pretty silver-etched locket on a fine chain lay within.

'B-but I haven't got you anything,' she protested. She hadn't dreamed for a minute that he'd buy her a gift.

'I don't want anything, just to know that you like it.'

'I truly love it,' she assured him, feeling very uncomfortable. 'Thank you so much, Richard, but you really shouldn't have.' His name had popped out before she thought about it and as he smiled at her he thought how pretty she looked with the colour in her cheeks. He was going to miss seeing her about over Christmas.

'I, er . . . I'd best get on,' she said hesitantly. 'I think Sister has got her beady eye on us. Will you still be here after Christmas?'

'I have no idea,' he admitted. 'But even if I'm not I shouldn't be gone for too long now. I'll write to you. Goodbye, and have a lovely Christmas.' He hesitated as if there was more he wanted to say but then, seeming to think better of it, he strode away leaving her feeling sadly deflated and frustrated. Much as she loved working at the hospital she wished they could have snatched a little more time together.

'You too,' she whispered to his retreating back before hurrying away to catch up with her mother and Ivy.

When they got back to the cosy little rooms above the flat, Emma showed Ivy the rest of the new clothes she had bought for her which made Ivy cry all over again. Her physical injuries were healing nicely but emotionally she was in a very fragile state, which was understandable.

'It's really kind of you,' she wept. 'But I really don't deserve it. I've been such a fool! Holly tried to warn me about him a few times in different ways but I wouldn't listen.'

'Love can make fools of all of us,' Emma told her gently. 'But now dry your eyes. I made a big panful of beef stew and dumplings this afternoon. Holly told me it's one of your favourites. It only needs heating up. And after dinner I have a suggestion to put to you.'

Ivy sank gratefully into the chair and sat staring sightlessly into the fire as Emma and Holly laid the table and got the dishes out. Despite making a valiant effort, Ivy ate very little that night and Holly grew even more concerned about her.

'You're eating for two now,' she told her friend.

'I know and I wanted to talk to you about that.' Ivy pushed a dumpling around the plate listlessly. 'The thing is, this baby will be a bastard when it's born.' She held her hand up as she saw the look of shocked horror on Holly's face. 'That's what everyone will call it,' she pointed out. 'And what do I have to offer it? So I was thinking, perhaps I could get it adopted? There are always childless couples who want a baby. I'm just not sure how to go about finding them though.'

'I think that's quite enough of that sort of talk for now,' Emma said sternly, waggling her spoon at Ivy. 'You wanted the baby until Jeremy, or Jimmy or whatever his name is, hurt you but that's no reason to take it out on the child. He or she is blameless in all this so let's wait until after the birth and see how you feel then, eh? Believe me, there's nothing in the world like the feeling a mother gets when she holds her baby for the first time. I can remember holding Holly as if it were yesterday. I could hardly believe that I had managed to produce something so perfect. And you'll feel like that too, you just mark my words.'

Ivy doubted that very much but she wisely didn't say anything. 'And how am I supposed to support it?' she queried, which gave Emma just the opening she had been hoping for.

When she had finished telling Ivy of her plan the girl was speechless for a moment.

'But why would you do that for me? And what will the master say when he finds out I'm havin' a baby?'

'We'd do it because we all love you, you silly goose,' Emma chuckled. 'And my father is fully aware of the situation you find yourself in. I shall quite enjoy having a baby in the house again and I have no doubt Cook will spoil it rotten. So, what do you think?'

'I'd love to go home,' Ivy said in a small voice. 'But I'd have to let the ladies in the suffragette office know I was leavin'. I don't wanna just go an' leave 'em all in the lurch.'

'I can go round there and do that in the morning,' Holly offered.

'Would you?' Ivy looked relieved that she wouldn't have to face them. She felt so ashamed of the situation she found herself in.

'Of course. Now, eat up and then you must go to bed and try to get some rest.'

Two days later Emma hired a cab to take them all to Euston Station. Ivy was quiet on the way, wondering if she would ever come back to London again. She and Holly had been happy there for a time, until Jeremy had come on the scene. Even now he still possessed a little piece of her heart but she had accepted that even if he were to come crawling on his knees begging for forgiveness, she could never trust him again. She had to finally face the fact that it was well and truly over and try to make the best of things for the baby's sake.

The journey home on the train was uneventful. Ivy was still weak and slept on and off for most of the way.

'Ivy, wake up, we're home,' Holly told her eventually and Ivy blinked awake. It was late afternoon and she was feeling absolutely exhausted. Her arm was still in a sling and her chest tightly strapped but it didn't stop her healing ribs from causing her pain.

'Just hang on to my arm, Mother and I can see to the bags,' Holly told her, eyeing Ivy's chalk-white face with concern. She worried that perhaps they'd made the journey too soon but at least it was almost over. As soon as they were off the train Emma hailed a porter to carry their bags and once outside he placed them in their cab.

'Right, my girls, let's get you home,' she said cheerily, keeping a close eye on Ivy. 'And then it's straight off to bed for you, miss.'

Ivy was so worn out that she didn't even complain and very soon the cab drew up outside the house and Cook rushed out to meet them.

'Just look at the state o' you,' she said to Ivy with a frown. 'I reckon I'm goin' to have to feed you up. You're as thin as a rake.'

Ivy grinned, suddenly feeling as if she had never been away. Perhaps things were going to work out after all – if the master would accept her that was.

Her fears on that score were set to rest when she entered the hallway to find Holly's grandfather standing there.

Ivy stared at him fearfully but he gave her a welcoming smile. 'Welcome home, I'm so sorry to hear of your troubles, my dear.'

'Th-thank you, sir.'

He turned to Holly next and without hesitation told her, 'And welcome home to you too. It's been far too long since we've seen you.'

Holly glanced at her mother uneasily then offered a faltering smile. Her grandfather paused, as if he was about to say something else, before he pottered away to his study.

'Crikey, he really has mellowed, hasn't he?' she whispered to Ivy who gave a nervous giggle. 'But come on, we can put our things away later. Let's go and scrounge a cup of tea off Cook and see if she has any gossip to tell us.' And so arm in arm the friends set off for the kitchen and suddenly Holly realised that she was actually feeling happy to be home.

Chapter Twenty-Two

On Christmas Eve, Emma announced that Walter Dolby and his family would be dining with them on Christmas Day. Holly was mildly surprised but her mother seemed happy about it and so she was too. Ivy was now back in her old room although it would be some time before she was fit to resume work so Holly had suggested she should dine with them, but Ivy insisted she would be far happier eating in the kitchen with Cook. Holly wasn't too pleased with the idea; while they'd been in London they had lived side by side and it felt strange to think that Ivy was going back to being a maid again.

On Christmas morning she woke and stretched luxuriously. She had forgotten how comfortable her own bed was and she had slept like a baby. After washing and pinning her hair up she dressed in the new day gown that Dora had made for her and for the first time she wore Richard's locket about her neck.

'That's pretty,' Emma commented when Holly joined her for breakfast and was amused to see the colour rise in Holly's cheeks as her hand rose to finger it.

'Thank you . . . It was, er, a present from a friend.'

Emma had a good idea who the friend might be but she refrained from saying anything as they tucked into the treats Cook had prepared them for breakfast.

Once they'd finished Emma, Holly and her grandfather gathered in the day room beside the Christmas tree to open their presents just as they had for as long as Holly could remember.

Holly was surprised to find that there was a gift for her from her grandfather, considering he'd already given her some money, and when she opened it she gasped with delight. It was a solid silver fob watch to clip on to the apron of her nurse's uniform.

'Oh, Grandfather, it's beautiful, and how thoughtful of you,' she told him, her eyes sparkling. 'I shall be the envy of every nurse on the ward.' Her grandfather really did seem to have changed, and she felt bad because it made the hand-kerchiefs and socks she had bought for him look very unimaginative but he seemed pleased enough with them. From her mother she had a lovely new coat in a rich red colour and again she was thrilled with it.

'This will certainly keep the cold out, I shall wear it this morning,' she said, smiling as she stroked the silky fur collar.

Her mother was also pleased with the pure silk scarf in autumn colours and the soft kid gloves that Emma had bought for her so Holly was in a happy mood as she skipped along to the kitchen shortly after to give Ivy and Cook their gifts before going to church with her mother.

However, she soon discovered that the mood wasn't so light in the kitchen. Ivy was huddled in the fireside chair staring moodily into the flames roaring up the chimney and as Cook caught Holly's eye she raised an eyebrow.

'She's proper down in the dumps,' Cook told her as she ladled her special sage and onion stuffing into a baking tin. 'Ain't hardly had one word out of her all mornin', I ain't.'

Ivy looked up and gave her a weak smile but her eyes were dull.

'Who would have thought I'd end up back here wi' a baby on the way an' no ring on me finger, eh?' she said glumly. 'An' I had all them high hopes of makin' somethin' of meself an' all. I can forget that now, can't I? Who will ever want me wi' an illegitimate baby? The more I think about it the more I think it'd be better all round if I just let it go for adoption.'

'And didn't we agree that we'd wait till the baby was here before you made that decision?' Holly scolded.

Ivy lowered her eyes guiltily and nodded.

'Then let's have no more of that sort of talk. Now here, open your Christmas present and try to cheer up.'

Holly had to help her in the end as one arm was still strapped in a sling and when Ivy saw the thick woollen scarf and matching gloves she did manage a smile.

'What wi' everythin' that's gone on I ain't had time to get you anythin',' she said with a frown but Holly merely laughed.

'The best present I could have had was having you back with me for Christmas Day, and I've got that,' she told her, giving her hand an affectionate squeeze.

Ivy promptly burst into tears again. 'Oh dear,' she blubbed, mopping at her streaming eyes with the hankie Holly pressed into her hand. 'I seem to spend half me life cryin' at the moment.'

'Well just remember, you're not alone,' Holly assured her, which only made Ivy cry all the harder as she thought how lucky she was to have such a special friend.

214

Holly and her mother left for church soon after, with Holly feeling very festive and smart in her new red coat. The Christmas service was beautiful and as Holly listened to the choir boys singing carols in their snow-white surplices, their pure young voices echoing from the rafters and the light from the myriad candles that had been set all about the church reflecting in the stained-glass windows, she felt happy and at peace, although at one point she did find her mind wandering as she thought of a certain young doctor and wondered what he was doing.

When they returned the sound of laughter and merriment wafted into the hall from the drawing room.

'Ah, it sounds like Walter and the children are here,' Emma said as she hung her coat on the hall stand. 'Although when I say children, Marcus, the oldest, is twenty. Then there's Florence, who's fourteen and Katie who's nine. I'm sure you'll like them.'

She took Holly to be introduced and just as she'd said, Holly did like them straight away. Marcus was quite tall like his father with fair hair and soft, twinkly grey eyes. Holly learned that he enjoyed working in the hatting industry with his father. It was hoped that one day when his father retired the business would pass to him but for now Marcus was keen to learn every aspect of the trade, which Holly thought was admirable. Unlike her brother, Florence was small and dainty with brown eyes the colour of warm treacle and a pretty smile. Then there was Katie, the baby of the family, who threw herself at Emma and hugged her soundly the second she entered the room. She was like a smaller version of Florence but slightly plumper and when she smiled Holly noticed her whole face lit up as bright as the candles on the Christmas tree.

'Look what Santa brought for me, Auntie Em.' Her face was animated as she pushed her new treasure towards Emma, who duly admired her new dolly.

'Why, she's beautiful,' Emma said. 'But now come and meet my baby. This is Holly, she's been staying in London nursing as I told you but she's home for Christmas.'

Katie clutched her doll as she stared solemnly at Holly for a moment then the smile was back as she declared, 'I think Holly is a really pretty name. That's what I'm going to call my new baby.'

'Thank you. I shall take that as a compliment,' Holly declared as she too admired Katie's new addition.

The rest of the morning passed in a blur of enjoyment. Much to her surprise even her grandfather was relaxed and happy, which was taking quite some getting used to. She was still quite wary of him, half expecting him to revert at any moment to being the stern man she remembered but he remained amiable and in high spirits. Holly wished that Ivy would have joined them but she still insisted on staying in the kitchen with Cook. Holly noticed how at ease Walter Dolby and her mother seemed in each other's company and it made her sad to think that they could never be more than friends. I'll speak to Dora again when I get back to London, and see if she's had any luck yet in tracing my father, she decided before giving herself up to enjoying herself.

Emma ushered them all into the dining room then; she had gone to great pains to lay the table earlier that morning and it looked truly beautiful. The crystal glasses sparkled as did the best silver cutlery and her finest china and all down the centre she had dotted bowls of freshly cut holly, their bright green leaves and startling red berries making a perfect contrast against the snow-white tablecloth.

She disappeared off into the kitchen then to help Cook bring in the meal. There was a perfectly cooked goose stuffed with Cook's own stuffing recipe, mounds of creamy mashed potatoes and roast potatoes, and turnips along with Brussels sprouts, broccoli and a jug of thick gravy. This was followed by a huge Christmas pudding that Cook had had soaking in brandy for weeks and by the time they had finished Holly was so full she was sure she wouldn't want to eat again for at least a month.

'Oh goodness me, I haven't enjoyed a meal like that for years,' Walter declared, stroking his stomach after a second helping of Cook's Christmas pudding and thick, yellow custard.

'Well I hope you have some room left because there's hot mince pies and coffee to come yet,' Emma teased him and he groaned, much to everyone's amusement.

Holly spent most of the afternoon playing tiddlywinks with Florence and Katie, until Walter and his family left at a little after six o'clock that evening with promises of coming back very soon.

'Well, that went well,' Holly said as she helped her mother to wash and dry the pots when everyone was gone. 'And as you said Mr Dolby and his family are very nice indeed.'

'Yes, they are. Katie is a little darling,' Emma answered wistfully. 'I've grown quite fond of her over the last few months.'

'I can see why, although she's a terrible cheat at tiddly-winks.' Holly grinned. They had all been invited to the Dolby's for lunch the following day but while Emma and her father had accepted the invitation, Holly had chosen to stay at home with Ivy. She was still very fragile both emotionally and physically and Holly was keen to spend as much time as she could with her before she had to leave to go back to London the following day.

That night she curled up on the end of Ivy's bed and asked, 'So will you be all right? When I go back to London, I mean.'

Ivy shrugged. 'Of course . . . but if you should see Jeremy—'

Holly sternly stopped her from going any further. 'If I see Jeremy I shall tell him in no uncertain terms what a cad he is,' she answered truthfully. 'And I most certainly won't tell him where you are.' When she saw the stricken expression on Ivy's face she went on in a softer voice, 'You have to try to put him from your mind now, Ivy, and accept that he was just using you as he uses all the women whose affections he toys with. He's probably already got some other poor fool to fall into his trap if he isn't still milking Lady Hamilton for all he can get that is.'

'I know you're right.' Ivy sniffed. 'But I loved 'im so much and I was so happy in London that I can't believe I won't see 'im no more. I loved being a part of the suffragette movement an' all. But I suppose once I've 'ad this baby and I get it adopted I can always go back and start over again.'

'You could if that's what you really want,' Holly agreed. 'But let's just wait and see, eh? Meantime at least I know

218

you're safe here. I think Mother and Cook will quite like having you to fuss over. In fact, you'll be in danger of being spoiled.'

Ivy shook her head. 'It's only till these ribs an' me arm are healed. I can't stand sittin' about all day wi' nothin' to do.'

Holly grinned before retiring to her own room. Exhausted from the day, she quickly slipped into sleep and dreamed of her and Richard wandering hand in hand across a lush green field dotted with wild flowers, with the sun shining down on them. He looked at her and smiled tenderly, squeezing her hand. Holly smiled back, and he bent to press a soft kiss on her lips. The dream felt so real that when she woke, she felt almost tearful when she realised she was alone.

The next day Holly said her goodbyes to her mother and grandfather before they set off for lunch with the Dolbys.

'I wish you didn't have to go back so soon, darling,' Emma said tearfully as she gripped her daughter's hands tightly in her own. 'It feels as if you only just got here and now you're leaving again.'

'I know, but I'll be back just as soon as I can,' Holly promised as they hugged each other fiercely. The goodbyes never seemed to get any easier.

It was her grandfather's turn to say goodbye then and she saw that he was struggling to know what to say.

'Goodbye, m'dear,' he muttered eventually. He paused; there was so much that he wanted to say but he found that the words wouldn't come so instead he simply cleared his throat and said, 'It, er . . . it's been good to have you home. And don't get worrying about Ivy. We'll take good care of her.'

She merely nodded. She was too full of emotion to speak but she did stand on tiptoe and give him a quick peck on the cheek, which made him blush furiously before he ushered her mother away. Holly then settled down to spend what time was left with Ivy before she had to catch the train back to London.

Ivy was in a tearful mood. 'Do you really have to go back today?' she asked.

'I'm afraid so otherwise Matron will have my guts for garters,' Holly told her with a smile. 'And seeing as there's only one train running today I shall have to be at the station early. I don't want to miss it. But you'll be fine, Ivy, and I'll come to see you again just as soon as I can get a little time off. I might even just come for the day one Sunday.'

Ivy sniffed and nodded and both studiously avoiding any mention of Jeremy they tried to enjoy the rest of the time they had. Cook did them a wonderful lunch of cold meat left over from Christmas Day and pickles, followed by mince pies and Christmas cake.

'Crikey, I'm so full I don't want to move now.' Holly grinned once she had carried the dirty pots through to the kitchen and washed them up for Cook, who was enjoying a glass of sherry with her feet up by the fire. 'But unfortunately I've got to go and pack my case and make a move.'

'I'll come to the station to see you off,' Ivy offered but Holly shook her head.

'I don't think that's a very good idea. You're still not able to walk too far with those broken ribs,' she pointed out. And so half an hour later Ivy trailed miserably behind Holly to the front door.

'I'm goin' to miss you so bloody much!' she declared.

Holly tried to make her smile. 'It won't be for long, I promise. Everything will work out, you'll see. But now I really do have to go. Take care of yourself, Ivy.' And with a huge lump in her throat she set off, blinking back fresh tears as she made her way to the station.

It was bitterly cold and dark by the time she arrived back in London and a thick smog hung across the streets. She found her way cautiously back to the flat, barely able to see more than a hand in front of her. As she inserted the key into the lock a wave of loneliness swept through her making her eyes smart. The rooms above would be cold and quiet with no welcoming fire to greet her and no one to talk to. Even when Ivy had moved out she had at least been close by, but now she was truly alone in the big city and it felt daunting.

Chapter Twenty-Three

'Ah, it's nice to see you back, Nurse Farthing,' Matron greeted Holly when she arrived at the hospital and reported for duty the next morning. 'I trust your friend is recovering from her injuries?'

'She's doing very well, Matron,' Holly answered politely, trying her best to conceal the sadness she felt inside.

Matron went over the list of new recruits from the Red Cross who would be arriving that morning and when they had finished, Holly went to greet them and settle them in their allocated wards.

It was two days before she caught a glimpse of Richard; two days of not knowing if he was even still at the hospital. But then at last she entered the canteen for a rather late lunch one day and there he was, standing at the counter being served. He looked a little tired and dishevelled, with his hair sticking out at odd angles, but to Holly, he looked just as handsome and dear as she remembered him.

She slipped in behind him with a wide smile on her face and when he caught sight of her his eyes lit up.

'So you're back.' He hastily paid the canteen assistant and lifted his tray. 'Won't you come and join me?'

'Of course.' Holly quickly bought a sandwich and a cup of tea then wove her way through to the tables to where he was sitting suddenly very aware of the locket he had bought for her which she always wore now beneath her uniform.

'So, did you have a good break? And how is Ivy?' he asked when she sat down opposite him.

'Still quite low in spirits but then I suppose that's to be expected. And yes I did enjoy my break, thank you. What about you?' She sipped at her tea, peeping at him over the rim of the cup.

'I only managed to have Christmas Day off, and I spent it with my family, which was nice. Well, if you can call spending the whole day with a tribe of younger siblings nice.' His eyes twinkled as he grinned at her. 'But now how about we arrange a meeting away from this place while we have the chance?'

There was no hesitation on her part this time and she nodded eagerly. 'I'd love it, when were you thinking?'

'I know we're a bit old for this sort of thing but there's a pantomime on in Drury Lane with George Greaves. I'm afraid I've never grown up and still love pantos. Do you fancy it? We could always do something else, of course, if you don't?'

'It sounds wonderful,' she told him and now her eyes were shining too.

'Right then, I'll go and get us two tickets when I've finished here this evening. Would Thursday or Friday night suit you?'

'Either.'

When they parted soon after, Holly floated back to the ward with her head in the clouds. They were finally going to spend an evening together, just the two of them and she could hardly wait.

When the big night arrived, Holly flung one outfit after another across the bed in an agony of indecision as to what she should wear. She had never been out with a man before and was suddenly nervous. What if they didn't get on? What if they found they had nothing to say to one another? Eventually she chose a pale green gown nipped in at the waist with a gently flowing skirt trimmed with a darker green braid. She then piled her long fair hair onto the top of her head in loose curls, and as she studied her reflection in the mirror she felt very grown-up all of a sudden. There was a knock at the door and her heart skipped a beat. Richard was here. She hurried down the stairs to let him in holding her skirt high so as not to trip and once he had followed her upstairs he looked around at her little rooms with a smile.

'You've certainly got this place very comfy and cosy,' he said approvingly, making her blush with pleasure at the compliment. 'And may I say you're looking very pretty tonight, but then you always do.' Before she could answer he went on, 'I've ordered us a cab for seven thirty. It's really frosty out there and I didn't want you slipping on the pavements. We see enough of hospitals as it is without ending up back there as patients.'

'In that case we've got time for a cup of tea,' Holly told him. 'If you'd like one, that is. I'm afraid I haven't got anything stronger.'

'Tea would be lovely.' He sat down in the chair as she pottered about putting the kettle on the hob and preparing the teapot. While they drank their tea, the conversation flowed easily and to Holly it felt as if they had known each

224

other forever, and before they knew it the cab was waiting outside and he was helping her on with her coat.

They enjoyed the pantomime enormously. In fact, Holly couldn't remember a time when she'd enjoyed herself so much and when it was finished he took her to a small restaurant for supper.

Soon, though, the night was over and it was time to go home. It seemed to have passed in the blink of an eye.

'I've had such a lovely time,' Holly told him as they stood on the icy pavement outside the flat. She would have liked to invite him up for a coffee but was worried it might make her look a little forward. 'Thank you so much.'

He smiled down at her thinking what a lovely girl she was. The glow from the street lamp was turning her hair to the colour of spun gold and her lovely blue eyes were shining. He was also thrilled to see she was wearing the locket he had bought her for Christmas, although he didn't comment on it.

'I enjoyed every moment,' he assured her and he meant it. 'Do you think perhaps you'd like to do it again sometime?'

'Whenever you like,' she assured him happily and then he was bending towards her and as his cold lips gently brushed hers, she suddenly felt as if they were on fire and she saw stars before her eyes.

'Goodnight then, Holly, sleep tight.' One last smile and he was marching away and she stood and watched until he was out of sight.

That evening proved to be the first of many outings they had together. On the following Sunday he took her ice skating on a frozen lake and Holly could never remember a time when she had laughed or enjoyed herself so much. On another occasion they went to the theatre and shortly after that on a boat trip on the Thames. Suddenly, almost without realising, they were spending every minute they could together. Then all too soon it was time for Richard to leave again to complete his training.

'Another six months and I'll be qualified,' he told her. 'And then I'll be coming back here as a fully qualified surgeon, if I pass my exams,' he added.

'Of course you'll pass and then we've got all the time in the world to be together,' Holly told him, although she knew that for her, the months before he returned would pass unbearably slowly.

It was the first week in March before Holly was able to go home again. Richard had been gone for two weeks so she was glad of the distraction. They had written to each other often and now she had all his letters tied with a blue ribbon in her drawer. She had read them so often that they were quite dog-eared and she missed him terribly. But now she had a whole weekend off, a very rare treat indeed, so she boarded the train and set off on Friday evening. It was late by the time she arrived in her home town but she knew the place like the back of her hand so it took her no time at all to walk home.

It was Ivy who answered her knock on the door and her face glowed at the sight of her, while Holly could only gape at her. In the weeks since they'd seen each other Ivy seemed to have ballooned to double her size.

'I know what yer thinkin',' Ivy groaned as she stared down at her rounded stomach. 'I look like I've swallowed a watermelon, don't I? An' I've still got about another two months to go, so God alone knows how big I'll be by then. I'm beginnin' to forget what me feet look like, but come on in. Yer mam's been on tenterhooks all day waitin' fer you an' I reckon Cook has some supper ready fer you.'

At that moment, Emma came out of the drawing room and gave Holly a fierce hug. Then holding her at arm's length she scowled. 'Are you eating properly? I'm sure you've lost weight,' she fretted. 'And why didn't you tell us what time your train would arrive, we could have come to meet you. I don't like the thought of you walking the streets alone in the dark.'

Holly grinned as she kissed her mother's cheek. 'I'm a big girl now, Mother. But where's that supper? I haven't eaten since lunchtime and then I only managed to grab a quick sandwich in the canteen. I'm starving!'

They went into the kitchen where Cook had a large bowl of leek and potato soup and some fresh crusty bread and butter waiting for her.

'So how long can you stay?' Ivy asked when Holly had finished.

'Only until Sunday, I'm afraid.' Holly was pleased to see that Ivy was looking much better. Her arm was healed now and her ribs were nowhere near as painful as they had been although as yet Emma would still only allow her to do light duties about the house.

'So how are things back in London?' Ivy asked eventually when Holly had finished her meal.

Holly shrugged. 'Much the same really. All I seem to do is work and sleep at the moment.'

'And have you seen anything of that nice Dr Parkin?' There was a mischievous twinkle in Ivy's eye and Holly flushed.

'He's away training,' she answered as nonchalantly as she was able to. She hadn't liked to tell Ivy too much about Richard because after what Jeremy had done to her, she felt guilty about telling her how happy he made her. 'But now tell me about you. It looks like my mother and Cook are taking good care of you.'

Ivy's face instantly became solemn. 'They are. Your mam made me see the doctor and she's got a midwife lined up already.'

'And have you got everything ready for the baby?'

It was Ivy who flushed and looked embarrassed now. 'Only essentials. There's not much point gettin' too much stuff together if I ain't plannin' on keepin' it.'

Holly sighed. She'd hoped that Ivy would have had a change of heart about keeping the baby by now but she clearly hadn't.

'I have to say yer mam an' yer gran'father have been really kind though,' Ivy went on. 'Yer mam is even makin' enquiries about the baby goin' for adoption, though she's made it clear she'd rather I kept it. She thinks I'll regret it if I let it go but I won't.' She stuck her chin out then. 'How could I ever love it or look after it after what its father did to me. Speakin' of which . . . have yer seen him?'

Holly shook her head. 'Not once,' she told her truthfully. 'But then he's going to keep well away after running out on you like that, isn't he?'

'I suppose so.' Ivy stared glumly from the window for a moment. 'But I don't half miss bein' part o' the suffragettes,' she admitted. 'Soon as ever this is born an' gone for adoption' – she patted her stomach – 'I shall go back to London an' hopefully get me old job back an' then it'll be like all this was just a bad dream.' She grinned ruefully as she admitted, 'I still can't think of Jeremy as a Jimmy.'

'That's understandable.' Although she didn't say it Holly was pleased that Ivy wasn't part of the suffragettes any more. At least at present she wasn't in a position to chain herself to railings or in danger of being arrested every time she went on a march with them. Only the month before she had read that Emmeline Pankhurst had been arrested after being involved in a bomb attack on the home of the chancellor, David Lloyd George. And then only days before that the suffragettes had been attacked by mobs in Hyde Park while they were protesting. No, as far as she was concerned, Ivy was well out of it!

On Saturday evening the Dolbys came for dinner and during the course of the evening Holly noticed that Marcus and Ivy seemed to be getting along famously. Ivy ate in the kitchen with Cook as she preferred to do but as soon as the meal was over she saw Marcus slip away to seek her out.

'They seem to be getting on well,' she commented to her mother when her grandfather and Mr Dolby retired to the study for a glass of port and a cigar.

'Mm, young Marcus is a regular visitor now.' Emma grinned. 'I think he's got a bit of a soft spot for our Ivy.'

'Really? And how do you think his father would feel about that if he had?'

'I don't think Walter would mind in the least, he's very broad-minded and not at all snobby,' Emma told her. 'But I don't think Ivy has even noticed yet. She's too preoccupied with the baby. She's still keen for it to go for adoption but we'll just have to wait and see how she feels after the birth.'

Holly nodded in agreement, although she hoped that Ivy would have a change of heart. The baby was the innocent in all this, after all, and would be a part of her, but only time would tell.

Chapter Twenty-Four

Early in April after Holly had taken a patient down to the operating theatre she was heading back to the ward when someone tapped her on the shoulder. Plastering a polite smile to her face, she turned, but when she saw who it was, her mouth gaped open in delight.

'Richard! You're back!' They were in the middle of a very busy hospital and it was all she could do to stop herself from launching herself into his arms. 'But why didn't you tell me you were coming?'

He chuckled. 'I didn't know myself till the middle of last week and I wanted to surprise you. I was going to come round to the flat this evening if I didn't bump into you at work.'

Her eyes were glued to his face. 'And your exams?'

He shrugged. 'Waiting for the results. They should be through by the end of next week but I thought while I was waiting for them I may as well come back to work.'

'Oh, I'm so glad you did.' From the corner of her eye, she spotted Matron coming along the corridor so she told him quickly, 'I'd better get back to the ward but hopefully I'll see you in the canteen at lunchtime.' She turned and walked on very sedately, although her heart was hammering with joy in her chest.

That evening she cooked them both a meal at the flat: his favourite lamb chops followed by a rhubarb crumble and custard she had made herself. When they had eaten she ignored the dirty pots and they curled up on the sofa together to catch up on all they had done since the last time they'd been together, not that there was much they hadn't already told each other in their letters. Holly had dressed in a pretty blue dress and left her fair hair loose, as he had always said he liked it, and now as he ran his hands through it she shuddered with delight. At last she could understand why Ivy had succumbed to Jeremy's embraces. Love was a heady feeling, but even though they had shared some very passionate kisses, they had managed to stop themselves from going any further.

'I've missed you so much,' she murmured as he covered her face in feather kisses and his hand stroked her back leaving trails of fire in its wake.

'Not as much as I've missed you,' he responded throatily.

She giggled. 'I bet you didn't even give me a thought with all those pretty nurses about.'

'There could never be any as pretty as you.' Suddenly he sat up and straightened his tie. 'I, er . . . think it's time I was going. You're making me forget myself,' he told her with a grin.

Long after he had gone she floated around the flat washing pots and tidying up with a smile on her face. She knew now without a shadow of a doubt that Richard was the one she wanted to spend the rest of her life with and she prayed that he felt the same way about her. But only time would tell. For now she was content to spend as much time as they possibly could together really getting to know each other.

It was the third week in April when Holly got home one evening and found Miss May waiting for her. 'Oh, Holly,' she looked concerned. 'I've hung back to pass a message on, my dear. Your mother just telephoned the shop, she didn't know how to get in touch with you at the hospital.'

'What's wrong?' From the expression on the woman's face, Holly was certain something was wrong.

'It's young Ivy. Apparently she's having the baby. In fact, she might have already had it by now and your mother said to let you know she'll keep you informed.'

'Thank you.' Holly watched the woman bustle away then, making a hasty decision, she flew upstairs, quickly changed her clothes and snatched up a bag. Ivy needed her and she intended to be there for her. In that moment she gave no thought to Richard, who she was supposed to be meeting that evening, nor to what Matron might say if she didn't turn up for work in the morning. She just knew that she needed to get to Ivy as soon as possible.

Thankfully, when she reached Euston there was a train due to leave for Nuneaton imminently so she hastily bought a ticket and climbed breathlessly aboard.

By the time it chugged slowly out of the station Holly had worked herself up into a right old state and could hardly sit still. Would Ivy be all right? What if something went wrong? A million questions to which she had no answers floated around her head as she stared impatiently from the window.

At last the train slowed and as it pulled into Trent Valley Railway Station she leapt from the carriage before it had barely stopped and set off at a run for home.

'Holly . . . what are you doing home?' Her mother gasped as she almost fell in through the front door.

Emma was taking yet another jug of hot water up to the midwife and was shocked to see her.

'I got your message from Miss May when I got home from work and I came straight away,' Holly panted as she tried to get her breath. 'How is she?'

Emma smiled. 'It shouldn't be long now, hopefully. Unfortunately first babies do have a habit of taking their time. The midwife is up there with her and we have the doctor on standby too but we're hoping we won't need him. She's done really well up to now and she's been very brave.'

Holly flung her coat at the cook who was hovering about like a nervous mother hen.

'I've put her in the room next to mine,' Emma told her as she started up the stairs and seconds later Holly raced along the landing and burst in.

Ivy was sitting up puffing and panting and the nurse in attendance smiled at her. 'Hello, you must be Holly. She's been telling me all about you between pains but I don't think she expected you to be here.'

Ivy looked up and tears instantly welled in her eyes as she held her hand out to her friend.

'Blimey, I ain't half glad to see you,' she welcomed her in a wobbly voice. 'This givin' birth don't half hurt.'

Holly grasped her hand. It was hot and sweaty and Ivy looked exhausted. She started to pant then and the nurse told her, 'Lie back down now, there's a good girl, and I'll have a peep at what's happening.' Ivy sank back against the damp pillows, her face chalky white as the midwife lifted the sheet and peered beneath it.

'Ah.' She smiled with satisfaction. 'I think we're almost there. Now on the next pain I want you to push down when I tell you. Do you think you can do that?'

Ivy gave a feeble nod and as the next excruciating contraction built she winced and clamped her mouth tightly shut but she didn't cry out loud. Beads of sweat stood out on her forehead and dribbled into her eyes and Holly had never felt so useless in her life. She had assisted midwives on a number of deliveries in the maternity ward back at the hospital but she realised now that it was a different thing entirely when it was someone you cared about giving birth.

'Right now,' the midwife urged encouragingly. 'Push with all your might!'

Ivy's chin rested on her chest as she did her best to do as she was told but her strength was waning now. Even so the midwife seemed pleased with her effort. 'That's it, good girl, now rest till the next one comes along and then I want you to do the same again.'

The same process was repeated seconds later and this time the woman smiled her approval. 'Well done, Ivy. I can see the baby's head now. You're almost there.'

'I . . . I don't think I can push any more,' Ivy whimpered. She was clutching Holly's hand so tightly that it had turned white.

'Of course you can,' the midwife told her in a no-nonsense sort of voice. 'One more mighty push should do it and it'll all be over, then you can meet your baby.'

'You can do it,' Holly told her, adding her voice to the midwife's. 'Come on, Ivy, don't let us down.'

And so as the pain became so bad that Ivy was sure it was going to rent her in two, Ivy made one last gargantuan effort and was rewarded when she felt something slither out of her into the midwife's waiting hands.

Holly dared to look then as tears of joy streamed down her face. 'Oh, Ivy, you've got a little girl and she's beautiful,' she breathed as the nurse laid the child on the bed. She quickly cut the cord and it was only then that Holly realised with a shock that was like a smack in the face that the child wasn't crying.

Ivy must have realised it at the same time because she lifted her head weakly and swiping the sweat from her eyes she shrieked, 'Why isn't she crying? What's wrong?'

Totally ignoring her the midwife swung the child in the air and after dangling her upside down she gave her a sharp slap on the back. Still only silence save for the sound of the logs spitting on the fire and the tick of the clock on the shelf. Emma had joined them now and she began to wring her hands anxiously. The nurse almost threw the baby onto the bed and pinching her nostrils together she began to breathe into the child's mouth. Still silence. She turned the child and slapped her smartly on the backside and suddenly the baby opened her mouth and her protesting wails echoed around the room.

'Oh, thank God.' Holly felt almost faint with relief. She had feared that the child was dead but she was certainly making her presence known now.

With a broad smile the nurse wrapped the baby in a towel

and laid her on her mother's chest before Ivy could protest. She had been adamant that she didn't even want to look at the child when it was born but now the strangest thing happened. Her arms cradled the baby instinctively and the look of shock changed to one of tenderness as she stared down at the indignant little face.

'Well, hello there,' she whispered with a look of awe on her face. 'You certainly gave us a scare then, didn't you?'

Holly and her mother both simultaneously sighed with relief. It was beginning to look like Emma wasn't going to have to search for any adoptive parents after all.

'Right, that's enough of that for now,' the midwife teased as she took the baby from Ivy's arms after a few minutes and plonked her into Emma's. 'We need to get this afterbirth delivered and get you cleaned up, so madam here can go for a bath too.'

Emma was only too delighted to do as asked as she skipped from the room with Holly close behind her.

In the kitchen the child was bathed and changed into the tiny clothes Emma had laid ready as Cook and Holly cooed over her. Even Holly's grandfather ventured into the kitchen to take a peep at the new arrival.

'Hmm, she's got a good pair of lungs on her,' he commented and hurried back to his study to leave them to what he called 'women's stuff'. Even so his eyes were damp as he thought back to the night his late wife had given birth to Emma and the utter joy he had felt as he had caught his first sight of her. He hadn't been able to believe that he could produce someone so perfect, nor believe now that he had been such a fool as to hold Holly at arm's length for all those years, just because her mother had chosen to disobey him when she met Holly's father. He sighed. There was nothing like old age and the awareness of your own mortality to force you to confront unwelcome truths about yourself. He just hoped it wasn't too late to make it up to her.

Once the baby was clean and dressed, Holly carried her back upstairs to her mother while Emma followed with a large tea tray and some shortbread biscuits.

Ivy had washed and changed by then and she held her arms out for her baby immediately, and Holly and her mother exchanged a relieved glance.

'I thought you might be a bit peckish after all that effort so I've brought you some biscuits,' Emma told her.

'Peckish? I'm bloody starvin',' Ivy declared in her own indomitable way. 'Just pass the tray over here!'

They all laughed as she balanced the baby in one arm while snatching at the biscuits with another.

'And when you've had your fill it'll be time to give the baby hers,' the midwife warned as she washed her hands in the bowl Emma had placed ready for her, but Ivy didn't even flinch let alone protest.

Minutes later the baby was suckling at her mother's breast and Ivy had a blissful smile on her face.

'So what are you going to call her?' Holly could hardly drag her eyes away from the happy picture.

Ivy frowned. 'Well, seein' as I weren't plannin' on keepin' her I haven't given it a lot o' thought, but somethin' will come to me.'

'Does that mean you are planning on keeping her now then?'

Ivy grinned sheepishly as she glanced up at her friend. 'Too bloody right I am! She's just perfect, ain't she?'

'Absolutely,' Holly and Emma agreed in unison and then they were all laughing again.

Chapter Twenty-Five

'And so she's decided to call the baby Alice. It's a lovely name, isn't it?' she said to Richard as they sat together in the hospital canteen a couple of days later. Luckily she had been able to telephone him at the hospital from her mother's to explain where she was when she had dashed off to be at Ivy's side. She'd also spoken to Matron who had given her a bit of a telling-off, but Holly was still pleased that she'd gone. She wouldn't have missed little Alice's birth for the world. 'She looks just like Ivy,' she gabbled on. 'And—' She stopped abruptly when she saw that Richard was laughing at her.

'Do you know you haven't stopped speaking about that baby for the last ten minutes? I'm beginning to get a bit jealous,' he teased.

'Sorry.' Holly grinned at him. 'But when you meet her you'll see why I'm so besotted with her.'

'Hmm, sounds to me like this little Miss Alice has turned you all broody. And if that's the case I shall have to make an honest woman of you, shan't I?'

When Holly almost choked on the mouthful of tea she was in the process of swallowing he thumped her on the back.

'Was that a proposal, Dr Parkin?' she squeaked when she'd got her breath back, her eyes like saucers.

'I think it was. Not the most romantic of ones I admit. But what do you say?'

Holly didn't even have to think about it. 'I say yes,' she breathed with all the love she felt for him shining in her eyes.

'In that case I suppose I'd better take you shopping on Saturday for a ring. But now I'd better get back to work. I don't want to get the sack if I have a fiancée to support, do I?'

Resisting the urge to kiss her because they were in full view of everyone in the canteen he went on his way and Holly followed on legs that suddenly felt as if they'd developed a life of their own.

As the afternoon wore on her elation began to wear off. What were her mother and grandfather going to say when she suddenly appeared with a fiancé that they'd had no idea about? And what about Matron? She had a strict rule that there should be no consorting between doctors and nurses. She was also very disapproving of any of her nurses being married, especially the younger ones. Perhaps she should suggest to Richard that she took him to meet the family before they bought the ring. At least then it wouldn't come as such a shock to those back at home.

She put the idea to him that evening. 'I'm not saying that I don't want to get engaged,' she assured him hastily. 'It's just that I feel it might be better if we do it this way. At least then my family will have met you. And as for Matron . . . perhaps we should keep it quiet at the hospital, for now at least. I wouldn't be allowed to wear my ring at work anyway.'

'All right, if you feel more comfortable doing it that way,' he agreed. 'The trouble is I'm not due a weekend off till the end of next month.'

'That will give me plenty of time to tell my family that I'm bringing someone very special home to meet them. But I'll bet Ivy will guess it's you before I say a word. I think that she knew I loved you even before I did.' She snuggled into his arms contentedly feeling like the luckiest girl in the world.

A few days later as Ivy settled down to read her latest letter from Holly, she grinned. Alice was fast asleep in the crib that Holly had slept in as a baby and Ivy glanced at her every few seconds as if to assure herself that she was still there. Already she couldn't imagine a life without the baby in it and she absolutely adored her. It was no wonder really, for Alice was a beautiful child with the sweetest nature. She never cried unless she was hungry and Ivy could hardly bear to let her out of her sight. In fact, little Alice had everyone in the house eating out of her tiny hand. Even Holly's grandfather had taken a shine to her and quite enjoyed a little cuddle whenever he could prise her away from her mother for a few seconds.

Ivy had read no more than two or three lines when the door burst open and Emma rushed in waving her letter in the air.

'Have you read yours yet?' she asked excitedly, then before Ivy could get a word in she rushed on, 'Holly is coming home for the weekend towards the end of May and she says she's bringing someone special with her to meet us. Whoever do you think it might be?'

Ivy grinned from ear to ear. She had a very good idea. 'I

reckon it'll be that young Dr Parkin. He was right took with Holly, I reckon, an' she were often mentionin' him.'

Emma giggled. 'Oh, how exciting. And it must be serious between them if she's bringing him home to meet us – although she doesn't really need to, after all, I've already met him. I can hardly wait.'

'Well, she could do a lot worse,' Ivy said. Alice stirred then and she rushed to tend to her. Good luck to Holly, Ivy thought a little later as Alice suckled contentedly. Holly was one of the most loving and giving people she knew and she deserved someone nice.

The week before they were due to travel to Nuneaton Richard visited the flat one night looking slightly sheepish.

'I've, er . . . bought you something,' he told her. 'I know we said we would wait and we can but I just wanted you to have it now although you can change it if you don't like it.' He self-consciously pulled a small velvet box from his pocket and handed it to Holly and when she flipped it open she gasped with delight. It was a single diamond set in a gold band that caught and reflected the light and she truly thought it was the most beautiful ring she had ever seen.

'Oh, Richard, it's perfect, but I'm afraid it must have been terribly expensive.'

He waved his hand airily. 'Only the best for my girl. I thought we could perhaps take it with us when we visit your family and then once I've talked to them you could wear it and we could make it official.'

Holly's eyes shone as she slipped it onto her finger – she couldn't resist at least trying it on.

'I think that's a wonderful idea,' she agreed, thinking how she couldn't bear to take it off again.

Just three days before she was due to visit home Holly was in the flat one evening when someone knocked on the door. Hoping it might be Richard finishing his shift earlier than he'd expected she rushed downstairs to open it only to find Dora standing on the step.

'Why, Dora, this is a nice surprise.' She took her elbow and led her upstairs. 'And what brings you out of an evening?'

'Well, as yer know I put the word out some time ago to try an' find anyone o' the name o' Farthin' in the area. Up to now I've had no luck whatsoever but then one o' me neighbours come round last night right out o' the blue an' said she thought she might know the person yer lookin' for. Or his wife at least.'

'Really!' Holly sat down heavily. He was married? she thought, stunned. But was he married before he met her mother or afterwards?

'The woman she thinks he were married to lives in Spitalfields now. She gave me her address, look.' She extracted a piece of rather grubby, screwed-up paper from her pocket and handed it to Holly. 'Now it could be yer settin' off on a wild goose chase o' course but I thought it were worth you checkin' it out. The woman's name is Belle.'

'Thank you, Dora. It's really kind of you. Now would you like a cup of tea?'

'No, duckie, thanks all the same, but I'd best get back to the little 'uns. The buggers run riot of an evenin' if I ain't there to keep 'em in order an' the old man's gone to the Horse an' Jockey for a jug of ale. G'night, luvvy, an' good luck.'

As soon as Dora had left Holly began to pace the room. Did she really want to try and trace her father after all these years when he had abandoned both her and her mother before she had even been born? No, her heart told her, but then if her mother could be free of him she would be able to start a new life. She deserved that so the only thing to do was visit the address Dora had given her, and, she decided, there was no time like the present so despite the fact she had been working since early that morning she hastily changed her clothes and set off.

She took a tram to the outskirts of Spitalfields and was soon heading for Dock Street. The area was in the heart of the East End and Holly was appalled at the poverty there. Once it had housed wealthy silk merchants but they had long since gone and now all manner of humanity lived there, mainly immigrants of every nationality. The once beautiful houses were divided into rooms, some of which housed whole families of ten or twelve people, and painfully thin, ragged children played in the gutters, their eyes dull and lacklustre.

By the time Holly arrived at the right place her heart was hammering so loudly that she was afraid anyone standing close might hear it, but she had come this far and she wasn't going to be put off. This address was part of a small row of terraced cottages, which looked strangely out of place amongst the once grander houses and she noted that it looked very clean and tidy compared to all of its neighbours. Before she could change her mind she rapped on the door and seconds later she heard footsteps pottering towards it. She found herself face to face with a woman who looked to be several years older than her mother, and noting Holly's neat appearance she smiled at her.

'H-hello . . .' Holly swallowed nervously before rushing on. 'Is your name Belle?'

'Yes, that's me,' the woman answered pleasantly. 'Can I help you?'

She was plainly dressed but clean with a large apron covering her skirt. Her hair was tied back into a neat bun and she had blue eyes that looked kind.

'I, er . . . wondered if I might speak to you about a rather delicate matter?'

The woman raised an eyebrow but held the door wide for Holly to step past her. 'Excuse the mess,' the woman said. 'I was just in the middle of baking but do come in and sit down.'

As Holly perched uncomfortably on the edge of the nearest chair she saw that the room, like the woman, was plainly furnished but very neat and tidy apart from the lump of dough on the table that she had been in the process of kneading.

'I'll just get these into the tins and put them on the hearth to rise then I'll be with you,' the woman said and soon she joined her and looked at her questioningly.

'The thing is,' Holly began cautiously, 'before I was born my mother eloped with a man and married him but then when he found out that she was having me he left her with no money. She has never seen him since. She returned to my grandfather's home in the Midlands and I lived there all my life until I came to London to nurse. I worked in a dress shop for a time when I first arrived and one of the seamstresses there gave me your address. She's been trying to help me trace my father and thought you might be able to help me?'

The woman looked slightly bemused. 'Really? How could I do that?'

'Well, my father went by the surname of Farthing—'

She stopped abruptly as she saw the woman's face drain of all colour. 'W-was his first name Michael?'

When Holly nodded, she sighed. 'In that case I think you've come to the right place,' she said quietly. 'And I'm afraid I have some rather bad news for you.'

'Oh?'

'Yes . . . you see, I was married to him too. His real name is Garrett but he left me for another woman with five children to bring up on my own. That woman was possibly your mother and I learned that he was going by the name of Farthing then. Of course, I attach no blame to your mother whatsoever, she could have had no idea what a cad he was. But do you realise what this means?'

Holly stared at her blankly.

'It means,' the woman went on gently, 'that your mother was never legally married to him . . . He is still married to me, you see? If he's still alive that is.'

Shock coursed through Holly as she tried to digest what the woman was telling her. If what she was saying was true it meant that she herself was illegitimate. But it also meant

247

that her mother was now free to move on with her life. There would be no need for divorce, for she had never been married in the first place.

'I . . . I see,' she stammered.

Seeing how shaken the young woman was, Belle Garrett hurriedly rose from her seat and went to fill the kettle at the sink. 'I think what we need is a good strong cup of tea,' she said kindly and all Holly could do was nod numbly.

Minutes later she was back with a tray and Holly wordlessly accepted the dainty cup and saucer the woman handed to her.

'Get that down you, it's good for shock,' Belle urged and Holly took a great gulp from the cup almost scalding her mouth.

'You mustn't feel badly about this.' The woman's voice was gentle. 'None of this was your fault and I can understand why your mother fell in love with him. Michael Garrett had the gift of the gab. He could have charmed the birds from the trees and I fell madly in love with him. I knew almost from day one that he wasn't the man he made himself out to be but love is blind. I would have followed him to the ends of the earth if he'd asked me to.' She sighed as memories rushed back. 'I was with him for five years before he left me, and it took me another five to get over him and accept that he wasn't coming back.' She shook her head.

'I had five children by then and somehow I had to try and keep a roof over their heads and food on the table. I was in a bit of a mess emotionally, which is probably why I was so vulnerable. Right from the day they met him my parents didn't take to him and made it clear that they would never accept him, but I wouldn't hear a word said against him so in the end we ran away.' She blushed prettily then. 'We lived together for a time and then when I discovered I was having my second baby he finally made an honest woman of me but my parents had already disowned me.' She smiled. 'Even so my firstborn, Richard, has done really well for himself, and the youngest has just left school so they're all in work now,' she told her proudly. 'Richard's just qualified as a surgeon and works at University College Hospital. Didn't you say you were a nurse? You might know him.'

Holly suddenly felt as if she was caught in the grip of a nightmare and she started to sweat as she asked unsteadily, 'Is his name Richard Parkin?'

'Yes, that's him.'

If, as his mother had told her, she and her father had lived together before getting married that would explain why Richard had a different surname. Parkin must have been Mrs Garrett's maiden name. It also meant . . . that Richard was her half-brother! They both had the same father!

She swayed in her chair and felt sweat break out on her forehead.

'Oh my dear, are you all right?' Mrs Garrett asked anxiously as Holly dragged herself to her feet.

'Yes . . . thank you, and thank you for your time. You've been most helpful but I really must go now.' And as the poor woman looked on with concern, Holly staggered towards the door and lifting her skirt she ran as fast as her shaking legs would allow her to. She had no idea if she was even running in the right direction. She just knew that she had to get away. But no matter how fast she ran the awful truth followed.

Richard is my brother, Richard is my brother. The words played over and over in her head like a mantra as tears streamed down her cheeks, but still she kept running and she didn't stop until a painful stitch in her side forced her to lean breathlessly against a dirty warehouse wall. She was on the docks and as she stared down into the flotsam on the sluggishly flowing water she had the urge to throw herself in and sink beneath it. At least then she would escape this awful pain in her heart.

Eventually she dragged herself away from the wall and made her way home on legs that felt as if they had turned to lead. Only hours ago her future had looked rosy. Now she had discovered that not only was she illegitimate, but that she was about to become engaged to her own brother. The wonderful life she had planned with Richard had gone in the blink of an eye. How was she to tell him? And how could she live without him?

Chapter Twenty-Six

As Holly turned the corner into Cavendish Street she groaned when she saw Richard standing outside the door of the flat, looking anxiously up at the window. She had forgotten that he was coming around this evening. But then she supposed it wasn't a bad thing. He would have to know sooner or later that they couldn't marry so she may as well get it over with. But what she wouldn't do was let him know about their relationship to each other. That would feel like a betrayal to his mother and Holly felt that the poor woman had gone through enough.

'Ah, here you are.' He smiled and hurried to greet her, but she ignored his outstretched arms and inserted the key in the lock.

'You'd better come up,' she said dully. 'I need to speak to you.'

He looked at her reddened eyes and frowned but followed without making a comment. It was obvious that something had upset her deeply.

When she reached the top of the stairs she marched straight into the little sitting room and turned to face him. He looked so handsome standing there that she almost faltered but then with a supreme effort she hardened her heart.

'I'm afraid I have something to tell you.' She paused to

lick her dry lips but went doggedly on. 'I've been doing a lot of thinking and I've decided . . .' Her resolve wavered for a second. 'I've decided that things are happening too fast.'

He scowled, looking confused. 'What do you mean? What things?'

'I mean us . . . I think we're too young to rush into marriage. We've both worked really hard to get where we are in our careers and I've decided I want to concentrate on that for a few more years before I even think of settling down.'

She saw the stricken look on his face and hated herself, but hardening her heart she went to the drawer and withdrew the box containing the diamond ring he had given her. 'I think you should give this to a girl who will be prepared to love you as you deserve to be loved.' She held the box out to him.

'But I . . . I don't understand,' he faltered. 'I thought you loved me.'

It was the hardest thing she had ever had to do but she stared back at him coldly. 'I thought I did too but then I realised we would be making a mistake.'

He stared at her for what seemed an eternity as if he didn't know her any more then slowly shook his head as he stared at the ring she was holding out to him. It had been meant to be a symbol of their love but now here she was calmly telling him that it meant nothing.

'Keep it,' he said in a husky voice. 'You're the only girl I've ever loved enough to give a ring to. I won't be needing it.' Turning abruptly he clattered away down the stairs slamming the door resoundingly behind him. Crumpling to her knees, Holly sobbed as if her heart would break.

Holly didn't go to work the next morning. She knew she wouldn't be able to bear it if she bumped into Richard and there were things she needed to do. She had lain awake all night with her mind whirling, but today she was calm.

As soon as the shop was open she went downstairs and asked Miss May if she might use the telephone.

'Why, of course you can, dear. But is everything all right? You don't look well,' the kindly woman said with concern.

'I'm fine but I need to ring my mother and go home for a few days.'

'Then I'll leave you to make your call in private.' Miss May pottered away as Holly lifted the phone and the operator put her through to the house in Nuneaton.

'Hello.'

At the sound of her mother's voice, Holly had to stop herself from bursting into tears again. 'It's me,' she said quietly. 'I was thinking of coming home for a few days today. Is that all right?'

'Holly, you should know you don't even have to ask, this is your home and your bedroom is always ready for you,' her mother scolded gently. 'But are you all right, sweetheart? You don't sound right.'

Holly almost laughed. She didn't sound right! Well she wasn't right. She would never be right again but her voice was level when she answered, 'I'm fine, but there's something

253

I need to speak to you about so I'll see you later. I'm going to get the first train out of Euston.'

'All right, darling, I can't wait to see you. Have a safe journey.'

She then rang the hospital to tell them that she wouldn't be coming in as she was sick, and half an hour later with a small bag she had packed with a few necessities, Holly was on her way. Once on the train she huddled in a corner of the carriage and stared fixedly from the window hoping no one would try to include her in a conversation. She didn't feel like talking; didn't feel like doing anything if it came to that, all she wanted was to be home.

Her mother was hovering in the hallway waiting for her when she got there and Ivy was close behind her with Alice wrapped in a pretty white shawl in her arms.

She allowed them to greet her then commented, 'Alice has grown, Ivy.'

'I know.' Ivy stared down at her little daughter. 'She seems to get bigger every day and she's such a little angel.'

Cook came bustling out of the kitchen then, all smiles. 'Here you are, an' just in time. I've made yer one o' yer favourite dinners.'

Holly didn't feel a bit like eating but she managed to raise a smile and told her, 'Thank you, I'm sure it will be lovely.'

'So now what was it you wanted to talk to me about?' Her mother helped her off with her coat. 'It must be something important for you to miss work and come all this way.'

'It is and I hope you'll think it's good news.'

'Ooh, is it something about that lovely doctor you're bringing home to meet us?' Emma asked excitedly.

Once again, Holly felt as if she had been kicked in the stomach. 'No,' she said flatly. 'He won't be coming now.'

'But why ever not?'

'I'll tell you about that later but first there's something else you need to know.'

Emma's hand flew to her mouth. 'You're not having a baby, are you?'

'Of course I'm not,' Holly snapped with an apologetic glance at Ivy. Ivy took the hint and disappeared as Emma led Holly into the drawing room. Her grandfather was there and actually looked pleased to see her.

'Why, this is a surprise.'

'Yes, I, er . . . have something I need to speak to Mother about.'

He put aside his newspaper and made to rise but Holly laid her hand on his arm and told him, 'No, please stay, Grandfather. This is something you need to hear too.'

Equally as intrigued as her mother he dropped back into the chair. Her mother sat beside him and Holly stood in front of the fireplace wondering where she should begin.

'As you both know, I wasn't aware that my father was alive until shortly before I left for London,' she began in a shaky voice. 'Mother told me that she knew he was from Whitechapel originally so I got one of the women who worked for Miss May to put the word around to see if I could find him.'

Emma had gone quite pale.

'Anyway, last night when I got home from work Dora was waiting for me and she gave me the address of a lady in Spitalfields who she thought might be connected to him. So

I set off to see her and sure enough she did know him. In fact he was married to her before he married Mother. He left her with five children when he met Mother but the thing is . . . Well, from what she told me, your marriage was illegal because if he's alive he is still very much married to her. They never got divorced.'

'Oh my goodness!' her mother gasped.

Emma smiled at her. 'But surely you realise that this is a good thing for you? Don't you see? You're free now to get on with the rest of your life. With Mr Dolby if that's what you want.' She smiled ruefully as her mother blushed prettily. 'I've noticed how close you've become on my last couple of visits,' she admitted. 'And now there is nothing to stand in your way. The more I've got to see of him the more I've realised he is in fact a very kind, gentle man. The only down-side to this discovery is that I now find I am actually illegitimate.'

She waited for her grandfather to rant and rave as he would have in the past. He had made no comment up to now so he shocked her when he said, 'If that is the case it is not your fault, nor your mother's,' he added hastily. 'The man was a trickster, a con man but it's all in the past now. Looking back I realise I behaved very badly to you both. I wanted your mother to make a good marriage and when she chose your father I couldn't accept it and I almost lost her. Even when she came home to have you I held you both at arm's length. I think I was still grieving for my wife, but that's no excuse. Now I just want to see both of you happy so all I can say is, I'm sorry.' He did something then that Holly could never remember him doing before.

He stood and took her in his arms and she sobbed on his shoulder.

'And what about your, er . . . friend?' Emma questioned and got a scowl from her father.

'It's obvious Holly doesn't want to talk about that so let's just leave it for now, and she can tell us if and when she's ready, eh? We've got enough to take in today with what's she's just told us.'

Ivy tapped at the door then and bustled in with a tray of coffee, looking concerned. She could tell that something was wrong but knew that Holly would tell her when the time was right. They had never kept secrets from each other. 'Cook says to tell you dinner will be ready in about half an hour,' she informed them and quietly went away.

Holly's grandfather left the room shortly after and Emma shook her head. What Holly had told her was just beginning to sink in now.

'I was such a fool to be taken in by him,' she muttered with a shake of her head. 'But I don't regret it. If I had never met him I wouldn't have had you and you're the most precious thing in my life.'

Holly smiled. 'Every cloud has a silver lining, that's what you always used to tell me when I was a little girl.' But she wondered now if the saying was true. All she could see on her horizon at the moment were dark storm clouds. She left to take her bag to her room, leaving her mother to think of the implications of what she had told her.

Emma had known for some time that she had feelings for Walter and she suspected that they were reciprocated but being the gentleman he was he had never spoken of it. Would he now, when she told him her news? she wondered. She would have to wait and see but she hoped he would.

It was later that evening when Holly addressed the second reason she had come home.

'I was wondering if I might come back here to live?' she said as they all sat together in the drawing room. It was a beautiful summer evening and the lace curtains were dancing gently in the soft breeze that came through the open windows. 'I thought I could carry on my nursing training at the cottage hospital. I've almost finished it now.'

'But of course you can,' Emma assured her quickly. 'But why this sudden turnabout? I thought you were really happy living in London.'

'I was but it isn't the same without Ivy.' Holly thought this sounded as good an excuse as any. She could never tell her mother the real reason; that she had fallen in love with her own brother. His ring was suspended on the chain holding the locket he had bought her about her neck. She would never wear it on her finger now but she could wear it close to her heart for always.

'Then you must come home just as soon as you like,' Emma responded and with a nod Holly stared into the empty grate.

Chapter Twenty-Seven

'Ah, Nurse Farthing,' Matron raised her eyebrow when she saw that Holly was not in uniform when she entered her office a few days later. 'Is there a problem?'

'I'm afraid there is, Matron.' Holly avoided the woman's eyes. 'Unfortunately I find that I must leave the hospital immediately.' She'd expected Matron's wrath but instead the woman looked disappointed.

'Surely not? You are highly valued, nurse, and should you leave you will be missed. Is it a problem that I could help you with?'

Holly shook her head. 'Regretfully not, Matron. I shall be returning home to the Midlands within the week.'

'I see, a family matter then.'

Holly didn't answer. It was far better for her to think that than know the truth.

'And is there no chance of you at least working a month's notice?'

'I'm afraid not. I'm so sorry,' Holly muttered.

'Then in that case I shall ensure that any wages owing are sent on to you and wish you luck for the future.' Matron rose from her desk and shook Holly's hand warmly. There was nothing left to say and Holly miserably left the hospital for the last time.

Now all that remained was to tell Miss May of her plans and she wasn't looking forward to that either.

'Oh no, surely not?' She too was dismayed when Holly explained that she would be leaving within the week. 'But you've made that little flat up there into a home,' she said. 'And what about all the furniture you've bought?'

'Whoever takes the flat is welcome to it,' Holly said. 'I'm going home so I shan't be needing it. But thank you for all you've done for me, Miss May. You gave me a job and Ivy and me a place to live and I'm very grateful for that.'

Miss May sniffed. She had never been blessed with a daughter but had she been she would have hoped for one just like Holly.

'Is there a man involved?' she asked then, and when Holly lowered her eyes, she sighed. 'I thought as much. Damn men, we can't live with them and we can't live without them. But do at least say that you'll come and see me from time to time if you visit London?'

'Of course I shall,' Holly promised and now the tears she had held back all morning trickled down her cheeks.

Miss May had her arms about her in a trice and her own cheeks were wet as she soothed, 'There, there now. Nothing can be that bad. Things will come right, you'll see.'

Holly doubted that very much. How could they in the circumstances? But she didn't say as much.

'I suppose I'd better go and start packing my clothes up then,' she said when she'd managed to pull herself together. 'But I promise I'll come and say goodbye before I leave.'

'You just make sure you do, my girl.' Miss May wagged a plump finger at her. 'Now be off with you before you set me off again. I have Lady Hamilton coming for a fitting in a minute and I don't want to be a blubbering wreck when she arrives.'

As a thought occurred to Holly she asked, 'Does she still have that young man in tow when she comes?'

Miss May grinned. 'Well, she has a young man in tow but I think she cleared the last one off. None of them last for long.'

Good, Holly thought as she made her way upstairs. Hopefully Jeremy or Jimmy was out on his ear now and it served him right after what he'd done to Ivy. Although now she came to think about it Ivy had perked up no end since Alice was born, especially when young Marcus Dolby called, which he seemed to do quite frequently. Could it be that they were developing a soft spot for each other? Holly hoped so. Marcus was a very likeable young man and she wanted Ivy to be happy, but she would just have to wait and see what developed. She smiled ruefully then. Hopefully in the not too distant future both her mother and Ivy would find happiness. And I, she thought, pushing all of the painful memories of Richard aside, will devote myself to nursing from now on.

Two days later Holly stood in the sitting room of the little flat and looked around for one last time. She and Ivy had spent some happy times there and she was sad to leave but she knew she had no choice. Staying would have meant having to see Richard at the hospital and she knew that she wouldn't be able to bear it. Her heart was well and truly broken. Far better to go and make a fresh start elsewhere somehow.

She closed the door and went down to the shop to hand the key back to Miss May and say her goodbyes to everyone. Dora and Enid, the seamstresses, both gave her a hug and a kiss as did Martha, Miss May's sister, then Miss May slipped an envelope into her hand.

'What's this?' Holly asked.

'You paid your rent till the end of the month,' the woman informed her. 'So I'm giving you some back plus a bit extra to tide you over until you start a new job.'

'Oh, but you really don't have to do that,' Holly objected as colour flamed in her cheeks.

'Shush now!' Miss May raised a finger to her lips. 'Just take it. You've been a wonderful tenant, I shall never get another like you. Unless our Martha decides to move in that is. Between you and me I think my Wilfred gets on her nerves a bit.' She giggled. 'I suppose it's understandable. He gets on my nerves at times as well. But now get on with you before I start bleating again and don't forget where we are. If ever you need anything, I'll be here for you.'

Holly felt her way to the door through a fog of tears. Over the last days she had convinced herself that she could have no more tears left to cry yet still they kept coming.

Soon after she boarded the train, and within minutes London and Richard were far behind her. One chapter of her life was closed and it was time to start another one. There was no turning back now.

The homecoming was all she could have wished for but she found no joy in it. She had left her heart behind in

London and was sure that she would never be happy again. That night she lay in bed thinking how cruel life could be. The chances of meeting and falling in love with your own brother must surely be a million to one and yet it had happened. Added to that she really wasn't sure who she was any more. If her mother and father had never been legally married, then her true name couldn't be Farthing. That hadn't even been his real name so was she Holly Elizabeth Garrett, her father's legal name, or Holly Elizabeth Mason, her mother's maiden name? She decided not to pursue that line of thought. The name on her birth certificate was Farthing so it would be easier to stick with that.

She had got used to sleeping in the little bedroom in the flat and it felt strange to be back in her own bed on a permanent basis. Pull yourself together, she silently berated herself. No good can come of feeling sorry for yourself, you just have to get on with things now. And that's exactly what she intended to do the very next morning when she would apply for a job at the cottage hospital.

The hospital was tiny compared to UCH with only twenty-six beds available for patients. It had been opened in 1900 by Lady Anne Emma Newdigate, the wife of Sir Edward Newdigate who owned Arbury Hall in Stockingford. Over breakfast Holly's mother informed her that an operating theatre had been funded by donations the year before but now the hospital was struggling for funds because of the miners' strike that had almost brought the local pits to a standstill some months before.

'I've heard of miners' families that have had to admit themselves into the Union Workhouse on the Bullring because their children were starving,' Emma told her gravely. 'It's been very hard for them, poor souls. Still, at least the strike is over now so hopefully things will improve for them. But whether there are any nursing jobs going at the hospital I couldn't say. Why don't you just have a few days rest before you go looking for a job? You don't seem yourself.'

'No, I'd rather be busy,' Holly answered as she helped herself to a slice of toast, and Emma wisely didn't say any more.

Soon after Holly set off and once she reached the hospital she was directed to Matron Connor's office. She was a small, plump woman with a sunny smile and a kindly nature, nothing at all like the strict matron in London who Holly had become accustomed to.

'You do realise that the staff here are very limited, don't you?' she said when Holly told her why she was there. 'I also have to fill the role of housekeeper as the hospital is run entirely on donations. We have five nurses and one doctor, Dr Nason, who is also the surgeon here. Last year we added two new wards, Victoria Ward and Mary Ward, which is for the children. Luckily for you one of our nurses is due to leave next week so perhaps you could take her place. I would need a reference though.'

'Oh, that isn't a problem,' Holly assured her. 'The matron at UCH told me that she would be happy to do one for me, or you could speak to her yourself on the telephone if you wish.'

Matron nodded and went on to tell Holly what would be

expected of her should she get the position. 'I'm afraid we are terribly underfunded,' she admitted with a sigh. 'And most of the children who are admitted here are beyond our help. The majority of their illnesses stem from poor diet and living conditions but we always try to make their end as peaceful as we possibly can.' She shook her head. 'That's why the mortuary at the back of the hospital is rarely empty. I'm not trying to put you off,' she added hurriedly when she saw the look of horror on Holly's face. 'I'm merely trying to be truthful. Of course we do have a measure of success with some of them, the trouble is when they are better we have to send them home to the slums again. Some of their parents could do with learning some parenting skills. But still, you will see for yourself hopefully. Perhaps you could come and see me again in a couple of days' time when I've had time to speak to your old matron and then we'll discuss working hours, wages, etc.'

'Thank you.' Holly stood up and shook the woman's hand then quietly left the hospital. Although it sounded very challenging, she had a feeling that she would enjoy working there and all she could do now was wait and hope that the reference the matron back in London gave her was good enough for her to get the job.

'I've no doubt you'll find it very different to working in a big hospital,' her mother commented over dinner that day. 'I can actually remember going to the opening of the place. My father took me along. It was Reginald Stanley's idea that the town should have a hospital. God bless him, that man has done so much good. He must own half of the businesses in town now but you could never begrudge him his wealth because he is always so generous to worthy causes. And to think that he made his fortune originally in America panning for gold. It was our good luck that he decided to make his home in Nuneaton when he came back.'

'Doesn't he own the brickworks in Stockingford?' Holly asked.

'Yes, but he also owns engineering firms and pits and employs hundreds of men. He was the one responsible for bringing in an architect from London to design the hospital and he funded a lot of the work on it himself.'

'Then he must be a gentleman with a big heart.'

'He certainly is,' Emma agreed. Alice started to cry then and there was a rush to see who could get to her first to pick her up. The little lady already had everyone in the house dancing to her tune.

When Holly returned to the cottage hospital two days later, as promised, she learned that the matron at UCH had given her a glowing report.

'So when would you like to start?' Matron asked her.

'Tomorrow?' It couldn't be soon enough for Holly. She had too much time to think about things at the moment. Matron agreed eagerly, much to Holly's relief; she could hardly wait to start.

Chapter Twenty-Eight

Within days Holly realised that working at the cottage hospital was indeed very different to working in London. The five nurses were expected to do shifts and so she was allocated a room where she could rest if all was quiet while she was working at night, which she very soon discovered was very rarely. Unlike UCH, here she tended to rush from one ward to another wherever she was needed and usually she was so busy that she didn't have a minute to herself.

As always the children's ward was the one that tugged at her heartstrings. As the matron had warned, many of the children were from the slum areas of the town and she soon found out that dealing with them when they were first admitted was far from easy. Most of them were filthy and crawling with head lice so the first job was to get them into the bath and into clean clothes ready for Dr Nason to examine them. The babies posed no problem but some of the slightly older children had never had a bath in their lives and could put up quite a struggle.

She had just started her shift one day when Matron informed her that she was to report to Mary Ward for an admittance – a six-year-old boy, badly malnourished with a hacking cough.

Holly hurried off to meet him and stared at him in dismay. Even from a distance she could see head lice running across the parting in his hair, which looked as if it had never had a proper cut in the whole of his life, and what she could see of his body was covered in sores.

She smiled at him and after lifting his notes she said, 'Hello, Robbie. How about we get you bathed and made more comfortable?'

He glared at her suspiciously, crossing his thin arms across his chest. 'I ain't goin' in no baff,' he told her stubbornly. 'I 'ad a wash last week.'

'Even so, I'm sure you'll feel much better when you've had one.' She took his hand and he begrudgingly followed her along the corridor to the bathroom. However, when she turned the taps on and he saw the water gushing into the bath, he stubbornly dug his heels in and refused to enter the room.

'If you fink I'm gettin' in there you've gorranoffer fink comin!' he declared with a mutinous expression on his face. 'I'll kick yer bloody arse if yer try an' make me!'

Holly's mind raced as she tried to think of a way to persuade him and then it came to her. 'Well, that's a shame. All the new admittances get a glass of milk and cake when they've got this bit over with.'

'What sorta cake?'

She could see that he was interested now. 'Hmm, I think I heard the cook say that it was cherry cake today. Ooh, I can tell you it's absolutely lovely. I had a piece myself yesterday and it's delicious . . . Still, if you're not hungry . . .'

He stared at her for a moment then cautiously entered the bathroom and dangled his hand in the water.

'That's too 'ot,' he said truculently.

'Oh, is it? Then let's put a little more cold in.' Holly quickly turned the hot tap off and now that he was close to her she heard his stomach rumbling ominously. Goodness knew how long it had been since the poor little chap had eaten.

'I ain't gerrin undressed wi' you in the room,' he growled and she nodded.

'That's fine. I've got to go and find you some clean pyjamas anyway. Then when I get back you'll be already in there.'

'An' 'ow long will I 'ave to stay in?'

Holly shrugged. 'Only as long as it takes for us to give your hair a good wash and get you clean,' she answered cajolingly.

She could see the indecision on his face but in the end the temptation of food was too great.

'A'right then. But when yer come back you ain't to come in till I say so.'

'I wouldn't dream of it,' Holly agreed and hurried away.

As she came back down the corridor minutes later she heard Robbie coughing and when she entered the bathroom she found him red in the face and fighting for breath. He was sitting in the warm water but when she hurried across to him he put up his hand to ward her off.

'I'll . . . be . . . a'right . . . in . . . a . . . minute,' he gasped, so after handing him a small towel which he held to his mouth she waited for the coughing bout to subside.

When he eventually handed it back to her she noted that there was blood on it but saying nothing she laid it aside and picked up a bar of carbolic soap.

'Let's hurry up and get this over with, eh?' she suggested

kindly. 'And then we can get you tucked up in a nice clean bed and get you that milk and cake I promised you.'

He had paled to the colour of putty and now that he was undressed she saw just how frail his poor little body was. However, as soon as she tipped the first jug of clean water across his head he began to scream blue murder and one of the other nurses came running to see what was wrong.

'Robbie here isn't too keen on having his hair washed,' Holly said breathlessly as she began to rub the carbolic soap into his hair. Already the bath water was the colour of mud and as she rubbed at his hair and body she saw that beneath the thick layer of grime his body was pink.

'Need any help?' the other nurse asked but Holly shook her head.

'No, we'll be done in a jiffy, won't we, Robbie?' she said encouragingly. 'And then I'm going to get him a great big slice of Cook's cherry cake and a lovely glass of milk.

The thought of the treat ahead seemed to calm him again and although he huffed and puffed his disapproval he allowed her to finish getting him clean.

'There now, that wasn't so bad, was it?' she asked as she finally handed him a towel.

He wrapped it around himself and scowled at her but at least he wasn't fighting her any more. 'Turn yer back while I get dressed,' he ordered and she immediately did as she was told. When she turned back he was dressed in clean nightclothes and looked very different to how he had minutes before.

'Now all we need to do is get that hair combed.'

He scowled as she produced a fine-toothed comb but

stood still as she began to run it through his lice-ridden locks. Dozens of the horrid little creatures came out with each stroke of the comb and Holly began to itch, but eventually she could see that he was weakening by the second and she stopped.

'I reckon that should be enough for now.' She laid the comb aside and took his hand. 'Let's go and get you tucked in now and I'll fetch your food.'

'But warrabout me cloves?' He stared down at the bundle of rags on the bathroom floor worriedly. They were all he possessed.

Holly knew they were too far gone to be salvaged, in fact they were so ragged they would undoubtedly fall apart if they were washed. 'Don't get worrying about those. When you're better and you go home we'll find you some smart new ones,' she told him cheerfully.

Thankfully the better-off local people donated clothes their own children had grown out of so there was usually a selection of good second-hand garments for the children who were admitted to the hospital to wear.

Robbie seemed to accept this. In fact he looked quite pleased at the prospect of new clothes so he allowed her to lead him to Mary Ward where a bed had been prepared and the sheets turned back for him.

Once he was tucked in Holly asked him, 'Will your parents be coming to visit you tonight, Robbie. I bet they'll hardly recognise you, you look so lovely.'

She thought for a fleeting moment that she saw the hint of a tear in his eye as he quickly looked away and shook his head.

'I ain't gorra dad, an' me mum goes out most nights. I 'ave to keep away while she fetches 'er men friends 'ome an' not go back till they've gone.' He started to cough again then so Holly went away to fetch his promised treat, her heart aching with sadness for him.

He was watching for her expectantly when she came back and when he saw the thick wedge of cake and the milk, his eyes lit up greedily.

He had cleared the lot in seconds and asked cheekily, 'Any chance of anuffer slice?'

Holly smiled at him indulgently. There was something about this little chap that struck a chord in her 'Not just yet. But it'll be dinner time soon. I think Cook has done a cottage pie, mashed potatoes and vegetables, then there'll be rhubarb crumble to follow.'

He nodded and slid beneath the sheets and by the time she carried the tray back to the kitchen he was sleeping like a baby, tucked up warmly in a clean bed for the first time in his life.

'So how is young Robbie Smith?' Matron asked a short time later. She was on the way to see him prior to the doctor doing his rounds.

'He's got a dreadful cough and his temperature is sky-high,' Holly informed her.

Matron nodded as she glanced down at his notes. 'Hmm, I wonder if we shouldn't consider having him admitted to the workhouse if we can get him better. Poor little boy would be a lot better off there than living with his mother, by all accounts. At least he'd be fed and have a warm bed to sleep in. His mother is a, er . . . prostitute and has no time for him according to the neighbour who brought him in.' She shook her head regretfully. 'Apparently he's just left to roam the streets half the time, he's had no schooling, nothing. But anyway, let's go and have a look at him. I hear he gave you a bit of a bad time while you were trying to bath him?'

'He certainly did.' Holly grinned. 'I had to bribe him with the promise of some of Cook's cherry cake.'

Robbie was still fast asleep when they reached his bedside and he didn't stir as Matron placed a gentle hand on his forehead.

'He is very hot. I shall be glad when Dr Nason has taken a look at him,' she said worriedly. 'If he has anything contagious we're going to have to move him. I can't risk whatever he has infecting any of the other children in the ward.'

'I understand.' Holly looked at the child on the bed. For all his bravado he was just a frail little boy and she silently prayed that he would get well.

'Hmm!' After listening to the boy's chest with his stethoscope later that day, Dr Nason straightened with a frown on his face. 'He has acute bronchitis and because of his weakened state it could very well turn to pneumonia.'

Holly's breath caught in her throat. The prognosis for Robbie did not look good.

The doctor turned to the matron and reeled off a list of medication he wanted Robbie to have, 'And you, nurse,' he turned back to Holly. 'I want you to sponge him down continually to try and bring his temperature down.'

'Yes, sir.' Holly stood to one side as Dr Nason moved on to check the other patients. He looked tired but that was hardly surprising. Because of the limited bed space at the hospital the doctor spent much of his time visiting the sick in their homes before he even got to the hospital each day and Holly thought it was no wonder he was so well respected. It was well known that he often waived his fee if he visited someone who was very poor and had even been known to slip the direst of cases a penny or two.

Holly turned her attention back to Robbie and smiled. 'You heard what the doctor said.' She grinned. 'It's a cool sponge-down for you I'm afraid.'

'But I'm cold already,' Ronnie complained, although beads of sweat were standing out on his forehead.

'That's because you have a fever. You were complaining of being too hot a few minutes ago.' He sighed as he drifted off to sleep again and she hurried away to fetch a bowl of cool water. He seemed to have deteriorated in the short time he had been there and she was gravely concerned about him.

For the next hour she sat at the side of his bed sponging his forehead and whispering soothingly to him but as the day progressed it was clear that he was getting no better. If anything he was getting worse and his breath was more ragged now. So much so that he even turned his head away from the meal that was offered to him at teatime.

During the afternoon Matron popped into the ward to check on his progress and whispered to Holly, 'The neighbour who brought him in has just been back to see how he is. He lives at number four cottage in the courtyards in Abbey Street.'

'And what about his mother?'

Matron shrugged. 'Either she doesn't know he's here or she doesn't care. I wouldn't mind betting it's the latter. I suppose I shall have to send someone round there to inform her just how poorly the little chap is.'

'I could call in and tell her on my way home, if you like,' Holly volunteered.

Matron gave her an approving smile. 'That would be a great help, if you wouldn't mind. Do tell her that because of his condition she may visit whenever she wishes. I don't like to be too strict about visiting times for the relatives of the patients who are very poorly and he might perk up a little if he sees his mother.'

Holly nodded and as she walked away the matron thought what an asset Holly was proving to be already.

Chapter Twenty-Nine

As Holly entered the courtyard where Robbie lived later that evening on her way home, she tried to hold her breath. The smell was appalling. At one end was a pigsty where a fat pig snuffled in the dirt. Throughout the year he was fed food scraps by the four families that inhabited the cottages, two on either side of a narrow cobbled yard, and come Christmas he would wind up on their plates as their Christmas dinner. Next to him was the ash toilet shared by all four cottages and badly in need of emptying if the stench was anything to go by. Holly marched up to number three and tapped at the door tentatively. From inside she could hear the sound of laughter so she knew someone was in. After a moment she knocked again, louder this time, and a voice shouted, 'Who is it? I'm busy so if it ain't important bugger off!'

'It is important, Mrs Smith!' Holly shouted back, suddenly angry. 'It's about your son, Robbie.'

She heard a scuffle on the other side of the door then it slowly swung open revealing a woman dressed in nothing more than a thin robe. Her hair was greasy and hung limply on her shoulders and her pock marked face was heavily made-up.

'So what's the little bleeder bin up to now?' she said gruffly. 'If he's bin caught stealin' by the coppers again I'll break his scrawny little neck. All he's gorra do is keep out o' the way for God's sake!' Then seeing Holly's uniform she stopped ranting and stared.

'He isn't in trouble with the police, Mrs Smith,' Holly informed her, trying hard to keep the disgust she felt for the woman from showing on her face. 'I'm sorry to have to tell you he's in hospital and very poorly indeed. He has acute bronchitis and the doctor is concerned about him.' The smell of cheap perfume, stale sweat and whisky radiating off the woman was almost worse than the smell from the privy and the pigsty but Holly managed to meet her gaze steadily.

'Oh . . .' The woman scratched her head. 'Well, at least he's in the right place, ain't he? What do yer want me to do?'

'I would have thought it was more of a case of what you wanted to do.' Holly could barely keep the contempt she felt for the woman from sounding in her voice now. 'Matron is more than willing to discuss his condition with you if you'd care to visit him.'

'What? An' risk catchin' it meself! No thank you very much. Just keep me informed of 'ow he is, eh?' And with that she slammed the door in Holly's face and seconds later the sound of bawdy laughter recommenced.

All the way home Holly fumed. How could a mother be so callous towards her child? she wondered. He was just a little boy, a very sick one, and his mother didn't appear to care at all!

Over the evening meal both her mother and grandfather noticed that Holly was even quieter than she had been ever since she returned from London and eventually her mother asked, 'Is everything all right at work, darling?'

'Yes, it's just . . .' And then it all came pouring out as

Holly told them of Robbie's sickly condition and the cold reception she had received from his mother. Ivy had just carried the main course in and she snorted.

'I ain't surprised. Havin' come from the courtyards meself I know how badly some o' the children are treated. Neither me mam nor me dad cared a hoot when I went off to London, they was just upset cos they weren't gettin' none o' me wages any more. Matron's right, Holly. If the little chap does get better he'd be better off in the workhouse.'

She made her way back to the kitchen then, leaving the family to serve themselves but she had to admit, what Holly had said had got her thinking. Her family didn't even know that she'd come home. Perhaps it was time to give them another chance? After all they had a brand new little granddaughter now. How could they possibly not love her? I'll pop round to see 'em on me next afternoon off, she decided, and having made the decision she felt slightly better. Family was family after all.

The next morning, Holly arrived at the hospital early. She was anxious to see how Robbie was but it wasn't good news. She found the night nurse at his bedside sponging his brow and when Holly approached she shook her head.

'He's delirious now,' she told her sadly. 'Poor little chap keeps trying to knock my hand away and cowering from me. I think he must be used to being knocked about.'

'Hmm, that would explain his bruises,' Holly agreed. 'But you get off now. I'll take over.'

'Are you sure?' the nurse asked. 'You're not due on the ward for at least another hour.'

'I know but I wanted to see how he was.'

The older nurse sighed. 'It doesn't do to go getting too attached, you know,' she told Holly kindly. 'Far too many of the children that come into this ward end up in the mortuary out the back. If we got too fond of every one we wouldn't be able to do our job.'

'I know.' Holly flushed guiltily. 'But there's something about this little chap that's touched me.'

'Well, don't say I didn't warn you.' The night nurse stifled a yawn then got up and stretched. She was stiff after sitting so long in the chair.

'I'll get off and get some sleep then. Dr Nason should be here soon. Matron asked him to pop in to look at Robbie before beginning his house calls.'

Holly sat down and took Robbie's hand in hers. It was burning hot yet clammy to the touch and his chest was rattling alarmingly.

Soon after Dr Nason arrived and instantly ordered her to get some bowls of hot water. 'Drape a sheet over the bed and get some steam round him,' he ordered. 'That might relieve his chest a little.'

Holly raced away to do as she was told but as the morning wore on he showed no signs of improvement.

'Has his mother been?' she asked the matron when she too came to see the child and she told her then of his mother's reaction when she had visited her.

The woman shook her head. 'But never mind. Let's just concentrate on getting him well for now. He wouldn't know if she was here anyway.'

After a while the steam did seem to ease his breathing and

just before lunchtime his eyes opened and he blinked. 'Where am I?' he asked groggily and Holly could have laughed aloud with sheer joy. It looked now like this little fighter might beat the illness after all.

'You're safe and you're here with me at the hospital.'

He frowned and nodded. 'Oh yeah, I remembers now. Yer give me some milk an' cake, cherry cake.'

'I certainly did. Would you like some now?'

He shook his head. 'No, but I's right firsty.'

She held a glass of water to his lips and he drank it greedily, then lying back against the pillows he drifted off to sleep again.

'I think the fever has broken thanks to your vigilant care,' Dr Nason told her when he visited again later in the day. 'Well done, nurse. Now just make sure he gets plenty of fluids down him and I'll be back to see him in the morning.'

Holly sighed with relief. Earlier in the afternoon one of the babies on the ward had died. She had seen its tiny lifeless body being wheeled away to the mortuary and she was sure she couldn't have borne it if it had been Robbie. But thank God now he should start to recover.

Every day that week she saw signs of improvement in him and one morning the matron called her into her office.

'I've just had a visit from Robbie's mother, Mrs Smith,' she informed her. 'I told her that he was doing really well and that if he continued to make progress he might be able to go home next week, and do you know what she said?' The woman's eyes were flashing with disgust and indignation. 'She had the nerve to ask could we keep him here for as long as we could because Robbie didn't get on too well with her latest man! The cheek of the woman! Anyway, I told her that if she didn't want him back at home I could possibly obtain a place for him in the workhouse. I expected her to argue but instead she was very happy with the idea. She said to go ahead, it would solve a lot of problems for her and sailed out of here without a care in the world!'

Holly chewed on her lip. Matron was such a jolly, happy person usually but right at that minute it was clear she was filled with rage and Holly didn't blame her.

It was a bright sunny morning in June when Ivy had her next afternoon off and, after putting baby Alice into her pram, she set off for her parents' home, stopping on the way to buy some groceries for them. She had been upset for days after reading of the death of Emily Davison, a suffragette she had known in London, who had stepped in front of the king's horse at the Derby races ten days before. Alice was her whole life now but sometimes she missed the suffragette women in London and she still wholeheartedly supported their cause. Still, hopefully today the visit to her family would be a happy distraction.

At the entrance to the courtyard that had once been her home, Ivy paused and frowned as the old familiar smells met her, but then she took a deep breath and pushed the pram down the narrow alley.

The door to her parents' cottage was open and inside Ivy could see her mother huddled in a shawl on the old horsehair sofa that had been there for as long as she could remember. She lifted Alice in one arm, the groceries in the other and stepped into the gloomy interior. Her mother had clearly been dozing but she woke with a start and peered towards the door.

'Who's there?' Then as Ivy stepped into the room she scowled. 'Oh, so yer've decided to come back an' show yer face then, 'ave yer? About time an' all. You ain't sent us so much as ha'penny piece fer months. Some daughter you are.' She stopped abruptly then as she saw the baby in Alice's arms and growled, 'An' whose sprog is that?'

'She's mine.' Ivy stuck her chin in the air. 'I thought yer might like to meet yer granddaughter. Her name is Alice.'

'Gran'daughter! Yer never told me you'd got wed,' her mother barked accusingly and when Ivy lowered her head she laughed scornfully. 'You ain't got wed, 'ave yer? She's a fly-blow, ain't she? Huh, yer silly little cow. Didn't I tell yer to keep yer legs shut till yer'd got a ring on yer finger!'

'It wasn't like that,' Ivy said as tears pricked at the back of her eyes. 'He said he loved me. We were goin' to get wed . . .'

'Ar, they all say that till they've had their leg over.'

Suddenly Ivy knew that it had been a mistake to come. Her mother had never had time for her so why had she thought that things might be any different now?

Dropping the bag of groceries onto the table she glanced around the room. It was exactly as she remembered it: dirty and unkempt. 'There's some food there for you,' she said, her voice calm now. 'But it will be the last you'll sponge from me. Goodbye, Mam, you'll not see me again.' And with that she walked from the cottage, laid Alice in her pram and walked away without once looking back.

Chapter Thirty

On Holly's day off she was pleased to see her mother's friend, Mrs Sunday Branning, arrive. She and her mother were of a similar age and had been friends for years. She often dropped in for coffee and a chat and was more than a little fond of Holly who she had known since she was a baby. Sunday was a very kind and caring woman and some years before she and her husband Tom had turned their lovely home in Hartshill into a children's home called Treetops. They were well known for taking in waifs and strays and treating them as their own and as a child Holly had spent many a happy day there. Today Sunday was looking very pretty in a smart two-piece costume in a soft blue colour that complemented her eyes and her lovely blonde hair was fastened into an elegant chignon beneath a matching hat that she wore at a jaunty angle on the side of her head. Anyone seeing her would have found it hard to believe that she was almost forty-three years old, for she carried her age well.

'Hello, love,' Sunday greeted her when Holly joined her and her mother in the drawing room. 'I came into town to get some new clothes for some of the children. I swear they grow like weeds.' She chuckled. 'Anyway, while I was here I thought I'd pop in to see your mam. It's a good excuse for half an hour's quiet. But how are you? Your mam tells me you're working at the cottage hospital now.'

Holly nodded. 'Yes, I am and I'm enjoying it although you see some sad sights.' As an idea suddenly occurred to her she asked cautiously, 'I don't suppose you have a spare place for another child at Treetops by any chance, do you?'

Sunday raised an eyebrow. 'Why do you ask? Do you know of an orphan that needs a home then?'

'Well . . . not an orphan exactly,' Holly admitted. 'Although he may as well be. There's a little boy in Mary Ward at the moment. He's six years old and his name is Robbie.' She went on to tell Sunday all about the position he was in as Sunday listened sympathetically.

'Poor little mite,' Sunday sighed when Holly was finished. 'And you say his mother doesn't even want him home?'

Holly nodded. 'That's right, she's an awful woman. Robbie was in a terrible state when he first came in and she didn't even bother to come and visit him. But he's on the mend now, although it was touch-and-go for a time whether or not he would make it.' She grinned. 'Mind you, I can't pretend he's an angel. The first time I met him he threatened to kick my arse if I tried to get him into the bath. He's a right little character. But now Matron is saying that she thinks she'll have to get a place for him in the workhouse. We can't just turf him out to go back onto the streets.'

Sunday shuddered involuntarily at the mention of the place. She herself had spent her early years in the Union Workhouse and none of the memories she held of it were good. 'Well, I would have to have a word with Tom as we are full at the minute but, saying that, I suppose we could always squeeze another little one in at a push. Leave it with me.'

Holly was delighted. If only Robbie could go to Treetops

she was sure it would be the making of the child. He had never had any love or stability in his life but she was sure he would blossom if Sunday took him under her wing. Holly had always greatly admired her and thought her life story was like something one might read about in a book. The poor soul had been abandoned on the steps of the workhouse as a newborn and it was many years later before she discovered that she was actually the daughter of Lady Huntley of Treetops Manor who had been led to believe by her late husband that her daughter had died at birth. A joyful reunion had followed and since then both Sunday and her mother had worked tirelessly to improve the conditions in the workhouse for those unfortunate enough to be incarcerated there. They were both on the board of guardians now and were well known for their charity work. Holly was sure that Robbie would be much happier living at Treetops and she prayed that Tom would agree to it.

'Well, I'm going to pop in and see Robbie in a minute,' Holly informed the ladies and Emma frowned.

'But, darling, it's your day off,' she pointed out.

'I know, but I just want to check he's all right.'

'This little chap has really got under your skin, hasn't he?' Sunday smiled. 'I'll tell you what. This was only a flying visit so why don't I come to the hospital with you? I could have a chat to Matron and meet the boy.'

Holly was all for the idea, so they set off in Sunday's smart new Morris automobile.

The matron was delighted to see them both and while Holly headed for the ward, Sunday went into the office with Matron to have a chat.

Fifteen minutes later they walked down the ward and Holly told Robbie casually, 'Ah, this is Mrs Branning, Robbie. She's a friend of my family and she's come especially to meet you.' She didn't want to raise his hopes until Sunday had had a chance to speak to Tom so she wisely didn't mention the possibility of him going to live with her.

'You must be Robbie,' Sunday said when she reached the bed. 'Holly has told me all about you, my dear. How are you feeling?'

He glared at her suspiciously. She looked very posh and he wondered why someone like her would take the time to come and see him.

'I's all right,' he answered guardedly. 'Are you one o' them from the work'ouse? I know yer plannin' to put me in there but I'll tell yer now I ain't goin' an' that's flat!'

'Robbie!' Holly was shocked. No one had mentioned the workhouse to him as yet as far as she knew. 'Whoever told you that?'

'Nobody,' he mumbled grumpily. 'I 'eard two o' the nurses on night duty talkin' about it when they thought I was asleep. They said me mam 'ad come to see Matron an' told 'er that she didn't want me back.' He swiped angrily at a tear that trickled down his cheek. 'But yer can forget that idea cos when I leave 'ere I can look after meself.'

Sunday's pretty face crumpled as she listened to the child and in that moment her heart was lost yet again. 'But you're very young to be thinking of fending for yourself,' she said gently. 'How would you manage and where would you live?'

Robbie shrugged his thin shoulders. 'The blokes leavin''

the pubs always chuck me a penny or two and I can sleep in shop doorways,' he answered sullenly.

In that moment Sunday made her decision and she was sure that Tom would understand why when she told him about the child. 'How would you feel about coming to live with me?'

Robbie's eyes almost popped out of his head. 'Live wi' you? Where?'

Sunday smiled at him reassuringly. 'I have a lovely big house in Hartshill on the edge of town all surrounded by woods and quite a few children live with me. There are big gardens to play in and you'd share a room with two other boys but you'd have your own bed. We have a cook who makes lovely meals and puddings. I heard you like cherry cake and she's especially good at making that, and three times a week Mrs Lockett, the vicar's wife, comes in to do lessons. You'd learn to read and write and do sums. I'm sure you'd enjoy that.'

Robbie looked thoughtful before asking, 'An' do we get the stick if we're naughty? Me mam uses the stick all the time, an' her men friends.'

'No, Robbie, we never use a stick,' Sunday told him gently, her heart aching for the poor little mite. 'So what do you think?'

He sniffed nonchalantly. 'I dare say I might come an' try it fer a time,' he answered, as if he was doing her some great favour and Sunday grinned.

'Right, well just as soon as Matron says you're well enough to leave here I'll come and fetch you, shall I?'

'If yer want,' he said airily and Holly felt as if she would burst with joy. Here, hopefully, was one little boy she wouldn't have to worry about for much longer.

Three days later when Dr Nason had declared Robbie well enough to leave Sunday and Tom arrived to collect him bearing new clothes.

'Wassup wi' me old 'uns?' Robbie muttered as Matron drew the curtains about the bed so that he could get dressed. But he put them on all the same and felt quietly pleased as he stared down at the smart new trousers and the soft leather shoes. Admittedly Sunday had had to guess the size and they were a little large for him but after his old ones that had leaked water and rubbed blisters on his ankles he felt as if he was walking on air. His pleasure increased when Matron and Holly followed them all outside to Tom's motor car.

'Are we really goin' in that?' he asked, his voice awed.

'We certainly are,' Tom told him as he ruffled his hair and winked at Holly who was feeling rather anxious. 'You'll have lots of rides in it in the future. How about you come up front with me? I'm sure Sunday won't mind sitting in the back.'

Robbie was smiling now as he turned to say goodbye to Matron and Holly. The matron smiled at him warmly and shook his hand making him feel very grown-up. And then it was Holly's turn and she found it difficult to speak past the lump that had formed in her throat.

'You be good now and do what Sunday and Tom tell you,' she said in a choked voice.

He stared up at her solemnly and nodded. Then suddenly he flung his arms about her waist and his voice was thick as he whispered, 'Thanks, Nurse 'Olly. Yer all right, you are.'

The next minute he was scrambling up into the seat next

to Tom and Matron and Holly stood and waved till the car turned a corner and was lost to sight.

'I think we can safely say that's going to be a very happy ending for one child thanks to you, nurse.' The matron smiled at her approvingly and they both returned to their duties.

Two weeks later Holly and her mother visited Treetops and were delighted to find Robbie had settled in nicely.

'Our teacher, Mrs Lockett, reckons I'm brainy,' Robbie told Holly gleefully when he had rushed out to meet her. 'I can count up to ten already an' I'm learnin' me ABC now!'

'Why, that's excellent,' Holly answered astounded at the change in him. His cheeks were glowing from the time he spent playing outdoors and he had gained a little weight. He'd also had a haircut, which he wasn't so happy about, much to their amusement.

'Tom took me an' one o' the other lads to the barber's,' he told them, solemnly stroking his shorn curls. 'An' Cissie went through me 'air every single night wi' a nit comb till she were sure all the nits were gone. Don't know why she boffered really. I were so used to 'em they didn't boffer me. But ooh, the grub 'ere is lovely!' He rolled his eyes in ecstasy. 'Cook makes smashin' dinners as well as cakes an' tarts an' we never 'ave to go to bed wi' a 'ungry belly. She reckons I've got 'ollow legs cos I eat so much but Sunday told her that's normal cos I'm a growin' boy.'

'So you're happy here then?' Holly asked and he grinned.

'Nor 'alf.' His attention was caught then by Ben, a child slightly older than him who was kicking a football about the lawn. 'Sorry, but I've gorra go.' His eyes were fixed on the ball. 'I'll see yer before yer leave, eh?' And with that he was gone like the wind as Holly watched him with a smile on her face that stretched from ear to ear.

She and Emma then spent a very pleasant hour with Sunday and her close friend, Cissie, in the drawing room but eventually Emma told them, 'I'm so sorry but I'm going out this evening so I really ought to be getting back to get ready.'

'Are you?' Holly was surprised. Her mother rarely went out in the evenings apart from to go to church. 'Are you going somewhere nice?'

Two spots of colour appeared in her mother's cheeks. 'Yes, I'm going with Walter to the theatre. Charlie Chaplin is on at the Hippodrome and Walter thinks we'll enjoy it.' She watched closely for Holly's reaction and when Holly smiled Emma almost sighed with relief.

'I'm sure you will and it's about time you got out a bit more.' She had no doubt that this might be the first of many times Walter Dolby took her mother out and she wished her well. It was time she had a little happiness in her life. Unbidden a picture of Richard's face flashed in front of her eyes and the pain was back, just as strong as it had been on the day she had said goodbye to him. He was still the first person she thought of when she opened her eyes each morning and the last one she thought of before going to sleep, but she knew she had done the right thing. Hopefully, Richard would meet someone who was worthy of his love in time but she knew she never would. If she couldn't have him she didn't want anyone, but at least she had her work and she intended to concentrate on that.

Chapter Thirty-One

Christmas was upon them before they knew it and Holly wondered where the months had gone. Walter was bringing his family for dinner and Cook was in a panic as she checked and double-checked that everything was just right.

'It will be perfect,' Holly assured her as she laid the table in the dining room with their best china and crystal. 'It always is.'

Mrs Bell, the cook, bustled back to the kitchen with a smile on her face at Holly's compliment. She was a small, round woman who had joined the household following the death of her husband just before Holly was born and she had been with them ever since.

'Yer mam seems a bit nervy today,' Ivy commented as she and Holly put the finishing touches to the table.

'Does she? I hadn't noticed.' Holly had been too busy thinking of Richard and wondering what he was doing. If he wasn't at the hospital he was probably at home with his family, or perhaps he had met someone else and was sharing his first Christmas with his new love? She wondered what she might be like, but the thought was too painful so she pushed it away and hurried into the kitchen to see if there was anything she could do to help in there.

Little Alice was contentedly sitting on a blanket surrounded by gaily painted wooden blocks and she held her arms out to be picked up the second Holly stepped into the room. The little girl had the whole household eating out of the palm of her hand, even Holly's grandfather, and she could play them all like a fiddle. She was eight months old now and bright as a button. Holly swung her up into her arms and tickled her making the child giggle.

'You're a crafty girl,' Holly told her and kissed her soft cheek soundly.

Their guests arrived before lunch and presents were duly exchanged and cooed over. Florence and Katie had been given new dresses for Christmas, and while Katie looked adorable, Florence, who was now fifteen, looked very grown-up, and soon Holly was busy keeping Katie entertained until dinner was ready.

The meal was a very light-hearted affair with all the usual trimmings to accompany the enormous turkey. Cook's Christmas pudding was a triumph but immediately after everyone had finished, Walter glanced at Gilbert, Holly's grandfather, and when the older man gave an almost imperceptible nod he rose to face them all with a wide smile on his face.

'Could I have your attention please?' He rapped his spoon on the table and all heads turned towards him. 'I'm delighted to tell you all that some days ago I asked Emma if she would do me the very great honour of becoming my wife and I'm happy to say, with her father's blessing, she has agreed. We thought we would wait until today to tell you all, seeing as it's such a special day, so now all that remains for me to do is to give Emma her ring and beg her not to be too long in choosing a date for the wedding.' Amidst cheers and applause,

Walter removed a tiny ring box from his jacket pocket and extracted a beautiful ruby and diamond ring. Turning to Emma, he slipped it onto her finger and kissed her soundly.

'Does this mean that Emma will be our new mother?' Katie asked innocently.

Emma tenderly stroked the child's cheek. She had grown to genuinely love her. 'I shall never be your real mother, she was irreplaceable,' she told the child gently. 'But I will be your stepmother and I hope that we will be the very best of friends.'

Gilbert rushed off to fetch a bottle of champagne that he'd had chilling in a bucket of water especially for the occasion and once the cork was popped and the drink poured they all raised a glass to the newly engaged couple, even Florence and Katie were allowed to have a sip, much to their delight.

Holly was thrilled to see her mother so happy, yet she couldn't help feeling a little sad and envious too as she thought of Richard and how things might have been. Even so she plastered a smile on her face and silently prayed that her mother and Mr Dolby might live happily ever after. They certainly deserved to.

'No wonder yer mam were nervy,' Ivy said with a smile when she and Holly were tackling the mountain of dirty pots later that afternoon. 'I ain't really surprised. I've seen the way the wind were blowin' fer some time now. A blind man on a gallopin' donkey could see that they were taken with each other. Just think, though, it could 'ave been you if yer grandfather had had his way.'

'That would never have worked.' Holly shook her head

as she carefully dried one of the crystal goblets. 'But I think they'll be happy together and the children are clearly thrilled with the news.'

'Hmm.' A thought had just occurred to Ivy and her hands became still in the soapy water. 'But what about you an' me? What I mean is, yer mam will no doubt move into Mr Dolby's house once they're wed but what will we do?'

'I can answer that question.' Gilbert Mason was bringing in yet more dirty pots and both girls started. They hadn't seen him come in. 'Things for you two will go on just as they are now if that's what you wish.' He smiled. 'I do understand, of course, that you may wish to go with your mother, Holly, and if that's the case I'll raise no objection. But if you prefer to stay here that's all right too. In fact, from a selfish point of view I'd prefer that you did. I quite enjoy our times poring over the newspapers together and discussing world affairs. And you, Ivy, well you'll still be needed to help Cook. Does that answer your question?'

'Yes, Mr Mason, it does.' Ivy flashed him a smile and he left to share a glass of port and a cigar in the study with Walter.

It had been a truly happy day but Holly was on night duty that evening at the hospital so at seven o'clock she set off, leaving them all to a game of tiddlywinks. It had been a cold but dry day with no sign of snow as yet so she made good time and on entering the hospital she found everyone in good spirits. The staff had pinned paper chains to the ceilings in the wards and even Matron had relaxed the rules just for this special day. A choir came into the wards at eight o'clock to sing Christmas carols and were served with hot mince pies and mulled wine and then it was time to get the children settled in Mary Ward.

As Holly tucked the babies into their cots she wondered what Robbie would be doing. She knew that Sunday and Tom always ensured that the children had a wonderful day and it gave her a little thrill to think that probably for the first time in his short life Robbie would be getting the sort of Christmas he deserved. Again, thoughts of Richard and how he was spending Christmas flashed across her mind but she pushed them firmly away.

On New Year's Eve the whole family were invited to Walter's for dinner but Holly was working once again. She had put her name down for every shift going over the festive period because while she was working she didn't have time to think of anything or anyone but the patients she was caring for.

It was just before midnight and most of the children on Mary Ward were fast asleep although a few of the older children were still awake, waiting to welcome the New Year in, when Dr Nason appeared with a young man.

'I thought I'd pop in to wish you all a very happy New Year,' Dr Nason told them. 'And also to introduce Dr Phillips who will be working with me from now on. He's come from a hospital in London especially to share some of my workload and I know he is going to an invaluable addition to our team.'

Holly could see the nurses preening as he made his way around them shaking their hands but she wasn't interested. There was only one man who she longed for in her life and if she couldn't have him then she didn't want anyone.

However, just as he reached her the clock struck twelve and everyone turned to the person next to them to shake their hand or give them a kiss.

'Well, it seems rude not to,' Dr Phillips laughed and without further ado he leaned forward and planted a kiss on Holly's cheek.

She felt her colour rise as his deep brown eyes twinkled with mischief. She had to admit that he was very handsome.

'Happy New Year, nurse, hopefully we'll be seeing a lot more of each other in the future.' He moved on then leaving Holly tongue-tied.

When he and Dr Nason had left and the nurses had finally got the patients settled for the night, Sylvia Conrad, one of the nurses, nudged Holly.

'Cor, he's a bit of all right that new doctor, isn't he? Fancy him giving you a kiss like that, you lucky devil. I notice that he didn't kiss any of the other nurses, me included, though I wouldn't have minded if he had.'

'Didn't he?' Holly answered nonchalantly and hurried about her business before any more could be said. The last thing she needed was to have her name linked romantically to the new doctor. She'd made her mind up that she didn't have time in her life for that sort of thing so she pushed it from her thoughts.

By the time she got home the following morning she was so tired that all she wanted was her bed but first she had to sit over a cup of tea in the kitchen and listen to Ivy who was excited because Marcus had invited her to go with him to Mr Leon Vint's Picturedrome, which had opened the year before. Many well-known vaudeville acts who had trodden the boards up and down the country were appearing there and it was becoming very popular.

'Cook has offered to look after Alice,' she said, then, her face becoming solemn, she asked, 'Do you think it's too soon to be going out with a young man? After what happened with Jeremy, I mean? I swore to meself that I'd never trust another bloke again as long as I lived but . . .'

'I'm just pleased you seem to be moving on,' Holly responded. 'And Marcus is a lovely chap so why shouldn't you go out and have a bit of fun? I have a night off tonight so I shall be here to help with Alice. Just go and enjoy it. You're only young once.'

Ivy raised an eyebrow. 'Ooh, hark at you. Ain't it about time you took a bit o' your own advice? I can't remember the last time you went anywhere apart from to work.'

'I enjoy my work,' Holly answered defensively and quickly changed the subject as she asked, 'So, have you thought what you're going to wear tonight? You'll want to look your best. Come on, we'll go upstairs and have a rifle through my wardrobe. There's bound to be something you'll like.' And looping her arm through her friend's she dragged her up the stairs before she could protest.

The following week the weather took a turn for the worst and by teatime each day everywhere was covered in a thick frost.

'Eeh, it's enough to freeze the hairs off a brass monkey,' Ivy grumbled as she lugged a bucket of coal into the kitchen. 'We'll have snow next, you just mark my words, an' that wind is enough to cut you in two.'

Holly, who was busily wrapping up warmly before setting off for work, nodded in agreement. 'You're right and it's causing havoc with people's health. There's a flu epidemic raging at the minute and we're bursting at the seams at the hospital. It's a good job Dr Nason took the new doctor on or he'd never have managed.'

Ivy gave a sly little grin. It wasn't the first time she'd heard Holly mention the new doctor. 'Nice, is he?' she asked innocently.

'Who?' Holly wound her scarf about her neck and yanked her gloves on.

'The new doctor, o' course? Who else would I be askin' about?'

'Oh . . . yes, he's nice enough, I suppose. I haven't really had that much to do with him, we've been far too busy but now I must get off or I'll be late. Just make sure you keep Alice in the warm.' And with that she left leaving Ivy with a smile on her face.

'Ah, Nurse Farthing.' Matron stopped Holly the second she set foot through the door of the hospital. 'I'm afraid I have a rather big favour to ask of you.'

'Oh yes? What's that then?'

'Well, apparently the inmates are dropping like flies up at the workhouse. Young Dr Phillips is there now and I wondered if you could possibly work there this evening to give him a hand. It seems that almost every child in the nursery is down with the flu and I'm sure he could do with some help.'

Holly paused. She had no objection to working at the workhouse but she wasn't so keen on having to work so closely with Dr Phillips. She could still clearly remember the way he had kissed her on New Year's Eve, not that he hadn't been a perfect gentleman ever since if their paths had happened to cross, of course.

Seeing her hesitation Matron hurried on, 'I'm only asking you because you are easily our best nurse when it comes to handling children.'

'Very well.' Holly reluctantly turned back to the door. She supposed that she should feel flattered that Matron had asked her, and she was probably just being silly regarding Dr Phillips. He could have had his pick of any of the nurses and even if he did like her she had no interest in him whatsoever so what did it matter if she spent the night helping him with sick children? With a sigh she set off for the workhouse.

Chapter Thirty-Two

When Holly arrived at the workhouse she removed her cloak and was shown up the stairs to the children's nursery. It was a large room with small beds and cots down either side of it. Most of the children were fretful and crying as some of the workhouse staff moved amongst them offering cold drinks and words of comfort. Dr Phillips was leaning across one bed containing a little girl who looked to be about one and a half to two years old. At a glance Holly could see that she was burning up with fever and her feelings towards the young doctor softened a little as she saw the genuine concern on his face.

'Ah, thank goodness, reinforcements.' He smiled with relief as he saw her striding purposefully towards him and rose to rub his aching back. 'Thank you for coming, nurse, I've been here since one this afternoon and if you wouldn't mind holding the fort for a while I could really do with a cup of tea.'

'Haven't you had a break?' she asked.

He smiled ruefully. 'Chance would be a fine thing. Some of these poor little mites are in a really bad way and I haven't felt able to leave them, but if I could just have half an hour . . .'

'Take as long as you like,' she told him, lifting a cloth to sponge the child's forehead. 'I'll do what I can for them while you're gone.'

'Thank you.' He looked at her for what seemed like a long moment then turning abruptly he left the room, closing the door softly behind him.

As promised he returned half an hour later looking slightly better for his short rest and for the remainder of the night they moved amongst the children doing whatever they could to make them as comfortable as possible. Sadly it was very little and as the night wore on and dawn kissed the sky, Holly was afraid that some of the weaker children would not survive.

'You look tired,' Dr Phillips remarked.

Holly smiled. 'I could say the same about you. You've been here much longer than me.'

They worked on in a companionable silence and she couldn't help but be impressed as she watched the compassion he showed to the young patients. At one point he even lifted a small baby from his cot and tenderly rocked him in his arms.

Eventually another of the nurses arrived from the hospital to take over and they made their way to the staff room for a well-earned cup of tea before heading for home.

Dr Phillips collapsed into a chair and stretched his long legs out while Holly poured boiling water into the teapot and left the tea to mash while she prepared the cups.

'I reckon I could sleep on a washing line,' he groaned. 'Thank you for all your help. Oh, and my name is Henry, by the way, but everyone calls me Harry. I hope you will too. It's so much less formal than Dr Phillips.'

Holly felt embarrassed as she spooned sugar into two mugs. 'I don't think Matron would appreciate that,' she answered primly. 'She's very strict about the nurses always addressing the doctors by their surnames.'

'Well, she wouldn't have to know if you only used my Christian name when we were away from the hospital, would she? Which brings me round to asking . . . would you like to go out with me one evening, for a meal or to the theatre perhaps?'

Holly's heart skipped a beat as she slopped milk all over the table and hastily mopped it up.

'That's very nice of you,' she answered as calmly as she could. 'But I, er . . . don't think so.'

'Oh.' Disappointment washed across his face. 'You already have a young man then, do you?'

She shook her head feeling decidedly uncomfortable now. 'No, I don't.' That much at least was true, she thought, not any more, and the pain of losing Richard sliced through her again. Was he missing her as much as she was missing him? 'It's just that I'm very dedicated to my job and I don't have time for that sort of thing.' She carried his tea across to him and he stared at her thoughtfully.

'That's very commendable but you should make time for a private life too.'

'I'm quite happy as I am, thank you,' she responded sharply.

He shrugged. 'Perhaps another time then?' Silence filled the air so Harry went on to a safer subject and they spoke of the various children they had nursed throughout the night and eventually they left to make their way to their separate homes.

Emma was waiting for her when she arrived and she

clucked with dismay. 'Oh, darling, you look worn out,' she told her worriedly. 'Go and get yourself tucked into bed and I'll bring you up a nice hot drink.' She smiled as she heard Alice wailing loudly in the kitchen.

'You're not the only one who's been up all night, poor Ivy has barely had a wink. Alice is teething and Ivy's spent half the night rubbing oil of cloves on her poor little gums.' She took Holly's cloak and shooed her away upstairs. When Emma carried the tea up to her some minutes later she found Holly wide awake.

'Matron sent me to the workhouse to nurse the children there all night,' Holly told her as she climbed into bed and took the tea. She frowned. 'The staff there do their best for the children, but I'm sure more could be done for the poor little mites.'

'Such as?'

'Well, they rarely if ever get a day out for a start-off and most of them have never even seen the seaside.'

'But that's awful.' Emma had always ensured that Holly had a week at the coast at least once a year, usually in Skegness or Southend in a boarding house.

'I was thinking that we might be able to form some sort of committee to raise funds for that sort of thing,' Holly said.

Emma thought it was a wonderful idea and nodded. 'I agree, but we can talk about it later when you've had a rest. Now get some sleep.'

Holly yawned, drank her tea and minutes later she was fast asleep.

It was mid-afternoon when she woke and after washing and dressing she went downstairs to find Verity Lockett,

Sunday Branning and her mother all having a tête-à-tête in the drawing room.

'Ah, here you are, darling, we were just having a chat about you.' Emma rose to greet her and after drawing her into their little circle she passed her a plate of Cook's home-made scones. Holly suddenly realised she was hungry and bit into one.

'So what's this?' she teased. 'A mother's meeting?'

'Actually I was just telling them about what you told me this morning – that most of the children at the workhouse have never seen the sea.'

'Yes, and it's made me feel ashamed,' Sunday admitted, helping herself to another scone. 'My mother and I have worked really hard to ensure that the little ones are treated with kindness and are adequately clothed and fed but we never gave a thought to day trips or holidays.'

'And so,' Verity Lockett piped in excitedly, 'we've come up with a few ideas to raise funds. For a start, we thought that we could visit the better-off members of the community to beg anything they have that they don't use any more. It could be clothes, knick-knacks, furniture, anything at all really, then we could put the items up for sale in the parish hall. I'm sure Edgar wouldn't mind.'

'Yes, and I thought that if I craftily put the word out that certain people have made healthy donations to a worthy cause I'm sure others would follow suit. Some of these ladies of leisure don't like to be outdone,' Sunday added with a wicked little smile.

Holly chuckled. 'You really have had your heads together, haven't you? And I think they're marvellous ideas.'

'In that case, we'll start just as soon as we're able to,' Sunday said and Holly had no doubt whatsoever that she would follow the ideas through.

Eventually the women drifted away back to their families and in no time at all Holly had to prepare for work again.

'So when are yer goin' to have a day off?' Ivy enquired as she jiggled a fractious Alice on her hip. The poor baby's cheeks were rosy red and she was grizzling, which was quite unlike her, she was usually such a happy little soul. 'You seem to have been workin' flat out for days on end.'

'It's because of the flu outbreak,' Holly explained as she fastened her cap in the mirror above the fireplace. 'We've been inundated with patients and now two of the other nurses have come down with it too. Matron has had to request temporary help from the Nuneaton and Hartshill Red Cross nurses.'

She kissed Alice soundly and set off to the hospital. It was six o'clock in the evening, pitch-dark and extremely cold and she pulled her cape closer about her as she hurried along. She had just reached the end of Manor Court Road when a motorcar pulled up beside her and, glancing towards it, she saw Harry Phillips grinning at her as he reached over to open the passenger door.

'Hop in, I'll give you a lift.'

Holly hesitated but realising that it would appear churlish if she refused she reluctantly climbed in beside him.

'So how are you feeling now?' she asked for want of something to say.

He grinned. 'Raring to go again now that I've had a rest.'

Holly searched her mind for something to start a conversation before asking, 'Didn't I hear you say you'd completed your training at Guy's Hospital in London?'

'I certainly did.'

Then before she could stop herself she blurted out, 'I don't suppose you knew a doctor called Richard Parkin? He'd be about your age, I should imagine.'

'Oh, I know Rick Parkin all right. We went through medical school together as it happens. But why do you ask?'

Holly was suddenly glad of the darkness as different emotions flitted across her face. 'Oh, no reason really. I just got to know him while I worked in London. He often visited the wards I worked on. Do you, er . . . still keep in touch?' She knew she shouldn't be asking such things but she couldn't seem to help herself.

As Harry glanced at her from the corner of his eye it came to him in a blinding flash. Holly had feelings for the chap, which was probably why she'd refused to go out with him. He could hear it in her voice and he felt a surge of jealousy.

'I saw him shortly before I came here, as it happens,' he said nonchalantly as he steered the car into the entrance to the hospital. 'He was out and about with a rather pretty young lady on his arm so we didn't get chance to say much.' He hated himself for lying the second the words had left his lips but realised that anything he said now could only make things worse.

'Oh!' Holly felt as if someone had punched her in the stomach. Richard clearly couldn't have thought as much of her as he'd said he did otherwise surely he wouldn't have replaced her so quickly. But then common sense told her that it was a good thing he had. He deserved to be happy and by making him think that she didn't love him at least she had spared him the shame of knowing that he had been courting his own sister.

'Here we are then.' Harry drew the car to a halt and switched off the engine. 'Let's go and see what Matron has in store for us tonight, shall we?'

She nodded numbly as he hurried round the car to open the door for her and went to report for duty. Thankfully their paths didn't cross again that night, which was a relief because she was busy torturing herself with visions of another girl on Richard's arm.

Her mother was grinning like a Cheshire cat when Holly got home the next morning. 'Walter and I have decided that we're going to get married this summer,' she told Holly joyously. 'To be honest, we had intended to wait until next year but then, we thought, we're not getting any younger so why not just go ahead and do it? We thought July would be a nice month for a wedding and we'd like you to be our matron of honour. And Florence and Katie will be brides-maids, of course. What do you think, sweetheart?'

'I think it's a marvellous idea.' Holly was genuinely pleased for her. It was time her mother had a little happiness.

'Oh good, we were hoping you'd approve,' Emma trilled. 'We're going to go and try to book a date at Chilvers Coton Church this afternoon and then Walter thought it would be nice if we had a little reception in the Bull Hotel in the marketplace afterwards. We don't want a big wedding though,' she rushed on. 'Just very close friends and family. Walter is talking about a honeymoon in Venice afterwards.'

Holly felt a lump form in her throat as she saw how happy her mother was. She looked ten years younger suddenly but she knew that she would miss her. She had been the most constant person in her life up to now.

'I hope you'll both be very, very happy,' she told her as she held her tightly and she meant every word.

Chapter Thirty-Three

By May Alice was sporting five teeth and was back to her normal smiling self, much to everyone's relief. The flu epidemic that had swept through the town was also over and with the better weather upon them the people of Nuneaton were feeling much more optimistic.

In addition, Holly and Dr Phillips were getting along much better now, and she had eventually agreed to have an evening out with him, but, as she had warned him, only as a friend and he seemed to have accepted that. Up to now anyway. If she was honest, though, Holly would have gone so far as to admit that she'd grown quite fond of him, but not in the all-consuming way she had felt about Richard. Her heart still ached for him, but knowing that she had done the right thing gave her some consolation.

Holly's grandfather, though, was not feeling quite so optimistic. 'There is a lot of unrest abroad,' he said gravely as he and Holly sat together in the garden reading the newspapers one evening after dinner. 'I fear that it may lead to a war.' He and his granddaughter had finally grown close since Holly had returned home and it thrilled him that he was able to converse with her on any subject from history to politics. He wondered now why he had never realised what an intelligent girl she was before.

'But it won't affect us surely, Grandfather?' Holly said.

He shook his head. 'I fear it might. The arms race in Europe is looming larger and Winston Churchill has made the largest navy budget ever to the Commons to ensure that we can put eight squadrons into service in the time that it takes Germany to build five. But that's enough gloom and doom for one evening, especially on one of your rare days off. How do you fancy a game of chess?'

She smiled. He had taught her to play chess some months before and now got quite touchy when she beat him.

'It's just beginner's luck,' he would grumble but he was secretly very proud of her, although he sensed that all was not well with her since she had returned home. It was nothing she said, just a look in her eyes sometimes as if her heart and her thoughts were far away, which, could he have known it, they were.

The following day Holly was making her first visit to London to visit Miss May since she had returned home and despite the painful memories there she was looking forward to it, so after once again beating her grandfather at chess she went to her room to lay out the clothes she would wear, as she intended to make an early start.

She was at the train station by nine o'clock the following morning and she boarded the train in a happy mood. She and Miss May were going to have lunch together, Holly's treat, and as the train chugged along she was trying to decide where she should take her. She decided on a little restaurant that had been a favourite of hers and Ivy's just off Oxford Street. When the train drew into Euston she found the station just as busy as she remembered it and she set off in the warm sunshine to walk to the shop. As she was walking across

Euston Square a couple strolling arm in arm in front of her caught her eye. There was something familiar about the man's walk and as he turned his head towards his companion, who was very pretty indeed, her stomach lurched. It was Richard, every bit as handsome as she remembered him. The couple were laughing at something the young woman had said and eager not to be seen Holly turned abruptly to walk the other way. But it was too late. Richard had seen her from the corner of his eye and he stopped in his tracks to stare at her. With a determined effort Holly drew herself up to her full height and as she approached him she smiled politely.

He took off his hat, his eyes fixed on hers. 'Hello, Holly. How are you? You're looking well.' Then suddenly remembering his manners he nodded towards the girl at his side, 'I'm so sorry. Holly, this is Melissa.'

Melissa gave her a charming smile and although Holly wanted to hate her she found that she couldn't.

'How do you do.' The girl had twinkling blue eyes and fair hair and seemed very pleasant.

Thankfully Holly was saved from having to speak to her when Richard commented, 'I, er . . . heard that you'd left the hospital. I trust you're enjoying your new post?'

'Yes, I . . .' Holly had been about to tell him that she had returned to live at home but thinking better of it she merely said, 'I'm enjoying it very much.' As their eyes locked Holly felt herself begin to panic. If she didn't get away from him very soon she knew that she might make a fool of herself and break down.

'Well, er . . . it's been very nice to see you, but I have an appointment so I really must get on. Goodbye, Richard,

311

Melissa.' She turned and moved quickly away, tears pricking the back of her eyes. She was sure she could feel his eyes burning into her back but she didn't turn once. It was only when she was a safe distance away and she was sure they wouldn't be able to see her that she sagged against a wall, taking deep breaths.

As she was standing there an old lady with a basket of heather on her arm approached her. 'Buy a sprig of 'eather from an old lady an' bring yerself luck, dearie?'

Holly gulped and fumbled in her bag then pushing a number of coins towards the woman she took the sprig of heather from her. The old woman stared at her solemnly for a moment then said quietly, 'I see a period of great hardship ahead fer you, me beauty. But never fear, you'll come through it. You're lovin' an' givin' an' one day you'll be together forever with the love of your life.' She turned and shuffled away then as Holly smiled wryly. What a load of rubbish, she thought. I wonder what she'd say if she knew that the love of my life was my own brother? She moved on but the day was ruined for her now.

Miss May and the women in the shop were delighted to see her and after leaving the shop in the capable hands of Miss May's sister, who was now happily living in the flat that Holly and Ivy had once shared, Holly took her old employer out to lunch.

'Do you miss living in London?' Miss May asked as they sat drinking coffee following the meal.

'I miss you but not particularly living here,' Holly admitted.

'Although I will admit it was strange when I first went home, getting used to the peace and quiet again.'

Miss May laughed. Having always lived in the capital she had never known anything but hustle and bustle. 'And what happened with that nice young doctor you were seeing?'

Holly's heart fluttered as if a little bird was trapped in her chest. 'Oh, we decided we didn't suit,' she answered vaguely.

Miss May raised an eyebrow. 'Really? I would have bet my bottom dollar that you two were meant for each other, but that's life, I suppose. Is there anyone new on the horizon?'

'No, not really.' Yet even as she said it a picture of Harry's face flashed in front of her eyes. Although they had been out together as friends, Holly was well aware that Harry would have liked to take their relationship a stage further. She enjoyed his company but for now she was happy for things to stay as they were.

'Hmm, not really in my books means there is someone in the wings,' Miss May teased but seeing that Holly was looking decidedly uncomfortable she changed the subject.

Eventually Holly walked back to the shop with her and went inside to say goodbye to the others. She had intended to do some shopping in Oxford Street but she wasn't in the mood after her meeting with Richard so she made her way back to Euston and waited for the next train home. All the way back images of the pretty girl with her arm threaded through his plagued her and she suddenly wished that she hadn't come. She supposed she should be happy that he had moved on with someone else, which brought her thoughts round to Harry. As Ivy had quite rightly pointed out, he was very handsome, and kind into the bargain. She had no doubt he would make a wonderful husband and despite the fact she had promised herself she would never marry now that she couldn't have Richard, she was beginning to wonder if she had made the right decision. Being around little Alice all the time had made her realise that she would like children of her own one day. But then would it be fair on Harry to marry him when her heart still belonged to Richard? The more she thought on it the more confused she became so eventually she lifted the *Woman's Life* magazine she had bought at the station and tried to concentrate on that.

She arrived home to find her mother and Walter in high spirits.

'We've chosen the date for our wedding,' her mother told her excitedly. 'It will be the second Saturday in July, the twelfth, so we're going to have lots to do now. I've already booked us an appointment at the dressmaker in town, then we have to choose the flowers. Oh, and what hymns we shall want during the service as well! I'm beginning to wonder if we've left ourselves enough time to get everything done!'

Walter smiled at her indulgently. 'Everything will be fine,' he assured her.

'An' me an' Alice an' Cook are comin' to the weddin' too,' Ivy piped up excitedly.

'But of course you are,' Emma said. Although Ivy was officially the maid Emma also considered her to be very much a member of the family now. Holly smiled and listened to her mother chatter on about what needed to be done and

314

when she eventually left the room, Ivy lifted Alice onto her hip and asked, 'So, what's wrong? An' don't say nothin' cos I can read you like a book an' I know there's somethin'. I thought you weren't comin' back till this evenin'?'

When Holly flushed she frowned. 'You saw Richard, didn't you?'

Holly nodded miserably and Ivy gave an exasperated sigh. 'Look surely if you still have feelins for him you could patch things up?' Holly had never told her the reason they had split up, which was surprising because they usually told each other everything.

'It's not as simple as that.' Holly lowered her eyes and played with the fringe on the chenille tablecloth.

'Then in that case, for goodness' sake give Harry a chance,' she scolded. 'He's clearly crackers about you an' good blokes like him don't come along every day.'

Holly knew she was right but she didn't want to talk about it, so after kissing Alice she went up to her room in a solemn mood.

A week later Harry took her out for a leisurely stroll through Riversley Park on a sunny Sunday afternoon, after which he hired a rowing boat on the River Anker.

'Have you ever done this before?' she asked anxiously as he helped her into the boat and lifted the oars.

'Huh! It'll be a piece of cake,' he assured her but minutes later she was laughing helplessly as they found themselves going round and round in circles on the sluggishly moving water.

'I, er . . . I'll get the hang of it in a minute,' Harry assured her as he battled with the oars, which only made her laugh all the more. The boat was rocking dangerously and Holly half expected to be pitched into the river at any minute.

'It's not quite as easy as it looks,' he panted. 'I think I've decided I'd rather be a doctor than an oarsman!'

Eventually they were back on dry land.

'Right, I think it's time we treated ourselves to an ice cream, don't you?' Harry asked.

Holly giggled. 'I think you've earned one after all that effort.'

They sat on the banks of the river to eat their ices beneath the shade of a weeping willow tree and Holly was shocked to realise that she was actually really enjoying herself. But Harry was on duty at the hospital that evening so soon he walked her home.

'Will you come in for a cup of tea?' she invited but after glancing at his pocket watch, a present from his parents for his twenty-first birthday, he shook his head.

'I'd love to but I'll be late if I stay and I don't want to get into Matron's bad books.'

Holly shocked both herself and him when she suddenly leaned forward and gently touched her lips to his. There was no explosion behind her eyes as there had been when she kissed Richard but she found that it was pleasant all the same.

'What was that for?' Harry touched his lips as if he could hardly believe what she had just done, suddenly feeling as if all his birthdays and Christmases had come at once.

'I just felt like it, and thank you for this afternoon. It's been really lovely. Now get off with you and no doubt I'll see you sometime tomorrow at the hospital.'

He grinned. 'Not if I see you first,' he said, then walked away with a spring in his step.

Chapter Thirty-Four

Holly got home from the hospital later in May to find Ivy poring over the newspaper. She was so engrossed and indignant about what she was reading that she didn't even give Holly a welcome.

'Would you just look at this!' She stabbed her finger angrily at the page. 'It says that fifty-seven suffragettes were arrested yesterday as they tried to reach Buckingham Palace to present a "Votes for Women" petition to the King! Emmeline Pankhurst, who has not been well, was amongst 'em!'

Holly leaned over her shoulder and commented, 'Yes but it also says that some of them were brandishing Indian clubs and that they were trying to break through a thousand-strong police cordon around the palace.'

'Well, what else are they supposed to do?' Ivy snapped as angry colour rose in her cheeks. 'Their right to vote was turned down again earlier this month but I'll tell you now they won't stop until they get it. Why should they?'

'All right, calm down, you'll frighten Alice,' Holly warned and Ivy was instantly repentant for her outburst.

'Sorry, it just makes me so bloody mad! I'll tell you now if I didn't have Alice I'd still be there, backin' 'em all the way.'

'Yes, but you do have Alice,' Holly pointed out as she removed the white cuffs from the sleeves of her dress. 'So now you have to concentrate on her and not on what the suffragettes are doing.'

'I s'ppose yer right,' Ivy grumbled as she lifted her daughter on to her lap. Then in a slightly happier mood she confided, 'Marcus is takin' me out this evenin'. We're goin' to the Picturedrome again then he's takin' me fer a fish-an'-chip supper.'

'How lovely.' Ivy and Marcus's relationship really seemed to be blossoming now, and Holly hoped that it would work out for them. Ivy certainly deserved to have a decent man in her life after the way Jeremy had treated her. Strangely enough, Ivy hadn't mentioned Jeremy for weeks now and Holly hoped that this was a sign she was getting over him.

'An' when are you seein' Harry again?'

Holly blushed. 'On Saturday; we've both got an afternoon off, but I don't know what we're doing yet.'

When Ivy nodded her approval she hurried away upstairs to get changed out of her uniform ready for dinner.

On Saturday Holly and Harry went to listen to the Stockingford Brass Band playing in the old bandstand in a recreation ground off Pool Bank Street in the town and soon their feet were tapping in time to the music.

'They're good, aren't they?' Harry shouted above the noise and Holly nodded in agreement.

'Excellent.' She had always wished that she'd been musically inclined but had never managed to master a musical instrument.

'So what would you like to do now?' Harry asked when the band began to pack up.

Holly could see that he was tired, he had been working double shifts at the hospital for most of the week, so she suggested, 'Why don't you come back to the house to have dinner with the family? It's time they met you.'

He stared at her intently for a moment, hoping that this meant she was ready to take their courtship another stage further. Harry had never met a girl like Holly and knew now that he had fallen deeply in love with her.

'But surely they won't be expecting me?'

Holly laughed. 'Oh, don't worry about that. Cook always makes far too much food so there'll be more than enough to go round and I'd like you to meet my mother and my grandfather properly.'

'In that case I'd be delighted to accept your kind invitation,' he answered and lifting her hand he kissed it gently before tucking it into his arm. It was turning out to be a good day, even if he was so tired he could have slept standing up!

Even though his visit was unexpected, the family greeted him warmly and over dinner Harry got on like a house on fire with Holly's grandfather as they discussed the ever-increasing unrest abroad.

'It'll lead to a war, you just mark my words,' Gilbert said as he bit into a juicy pork chop covered in apple sauce, just the way he liked it.

'Father, please!' Emma glanced at Harry apologetically. 'This is really no topic for the dinner table.'

'Hmph! I suppose you'd rather talk about the plans for

the wedding,' he grunted with a wicked wink at Harry. 'You don't know what I have to suffer,' he confided with a martyred sigh. 'The women are runnin' about like headless chickens getting everything organised. This should turn out to be the weddin' of the century! An' she said she didn't want a fuss when they first got engaged an' all. Women, eh?'

Harry smiled good-naturedly. 'I do believe it's supposed to be one of the happiest days of a woman's life, or so my mother tells me. She's always dropping hints about when it will be my turn,' he added with a twinkle in his eye as he glanced towards Holly who blushed furiously. Suddenly she wondered if inviting him to meet the family had been such a good idea after all.

As soon as he left, her mother told her, 'What a delightful young man. And a doctor too!'

'Now don't go reading too much into it,' Holly scolded. 'Harry and I are merely good friends.'

'Hmm . . . merely good friends,' her mother teased but then thankfully she had to dash away to get ready for Walter to call for her.

Ivy had more than a word to say about the situation too when she caught Holly alone in the dining room. 'You're a dark horse.' She grinned. 'Why didn't you tell me it had got to the stage where you wanted him to meet the family?'

Holly groaned. 'Oh, not you as well. I invite a friend to dinner and the next thing you lot are marrying me off!'

'Well, from what I saw of him yer could do a lot worse,' Ivy remarked as she loaded the dirty pots onto a large wooden

321

tray, then she sailed from the room with an amused gleam in her eye.

❧

Over the next few weeks there didn't seem to be a spare minute in the day. Holly was either at work, helping her mother with her wedding plans or helping with the various fund-raising activities Emma and Sunday Branning had planned to raise money to get the workhouse children to the seaside. On one particular Saturday the women held a second-hand clothes sale in the parish hall and as soon as they opened the door, they were nearly trampled by the local women as they pushed and shoved their way in to get first pickings.

One woman grabbed a cardigan just as another woman was reaching for it and Sunday had to intervene to stop a fight from breaking out.

'Now, ladies, I'm sure there will be something for both of you,' she panted as she tried to hold them apart.

'I bleedin' seen it first,' one of the women protested loudly. 'Give it 'ere else I'll black yer bleedin' eye!'

Holly and Ivy, who were standing beside one of the stalls, watched with amusement as Sunday hastily handed the garment over.

'Don't blame her,' Ivy whispered. 'That's Mrs Davis. She's from the courtyards an' she'd knock yer down soon as look at yer!' Thankfully the rest of the women were a little better behaved although some of the foul language they used as they snatched at various items of clothing was enough to turn the air blue.

By the time everything was sold and the women had left,

Emma felt as if she had been on a battlefield and her nerves were in shreds but when they counted the money, they were delighted to find that they'd raised almost ten pounds.

'We'll have those children to the seaside in no time at this rate,' Verity Lockett chirped happily.

On 28 June a tidal wave of horror swept through the country as word reached the people that the Archduke Franz Ferdinand, the heir to the Austro-Hungarian throne, and his wife, the Duchess of Hohenberg, had been assassinated as the car carrying the royal couple through the streets of Sarajevo was attacked by a young man who ran from the crowd and fired a gun at them. The first bullet got the duke in the neck, the second got his wife in the stomach and she died almost instantly, the duke ten minutes later.

'I fear this will have serious repercussions on all of us,' Gilbert said gravely.

'Surely not, Father,' Emma said. 'How could something that has happened so far away possibly affect us?'

Not wishing to spoil the lead-up to her wedding, which was only two weeks away, the old man held his tongue but in the weeks to come they would all think back on his prediction.

Emma's wedding day dawned bright and clear and as they set off for the church everyone was in a happy mood. Emma was wearing a sky-blue satin dress with a little matching hat and she carried a small posy of sweet-smelling freesias. Those watching as she walked down the aisle on the arm of her proud father all agreed that they had never seen a more radiant bride. She kept her eyes fixed on Walter, who was waiting for her at the front of the church before the altar, and at the sight of his bride his face lit up with love for her. Holly, Florence and Katie looked stunning in their matching bridesmaids' dresses, which were in a lighter shade of blue to the bride's. The service, conducted by Verity Lockett's husband, was touching and as her mother made her vows, Holly prayed that she would at last find happiness.

When the happy couple eventually emerged from the church to the joyous peal of bells they were showered with rose petals and rice and the mood was light. Emma turned her back and tossed her posy into the air and when it landed in Holly's hands everyone cheered.

'Looks like you'll be the next bride,' little Katie declared delightedly and they all laughed as Holly blushed to the roots of her hair.

The reception that followed was equally as joyful and when Walter made a very touching speech and toasted his bride there was hardly a dry eye in the house. No expense had been spared and the meal was delicious as was the three-tier cake that the happy couple eventually sliced into. Then the tables were cleared and the serious business of everyone enjoying themselves began in earnest. Walter had booked a four-piece band and soon they were all dancing as the wine flowed freely. Holly was happily watching everyone have a good time when she suddenly became aware that her grandfather had come to stand beside her.

'She looks happy, doesn't she?' he said softly as his eyes followed his daughter around the room in Walter's arms.

Holly smiled. 'Yes, she does.'

He looked at her then and she was surprised when he took her hand and gently squeezed it. 'I owe you an apology, my dear.'

She shook her head and opened her mouth to deny it, but he held his hand up. 'Please, let me say it. I realise now that I was wrong when I first tried to get you married off to Walter. I've known him for a long time and I knew he was struggling without his wife so I thought he would make a suitable match for you. Ridiculous, I know. He was far too old for you for a start and to give him credit he was very reluctant to even come and meet you when I first suggested it. I don't blame you for leaving home. It wasn't my place to say who you should or shouldn't marry. But at least all's well that ends well. I think Walter and your mother are a true love match, don't you?'

'Oh definitely,' Holly agreed.

'So . . . do you think you can ever forgive me? My reasons for doing what I did were not entirely selfish. I'd had to stand by and watch the appalling way your father treated your mother and I couldn't bear to think that that might happen to you too. After she came home when she was carrying you, I shut myself off from the pair of you and that was my loss. But perhaps it's not too late to put things right, eh?'

Holly smiled up at him and gently returned the pressure on her hand before standing on tiptoe to kiss his cheek. 'It's never too late,' she told him softly and she had never felt closer to him.

Emma had tried to talk her into inviting Harry to the

wedding but Holly had declined. She continued to feel uncertain about him and the memory of Richard was still far too painful, but she had invited him to join them at the reception that evening and when he arrived he found the dance floor full of people dancing and singing along to Al Jolsen's, 'You Made Me Love You', and he grinned as he spotted Holly.

'Crikey,' he shouted to make himself heard above the din. 'Looks like everyone's having a good time.'

'It's been a lovely day,' she agreed as she took his hand and led him to the bar. 'Now, what would you like to drink. Oh, and there's a buffet laid on in the next room if you're hungry.'

He looked her up and down approvingly. 'You look beautiful,' he told her. 'That colour really suits you.'

Holly grinned as she glanced down at her dress. 'I dare say it is an improvement on my uniform.'

They got him a drink and soon after they joined in the dancing and the evening seemed to pass in the blink of an eye. Finally somebody shouted, 'The car's here!' and the guests trooped outside to watch the newly-weds leave, laughing as they saw the trail of tin cans someone had tied to the back of the car.

Walter shook the men's hands as Emma hugged her daughter and there were tears in her eyes.

'I shall miss you so much,' she said in a choked voice.

Holly was feeling tearful too. 'But it isn't as if you're going to be a million miles away,' she pointed out bravely. 'And we'll still see each other often.'

'Of course we will but look after yourself, darling.' And then Walter was there helping her into the car and as it drew away taking the couple to a hotel for the night everyone cheered and waved. They would be leaving for their honeymoon in Venice in August.

'Goodbye . . . goodbye . . .' Holly's voice trailed away and a comforting arm came about her shoulders and she looked up into Harry's sympathetic eyes.

'Don't take any notice of me, I'm just being silly and sentimental,' Holly sniffed as she mopped at her eyes with the large white handkerchief he handed to her.

'There's nothing wrong with having feelings.' She was still looking up at him and he bent towards her and kissed her softly on the lips, and for the very first time she found herself responding. He could never take the place of Richard but perhaps there was a future ahead for them after all.

Chapter Thirty-Five

Early in August, Emma sat with Holly and Ivy in the drawing room speaking of her forthcoming trip to Venice. She had blossomed since her marriage and anyone could see that she and Walter adored each other.

'I can't believe that it's only a few more days until we go,' she said, her eyes shining. 'I did try to persuade Walter to let Florence and Katie come with us but he wouldn't hear of it. He says we'll share all the rest of our holidays with the children but this one is just for us. He really is so considerate.'

Holly and Ivy exchanged an amused smile. Emma was clearly very happy and that made them happy.

The door opened then and Walter and Gilbert appeared.

'Oh, darling, I was just telling the girls about where we're hoping to visit while we're in Venice and . . .' Emma's voice trailed away as she saw the grave expressions on the men's faces.

'Is there something wrong?' she asked.

It was her father who nodded. 'I'm afraid so, my dear. The prime minister, Herbert Asquith, has just announced that we are now officially at war with Germany.'

Emma's hand flew to her mouth. 'Oh no, surely not?'

'I'm afraid it's true, my darling,' Walter told her solemnly. 'And in light of this I think we should postpone our honeymoon until we know what's going to happen. I wouldn't wish to take you anywhere you might be in any danger.'

'Apparently people are already surging through London gathering outside Downing Street and Buckingham Palace singing the national anthem,' her father went on. 'Recruitment centres are being set up all across the country even as we speak and all young men are being encouraged to enlist. Germany invaded Belgium this morning on their way to Paris so sadly the fighting has already started.'

Unable to take it in, Emma shook her head as she thought of Marcus. She had already grown very fond of Walter's children. 'But what about Marcus?'

Walter shrugged, his face pale. 'I would much rather he didn't enlist unless he had to,' he admitted. 'But he must make his own mind up and I shall stand by his decision. He's a young man now, after all.'

It was Ivy who paled now. She and Marcus had grown quite close but it was only when she thought of him possibly going to fight that she realised just how much he had come to mean to her.

'I'll talk to him. He won't go if I ask him not to,' she said in a wobbly voice but Walter wasn't so sure.

'We'll have to wait and see what his decision is,' he said quietly, then he turned to his wife. 'Are you ready, darling? I think I'd like to get home now.'

'Of course.' Emma snatched up her bag and after saying their goodbyes she and Walter departed.

'I've had a horrible feeling this was going to happen for some long time,' Gilbert said when they'd gone. 'But don't look so frightened. Hopefully it will be all over in no time with not too much harm done.' And he left the room leaving the girls to their gloomy thoughts.

The next morning on her way to the hospital. Holly could hardly believe her eyes. A recruitment centre had appeared in the town centre and young men were queueing outside it, eager to enlist and go to war. They were laughing and happy as if they were about to embark on some great adventure and she felt sick as she wondered if they realised they might never come home.

'The whole world has gone mad!' Matron declared worriedly when Holly arrived. 'Did you see those young boys in the town signing up to go to war? Some of them didn't look older than fifteen or sixteen, they must be lying about their ages to get in. There will be no young men left in the town at this rate.'

'I know.' The sight had upset Holly too but there was nothing she could do about it so she quietly went about her work.

Harry came to the hospital later that day. 'You aren't thinking of signing up too, are you?' Holly asked him.

He shook his head. 'Not exactly, but if doctors are needed to treat the wounded abroad then I may well go.'

'Oh, Harry, it's all so senseless.' She leaned heavily on the office desk. 'Surely someone can do something to stop this madness.'

'I think it's gone too far for that now. The prime minister did give Germany a chance when he asked them to respect the neutrality of Belgium but they chose to ignore it. The newly appointed secretary of war, Lord Kitchener, has already called for at least 100,000 men to start a new army and the Royal Navy has been put on a war footing with orders to be prepared to open fire on the enemy at any moment.'

Harry was usually such a happy-go-lucky chap that it was strange to see him looking so sombre.

'Try not to worry,' he told Holly as he saw her nervously nibbling at her lip and without another word he went to see his patients.

Emma and Walter visited again at the weekend, and Walter was concerned. 'I won't have any men at all working for me at this rate,' he told Holly's grandfather. 'They're all going to sign up for the army.'

'It's the same in the mill and the pits from what I can make of it,' Gilbert replied worriedly. 'How everyone is supposed to keep the businesses going is a puzzle to me.'

'I believe the prime minister has stated that women will be expected to take over the roles of some of the men for the dur-ation of the war.' Gilbert shook his head. It made him wonder what the world was coming to. After all, how could women possibly do men's jobs?

'And why shouldn't women do men's jobs?' Ivy asked heatedly. She had just carried a tray of coffee and biscuits in and was instantly on the defensive. 'The trouble is most men think all women are fit for is standing at the kitchen sink and bringing up babies.'

'Not all men think like that,' Holly said soothingly, seeing that Ivy was getting riled.

'No, but most of them do,' Ivy snorted indignantly. 'That's why the suffragettes are havin' to fight to get us equal rights.'

Holly flashed her a warning look and Ivy had the grace to flush. 'That's my opinion anyway,' she mumbled and shot out of the room.

Luckily, Walter seemed quite amused by her little outburst. 'I do understand what she means,' he said. 'When I first bought the hat factory there were both women and men there doing exactly the same job and yet the women's wages were far lower than the men's. I didn't think it was fair so they're paid the same now.'

Emma looked at Walter adoringly. Married life to a good man was suiting her and she had never been happier, apart from worrying about the war that was. Only the night before she had asked him if he would have to go and fight and he'd tried to allay her fears.

'At the moment they want the younger men,' he'd told her gently. 'But of course if it went on for any length of time there is a possibility that they would want men my age.'

'I wouldn't let you go and risk getting killed,' she'd informed him with tears in her eyes but deep down she knew that if it came to that she wouldn't be able to stop him. Walter was a very honourable man and he certainly wouldn't want to be branded a coward or be presented with a white feather.

Thankfully Ivy came back in carrying Alice at that moment and everyone's attention was immediately diverted to the little girl. She was now a happy little toddler into all sorts of mischief and Ivy often said that she needed eyes in the back of her head.

Emma produced a chocolate bar from her bag – she never came without one – and within minutes they were all laughing at Alice who fell on it as if it was the first treat she had ever had and the sombre mood lifted.

Throughout the month training camps appeared as if by magic all over the country. The first lot of new recruits left the train station to the sound of a brass band and so many people waving them off that families were standing shoulder to shoulder on the little platform. There were mothers and fathers, sisters, brothers, wives and sweethearts all waving wildly and praying silently that this would not be the last time they saw their loved ones. Once the train had disappeared from view, the mood became sombre and the crowd drifted away with heavy hearts.

In no time at all the British troops, alongside their French and Belgian comrades, were engaged in a bitter struggle for the town of Mons in France. The British Expeditionary Force, consisting of some 70,000 men, had crossed the Channel in a highly secret navy operation but despite their best efforts and skills the enemy proved too much and on 23 August the retreat began and civilians in Mons, who had been innocently attending a church service, were caught in the cross fire. Bloody battles were already being fought along an ever-shifting line from Belgium in the north to Alsace and Lorraine in the south, where the French opened their main thrust. The main danger lay in the north, for in less than a month the Germans had swept over most of Belgium, crossed the Sambre and Meuse and forced a

French retreat to the Somme, which was the last barrier before Paris.

Slowly the victims of the war began to be shipped home and suddenly the little cottage hospital was bursting at the seams. There were young men with horrific injuries, some of them life-threatening, and the doctors and nurses were working almost around the clock to care for them.

It was reported in the newspapers that in London the Metropolitan Police had rounded up and detained over three hundred Germans who were suspected of being spies and they were now being kept in the vast Olympia complex in Kensington, which had been turned into a prisoner-of-war camp.

'But what if they're innocent?' Holly asked her grandfather as they sat at the dining table. She had just finished a fourteen-hour shift and was almost dropping with fatigue. And she was due back on duty at six the next morning.

'For now the prime minister can take no chances,' he answered gravely. 'All Germans must be treated as the enemy.'

Holly shook her head and drained the tea in her cup before going upstairs to drop into bed, exhausted.

The following month brought no better news from abroad when German submarines sunk three British cruisers off the Netherlands. A number of neutral ships and fishing vessels were also struck by mines in the North Sea. Suddenly it seemed that nowhere was safe and people lived in fear of what might happen next, and still the young men went in droves to fight for their king and country never realising that most of them would never come home.

Chapter Thirty-Six

'Prepare him for theatre, nurse. I'm afraid this leg will have to be amputated.' Harry wearily straightened from a young soldier's bed and managed a small smile for Holly.

'But he's so young,' Holly whispered as she gently sponged the boy's feverish brow.

'It's gangrene and it's gone too far for me to do anything,' Harry answered. 'It's either his leg or his life, which do you think he'd prefer?'

'Oh, I wasn't questioning you, doctor,' she assured him hastily, hearing the note of irritation in his voice.

'Sorry.' He knuckled his tired eyes. 'I'm just shattered. Still, once we've got this boyo sorted I might be able to snatch a few hours' sleep. I'll leave you to it now while I go and ask them to get theatre ready.'

She watched him walk away and sighed. All of them were worn out and with still more casualties arriving daily she wondered how the hospital was going to cope. They had already had to ask for help from the Nuneaton and Hartshill Red Cross nurses to provide the extra staff but soon they wouldn't be able to squeeze any more beds into the wards. The young man in the bed winced then and when she looked down at him she saw that his eyes were open.

'I heard the doctor say somethin' about goin' to theatre?' he said in a shaky voice. 'Was he talkin' about me?'

Holly nodded, not sure what she should tell him. How did you tell someone, who until recently had been young and active, that he was about to have a limb amputated?

'But why?' His eyes were tight on her and she felt hot colour creeping up her neck into her cheeks.

'I think it might be best if I get Matron to come and explain,' she told him and before he could object she hurried off to find her.

They arrived back at the bedside within minutes to find the young man anxiously waiting for them. 'What's wrong? What are they gonna do to me?' he asked.

Matron gently laid her hand on his arm. 'I'm afraid your leg is gangrenous below the knee,' she told him in a hushed voice. 'And the only way we can prevent the infection from spreading is to remove it.'

Stark fear shone in his eyes as his head wagged from side to side. 'NO! I ain't havin' me leg off,' he protested. 'I'm too young to be a cripple. Me life will be over.'

'I'm afraid if you don't you will die,' she told him bluntly but still he shook his head.

'I won't give you permission to do it,' he protested strongly. 'I don't wanna be butchered.' At that moment they spotted his girlfriend standing at the end of the ward. She had come to see him every day since he had been there.

'Let's talk to your girl and see what she has to say about it,' Matron suggested, and minutes later the girl, a pretty, petite blonde, was at the side of the bed holding his hand tightly as Matron explained the position to her. Tears trickled down her cheeks but when she turned to the young man lying on the bed her voice was strong.

336

'You must let them do it, I'd rather have you with a leg missing than not at all.'

'What? You mean you'd still want me?'

'Of course I would.' She smiled at him through her tears. 'Lots of people learn to cope with only one leg and you're strong. You'll do the same.'

He stared at her for a long moment before slowly nodding. 'Very well, go ahead.'

Matron led his young lady away to wait anxiously as Holly quickly prepared him for theatre but her heart was heavy as the full implications of the effect the war was having on so many people came home to her. Here was a young man with his whole life in front of him who from now on would never be able to do some of the things he had done before. And yet he was one of the lucky ones. At least he had come home. Many had died already and now the sight of the boy pedalling furiously along the streets to deliver telegrams to inform mothers and wives that their loved ones would never return struck fear into the hearts of everyone who saw him.

'You look tired,' Ivy remarked when Holly arrived home late that evening.

'I am tired.' Holly dropped onto the nearest chair and wiped her weary eyes. They felt as if they were full of grit and her legs ached from being on them all day.

'I'll go an' make you a nice hot mug of milk. It'll help you sleep,' Ivy volunteered kindly.

Holly snorted. 'Thanks, but I don't think I'll need any rocking off tonight. I reckon I shall be out like a light the second my head hits the pillow.' She eased her feet out of her shoes and wiggled her toes as she waited for Ivy to come back, then noticed that Ivy didn't seem her normal cheery self.

'Is Alice all right?' she asked as she sipped at her drink.

'Oh yes, she's fine, tucked up safe and warm but . . .'

'But what?'

Ivy sniffed. 'Walter came round earlier and I heard him telling your gran'father that he thought Marcus might be thinking of enlisting.'

Holly wasn't surprised. Marcus wasn't the sort of young man who would want to be seen as a coward. 'And would it bother you very much if he went?'

Ivy considered for a moment before nodding. 'Actually, yes, it would. I mean I know I'm being silly thinking anything serious could ever come of our friendship. He's from a well-to-do family an' I'm just a maid wi' an illegitimate daughter into the bargain . . . and yet I've grown fond o' him. I didn't realise quite how much till I thought of how I would feel if he went away.'

'I think the war is doing a very good job of doing away with class distinction,' Holly pointed out. 'But what about your feelings for Jeremy? You were so devastated when he left you.'

Ivy shrugged. 'I think I just had my head turned by all the attention an' flattery he gave me,' she admitted. 'I'd never really had much to do wi' chaps until he came along an' he just sorta swept me off me feet. To be honest, I think I always knew he weren't the man I'd thought he was, but by the time I finally admitted it to meself, Alice were on the way so I didn't know how I could walk away from him.'

Holly smiled at her sympathetically. It seemed that the path to true love wasn't going to be a smooth one for either of them. Her hand unconsciously rose to touch the ring hanging on the chain about her neck beneath her blouse and she sighed. She'd accepted that Richard was a part of her past, but it didn't stop her missing him and somehow she couldn't bring herself to take it off even though her relationship with Harry was slowly developing into something a little more than friendship. He was a good man and she knew that more than a few nurses at the hospital would have given anything to be in her position, yet still she couldn't feel for him as she had for Richard.

'I dare say everything will sort itself out in the end,' she said.

Ivy sighed. 'Hmm, I dare say it will.'

When Holly arrived at the hospital the next day she found Matron waiting for her. 'Ah, Nurse Farthing, could I have a word, please.'

Holly followed her into her office where the matron asked her, 'I was wondering if you would do some of the house calls that Dr Nason and Dr Phillips usually do? As you're aware we are having to limit the number of people we admit to keep the beds for the military wounded and both Dr Nason and Dr Phillips are having to spend so long in theatre they simply don't have time to visit people. Most of the calls would be dealing with coughs and colds, childhood illnesses like chickenpox and measles, and boils that need to be lanced. I know you are more than capable of handling things like that, although I would of course expect you to use your discretion, and if you thought that someone really needed to be admitted you must report back to me immediately. I think by doing this it would give you far greater experience in the practical side of nursing because I know when you are on the wards a lot of your time is spent giving bed baths and emptying bedpans. What do you think, nurse? Would be prepared to give it a trial? It would help enormously.'

Holly stared at her warily. 'But what if I went out to someone and I wasn't sure what was wrong with them? I'd hate to give a wrong diagnosis in case anything went wrong.'

'In that event you would of course consult with myself or one of the doctors and if need be they would go out with you. In fact, until you are feeling a little more confident I would prefer that you erred on the side of caution. And of course we wouldn't dream of sending you out on your own to a patient who we thought was seriously ill.'

'In that case I suppose I could see how I go on,' Holly agreed cautiously.

Matron beamed. 'Excellent. As it happens I've already made you a list of the people I wish you to visit and they all appear to have fairly straightforward symptoms. Come along with me and I'll make you up a bag of things you may need.'

Holly dutifully followed Matron to the medicine cabinet and listened carefully as she explained what each of the drugs she placed in the black bag were for.

'Now, when you've completed the house calls I'd like you to report back to me with the symptoms of each of the patients you have seen. I am quite aware that you are on foot so it will take you some time to get from one patient to another, so I shall leave it to you to work out your own route, but I thought that if you are happy doing this for now we might be able to find you a bicycle to speed things up a little for you. Have you ever ridden a bicycle, nurse?'

Holly grinned. 'Not since I was little but I'm told that once you've ridden one you never forget so I dare say I could manage.'

'Excellent.' Matron produced a list of names and addresses and after perching her gold-rimmed glasses on the end of her nose she stabbed her finger at one address.

'This Mrs Murdoch lives in the courtyards in Abbey Street. She reports that three of her children have a rash. It sounds like chickenpox or measles to me. That might be a good place to start as it's fairly central but as I said I'm quite happy to leave it up to you. Now, is there anything you need to ask me?'

Holly shook her head. 'I don't think so.'

'In that case I suggest you make a start, nurse.' And with that Matron handed her the loaded bag and Holly set off with the list of patients gripped in her hand wondering just what on earth she had let herself in for.

Chapter Thirty-Seven

'Mrs Murdoch?'

'Aye, that's me.' The gaunt-looking woman peering warily round the door opened it wider when she saw the nurse's uniform and Holly stepped into a tiny room that looked to be little more than a hovel. A bed with an iron frame stood against one wall with three young children huddled together in it and as Holly approached them she saw that they were indeed covered in spots.

'Tim started first wi' spots behind his ears,' Mrs Murdoch informed her. 'An' now there's three of 'em covered from head to bloody toe. They're itchin' like hell an' all.'

'It's chickenpox,' Holly said as she inspected the nearest child to her and noted the small blister-like spots. She searched in her bag and produced a bottle of calamine lotion. 'Dab this on their spots, it will help with the itching,' she advised. 'And keep them cool and see that they drink lots of liquid.'

'Is that it?' the woman asked and Holly nodded as she snapped the bag shut and crossed to the sink to wash her hands.

'I'm afraid so but now that the spots have come out I think you'll find that they'll be feeling much better.'

'An' what about your fee?' the woman asked worriedly. She was clearly very poor.

'The doctor will send you a bill, but don't go worrying about it, it won't be very much,' Holly informed her, wishing she could just waive the fee. As she left she prayed that this wouldn't be the start of an epidemic.

Holly's next stop was in Willington Street in Abbey Green where a very old lady admitted her.

'It's me 'usband, dearie,' she told Holly worriedly. 'He's over there in the chair, see, sittin' on a cushion.'

'I see, and what appears to be the problem?'

'Well . . .' The old woman flushed. 'It's a bit embarrassin', but the poor old sod's got a boil.'

'And where is it?'

The old woman pointed to her skinny backside. 'Right there, I'm afraid.'

Holly gulped but managed to keep her expression calm. 'Right, we'd best take a look,' she said as she approached the old man's chair. 'Hello, Mr Day, and how are you today?' she asked cheerfully.

'Eh? What did yer say, dearie?'

'He's deaf as a post an' all,' the old woman confided, then addressing her husband she shouted, 'Pull yer clouts down, Horace. This young lady 'as come to look at yer boil.'

'What? Arr . . . all right.' The old man turned on his side and after undoing his flies he yanked his trousers down revealing a very skinny backside on which stood a huge boil that looked like a volcano.

'Oh my, that must be so painful,' Holly said sympathetically. It was no wonder the poor old soul was sitting on a cushion. All around the boil was red and angry-looking and the middle was full of yellow pus. 'I'm afraid that needs to

343

be lanced then we'll put a dressing on it and hopefully you'll be a little more comfortable.' Turning to his wife, she asked, 'Could you bring me some hot water, please, and a clean cloth.'

Twenty minutes later as she finished dressing the wound, the old man smiled at her appreciatively. 'Cor, that don't 'alf feel a lot better, me dear,' he thanked her and Holly managed a wobbly smile. It hadn't been the nicest of jobs but then, as the matron had pointed out, it was all good experience.

The next visit was in Fife Street to a young woman who had thought she was going into labour with her first child. Thankfully it had been a false alarm so she set off for Tuttle Hill next to see a young girl who had cut her leg climbing a tree.

'If I've told her once not to be such a tomboy, I've told her a dozen times,' her mother grumbled as Holly tried to calm her young patient.

'Unfortunately it's going to need a couple of stitches,' Holly told her as her stomach turned over. During her training she had watched the doctors stitch people up dozens of times but she had never actually done it herself. Still, she told herself as she threaded the needle that had been packed for her, there's a first time for everything and when it was finally done she felt a little glow of pride. It was very neat, even if she did say so herself. It wasn't until she was washing her hands that she realised how much she was trembling but she kept her smile in place and after telling her patient how brave she had been she headed for the next call.

Much later that afternoon when there were only two more names on her list she arrived at a house in Shepperton Street in Chilvers Coton and a worried-looking woman answered the door to her knock.

She looked mildly surprised to see a nurse standing there and glancing over Holly's shoulder she asked, 'Is the doctor not with you?'

'No, both of the doctors are in theatre today so I'm doing the house calls. How can I help you?'

The woman ushered her inside and closed the door quickly then chewed on her lip before telling her, 'It's me daughter, Annie. She, er . . . ain't well.'

'Oh? What appears to be the problem?'

'It's, er . . . her monthlies. She's bleedin' really heavy an' I can't seem to stop it.' The woman led her up a steep, narrow staircase and as Holly saw the young woman lying on the bed with a blood-soaked towel between her legs she frowned. The girl's eyes were rolling back in her head and beads of sweat stood out on her forehead as Holly quickly crossed to her and took her pulse.

'Are you sure she hasn't miscarried?' Holly asked carefully. The girl was in a very bad way and she saw at a glance that this was no normal monthly period.

'O' course she ain't, she ain't even wed.' The woman was a bag of nerves but Holly guessed instantly what had happened. The poor girl had been butchered by a backstreet abortionist, probably at her mother's insistence so that she wouldn't bring shame on the family.

'I'm afraid I'm going to have to get an ambulance,' Holly told the woman, trying her best to stay calm. 'She needs to be in hospital as soon as possible.'

'B-but couldn't yer just treat her here?' The woman's hands

plucked nervously at the buttons on her blouse as she stared at Holly fearfully.

'I'm afraid not. Stay with her and I'll be back with an ambulance as soon as I can.' She hurried from the room knowing all too well that every minute counted. She had seen a young girl brought into the hospital just a few weeks before in the same condition but sadly there had been nothing the doctors could do for her and she had passed away. She didn't want that to happen to this poor soul. She ran as fast as her legs would take her all the way back to the hospital and when she finally flew into the corridor, she rapped on Matron's door and breathlessly told her about the girl.

'Well done for realising what had happened,' Matron praised her. 'Luckily Dr Phillips has just come out of theatre so he can go with the ambulance to fetch her. Meantime, you sit there, I shan't be more than a minute or two. And feel proud of yourself because your quick thinking may well have just saved that young lady's life!' She hurried away to organise the transport and when she returned she found Holly a little calmer.

'So apart from the last patient how did your first day go?' she enquired.

'Well, I still have one patient left to see,' Holly explained as she took the list from her pocket. 'And I haven't had time to write my notes up yet, but I didn't want to delay getting the girl admitted.'

'You did absolutely right.' Matron smiled at her. 'But now before you go out to the last patient I insist you have a sandwich and a hot drink in the kitchen. The cook will be happy to rustle something up for you. I bet you haven't had any lunch, have you?'

'No, I haven't.' Holly gave her a guilty smile. 'I was worried about not having time to get to everyone so I just kept going.'

'We really do need to get you a bicycle. I shall speak to Dr Phillips about it this very evening. Now go and have something to eat and don't worry about the notes. You can do them this evening at home and hand them to me in the morning. Well done, nurse.' And with that she left Holly feeling rather proud of herself.

Just as Holly had feared, over the next week there was an epidemic of chickenpox amongst the children in the court-yards and almost every visit she made was to one of them. Some of them were so weak and malnourished that it made them desperately ill and Holly wished she could do more for them.

She arrived at the hospital one morning to collect her list of house calls to find Matron waiting for her with a broad smile on her face. 'Come with me,' she instructed and led Holly to the very back of the hospital where the mortuary was situated. 'There, will that help?' She pointed to a bicycle with a large basket balanced above the front wheel and Holly smiled.

'That will do very nicely,' she answered. 'And my bag will fit in the basket. I shall be able to get to my patients in half the time now. Thank you, Matron.'

'It's Dr Phillips you have to thank, really,' Matron admitted. 'He knew of someone who was selling it so we bought it out of the hospital funds but I've no doubt it will pay for itself in no time. Oh, and by the way, you might like to know that thanks to you the young lady you had sent in after a backstreet abortion looks like she's going to pull through.' She shook her head sadly. 'Unfortunately whoever performed the operation was a butcher. She admitted that they used a knitting needle to rid her of the child and then an infection set in so it was touch-and-go with her for a while there. She won't tell us who did it, however, so the maddening thing is that some other poor girl will no doubt suffer the same fate. Also it looks doubtful that she will ever be able to have any more children but I suppose that's a small price to pay for her life.'

Holly nodded in agreement, feeling desperately sad for the girl. Just then Harry appeared from the rear door and lifted the mood when he asked, 'What do you think of her then?' He nodded towards the bicycle and Holly giggled.

'She's a beauty. I just hope I can remember how to cycle.'

'You'll soon get the hang of it again,' he assured her and she hoped he was right.

Her first attempts at riding the bicycle were somewhat wobbly to say the least but she soon mastered it and within days she was a regular sight zooming about the town with her little black bag sitting in the basket and her cloak flying out behind her as she went from one patient to another.

Her first call one particular morning was to one of the children suffering with chickenpox in the courts. She was a very fragile little girl whom Holly had already called on a number of times but sadly no matter what she did the child was showing no signs of improvement and she was gravely concerned about her.

'How is she today?' Holly asked the child's mother as she entered the tiny cottage and placed her bag on the table. The woman was eking out a meagre amount of porridge amongst her other offspring and she nodded towards the truckle bed that stood against one wall.

'She was really poorly till about three this mornin' but then she dropped off, thankfully, an' I ain't heard a peep out of her since.'

'I see.' A cold finger played up and down Holly's spine as she approached the bed and she saw almost immediately that her worst fears had been realised. Without even touching her she could see that the little girl was dead. Her face was the colour of wax, making the red blister-like spots that covered her skin stand out in stark contrast.

Holly quietly felt for a pulse. The child was as cold as ice and her heart sank. She stood silently until the children were hungrily eating their food at the wobbly table that took up the centre of the room before calling the mother over to her.

'I'm so sorry, Mrs Land, but I'm afraid she's gone,' Holly told her gently. 'I think she must have died some hours ago.'

The woman wiped her hands on her apron and shook her head in shocked denial. 'But she can't have. She looked so peaceful when she went to sleep.' Yet even as the words left her lips she could see that Holly was telling her the truth and she began to cry, great racking sobs that shook her thin frame. 'It's my fault,' she choked. 'I should 'ave watched her more closely but when I thought she were sleepin' peacefully I snatched a couple of hours' sleep meself.'

Holly laid a hand on her arm. 'You mustn't blame yourself, you did all you could.' She gently pulled the worn sheet up across the child's face. Somehow that simple act made the little girl's death all the more real and the woman cried harder. 'Would you like me to call at the undertaker's and get him to come?' she asked then. 'I shall have to go and report her death to Matron before I go to any of my other patients. But I could lay her out for you, if you like?'

The woman shook her head vehemently. 'No . . . thank you, but I'd like to do that meself. It's the last thing I can do for her . . . but you could ask the undertaker to come.'

'Very well.' Holly lifted her bag but paused at the door to say, 'I'm so sorry, Mrs Land.' She went outside and climbed onto her bicycle and as she rode away there were tears on her cheeks. She had witnessed other deaths on the ward at the hospital but somehow when the grim reaper came for someone she had been personally caring for it was all the harder to bear.

Chapter Thirty-Eight

In October the government issued instructions on what to do in case of an air raid and suddenly the war seemed very real and everyone lived in fear of an invasion.

'It scares me to think of it,' Ivy said worriedly as she cradled Alice protectively to her.

Marcus smiled at her. She'd been quite surprised to see him when he had suddenly put in an appearance that morning, he usually visited of an evening after work but before very long she knew the reason why.

'Actually . . .' Looking uncomfortable, he shifted from foot to foot as she stared at him with prickles running up and down her spine. 'I, er . . . wanted you to be the first to know, after my father of course, that I joined up this morning. I shall be leaving for army training in a week's time.'

Ivy plonked down heavily onto the nearest chair. She felt as if all the air had been sucked out of her lungs, although she didn't know why she was so shocked. Wasn't this exactly what she had been fearing he would do for some time now?

'I see . . .' Her voice came out as a croak. 'And how does your father feel about it?'

Marcus lowered his head and shrugged. 'Well, obviously he's not happy about it but he says it's up to me. Nearly all the chaps from the hat factory have gone already. And the thing is, Ivy . . . I couldn't bear it if I was given a white feather. Try to understand, please.'

'I think I do understand.' A tear trickled down her cheek and Alice's plump little hand instantly came up to wipe it away. 'It's just that . . . I'll worry about you . . . and I'll miss you.'

'I'll miss you too.' He gently lifted Alice from her lap and put her on the floor and as the child tottered away he took Ivy in his arms. 'I think the world of you, Ivy, you must know that by now. And if it weren't for the fact that I might not come back I'd ask you to be my girl.'

Her heart swelled as she stared into his eyes. 'But I want to be your girl, and you will come back, you must!' she told him firmly.

He stared at her intently for a long moment then said, 'In that case, will you wait for me? And if I do come—'

'Shush, yer daft ha'porth an' kiss me,' she told him sternly, placing her finger on his lips. 'If we only have a week till you leave then we'd best make the best of it.'

Marcus was only too happy to do as he was told, and as his lips found hers her heart soared.

'So where will yer be goin'?' she asked eventually when they came up for air.

'I have to report to Budbrooke Barracks near Warwick then I'll be sent to train on the Isle of Wight. I shall be in the second battalion of the Royal Warwickshire Regiment.'

She nodded as she digested what he'd told her. 'But why didn't yer say somethin' about how yer felt about me before?' she asked as they sat with their arms about each other.

'Why didn't you?'

'Because I didn't think someone o' your class would look twice at a girl like me who has a baby born the wrong side o' the blanket.'

'And I was worried that you might still have feelings for Alice's father.' Placing his finger gently beneath her chin he tilted her face and kissed her again. 'And class doesn't even come into it. I knew you were the girl for me the moment I clapped eyes on you, and when I come home we'll be a family.'

'Is that a promise?'

He nodded solemnly.

'In that case I'll wait forever if need be.'

'And about time too,' Holly chuckled when Ivy told her the news later that evening. 'I was beginning to think you pair were never going to get around to admitting how you felt about each other. It's as plain as the nose on your face that you'll be perfect together.'

'Ooh hark at the pot calling the kettle black!' Ivy's eyes sparkled with mischief. 'An' what about you an' Dr Phillips?'

'We're still just good friends,' Holly said quickly. 'Which is just as well because he's talking of going to work in one of the field hospitals they've set up in France.' She swallowed nervously and went on, 'And actually, I'm thinking of going with him. I've been considering it for a while and when he said he was going it helped me to make up my mind. I've already spoken to Matron about it and she said that although she'll be sad to lose me she thinks it's a good idea. As it happens, there's a load of Red Cross nurses and doctors being shipped out there shortly before Christmas so I might go then. I was going to tell my mother and my grandfather first but you may as well know now.'

'Well, I'll be!' Ivy looked as if she had well and truly had the wind taken out of her sails. 'But won't it be really dangerous working close to the front?' It seemed that today was full of surprises, and not good ones!

'The hospitals aren't right on the front,' Holly pointed out. 'And there's such a desperate shortage of doctors and nurses out there that I feel I ought to go.'

'Then if you've made yer mind up I dare say there's nothin' I can say to change it, is there?' Ivy answered resignedly.

Holly shook her head. 'Not really, but don't worry, I shall be fine, and so will Marcus. Everyone is saying that the war will be over in no time then hopefully everyone can get back to some sort of normality.'

Ivy could only pray that she was right.

By November, word from the soldiers at the front was grim. They were being forced to spend hours in dirty trenches ankle-deep in icy water and frostbite had become a real danger. It was reported that men's toes were turning black and dropping off, and they were the lucky ones, for others, as infection set in, there was no hope. Men all along the front were dropping like flies and the rats that infested the trenches were feasting on their bodies. The field hospitals were struggling to cope with the number of casualties each day and mass graves were having to be dug for those who died at the enemy's hands.

The conditions that the men had to live in left a lot to be desired as well. Rows of tents with no protection from the bitter cold were their only shelter, not that it troubled them much. Usually by the time they returned to them after fighting they were too exhausted to care where they slept.

A continuous line of trenches full of weary soldiers now stretched from the North Sea to Switzerland but there had been little movement since the Germans had failed to reach Paris. It seemed that there was a stalemate amid the mud and barbed wire and nobody had yet developed a tactic to break the deadlock; the number of dead continued to rise, and every day now, the telegram boy could be seen furiously pedalling about the town delivering the news that someone's loved one had fallen in battle.

At home, the chancellor, David Lloyd George, announced in his war budget that income tax would be doubled to one shilling and sixpence in every pound in the year ahead, beer and tea duties would also go up to help pay for the war. Already there were shortages of certain goods that could no longer be shipped in from abroad and now everyone was having to tighten their belts. Claridge's Hotel in London had opened its doors to sewing guilds where women congregated to make clothes for the servicemen and other women were busily unpicking any old woollens they could get hold of and reknitting the wool into socks for the troops. Even the Boy Scouts had been given jobs to do, and they were placed on what was termed Special Service, which involved them guarding gas works, electric substations and telegraph lines, although as Holly's grandfather quite rightly pointed out, what were the boys supposed to do if they were under threat of being bombed?

Then in mid-December, soon after dawn, three German warships loomed out of the mist off the east coast and began shelling the towns of Scarborough, Whitby, Hartlepool and West Hartlepool causing the deaths of over a hundred civilians and injuring a further two hundred. British destroyers were deployed to drive off the German force but two of them were hit, resulting in the deaths of four seamen. During the raid over two hundred shells struck the towns, damaging homes, resort hotels and churches, and that evening West Hartlepool was in total darkness because of a direct hit on the local gasworks.

'It's so scary,' Ivy said as she read the newspaper report out to Holly's grandfather the next day. She lived in a constant state of anxiety now, fretting about what might happen to Alice if they were invaded and worrying if Marcus was safe. He had been to see her just once after doing his training before being shipped abroad and he had looked so handsome in his uniform that she couldn't help but be proud of him, although she had wept when he had to leave again. She knew that he was somewhere in France but had no idea what area because the letters she had received from him were so heavily censored that it was difficult to be sure. And now that Holly was insisting she wanted to work in a field hospital near the front, that would be one more for her to worry about!

'I thought when war was declared that everyone said it would be over by Christmas,' Ivy grumbled and Gilbert shook his head sadly.

'That is what everyone hoped but it clearly isn't going to happen now.' He sighed heavily and they both sat silently thinking of the effect the war might have on their loved ones.

'I just wish I were younger so I could go and do my bit for king and country,' he said regretfully.

Ivy shook her head. 'An' that'd be another one I'd have to fret about.' She smiled at him; it was hard to believe this was the same man who used to strike terror into her heart. He had changed so much and she'd grown fond of him; in fact, sometimes she forgot he was actually her employer. She knew that, like herself, he was dreading Holly going away and was hoping she'd have a change of heart, but at least Ivy could be there for him if Holly did leave. That at least gave her a little comfort.

The day after this exchange, Holly arrived home from the hospital with bad news for them.

'I shall be shipping out to France next week,' she informed her grandfather as they sat eating their dinner in the kitchen with Ivy, Alice and the cook. They rarely bothered to use the dining room now; it just meant another fire to light for Ivy and it was cosy in the kitchen.

Ivy almost choked on the mouthful of soup she was eating. 'But it's the week before Christmas! Surely you could at least wait till the New Year.'

'I suppose our soldiers fighting out there would like to be home for Christmas too,' she answered flatly, and Ivy flushed. Holly did have a point.

'Unfortunately we are needed as soon as possible so three of us from the hospital are sailing on a military ship from Portsmouth next Monday. There will be Harr . . . Dr Phillips, myself and another Red Cross nurse, Angela Dewis.'

Her grandfather, who had said nothing up to now, looked dismayed but all the same he raised a smile and told her solemnly, 'I'm very proud of you, my dear, more than you will ever know.'

The unexpected show of affection brought a lump to her throat and the rest of the meal was finished in silence as they all tried not to think of what might lie ahead for Holly.

Chapter Thirty-Nine

'Now, are you quite sure you have everything you need?' Emma asked her yet again on the morning of Holly's departure. She had come to see her off and was very tearful. She stared at the small carpet bag Holly had packed with a frown. There certainly didn't seem to be much in there.

'All I need is my clean underwear and nightwear, one civilian outfit, just in case, toiletries and my other uniform,' Holly assured her. 'I'm not going on holiday, Mother!'

Emma sniffed and Holly softened and leaned over to give her an affectionate hug.

'So can't I at least come to the station with you to see you off?'

Holly shook her head. 'I'd rather you didn't. I'm meeting the other two there and once the train gets to Portsmouth we have to get on the hospital ship that will take us over to France. I have a feeling it will be packed with doctors and nurses from all over the country.'

'Then this is it.' Emma couldn't prevent a tear from trickling down her cheek as Holly lifted her bag. 'Promise me you'll be careful and that you'll write regularly.'

'That goes without saying, of course I will.' Holly stood on tiptoe to kiss her grandfather's whiskery cheek.

'Just take care,' he said gruffly as she turned to the cook

and Ivy. Ivy was crying freely and even Mrs Bell had a tear in her eye.

'Look after him for me,' Holly said softly as she embraced Ivy, who nodded tearfully. She said the same to Mrs Bell, and then, after kissing her mother and baby Alice she hurried towards the door keen to get the goodbyes over with. She was feeling rather emotional herself.

She paused just once at the end of the street to take one last look at her home, wondering if she would ever see it again, then she straightened her back, swallowed the lump in her throat and strode purposefully towards the train station.

Harry and Angela were already there waiting for her and she saw at a glance that Angela, a pretty brunette with soft grey eyes, had been crying too. Harry, however, seemed in fine spirits. He was dressed in a navy pinstriped suit and a white shirt with a navy tie and looked very handsome.

'That's good timing,' he said. 'The train should be here in five minutes or so. That's if there haven't been any delays.' All the train stations had now removed the signs just in case the Germans invaded, but seeing as they were going all the way to the coast he didn't envisage them having a problem in knowing where to get off.

Immediately the train entered the station they found a carriage where they could sit together and soon discovered that over half the men on the train were in uniform. Some of them were returning to their units after a precious few days leave, others were returning after recovering from injuries they had sustained in battle. One young boy in particular, who looked to be no more than sixteen or seventeen years old, caught Holly's eye. He was huddled in a corner staring from the window and he looked terrified.

Harry had also noticed him and after a time he asked kindly, 'Off to join your unit are you, son?'

For a moment he thought that the lad wasn't going to answer but then he nodded. 'Yes, I was sent home after an injury but the doctors think I'm well enough to be shipped back out again now.'

Harry saw that the poor soul was on the verge of tears. 'Rough out there, is it?'

The boy gulped, making his Adam's apple bob up and down. 'It's like being in hell on the front. Just before I got shot in my leg I saw my best mate blown up by a mine . . . Scattered all over the field, he was!'

'I'm sorry.' Harry patted the lad's arm. There were beads of sweat on the boy's forehead now as the terrible memories rushed back and he was shaking. He might have recovered from his physical injuries but it was apparent that he was nowhere near ready to go back mentally. It made Harry wonder if the lad would survive in the frame of mind he was in, not that there was anything he could do about it.

'So will you be going back on one of the hospital ships?' Harry asked.

'Yes, they'll sail tonight when it gets dark.' The lad shuddered. 'There's less chance o' bein' attacked at sea that way. Then soon as we land they'll be loadin' the next lot of injured on board to come back here tomorrow night. Not that all of 'em will make it.' He shook his head. 'They're packed in like sardines in a can an' the medical staff do their best but they can't work miracles.'

Angela looked truly horrified. She had imagined it was going to be quite an adventure working with so many handsome doctors and soldiers but now, if what the young man was saying was anything to go by, she wasn't so sure. She quickly fumbled in her bag and grabbing her lipstick, she quickly applied a bright red layer in the hope of making herself feel better. Matron had strictly forbidden the nurses from wearing any sort of make-up while in uniform but she wasn't there to see her now, was she? Angela reasoned.

A couple of hours later Holly unpacked the sandwiches that Cook had insisted she bring and handed them round. Brian Hackett, as the young man eventually introduced himself, refused one politely and Harry grew even more concerned about him. He looked like a rabbit caught in a car's headlights.

'Why don't you let me have a word with the medical staff when we get to Portsmouth?' he suggested. 'I don't think you're quite ready to go back yet and they might listen to me.'

Brian shook his head. Admittedly he was scared at the thought of what was ahead of him but he was even more terrified of being shot as a coward. He'd seen that happen to one poor bloke who had lost his nerve and turned tail to run as they approached the enemy across a muddy field and he would never forget it for as long as he lived.

'Nah, thanks but I'll be all right,' he answered and Harry could only shrug. They washed the sandwiches down with a bottle of lemonade, another gift from Cook, then they sat in silence, dozing and staring out of the window as the train took them further and further away from home.

At last an announcement came over the tannoy, 'The next stop will be Portsmouth.'

They all began to gather their things together and when the train finally drew into the station, Brian lifted his kitbag, doffed his cap and disappeared into the throngs of soldiers on the platform.

'Poor little sod, I don't reckon he stands a dog's chance of surviving in the frame of mind he's in,' Harry commented but soon they were pushing their way through to the station exit and there was no more time for talking.

It soon became clear that they were not the only medical staff going abroad that day as they spotted several Red Cross uniforms dotted here and there.

'Probably being sent from different hospitals,' Harry said as they tried to flag down a cab. Eventually they found one that took them straight to the docks then they spent half an hour trying to find the ship they would be sailing on.

At last all their papers had been checked and they were directed up a gangplank.

'Where exactly are we going?' Holly asked one of the crew but he shook his head.

'I doubt you'll be told that, luvvie,' he answered. 'The least yer know the better.'

'But how will we be able to write home if we don't even know where we are?' she asked in dismay.

The seaman smiled at her. He had a daughter about Holly's age and he felt sorry for her. 'Don't get frettin' about that. You hand all your mail into a box at the hospital you end up in and it will be forwarded on for you. Then your family will be given a post box number they can write to.'

'I see.' Holly patted Angela's hand. She had turned a sickly shade of grey already and Holly feared the girl wasn't going to have a very good crossing if just the slight swaying of the gangplank could make her feel sick.

On deck, Harry was led off one way and the girls another and soon they found themselves in a cabin flanked with bunk beds on either side. There were no windows apart from a tiny porthole and the place stank abominably of dried blood from the injured soldiers who had occupied it before them. It was very cold too and their breath hung on the air.

'Seeing as we're going to be sailing through the night, I dare say we should try and get some sleep,' Holly suggested.

Angela eyed the bunks with distaste. Many of them had blood on the sheets but she supposed that the crew wouldn't have time to change them every time they brought a shipload of injured men home. They would probably be more concerned about getting the patients to hospital.

'Not exactly the Ritz, is it?' Angela said glumly, throwing her bag onto the nearest bunk. 'And what is that awful smell?'

'I think it's better that we don't know. But come on, let's see if there's anything to eat in the dining cabin. I'm starving.'

Angela groaned. Just the thought of food at the minute made her feel nauseous. 'No, you go,' she encouraged. 'I reckon I'll just wait here.'

'But it's stuffy down here,' Holly pointed out. 'At least up on deck you'd get some fresh air.'

Seeing the sense in what she said, Angela reluctantly agreed and they set off to explore.

Many parts of the ship were out of bounds, but they soon found the deck. 'I wonder if Harry's coming for something to eat?' Holly mused once they were out in the open. A thick sea mist had rolled in and already it was pitch-dark, although it was only late afternoon. It was icily cold too and both girls shivered as they asked one of the crew the way to the dining cabin. They'd quickly decided it was far too cold to stay outside longer than they had to.

At least it was warm in the dining cabin and on entering they saw Harry already deep in conversation with another man who had his back to them.

They approached the table with smiles on their faces but when the person Harry was speaking to turned to look at them Holly felt the colour drain out of her face. Richard!

'Ah, here you are,' Harry welcomed them. 'I believe you know my old friend Richard Parkin, don't you, Holly? Didn't you say you were both at the same hospital in London?'

'Y-yes I did,' Holly croaked. 'Hello, Richard.' Her hand rose to finger the ring he had given her which she still wore close to her heart.

He rose to greet her. 'How are you?' he asked formally, and Holly wanted to weep. He seemed so cold and stand-offish, but then what could she expect after the way she had ended their relationship so abruptly.

'I-I'm well.' She hurriedly looked away from his eyes, terrified that he might see the love she still felt for him reflected in them but she needn't have worried. He had already turned his attention to Angela, who was staring at him admiringly, and, holding out his hand, he formally introduced himself: 'Dr Richard Parkin.'

'Angela Dewis.' She shook his hand and he smiled at her. 'So it seems that we're all going to be working together.'

365

Angela simpered and held onto his hand a fraction longer than was necessary and Holly felt a surge of jealousy.

'I can recommend this beef stew,' Harry said, breaking the fraught atmosphere and Holly hurried away to order some for herself and Angela, glad of the chance to gather her wits. She couldn't believe what had happened and wondered how she'd ever be able to see and work with him every day without showing that she still loved him. And she did still love him! Seeing him again had only reinforced that fact. Still, knowing how hopeless it was, somehow she was going to have to harden her heart.

Some minutes later when she carried the two bowls of stew back to the table she found Richard and Angela deep in conversation and when she took a seat Harry put an arm possessively about her shoulders, making her squirm with embarrassment as she noticed Richard glance over at them.

'Come on now, get some of that inside you,' Harry said cheerily. 'I don't want my best girl being ill.'

Again she could feel Richard's eyes boring into her. What must he be thinking of her? Suddenly her appetite had gone and while the others made small talk and Angela flirted outrageously with Richard all she could do was push the food about the bowl. She felt thoroughly miserable, and this was only the beginning. From now on, for an indefinite period, she would probably see him daily. She had truly thought that she had managed to move on; had even considered a future with Harry for a time but now she knew that this could never happen. How to let Harry down gently was the problem.

Chapter Forty

'Crikey, that Dr Parkin is gorgeous, isn't he?' Angela sighed when the meal was over and they were heading back to their cabin.

Holly remained tight-lipped but it didn't really matter. Angela was clearly so besotted with the handsome doctor that she didn't even notice.

'I thought you were feeling queasy?' Holly said and Angela giggled.

'I was but he's so handsome I reckon he's taken my mind off it. But what time do we set off?'

'Should be any time now,' Holly answered, happy to get off the subject of Richard.

'In that case I think I'll try to get some sleep.' Angela yawned, tired after the long train journey. 'I'm going to keep my clothes on though.'

Despite the fact they had both wanted to come, they were painfully aware that many of the British military ships were being targeted out at sea and they were both feeling rather apprehensive. Angela had even written a letter, which she had hidden in her bag, to be delivered to her mother if she died – although she hadn't told Holly this. They removed their capes and crept under the blankets fully dressed and surprisingly they both dropped off to sleep in no time. The sudden movement of the ship brought Angela springing awake some time later and her face instantly turned a sickly shade of green.

'I reckon we're moving,' she squeaked.

'W-what?' Holly was awake now too, conscious of the ship rolling as it set out to sea.

'I don't feel well,' Angela bleated and Holly hurriedly fetched a bowl from by the sink and handed it to her. It was just as well she did because seconds later Angela brought up everything she had eaten that day.

'Oh Lord, I'm dying,' she groaned and Holly couldn't help but smile.

'No, you're not dying, you're just a bit seasick that's all. Once we get out to sea and the ship stops rolling so much you'll probably be fine.'

Holly took back her words when halfway across the Channel they sailed into a storm and suddenly the boat was pitching dangerously from side to side. They had to grip the sides of their bunks to prevent themselves from being thrown over the edge and Angela was almost hysterical.

'If the bloody Germans don't sink us this storm surely will,' she wailed. Her eyes were huge with terror in her pale face but Holly couldn't even manage to stand to comfort her without being thrown about the cabin like a rag doll.

'The crew are very experienced,' she said weakly. 'And the storm's bound to blow over soon.' But Angela didn't hear a word she said. She was too busy retching and moaning over the bowl.

Which was probably just as well, because though she'd tried to sound confident, Holly was just as frightened as Angela and the constant pitching and rolling was making her feel sick as well. Each time the ship crested the treacherous waves it would then drop like a stone and whenever it did this, both girls felt as if they had left their stomachs up in the air.

They were within sight of the French harbour early the next morning when the storm died away as quickly as it had started but by then both girls were exhausted and looking far from well.

Holly tentatively rolled to the edge of the bunk and placed her foot on the floor, relieved to find that she could stand again, albeit on very wobbly legs, without being thrown about.

When the ship's foghorn sounded she breathed a sigh of relief. 'We must be nearly there,' she told Angela but the girl was still feeling too sick to care. 'Let's go up and see if there's any sign of Harry and Richard on deck,' she suggested, feeling the need to feel fresh air on her face, but Angela shook her head.

'No you go . . . I'll stay here.'

'Are you sure you'll be all right?' When Angela nodded Holly snatched up her cape and headed for the steep, narrow wooden stairs that led to the deck. If anything the fog was even denser than it had been the day before and she suddenly had the eerie feeling that she was the only person left on board. Warily she felt for the rails and peered ahead with narrowed eyes but she could see no more than a few feet in front of her. In addition to this, the wind was icy so after a few minutes she turned to go back to the comparative warmth of the cabin only to find Richard standing just a few feet away from her.

'Oh . . . I didn't see you there.' Her heart was thumping wildly and she hoped that he wouldn't be able to hear it. 'That was some storm, wasn't it? Angela's been ill for most of the way.'

'And yourself?'

'I'm all right, thank you.' She stifled the urge to reach out and touch him before saying, 'I, er . . . ought to get back to check she's all right though.'

'Of course.' He stood aside and made no attempt to stop her as she scuttled past like a rat with its tail on fire. I've got to stop behaving like this every time I see him, she scolded herself, but she had the feeling that it was going to be easier said than done.

Angela was sitting on the side of the bunk looking slightly better when Holly arrived back at the cabin. 'Perhaps some tea would settle your stomach a little. Would you like me to fetch you a cup?' Holly suggested.

'No, thanks.'

'Then in that case we'd better get ready to go ashore. I don't think we're far off now.'

Sure enough, half an hour later a small tug guided the military ship into the harbour and soon they heard the engine stop, followed by the sounds of the crew manhandling the gangplank into position.

'Thank goodness for that,' Angela said. 'I can't wait to feel my feet on solid ground again and one thing's for sure, when this damned war is over I won't be putting my name down for any cruises. How anyone could derive any pleasure from being at sea is totally beyond me.'

There was a tap on the door and one of the crew called that they were to report up on deck.

Angela followed Holly on legs that felt like jelly and when they arrived they found Harry waiting for them, although Holly was both relieved and dismayed to find that there was no sign of Richard.

'I reckon Richard might be being posted to another hospital,' Harry informed her as he saw her glancing about and she had the uncanny feeling that he could read her mind.

'Oh, I hadn't really thought about it,' she answered nonchalantly but she had the feeling that she hadn't fooled him one bit. They were surrounded by swarms of nurses and doctors from other hospitals all eager to disembark but Holly noticed that the mood was sombre now that they had all almost reached their destination. It was one thing to feel brave before the event but quite another now that they were faced with the reality of war.

Eventually they were led down the gangplank like a herd of cattle and at the bottom two military men with clipboards asked them for their names. They were then pointed towards the transport that would take them to the various hospitals.

'Farthing, Dewis, Parkin and Phillips, truck number three,' the soldier told them and they battled their way through the throngs of people on the dock. Holly's heart was racing now that she knew Richard was to join them, although outwardly she appeared calm. They clambered awkwardly into the back of the trucks and squatted on the hard wooden benches that ran along either side.

'Crikey, I hope we don't go over any bumps if we have to sit here for long,' Angela grumbled. 'These seats are as hard as rocks. I bet my bum will be bruised by the time we get wherever we're going!'

Holly said nothing, she was too intent on trying to get warm but when Richard climbed in and sat beside her suddenly she could feel her cheeks flaming. Harry was sitting the other side of her and she hardly dared turn her head because he was watching her intently. Another couple of Red Cross nurses joined them shortly after and at last they set off. They had no idea where they were going and could see nothing because of the large canvas that covered the back of the truck. Angela moaned and groaned as they bounced up and down on the hard wooden benches and another young nurse was crying softly. Eventually the town roads gave way to what felt like country lanes and they had to cling to the edges of their seats and dig their heels in to prevent themselves being thrown off.

'Bloody hell, this is torture!' Angela complained as they rattled along. They seemed to have been going forever when, far off in the distance, above the sound of the engine, Holly heard what sounded like gunshots.

'We must be getting close to the hospital. It won't be all that far away from the front,' Harry told her solemnly. The sound was enough to make even Angela stop moaning as they tried to imagine what it must be like for the people fighting. At last the truck slowed and stopped with a grating of gears and the canvas was drawn aside. It was mid-morning by now but the sky was grey and overcast and a cold drizzle was falling.

'Nurses' quarters that way, doctors' that way,' a young lieutenant guided them.

Holly and Angela set off, careful to keep to the duckboards that seemed to be floating in a sea of mud. A row of large tents was before them and Holly realised with a sinking feeling that this must be their accommodation.

'It's pretty grim, isn't it?' Angela hissed and Holly could only nod in agreement. They found a young nurse waiting for them in the first tent and after ticking their names off her list she told them, 'You're both in number three. Choose whichever beds you like. You'll see which are already taken.'

Once again they set off across the duckboards and on entering the tent Angela groaned. It was even worse than she had imagined it would be, completely lacking in comfort save for a stove which stood in the centre of the tent. Its chimney went up through a hole in the roof and there were a number of logs piled at the side of it so she quickly opened the door and threw one on.

'Looks like we're responsible for keeping that going,' she said miserably, making her way to the bed nearest the fire. Even there it had little effect on the cold. They looked about and found a screen in one corner behind which was a jug and bowl and a number of faded towels.

'And this must be where they expect us to wash,' Angela snorted in disgust. 'But what do we do for hot water and how do we take a bath?'

'I've no idea,' Holly admitted, dropping her bag on the bed next to Angela's. 'But let's go and find where we eat now. I'm hungry after all that jolting about and I'd do anything for a cup of tea.'

Holding their capes closely about them they stepped out of the tent and asked a young soldier who was passing by, 'Could you tell us where we can get something to eat, please?'

He pointed across a patchwork of duckboards. 'That's the mess over there. The cook's usually got something warm on the go.'

They thanked him and made their way cautiously towards it, very aware of the gunfire in the distance. 'Blimey, you're taking your life in your hands trying to get across these things without slipping,' Angela commented.

'Hmm, and I wouldn't fancy our chances if we were to slip into the mud,' Holly agreed.

The mess, as the young soldier had referred to it, turned out to be another, larger, tent and as they entered, the warmth from the stoves positioned to one side of the tent met them. There were tables and chairs arranged in two lines down the length of the room and weary, filthy men with dull eyes were sitting at some of them sipping hot, sweet tea.

'Ah, newcomers I presume,' the cook greeted them, his brown eyes twinkling. He was enormous in both girth and height and seemed friendly.

'Yes, we are,' Holly admitted. 'And we've travelled through the night to get here so we're quite hungry.'

'Then you've come to the right place,' he told them cheerfully as one particularly loud explosion echoed around the tent, making them start. 'How about a nice plateful of my cottage pie? There's nothing like it on a cold day like today.'

Both girls nodded, their eyes huge as they tried to ignore

the sounds. Minutes later they were seated at a table with piled plates and steaming mugs of tea in front of them. The food was plain and simple but surprisingly tasty.

'I wonder what we should do next?' Angela mused.

Holly wasn't sure either. 'I dare say someone will come and tell us, but let's go back to the tent when we've eaten and wait there.'

Some more of the newly recruited nurses were drifting in by now and they all smiled at each other. When the two girls had finished they made their way back along the duckboards and managed to find the right tent eventually. The trouble was they all looked exactly the same from the outside so they wondered how they would find their way back to their own tent in the dark as there didn't appear to be any lights. They were both beginning to wonder what they had let themselves in for and home suddenly felt like a terribly long way away.

Chapter Forty-One

Some other newly arrived nurses were also in the tent when they finally found it, along with a sister in a navy-blue uniform with a starched white cap, although she looked rather grimy to say the least.

'Names?'

'Farthing and Dewis, Sister.'

'Ah yes, here you are.' She ticked their names off the list in front of her before telling them, 'I'm Sister Flynn, and you two are to come to the hospital with me now. The rest of you, get settled in, have something to eat and I shall return for you shortly.'

They followed her silently along what felt like miles of muddy duckboards, then turning a corner they saw an enormous tent ahead of them. This, they rightly guessed, must be the hospital.

As they followed her inside they both suddenly felt as if they had been transported into hell. Rows and rows of beds stretched down either side of the tent and in each one were men with wounds of varying degrees of severity. Some of them were rambling and crying like babies, others lay still, their faces deathly white, their eyes dead. Nurses were flitting about carrying bloodied bandages and bedpans, looking exhausted themselves.

'You two.' The sister signalled to the two nearest nurses.

'Get yourselves off for some rest now. You've both just done fourteen-hour shifts. Report back for duty at six o'clock in the morning.'

The nurses nodded, only too keen to do as they were told. 'Now, you two.' Sister Flynn turned her attention back to Holly and Angela. 'You will each be in charge of the beds on one side of the ward. Do whatever you can to make the patients as comfortable as possible and report to me immediately if you have any concerns. They will all need a bed bath and possibly bedpans. I will advise you on what medication each of them needs later in the day. The sluice is through that canvas there. You'll find it somewhat primitive compared to what you've been used to at home but as you'll soon discover, out here we can only do the best we can with the facilities available to us. ' She pointed to a flap in the wall. 'You'll find all the patients' notes on the end of their beds. Now run along.'

The girls instantly separated, Holly to the right, Angela to the left. Neither of them quite sure what they should be doing.

The first patient Holly came to was a very young man with a cage covering his bottom half. His eyes were closed and sweat stood out on his brow. She quickly read his notes and discovered that he had trodden on a landmine which had resulted in him having to have the whole of one leg amputated and half of the other one below his knee. He was marked urgent which meant that he would be sent back to a hospital in England on the first hospital ship that had a bunk available, if he survived that long. He had developed an infection and was now seriously ill and Holly's heart went out to him. He

377

was so young but even if he did survive she wondered what sort of future was in store for him now? He would never be able to run or dance again and it seemed such a pointless waste. Even now the distant sound of gunshots could clearly be heard and she wondered if there was ever any respite from it. With a sigh she quickly went to find the trolley containing everything she would need to bath him. It was only when she was about to begin that she realised there were no curtains about the bed. There was clearly no room for modesty here so she washed him as quickly and gently as she could and throughout it all he didn't even open his eyes. Slowly she worked her way along the row, offering bedpans and comfort where she could.

'This must be what it's like in a bloody slaughterhouse,' Angela whispered to her when they both finally reached the end of the rows. 'And that constant noise in the background is giving me a headache. What must it be like for those fighting on the front? It's a wonder the noise doesn't deafen them.'

'If you think this is bad now just wait till it gets dark and everything goes quiet,' a nurse who had been working with them said in the sluice room, which stunk to high heaven. It was actually nothing more than rows of buckets that they emptied the bedpans into until someone had time to empty them into a cesspit. The bedpans were then rinsed out under a single cold-water tap. 'At the end of each day the stretcher-bearers go out onto the field to bring in the dead and injured and that's when the work really starts. The doctors usually end up working through the night operating on those who are still alive, poor sods.'

Angela shuddered at the picture she was conjuring up. 'And what happens to the dead?'

'The lucky ones are transported to a graveyard where their resting place is marked with a simple wooden cross bearing their name. If there are too many of them they have to go into a communal grave. Obviously the corpses can't be kept for too long, although it's not so bad at this time of year when it's cold. But in the summer it's awful and the rats have a feast.'

Angela's face was bleached of colour again so Holly asked quickly. 'And do we ever get any time off?'

The nurse grinned ruefully. 'Now and again but not very often. The last time we got a night off me and some of the other nurses went to a dance in the nearest French village hall but the trouble was none of us could speak much French so it wasn't too successful.'

'I can speak French.'

Angela stared at Holly. 'You never told me that!'

'Well, you never asked me. I had a private tutor for many years, who refused to speak to me in anything but French as a way of making sure I learned to speak it fluently. But come on, we'd better get back onto the ward and see what sister wants us to do next. We don't want to get into her bad books on our first day.' They all trooped back and soon they were busy administering tablets and medication under the sister's supervision.

It was early evening and pitch-black when Holly suddenly noticed the silence save for the moans of the patients.

'That's it for another day by the sounds of it,' the nurse they had spoken to earlier, who introduced herself as Laura, said. 'Give it another half an hour and you won't know if you're on your arse or your elbow we'll be that busy.' She wiped her hands down her blood-smeared apron and hurried away to fetch a bowl for one of the patients who was hanging over the side of the bed being violently sick.

Looking around, Holly noticed that the young man she had bathed earlier was crying out so, rushing across to him, she gripped his hand and gently stroked the damp hair back from his brow. His eyes were open but she could see that he was very feverish.

'Tell me . . . mam . . . that I'm sorry,' he appealed. 'She didn't want . . . me to join up but I thought I . . . knew best an' I wanted her to be proud o' me.'

'I'm sure she is but just rest now and save your strength,' Holly soothed but his head moved from side to side. Realising that he was in a bad way she ran to find the sister who came back to the bed with her and took his pulse. She drew Holly slightly away from the bed and whispered, 'Poor soul won't last the night. Will you sit with him? I hate to think of any of the patients dying without someone by their side. Just offer what comfort you can.'

'Of course.' Holly went to find a chair and after placing it at the side of his bed she gently took his hand.

He turned his head to her to ask, 'Will you write a letter . . . for me. To me girl? And see that she gets it?'

'Of course I will.' Holly had a lump the size of an egg in her throat as she went off in search of pen and paper, which the sister supplied her with.

'Right, what would you like me to write?' she asked.

He licked his lips, and began haltingly:

380

Dear Jeannie,

I just want you to know that after I met you I always knew that you were the girl for me. Remember how we used to talk about the children we would have one day? Two boys and two girls? And the little cottage in the country we were going to buy? Sadly I don't think that will happen now. I've lost me legs and even if I come home I wouldn't want you to be tied to a cripple for the rest of your life. So what I want you to do now is put away the ring I gave you and when the war is over settle down with someone who will love you as much as I do. Please go and see me mam and tell her that I love her, and me brothers and sisters, and never forget that I love you with all me heart. You were the best thing that ever happened to me so be happy, sweetheart, and have a good life,

All my love forever, Tom xxx

By the time the letter was finished tears were rolling down Holly's cheeks. What was left of his legs was clearly terribly infected and Holly was experienced enough to realise that the sister was right, there was little hope for him now. She lay his letter aside and after drying her tears she asked him cheerfully, 'So, what is your Jeannie like then? Is she pretty?'

A smile instantly lit his pallid face. 'Oh yes, the prettiest girl I've ever seen. Her hair . . . is like a coppery colour . . . and her eyes . . . are the colour of bluebells . . .' His breath was laboured but even so, talking about his fiancée had clearly cheered him. 'She comes up to just below me shoulder . . . or at least she did . . . till I lost me legs . . . and she's kind

. . . so kind . . .' His eyes gently closed but Holly sat on holding his hand and watching his chest rise and fall errat- ically, while all around her the ward was in mayhem. Just as Laura had predicted, stretcher-bearers were bringing in the wounded from the battlefield now, passing through the ward she was on to others beyond where the weary surgeons were waiting to assess who needed to go to theatre first.

At some point Angela came to find her. 'Sister says we can go now. There are some more nurses here ready to take over.'

Holly shook her head. 'You go on. I'm staying with Tom here for a while longer.'

'But it's gone nine o'clock.'

'It doesn't matter,' Holly said stubbornly, so with a shrug of her shoulders Angela went off to try and find the mess in the dark for a hot drink and something to eat before she went to bed.

It was just after midnight and Holly was desperately trying to keep herself awake when she suddenly became aware that Tom's grip on her hand had weakened, and as she glanced at his face she saw that his eyes were staring and there was a smile on his face. Sister Flynn, who was just going off duty herself after a very long day, paused at the end of the bed.

'I . . . I think he's gone,' Holly said sadly.

The woman nodded. 'Yes he has, but hopefully thanks to you he went thinking happy thoughts. Look how peaceful he is now and the smile on his face. Close his eyes, nurse, and I'll get someone to take him out to the morgue. Leave the letter at the nurses' station and I'll make sure it's forwarded on to his loved one in the morning.'

She patted Holly's shoulder. 'Well done, Farthing. I can see you're going to be an asset. Now go and get some rest.'

Holly nodded and left feeling heartsore at such a pointless waste of life.

⚜

'It's hard to believe it will be Christmas Day tomorrow, isn't it?' Angela said wistfully as they were getting dressed ready to go on duty on Christmas Eve morning. 'My mum will be getting everything ready before all the family go around tomorrow.' They had both taken it in turns washing in icy-cold water behind the screen to one side of the tent.

'I know what you mean,' Holly admitted. 'I think my family will all be having dinner at my grandfather's house. There'll be a big turkey with Cook's home-made stuffing and crispy roast potatoes and—'

'Oh, please don't say any more,' Angela groaned. 'You're making my mouth water!'

Holly giggled. 'Well at least we have a chicken dinner to look forward to. One of the Frenchmen in town who owns a smallholding gave some chickens to the cook. I've seen him here a few times talking to one or another of the officers although I have no idea what they could be discussing. But anyway, we'd best be going. Sister won't like it if we're late reporting for duty.'

'I wonder sometimes if that woman is even human.' Angela pulled her cloak across her shoulders. It was bitterly cold outside and it wasn't much better in the tent. Some of the other nurses were sleeping, having come off night duty, so the girls slipped out of the tent as quietly as they could and

383

set off across the duckboards. There had been a sharp frost during the night and now the mud beneath their feet was treacherously slippery.

'It's a wonder one of us doesn't end up in hospital ourselves,' Angela grumbled but then she spotted Harry and Richard heading towards them from the doctors' quarters and she instantly brightened. Holly, on the other hand, felt uncomfortable. It was the first time they had seen either of them since they had arrived and she'd been hoping it would stay that way.

Harry's eyes instantly settled on Holly and he smiled as he quickened his steps. Angela meanwhile was batting her eyelashes at Richard, although he showed no reaction whatsoever.

'Ah, here you are.' Harry seemed so genuinely pleased to see her that Holly cringed, especially as she was aware that Richard was watching them closely. 'I was wondering when I was going to see you. We've been so busy in theatre that we've had no time for anything but catching a nap here and there. We've been told that a truce has been called for tomorrow, though, so perhaps we could have dinner together in the mess?'

'I er . . . don't know what Sister's got planned for me,' Holly hedged uncomfortably.

'Well, apart from the ward rounds there won't be any casualties brought in tomorrow so I'm happy to wait until you're free,' Harry told her persistently. She could feel Richard's eyes boring into her and felt the colour rise in her cheeks.

'I'll let you know when Sister's told us what hours we'll

be working,' she answered then scuttled away like a frightened deer.

'Here, what did you have to shoot off like that for?' Angela said crossly when they were out of earshot.

Embarrassed, Holly shrugged and hurried towards the ward.

The casualties brought in from the field at the end of the previous day had been particularly high so it was late evening before Holly finally made it to the mess to grab something to eat. Angela had been assigned to another ward so she hadn't seen her all day and there was no sign of her now. However, Holly's heart sank when she saw Richard sitting alone at a table. Deciding to pretend that she hadn't seen him, she went to the counter where cold food had been laid out for them and loaded some sandwiches and a hot drink onto a tray. She'd intended to creep to one side of the room but she had carried her meal no more than a few steps when Richard's voice halted her.

'Won't you join me?'

She gulped before forcing a weak smile. 'Oh yes . . . yes, of course. I didn't see you there,' she lied as she reluctantly placed her tray down on his table.

She sipped at her drink as silence settled between them until he eventually asked, 'So, how have you been?'

She was suddenly aware of the mess she must look. Some of her hair had slipped from beneath her cap and her apron was bloodstained. 'As well as could be expected, I suppose. Although I think I'd give anything to wash my hair and have a hot bath. I've forgotten what it's like to feel clean.' She was painfully aware of the ring she wore on a chain close to her heart and wondered what Richard would think if he could see it. 'But how are you doing?' They were behaving like polite strangers and anyone seeing them would never have guessed that they had once meant the world to each other.

'About the same as you.' He shook his head sadly. 'It's like working in a slaughterhouse. I lost two young men on the operating table tonight. Some Christmas it's going to be for their families when they receive their telegram.'

She nodded in agreement. At least they were on safe ground while they didn't discuss their personal lives. She noticed that he had finished his meal but now the sandwiches she had chosen tasted like sawdust and she was having problems swallowing them.

'Harry tells me you're having Christmas dinner in here with him tomorrow.'

'I . . . didn't say that exactly,' she answered, almost choking on a mouthful of tea.

'Well, he seems to think you are. In fact he's more than a little fond of you,' he said and she thought she detected a touch of sarcasm in his voice. But then why wouldn't he be angry with her? she reasoned. They had thought they would be spending the rest of their lives together until she'd dropped him like a hot brick. She could think of nothing to say and after a few more minutes he pushed his chair back and rose from the table.

'I'll wish you goodnight then. Have a good Christmas, Holly . . . or at least as good as you can out here.' Then he was gone and as she watched him stride away her heart broke afresh and she had to blink rapidly to stop the tears that were threatening to fall.

Chapter Forty-Two

Both Holly and Angela were given the whole afternoon off when they reported to the ward the next morning. It was the first day since Holly had been there that there was no gunfire in the background and it felt unnaturally quiet. The staff had done what they could to make the ward look festive with holly and mistletoe scattered here and there, and as they went about their duty that morning more than one of the men offered a kiss to the nurses, holding up little sprigs of mistletoe and Holly was happy to oblige. As they were confined to bed, some with horrific injuries, and so far away from their loved ones it seemed the least she could do. The patients too were going to be served with a Christmas dinner and many of them were looking forward to it.

'I bet it won't be as nice as my Ada makes, though,' one man, whose head was swathed in bandages, commented, as Holly gave him a bed bath. She was so used to doing it now that it no longer embarrassed her. In fact, as she'd commented to Angela, 'When you've seen one, you've seen them all.'

'Even if it isn't, it won't be long till you're home now,' Holly comforted him. 'Sister has you down for a place on the first hospital ship available. I wouldn't be surprised if you weren't home to see the New Year in with her.'

He gave a sigh of pure joy as he thought of it and after making him comfortable again, Holly moved on to the next patient. She had almost finished washing him when Sister appeared at the head of the ward to inform them all with a smile, 'I'm delighted to say we shall be having a choir of French carol singers in to entertain you all later this afternoon. It's very generous of them to give up their time and I hope you'll enjoy it.'

There was a short burst of applause from the men and Holly was feeling almost happy until she reached the next bed and saw at a glance that there was something very wrong with the young man lying there. He had been brought in the day before with horrific burns to his face, he'd also had to have his right arm amputated from the elbow down but now he was lying strangely still and Holly knew immediately that he had passed away. She checked his pulse to be sure before hurrying off to inform the sister who would have his body moved to the morgue as discreetly as possible.

'The poor boy. It seems that the grim reaper has no respect even for religious days,' the sister commented sadly as they stared down at him before gently pulling the sheet up over his face. 'Go about your business, Nurse Farthing. I shall see to this.' And so Holly did but her heart was heavy. That young man had been someone's son or possibly husband. Life could be very cruel, she pondered.

By lunchtime Holly's jobs were done and the sister excused her for the rest of the day. 'You've worked tirelessly, over and above what was expected of you ever since you arrived,' the woman told her with a rare smile. 'So you certainly deserve a few hours off.'

Holly smiled and set off back to the tent hoping to tidy herself up before going for lunch in the mess. Angela was already there and had boiled the kettle that stood on top of the stove and washed her hair. Now she was sitting in front of the fire wearing just her underskirt, rubbing it dry with a towel.

'Ooh, not as good as a nice hot bath admittedly but I don't half feel better for a thorough strip wash, and in warm water too.' She grinned.

Her hair was shining as it dried and with her cheeks glowing Holly thought how pretty she looked. She had clearly set her cap at Richard and Holly wondered how she would feel if he responded to her advances. But there was no time to ponder on that now because Angela had thoughtfully boiled the kettle for her, so she too disappeared behind the screen to wash herself and her hair.

When both girls were ready they set off for the mess.

'It would have been nice if we could have worn our civvies,' Angela commented as they cautiously picked their way across the duckboards once more. 'But at least we had a clean uniform to put on.' The uniforms were washed and ironed by a Frenchwoman in the nearby village and luckily the clean ones had been delivered back to them the day before. Unfortunately, as they only had two of each item, they often had to go onto the ward in blood-spattered uniforms but at least they felt clean today. The mess had a festive air about it too thanks to some bottles of home-made wine another villager had donated. The meal was surprisingly tasty: succulent chicken, crispy roast potatoes and a mountain of vegetables with thick gravy, and if either of the girls were feeling homesick and thinking of their families back home neither of them mentioned it. Everyone was in the same boat here so all they could do was make the best of it. They had almost finished eating when Richard and Harry appeared and after fetching their meals from a rosy-cheeked cook they joined them at their table.

'Merry Christmas,' Harry said brightly, raising his glass of wine. Then feeling in his pocket he produced a small, beautifully wrapped package which he passed across the table to Holly as Richard looked silently on. 'I bought this before we came here,' he told her. 'And as you can't go all the way back to England to change it, I hope you like it.'

Holly blushed to the roots of her hair wishing that the ground would open up and swallow her. 'B-but I haven't got you anything,' she protested.

Harry waved aside her concerns as he lifted his knife and fork and tucked into his dinner. 'I didn't expect anything, so just open it, will you?'

Holly was all fingers and thumbs as she undid the ribbons to reveal a long, slender box. She sprang the lid and gasped as she stared down at a pretty gold bracelet. 'B-but I can't accept this,' she said uncomfortably. 'It's far too much.'

Harry grinned. 'Don't worry about that. Do you like it?'

'Well, if she doesn't, I'll have it.' Angela giggled enviously.

'Er . . . why don't you keep it safe for me until the war is over,' Holly suggested tactfully. 'It's not as if I can go anywhere to wear it out here is it?'

Harry looked hurt and she felt dreadful. It was a very kind thought but she wished that he hadn't done it.

'I suppose I could if that's what you want but are you sure you like it?'

'Who wouldn't?' Holly thrust it back at him, more

forcefully than she meant to, and reluctantly he tucked it back into his pocket as Angela stared at her as if she had gone mad. There was no way she would ever have given back such a beautiful present. There was an influx of officers and nurses then and thankfully the atmosphere relaxed as they all tried to make the best of things.

'So what are you girls planning to do with yourselves this afternoon?' Harry asked when they'd finished eating and drinking. Holly had drunk two glasses of wine by then and was feeling quite tiddly.

'We don't have a lot of choice, do we?' Angela pointed out. 'So we may as well go and listen to the carol singers. Cook was saying he's made them all some mulled wine and mince pies.'

They all headed back to the hospital and within minutes of them getting there the carol singers arrived and, spreading themselves down the centre of the ward, they began to sing some well-loved carols. Everyone smiled when they realised that they were singing them in French, but even so those that were able to soon joined in in English and the air echoed with the sweet strains of music. There were about twelve singers in total, ranging from a little girl who looked to be about ten years old who had the voice of an angel to an elderly man who Holly judged must be at least eighty. The men were wearing berets and warm jackets while the women wore gaily coloured scarves and shawls. It was when they began to sing Holly's all-time favourite carol, 'Silent Night' that she suddenly stepped up to join them and began to sing along in perfect French. Her pure voice floated on the air and Angela's eyes almost popped out of her head.

'Blimey . . . she's good, isn't she?' she whispered to Richard who was watching Holly closely and he nodded never taking his eyes off her for a second. He wasn't the only one and when the carol was finished there was a round of applause from patients and staff alike.

'That was very impressive,' Harry told her when she rejoined them.

Holly merely smiled as Richard watched her with a thoughtful expression on his face. Shortly after she saw him speaking to one of the Frenchmen who had been in the choir and she recognised him as the one she had seen about the hospital from time to time speaking to officers, although she didn't really give it much thought.

The next day it was business as usual and when Holly woke to the sound of distant gunfire she silently groaned. Yet more blood would be spilled today.

That evening, amongst the many wounded admitted to the hospital was a young man who was delirious.

'Get the rats off me!' he screamed in terror as Holly was trying to bathe his wounds to see the extent of them. He was lashing out blindly at something only he could see, poor lad, and the man in the next bed shook his head sadly. After removing his boots Holly found that all his toes were black with frostbite and she knew instantly that they would all have to be removed if he were to stand a chance of survival.

'It's the rats in the trenches he'll be talking about,' the patient in the next bed told her. 'Most of the trenches are ankle-deep in freezing water and the rats swim along them, bold as you like, feeding on the fallen.'

Holly looked horrified.

'Trouble is, there's no chance to remove the bodies till ceasefire and by then the rats have had a feast. It's the same on the field. There's as many horses as men fallen so the rats round here are as big as cats.'

Holly continued to undress the young man, avoiding his wildly flailing arms. When she'd finally stripped him to his long johns she said to the man who'd been talking to her, 'I'd best get the sister. I think he'll need to go to theatre as soon as possible.'

The sister agreed with her when she came to examine him. 'Prepare him now, and make sure he doesn't have anything to eat or drink,' she told Holly soberly. 'I'll go and put his name on Dr Parkin's list. He's doing an arm amputation at present.'

Richard's name set her heart pounding but she calmly did as she was asked and just under an hour later the young man was wheeled away to theatre, still desperately swatting at the rats he imagined were crawling over him.

Each day was much the same now. One victim after another was brought in after dark and sometimes the doctors had to work all through the night to deal with them. Two weeks after Christmas, just when Holly felt that she couldn't take much more, her spirits were lifted when she received two letters from home, one from her mother and one from Ivy. They were given to her as she arrived at the hospital so she stuffed them into her apron pocket and looked forward to reading them at lunchtime.

When she finally sat down in the mess later that day, she opened Ivy's first.

Dear Holly,

I hope this finds you well, as we all are. Alice is still growing like a weed. I swear this child has hollow legs because we can't seem to fill her up. I've had a letter from Marcus and thank God he is managing to cope. He's somewhere in France but I'm not exactly sure where. Your grandfather asked me to send you his love and apologises for not writing himself but he says you know he's never been much of a letter-writer. Your mother and Mr Dolby and the children all came here for Christmas dinner and it was lovely although we all missed you very much. I worry about you all the time and can only imagine how awful it must be for you out there. The horror stories we read in the papers scare your mam to death and she's constantly on edge, only happy when she gets a letter from you. Still, God willing this awful war will be over soon. So much for everyone saying it would be over for Christmas, eh? They've been taking all the horses from the town recently and shipping them out to the front, poor things. There's hardly one to be seen now except the old ones. Cook sends her love and says to tell you that soon as you come home she'll cook you your favourite apple pie and custard. I can't wait to see you again. Is there any chance of you getting leave soon? Please take care of yourself, and may God keep you safe. Please write as soon as you can and know that we are all thinking of you.

Your loving friend,
Ivy xxx

Holly sniffed back tears and gave a wry smile. The letter was beautifully written following all the evening classes Ivy had done in London. She then returned the letter to its envelope and opened the one from her mother. It said much the same as Ivy's and a wave of terrible homesickness swept through her. Despite this, Holly didn't regret coming; she was needed here, and her only regret was that by some cruel twist of fate she and Richard had landed up at the same place and it was painful to be so close to him. Still, this was nothing compared to what the injured were going through so, like Ivy, all she could do for now was pray that the damned war would soon be over.

Towards the end of January Sister Flynn pulled her to one side one evening and whispered, 'I need to speak to you, Nurse Farthing . . . in private. Could you come to my room in half an hour?'

'Of course, Sister.' Holly frowned as the woman walked away, wondering what she might have done to warrant her wishing to speak to her alone, but then one of her patients called out for her and rushing to his side she tried not to think of it. At least she didn't have long to wait to find out what the sister wanted, her but she was intrigued and slightly apprehensive all the same.

When she reported to Sister Flynn's office shortly after, she was surprised to find Richard and the Frenchman who she had seen about the hospital also there.

'Come in,' Sister invited and after glancing at Richard she began, 'I am going to put something to you because I feel of all my nurses you are the most hardworking and the most trustworthy, but I want to make it clear that if you don't wish to do what I'm proposing you are under absolutely no obligation.'

Holly nodded and swallowed. Whatever it was it sounded serious.

'The thing is . . . we have, shall we say, a "safe house" for our injured airmen who have been shot down behind the enemy lines. Monsieur Le'Fete here has a smallholding where he keeps them safe until they are well enough to be brought here. Every day he risks his life to help us. Sadly an airman whose plane was shot down was found hanging in a tree from his parachute close to the monsieur's farm shortly before Christmas. Usually the monsieur and his wife can tend them and get them well enough to be smuggled to us but this time the airman's injuries are too serious. It appears that his leg is badly broken and an infection has set in. Dr Parkin has volunteered to tend to him but he will need a nurse to assist him and I thought of you, especially when I discovered that you can speak fluent French. You and Dr Parkin would have to pretend that you were newly-wed relatives of the monsieur should you be questioned. I will not lie to you, it is a very dangerous mission I am asking you to undertake. Should it ever become known to the enemy what the monsieur does he would be taken out and shot, as would anyone else involved, including his family and yourselves. I know it is a lot to ask, but do you think you could do it? I assure you I will think no less of you if you consider it to be too dangerous.'

Holly flushed, very aware of Richard watching her closely but she didn't even have to think about it as her chin went up in the air. 'I'll do it,' she said bravely.

Chapter Forty-Three

There were so many questions she wanted to ask and she began with, 'When will we be leaving?'

'Late tonight, under cover of darkness.'

Holly's breath caught in her throat. She hadn't expected it to be so soon, but then if the airman was as critical as they suspected then of course time was of the essence.

'And how will we get there and where exactly are we going?'

'Monsieur Le'Fete has a small wagon which he uses to supply us with seasonal vegetables. I am afraid you will have to travel in the back of that beneath sacks. It is the safest way. The enemy are used to seeing him in it so hopefully no questions will be asked. As to where you're going, I think it's best if you don't know. But you must swear to me that you will say nothing of this to anyone. You will be risking your own life and the lives of monsieur's family if you do.'

Holly nodded. 'Of course, but what shall I tell the nurses and Angela? They're bound to notice if I just disappear.'

'You won't leave until the rest of the nurses are all asleep then you'll change into clothes we have ready for you. I shall tell them that I transferred you to another hospital temporarily in the night because of an emergency.'

It seemed that she had thought of everything. 'Very well,' Holly agreed.

Richard spoke for the first time since she had entered the room. 'I'm really not happy about putting Holly's life at risk,' he told the sister. 'Surely I could do this alone?'

Sister Flynn shook her head. 'It will definitely need two of you to give the airman round-the-clock care. Holly, as soon as everyone in your tent is asleep report to me here. I shall have a change of clothes waiting for you . . . and thank you, you are a very brave girl. Now go and get some food and a rest. You have a long night ahead of you.'

Holly inclined her head and slipped away hardly able to believe what she had just agreed to, but she had agreed and now she intended to see it through to the bitter end no matter what the outcome. She would rather die than let Richard think she was a coward.

When she got back to the tent, Angela was already in her nightwear ready to hop into bed. So were most of the other nurses who had worked throughout the long day. One by one they snuggled down and dropped off to sleep until at last there was nothing but the sound of their gentle snores to be heard. Very quietly Holly crept out of bed and snatched up her uniform before slipping her feet into her shoes and putting her cape on. It wouldn't do to leave the uniform there, even if she was to change into civilian clothes, Angela would be suspicious, so she would leave them with the sister. Once outside she gasped as the cold air took her breath away and then she tiptoed across the duckboards in the darkness praying that she wouldn't slip off them into the mud. At last she reached the hospital and sidled into the sister's office, very conscious that she was in her nightclothes.

Sister Flynn quietly pointed to a pile of clothes she had

laid across a chair for her and Holly scrambled into them as fast as she could, although she had to keep her own shoes on because the ones sister had found her were so big that she was nearly walking out of them.

There was a somewhat shabby skirt, much darned and faded, and a blouse of an indistinguishable colour over which she would wear a thick woollen shawl and a head square. They were not like anything Holly had worn before but were typical of what she had seen the village Frenchwomen dressed in. Once she had scrambled into them Monsieur Le'Fete and Richard appeared and she had to stifle a smile. Richard was also dressed as a French peasant with a beret on his head and worn work clothes.

'We have decided that as Dr Parkin can speak no French we shall say that he is dumb,' Monsieur Le'Fete told her in his own tongue and solemn again now, Holly nodded.

'Now, are there any questions you would like to ask?' the sister, who had just entered the room behind the men, asked her.

'How long do you think we will be gone?' Holly said falteringly. Nerves were kicking in now and she felt faintly dizzy.

Monsieur shrugged his shoulders. 'There is no way of knowing, mademoiselle. It will depend on how quickly the airman recovers, or even if he survives. He ees in a very bad way.'

Holly nodded. 'Very well. I'm ready to go.'

Richard surprised her then when he said, 'I'm really not happy about this. You do realise that you'll be risking your life, don't you?'

His concern for her made her heart hammer but her face gave nothing away as she nodded. 'Yes, I do, but I want to do it.'

'There ees no more to be said then.' The monsieur jammed his hat on and ushered them towards the door. 'My wagon is parked just outside the hospital,' he informed them. 'Once we cross the enemy line you must be very quiet and still. Should they spot me they will think nothing of it. They are used to seeing me delivering food to the hospital but if we should be stopped and they discover you in the back of the wagon you must say nothing. Leave the talking to me, do you understand?'

Richard and Holly nodded and as they left Sister Flynn stopped Holly at the door where she gave her a swift hug. Holly was shocked and touched to see that there were tears in her eyes. 'May God keep you safe,' the woman said in a choked voice. 'You are a very loving and giving young lady, Nurse Farthing. Now go quickly.'

Seconds later they were out in the bitterly cold night and the monsieur pointed to a wagon. An old horse contentedly munching on a nosebag with a blanket thrown across his back was tethered to it and as his master approached he raised his head and whinnied softly.

Holly and Richard quickly scrambled into the back of the cart and the monsieur covered them in thick layers of sacks that smelled of earth, fruit and vegetables.

'Now be still,' the elderly man advised them. 'I shall not speak until we arrive at the farm. You never know who may be listening.'

Richard and Holly were lying so close that she could feel

his warm breath fanning her cheek and she was glad of the darkness to hide her blushes. They heard the monsieur talk to the horse before climbing onto the driver's bench seat and then they were off. It was very uncomfortable and as the wagon rattled across the rough ground they were thrown from side to side but neither of them said a word. Shortly after, the ride became smoother as they went through the streets of the town but then it grew rough again and they knew that now they were in enemy territory. Despite trying to be brave Holly's heart began to pound with fear and when Richard reached out beneath the sacks to hold her hand and squeeze it reassuringly, she clung to it like a leech, his comforting touch enveloping her. She was all too aware that should the enemy discover them they might well be shot and it was a terrifying thought. However, the wagon rattled on its way for what seemed like an endless time with no one stopping them as they were rolled about all over the place. They had no way of knowing how long they lay there but at last they heard the monsieur speak softly to the horse and it came to a halt. Holly felt stiff and sore but she made no complaint and remained silent until the monsieur whipped the sacks off them. She saw that they were in a large barn and the horse was already cropping at some hay.

'Well done,' the monsieur praised them. 'Now, you must come into the farmhouse to meet my family. They will be relieved that you 'ave arrived safely. Come.' He helped Holly down from the cart and as she looked down at her skirt and shawl she smiled ruefully. There were bits of straw and dirt all over her but at least they had arrived safely. She and Richard followed the man across a farmyard and entered a kitchen where a plump, middle-aged woman and a very pretty younger girl were waiting for them.

'Ah, Pierre, at last, I 'ave been so worried.' The older woman hurried over to throw her arms about her husband and he smiled at them across her shoulder. 'This is my wife, Claudette, and that is my daughter, Francine.' Turning his attention back to his wife he told her mock sternly, 'Come, woman, these people are cold and hungry. Where are your manners? Fetch them some hot soup immediately.' He patted her ample backside and she skittered off, giggling like a girl. It was clear that they had a very loving relationship. Her dark hair was streaked with grey at the temples but her eyes were kindly and she was still a very attractive woman. Francine, however, was stunningly pretty, Holly thought, as the girl offered her a shy smile. Her long black hair hung down her back like a shimmering cloak and her eyes were a curious mixture of grey and blue. She was tall and slender and placing his arm affectionately about her, the monsieur informed them proudly, 'Francine is the baby of the family. The rest of our children have grown and flown the nest. But ah, here is some food. Please sit down and eat and then I shall take you to the airman.'

They obediently sat at the large, scrubbed pine table that took up the centre of the room as Claudette placed steaming bowls of soup in front of them. While she was eating, Holly discreetly looked about the room. It was a typical farmhouse kitchen, low-beamed with a flagstone floor and a fire blazing in the inglenook above which shiny copper pans were suspended. Old, much-loved wing chairs covered in colourful cushions stood either side of it and a large pine dresser holding Claudette's cherished china stood against another wall. Brightly coloured rag rugs were thrown down on the floor and pretty flowered curtains hung at the tiny leaded windows, tightly drawn against the bitter night. It was far from salubrious but very warm and cosy. The soup was delicious too and she emptied her dish in minutes. Now they had arrived safely she was suddenly so tired she could have fallen asleep where she sat but she knew that the real work must begin straight away if they had any chance at all of saving the airman.

I wonder where he is? she thought to herself. Surely the Le'Fetes would not be foolish enough to have him staying in their home? If they did and the enemy discovered him there they would be signing their own death warrants. And then her unspoken question was answered when Monsieur Le'Fete dragged the table to one side and folded back the carpet beneath it to reveal a trapdoor, and when he opened it, Holly could see a flight of steps leading down into darkness. 'Put the table back until I knock, just in case,' he said to his wife as he lit an oil lamp so he could show them the way. He knew that he could never be too careful.

Richard followed Monsieur Le'Fete with Holly behind negotiating a very steep, wooden staircase. When they reached the bottom of it she was shocked to see how huge the cellar was. It must have run the whole length of the cottage and although it could never be classed as warm it was nowhere near as cold as she had expected it to be.

She noticed the beds then, four in a row along one wall, all with iron frames and gaily coloured patchwork quilts on them. There was also a table and chairs and various other bits of furniture dotted about including a small screen with a bucket standing behind it that they could use should it not be safe for them to use the toilet outside. The Le'Fetes had clearly gone to a lot of trouble to make the room as comfortable as they possibly could. On the end bed they saw the patient. He looked to be somewhere in his mid- to late twenties and his face was beaded with sweat. His dark hair was also damp and his breathing erratic so Richard wasted no time in hurrying across to him to take his pulse, which was racing dangerously fast.

'Let's have a look at this leg then, old chap,' he said cheerfully, although he suspected that the airman couldn't hear him. When he turned back the sheets Holly gasped as she stared down at his leg and the vile smell issuing from it hit her full force. It was clearly badly broken just below the knee and she could see a bone poking out of his skin.

'That's a really nasty break,' Richard cursed. 'Before I do anything else I'm going to have to realign the bone and strap it as best I can. Then we'll have to see what we can do about the infection, but first the wound must be thoroughly cleaned with hot water. If he had come into the hospital like this I think I would have been tempted to amputate beneath the knee but here we don't have the facilities.'

Monsieur pointed to a small sink and cooker at the end of the room telling them that they could get the water there and Holly quickly translated for Richard.

'I am so sorry,' he apologised. 'I tend to speak my native tongue without theenking about it but I will try to remember to speak in English in future.'

Holly had already hurried away to boil a kettle and Richard

404

now asked the monsieur, 'Would you have any sheets that I could tear up and use as bandages? I shall need as many as you can spare.'

The man nodded and mounted the stairs, returning minutes later with three snow-white, if somewhat threadbare, sheets.

Richard quickly crossed to the sink and washed his hands thoroughly while Holly began to tear the sheets into strips.

'Do you think you'll be able to save him?' she asked.

Richard sighed. 'It's hard to tell. I'm just praying we don't end up having to amputate his leg. I only have the equipment I was able to bring in my bag. What we really need to do is get rid of that infection, if we can't then I fear we're in trouble.'

The kettle began to gently sing and after bringing a bowlful of water to him she asked, 'What do you want me to do now?'

'Get some chloroform out of my bag and soak a rag in it then hold it under his nose. What I'm going to do is going to hurt like hell so it's best if he's out of it.'

'May I go now if you have no need of me?' Monsieur Le'Fete asked and Richard nodded.

'Of course.'

'Please feel free to rest on the beds when you can,' the monsieur told them. 'And I will make sure that you have food and drink brought to you first thing in the morning. But please, if you hear anyone other than my family upstairs remain silent, even if you have to gag our friend here. Oh, and from now on please call me Pierre.'

He left them and as the trapdoor closed behind him and

405

Holly heard the table and chairs being dragged back into position she suddenly realised how dangerous what she had agreed to do was and a finger of fear chased up her spine. Even so, she grit her teeth and held the chloroform-soaked rag beneath the airman's nose. Now that she was here she would do everything she could to help Richard to save him.

Chapter Forty-Four

Even though the airman was heavily sedated he winced and writhed about as Richard set his leg as best he could. He then cleaned the wound thoroughly before binding it as tightly as he was able.

'That's about all we can do for now,' he said wearily as he straightened from the bed and wiped his brow. He had been working for almost twenty-four hours and looked fit to drop.

'Then you lie down and get some sleep. I can watch him,' Holly offered.

He was so exhausted that he didn't even argue but headed for the nearest bed.

'Thank you, but while I'm resting can you get as much fluid into him as you can. If he won't take it use a syringe out of my bag to get it into him. We don't want him dehydrating on top of everything else.'

Holly went to his bag to do as she was asked and when she next turned back, Richard was already fast asleep. She paused to stare at his peaceful face for a moment and had to resist the impulse to reach out and stroke his cheek, and in that instant she knew without doubt that she still cared deeply for him. But now was not the time for such thoughts so she forced her attention back to the patient.

It was one of the longest nights that she could remember as she constantly mopped the airman's brow and syringed water into his mouth. Eventually he began to come round and Holly had to hold the bowl to his chin as the effects of the chloroform made him vomit. And then his eyes blinked open and he stared at her fearfully for a moment.

'It's all right, you're safe,' she reassured him gently. 'Your plane took a hit and you had to jump. Do you remember? You landed in a tree in your parachute and I'm afraid you broke your leg.'

'B-but where am I? Is . . . this a hospital?'

'No, we are behind enemy lines still, but a French farmer found you and brought you here to recover. Dr Parkin over there and myself will look after you now until you're well enough to be transferred to the field hospital.'

He managed a weak smile and then his eyes closed again and Holly continued to mop his brow. She had no idea how long she sat there. Time seemed to have no relevance in the cellar; she didn't even know if it was still night or day. The sounds from above had ended long ago when the family went to bed but eventually she became aware of footsteps again and then the trapdoor was opened and a weak light flooded down the stairs. Claudette appeared clad in an old woollen dress and large shawl with a tray in her hands.

Unlike her husband she could speak no English so she gestured to the pot of tea and the toast and porridge.

'Merci,' Holly told her and the woman looked relieved.

'Ah, you speak French?'

Holly nodded as Richard stirred on the bed.

'And how is the patient?' Claudette asked as Richard sat up and knuckled the sleep from his eyes.

'Richard set his leg last night as best he could and he has

408

woken so now we'll just have to wait and see,' Holly told her in French.

The woman nodded and hastily retreated back up the stairs. It wasn't wise to leave the trapdoor open for long.

Holly and Richard tucked into the food and drank the steaming hot tea with little said between them. They were still uncomfortable in each other's company but when they had finished he told her, 'Now it's your turn to get some sleep. I'll check and see if the infection looks any better.'

She needed no second telling and was asleep almost as soon as her head hit the pillow with no idea whatsoever that Richard was watching her while his heart broke afresh. He had been so sure that she loved him as much as he loved her but she had dropped him like a hot potato and every time he remembered, it hurt bitterly. Still, he scolded himself, this wasn't the time or place to be thinking of his own feelings. He needed to concentrate on the airman. Throughout the next couple of hours as Holly slept he constantly washed the wound with disinfectant, but it still looked angry and sore and Richard grew increasingly concerned. There was a vicious red line running from the wound up the airman's leg above the knee now, which told him one thing. If he was to save the chap's life he was going to have to amputate whether he liked it or not.

Francine brought them down a pot of coffee and home-made scones thick with jam and butter mid-morning and although he hated having to do it he nudged Holly awake.

'I'm sorry, but I need you to tell Francine to ask her father if he could go to the hospital to get the tools I shall need to do an amputation,' he explained solemnly.

Holly stirred, then taking in his words, quickly told Francine what he had said. Not understanding a word they were saying, Richard grew increasingly frustrated as he listened to them both jabbering away in French but at last Holly told him, 'Unfortunately, her father is out delivering supplies to the Germans. Because he supplies them they turn a blind eye to him also supplying the hospital.'

'And how long will he be?'

Francine informed them that he would be home possibly mid-afternoon but Richard realised that they may not be able to wait that long. Every second counted now if they were to save the airman's life.

'Tell her I need the sharpest, biggest knife they've got and some whisky or brandy,' he said grimly.

Holly quickly relayed what he had said and Francine hurried away to get the things he had asked for. She was back within minutes with a half-bottle of brandy and the biggest, most terrifying-looking knife that Holly had ever seen. Richard immediately began to undo the bindings on the airman's leg and soak yet another rag in chloro-form. Realising what he was about to do Francine scuttled away like a frightened rabbit, closing the trapdoor behind her with a bang.

'This is not going to be nice. Are you sure you're up to it?'

Holly swallowed and nodded. She had assisted in theatre many times before but never in such primitive conditions as this.

'We shall need to boil that knife and wash our hands thoroughly,' he said as he took a large needle from his bag

410

and began to thread it. 'Oh, and boil this needle while you're at it would you? We can't afford for him to get another infection.'

Soon a pan of boiling water containing everything Richard might need to perform the operation was bubbling on the stove. By then he had placed a thick wad of sheet beneath the patient's knee and as soon as he was happy that the instruments he would need to use were thoroughly sterilised he would be ready to begin. Thankfully the poor chap was only semi-conscious and was rambling incoherently so had no awareness of what was about to happen to him.

'Right,' he said as he stood poised with the knife. 'Hold that chloroform rag under his nose and keep it there until I tell you to stop.'

Holly did as she was told and soon the airman was breathing deeply. 'Good.' Taking up the pen he had carried in his bag Richard carefully drew a line where he wanted the amputation to be and then the knife glinted in the light from the oil lamp as the operation began.

'That's it,' he said an hour later as he stepped back from the table. The rotting limb was lying on the floor at the side of the bed and what was left of the airman's leg was stitched up as neatly as Richard could manage. A large pile of bloody cloths had also been thrown to the ground and the bed resembled a bloodbath.

'Keep the pressure on those stitches till the bleeding slows down,' he told Holly. 'He's already lost far more blood than I would have liked him to but we can only do our best under these circumstances.'

Obediently she pressed one cloth after another to the

stump, discarding them and reaching for yet another when they became soaked through, but at last the bleeding began to slow and she sighed with relief.

'I think that's the worst over now,' she informed him and he looked pleased.

Then unexpectedly he tipped Pierre's fine French brandy all over the stump, telling her, 'Alcohol is a wonderful cleanser and seeing as it's the only one available it'll have to do.'

Holly suddenly giggled. 'What a waste!' and when he laughed too, just for a moment the old closeness between them was back.

Over the next two days the airman showed signs of improvement although he sobbed brokenly when Richard had to explain to him what he'd had to do.

'I'm so sorry, old chap,' Richard apologised. 'But it was either that or lose you.'

The airman sniffed and held out his hand. 'I understand, thank you, doctor. I'm Sam Wright, by the way.'

'Dr Richard Parkin, and this is Nurse Holly Farthing, she assisted during your operation as well as sat by you for hours on end ensuring you didn't dehydrate.'

Sam inclined his head to her and Holly smiled. It was so nice to see him awake although she knew they were far from out of the woods yet. There was still time for an infection to set in and if it did they'd be in very deep trouble. He really needed to be in the hospital where he could receive the proper medication but she doubted he would be well enough to travel for at least another couple of days.

Suddenly they heard a loud banging on the door upstairs and they all froze. They could hear a door opening and a German voice. Holly began to tremble and held her breath as Richard crossed to the oil lamp and extinguished it, holding a finger to his lips to tell her and the airman to remain silent. They had now been plunged into darkness and without thinking Holly's hand sought Richard's for reassurance. They could hear Claudette talking loudly to whoever was up there then there was the sound of something being hauled across the floor and the door slamming. All was quiet again but still they sat on until they could be sure that it was safe to speak.

At last the trapdoor opened and Francine appeared pale-faced, 'Maman said to tell you that the pigs came for a sack of winter cabbages but they are gone now. It is safe again.'

Richard sighed as he fumbled with the matches and relit the oil lamp. Meanwhile Holly's heart gradually slowed to a steadier rhythm. What stories she would have to tell her mother and Ivy, if and when she ever got home.

Chapter Forty-Five

Over the next few days Sam gradually improved until at last Richard told him, 'I think you could just about manage the journey to hospital now, providing Pierre doesn't jolt the wagon too much.'

Holly had lost all sense of time by then. Down in the semi-darkness every hour was the same, although she had spent some of the time up in the kitchen chatting to Francine who she now considered to be a friend. Being a very similar age they had a lot in common and Holly knew that she would miss her when they left. She was full of admiration for the girl and her family who were risking their lives every time they tried to help people such as Sam who had been shot down behind enemy lines. Had Pierre not found him he would have died where he fell or, worse still, been shot by the Germans if they came across him. And now Holly realised that this was not the first time the family had stuck their necks out to help the British soldiers.

'You all deserve a medal,' Holly told her sincerely. 'And I really hope that when the war is over you receive one.'

Francine giggled mischievously. 'I would rather 'ave a big diamond from a 'andsome man!'

'Oh yes, and would this handsome man happen to have a name or be anyone in particular?'

Francine blushed prettily. 'His name is Marc and we are

betrothed. God willing when the war is over we shall be wed but for now he is part of our French resistance. He works tirelessly helping our allies to get to safe houses such as this if they should find themselves behind enemy lines.' Her lovely face had become solemn as she continued, 'He risks his life every single day and all I can do is pray that he will remain safe.'

Holly could find no words of comfort and so merely squeezed her hand gently and from then on they had become close. But now it seemed that they would be returning to the hospital soon as Sam continued to improve and despite the fact that Holly admired the Le'Fetes enormously she couldn't help but be relieved, for every second they spent there was putting the lives of the Le'Fetes and themselves at risk.

That evening Richard left Holly to watch over Sam while he went upstairs to discuss moving Sam to the hospital with Pierre. When he came back he told her that they would be leaving the following evening.

The next day dragged by painfully slowly but at last Pierre appeared at the trapdoor to tell them the wagon was ready. Earlier in the day he had carried a door down to the cellar and now he and Richard loaded Sam onto it and somehow managed to manoeuvre him up the steep, narrow staircase. It was no mean feat and by the time they reached the kitchen the men were sweating profusely despite the bitter cold night outside.

Sam shook the hands of the family in turn and thanked

them several times over before being carried outside, leaving Holly to say her goodbyes. There were tears in Claudette's eyes as she hugged her and kissed her soundly and Francine was openly crying.

'I shall miss you, Miss Holly.'

Holly was tearful too as she embraced her. 'And I shall miss you too. Thank you for everything and please stay safe. You are a very special family.' And then she was being ushered towards the door and it wasn't safe to talk any more so she clambered silently into the back of the wagon next to Sam. Richard joined them and once again they were covered in sacks and the wagon set off. On the way Sam's stump began to bleed again. Holly could feel the dampness of the blood against her skirt but there was nothing she could do about it apart from apply pressure to it as best she could and place a reassuring arm about his shoulders. And then what they had all dreaded happened. The cart came to a halt and a German voice asked Pierre, 'What is your business?'

Pierre was as cool as a cucumber as he replied, 'I am delivering supplies to the hospital. I delivered yours to your headquarters this morning.'

'Very well, move on.'

Pierre clicked his tongue and the old horse pulled off again as tears of relief ran down Holly's pale cheeks. That had been a little too close for comfort. She was sandwiched between Richard and Sam and when Richard's arm came around her and he held her to him comfortingly it was all she could do to stop herself from turning to him and blurting out why she had been forced to end their relationship. Being so close to him was torture but she bit her tongue as the old horse and wagon clattered on through the night. There was a dense fog but thankfully the horse seemed to know the roads and after what felt like an eternity Pierre's voice came to them. 'We are safe and back inside the grounds of the hospital.'

Holly gave an audible gasp but then everyone's attention was focused on Sam again. They had to get him on to the ward as quickly as possible now.

Richard helped her down from the wagon as Sister Flynn appeared from the fog to tell her, 'Follow me, you can change back into your uniform in my office. It's imperative that you are not seen.'

Holly thought the likelihood of that was slim as it was now the early hours of the morning. The nurses who had worked the day shift would be fast asleep and the night nurses would hopefully be busy on the wards. She followed the sister into her office while Pierre and one of the male nurses got Sam into a ward. Richard had already hurried away to get changed.

Sister Flynn turned her back discreetly as Holly struggled into her uniform and when she had finished she turned to her and smiled. 'Well done, nurse. You've done a remarkable job. But remember, not a word to anyone. Walls have ears and should it ever become known what the Le'Fetes do I have no need to tell you what would happen. Everyone has been told that you and Dr Parkin were transferred to another field hospital further up the line because of a temporary shortage of staff. Stick to that . . . Oh, and by the way, I have applied for two weeks leave for you. I rather think you deserve it.'

Holly's heart soared as she thought of her family. It would be so good to see them again and she was grateful. 'Thank you, Sister, thank you ever so much.'

'No, my dear, it is I that should be thanking you. You put your life at risk to go on this mission. But now go and get some rest and take tomorrow off. I dare say you've had little sleep for the last few days and when your leave pass is approved I shall let you know. Goodnight.'

'Goodnight, Sister Flynn.' Holly set off for her tent with a smile on her face. The last days had been fraught with danger and anxiety but they had earned her a visit to her family. She would not say no to it.

Chapter Forty-Six

Holly didn't see Angela again until the following afternoon in the mess. She had been fast asleep when Angela had got up that morning and she had stayed that way for most of the day.

'Ah, so here you are,' Angela greeted her as she carried her tray to Holly's table. 'How was it working in the other hospital?'

Holly averted her eyes and crossed her fingers under the table. 'Much the same as in this one . . . but it's good to be back with people I know.'

'It's good to have you back,' Angela answered. 'And guess what? There's going to be a dance in the village hall this Saturday and me and some of the other nurses are going. You'll come, won't you?'

'I'll see a bit nearer the time,' Holly replied. Going to a dance was the last thing she fancied after what she'd done that week.

Angela frowned. 'Now come on, you know what they say? All work and no play makes Jack a dull boy! It'll be lovely to wear our own clothes again, even if it's only for a few hours. There might be some handsome Frenchmen there, not that Harry would let one near you. He's been none too pleased about you not being here I can tell you! Oh, please say you'll come!'

Holly sighed. She would have to tell Harry that there could be no future for them, and soon. And regarding the dance, Angela could be very persuasive when she had the bit between her teeth.

'I think all the Frenchmen you'd be interested in will be away fighting the war,' she pointed out. 'But all right, yes, I'll come if it makes you happy. Providing I'm not on duty that is.'

Angela grinned from ear to ear. She could hardly wait. 'And did you see much of that dishy Dr Parkin while you were working away with him?' she asked.

Holly lowered her eyes to flick an imaginary speck of dust from her apron, 'Not really,' she said nonchalantly. 'But now, tell me what's been happening here.' And thankfully the conversation turned to another topic, for the time being at least. The next person she saw was Harry when he strode into the mess looking none too pleased, as Angela had warned her.

'So you're back then, are you,' he said peevishly. 'I had to hear from Sister Flynn that you'd been transferred. You could have told me.'

'I didn't get a chance to,' Holly answered coolly. 'You were in theatre when I was told that I was going and I had no way of getting word to you.'

He looked slightly repentant and offered a guilty smile. 'In that case, I apologise. I was just worried about you, that's all.'

'I don't see why you should have been. It was no more dangerous at that hospital than it is at this one and I could hardly refuse an order.'

'Of course you couldn't.' He sat down and reached for her hand across the table as Angela giggled.

'Ooh, that's my cue to go! I don't want to be a gooseberry. See you later, Holly.'

Once she was gone Holly pulled her hand from his and bit her lip. This had gone on for quite long enough and she knew that it wasn't fair to give Harry false hope any longer.

'Harry . . .' she began tentatively. 'I'm really sorry because I'm very fond of you . . . but the thing is . . . I don't love you and I think you deserve a girl that does. I admit for a time I thought we might make a go of things but I realise now it wouldn't be fair on you, I'm so sorry.'

His face hardened. 'And what's brought this about all of a sudden? Things were fine between us before you went. Is it Richard? I'm no fool and I've seen the way you look at him.'

'No, it's nothing to do with Richard,' she denied. 'But there was never anything official between us and I just don't think you and I have a future together. I . . . I'm so sorry.'

'So am I,' he said as he slammed his chair away from the table so quickly that it almost overturned. 'You've been stringing me along and I don't appreciate that. But never mind, there are plenty of nurses to choose from who hopefully won't be as cold as you are.' And with that he was gone, leaving her feeling bereft. Harry was a good man but she knew more than ever now that he could never take Richard's place in her heart. No one could, so it looked as if there was a very empty future ahead of her.

There was great excitement in the nurses' quarters on the following Saturday as those of them who were off duty prepared for the dance. Unknown to Angela, Holly had actually volunteered to work the night shift.

'Oh, I wish you were coming,' Angela groaned as she applied a layer of lipstick in the mirror above the fire. She was all done up in the only civilian dress she had brought with her and after weeks of wearing her uniform she felt like a different girl.

'Don't worry about me, just go and enjoy yourself.' Holly was fastening her cap ready to go on duty. 'I've no doubt looking like that you'll have a queue of men wanting to dance with you.'

Angela preened as she studied her reflection in the mirror again and pouted. 'Do you really think so? Just so long as one of them is Dr Parkin.'

Holly's stomach did a little somersault as she thought of Angela in Richard's arms but she didn't say anything.

She was just entering the ward when Sister Flynn waylaid her with a smile on her face. 'Good news, Nurse Farthing. You have been granted leave from the first of February for two weeks. We've arranged for you to return home on one of the hospital ships that will be sailing that morning and I've no doubt you won't mind tending the patients on the crossing?'

'Of course not,' Holly answered with a smile. She was ready for a rest. She went to check on Sam first, who was improving by the day. Of course no one knew that it had been she and Richard who had looked after him before he had been admitted so she had to be very professional when speaking to him.

'How are you today, Mr Wickes?' she asked as she lifted the notes from the end of his bed and scanned through them. Heart rate normal, pulse normal. He really was on the mend.

'Fine and dandy, thank you, nurse. In fact I'm being shipped home on the morning of the first of February.'

Holly's head snapped up and he gave her a crafty wink. No wonder the sister had said she could help with the patients on the crossing. She would be travelling back to England with Sam.

'I'm very pleased for you,' she answered, her eyes twinkling and she went on her way with a little spring in her step.

Angela was somewhat the worse for wear the next morning after partaking of rather too much home-made French wine but she'd clearly had a wonderful evening.

'You were right,' she told Holly as she got into bed and Angela got out. 'There were hardly any Frenchmen there, well, not young ones anyway, but there were loads of very handsome soldiers and I got to dance three dances with Dr Parkin an' all.'

'Sounds wonderful,' Holly said in a clipped voice as she felt tears pricking her eyes. 'But now I must get some sleep. It was really busy on the ward last night. We lost two of the patients, unfortunately. You can tell me all about the dance this evening. I'll meet you in the mess when you've done your shift.' With that she snuggled down under the blankets and stayed there until Angela had left, torturing herself as she imagined Angela in Richard's arms.

As she was waiting for Angela to join her in the mess that

evening she saw Richard for the first time since they had got back from the Le'Fetes and to her surprise he joined her at the table.

'You missed a good night last night. I thought you'd be there.'

She shrugged. 'I had to work but Angela told me you both had a good time.' She silently cursed herself. That must have sounded like she cared and of course she didn't!

Seeing her discomfort he grinned. 'As luck would have it she's a very good dancer,' he replied and just at that moment the person they were discussing appeared.

'Hello, Dr Parkin,' she said cheerily. 'Can I get you anything? Tea? Coffee?'

He rose hastily from his seat. 'No, thank you, nurse, I must be off now. It looks like it's going to be another busy night in theatre after the influx of wounded we've had in today.'

'Oh bugger!' Angela pouted as he disappeared. 'I thought he'd come to have dinner with me.'

Holly said nothing as Angela went off to the counter to fetch her meal but she couldn't stay the little worm of jealousy that was wriggling in her stomach. How would she bear it if Richard and Angela did become a couple? She would just have to wait and see.

'Lucky thing,' Angela grumbled as Holly prepared to leave for home. 'If I'd known getting transferred to another hospital would get me two weeks leave I'd have volunteered for it.'

Holly smiled as she crammed the last of her things into

her small bag. 'I'll be back before you know it. Just don't do anything I wouldn't do,' she teased with a wink as she headed for the flap in the tent that served as a door.

'I should be so lucky,' Angela retaliated but she grinned and came to give her a hug. 'Have a safe journey and I'll see you in two weeks.'

Holly sprinted away to climb aboard the military vehicle that would take her and the patients that were going home to the hospital ship and soon the field hospital was far behind them. On the journey it was heart-breaking to pass through the once quaint little villages, all flattened and bombed by the enemy and Holly couldn't help but think of the poor people who had once lived in them and loved them.

Sam Wickes was following in an ambulance and she wondered how he would cope when he was fully recovered from his amputation. His flying days were well and truly over now but she supposed he was lucky to be alive and knowing Sam, she was sure he would find a job he could do with one leg. In fact he would probably return home a hero and as he was still a very attractive man she had no doubt he would never be short of female admirers. He was already talking about getting a prosthesis made and she was glad that she had helped to save his life, although Richard had done far more for him than she had.

By lunchtime they were all aboard the ship and Holly helped the other nurses settle the patients for the voyage. Most of the men would go into one of the army hospitals dotted along the coast and stay there until they were fully recovered. It was dark when they docked and from there it was up to Holly to find her own way home, but first she wanted to say a final goodbye to Sam. It was highly unlikely she would ever see him again. She found him about to be stretchered out to a waiting ambulance and hurried over to him.

'Goodbye, Sam, take good care of yourself,' she said, and he caught her hand.

'You too, Holly . . . and thanks. If it weren't for you . . .' His voice trailed away but there was no need for words, they both knew what he meant.

'Goodbye, Holly, have a good life. I'll never forget what you and Dr Parkin did for me.'

Holly felt a lump in her throat as he was carried away. She could only hope for the very best for Sam and she silently said a prayer for him as he was swallowed up by the crowds on the dockside.

As soon as she had composed herself she hurried towards the train station, praying that she was not too late for the last train, and was delighted to discover that there was one due any minute. She hastily paid for her ticket and climbed aboard and soon found herself surrounded by men in uniform, many of them like herself going home on a short leave before heading back to the fray.

As she looked around at the haggard, haunted faces she couldn't help but compare how the men looked now to the day she had watched the young men from her home town climb aboard the train at Nuneaton, eager to start their training. They had discovered all too soon that rather than being the adventure they had envisaged, it was instead a living nightmare. They had been forced to live in muddy, filthy trenches, seen their fellow men gunned down in front of their very eyes and been forced to kill to save their own skins. It was no wonder that some of them would never be the same again. They had seen sights that no one should ever see and it showed in their stance as they sat staring numbly ahead, poor things. But these were the lucky ones, for at least they were going home, she thought.

It was very late at night when the train pulled into the station and Holly was almost dropping with exhaustion. Still not far to go now and I shall be home, she thought, forcing herself to put one foot in front of another. And then there it was, her home, thankfully with a light still shining dully from the drawing room window.

She tapped at the door, which was opened by Ivy who was in her dressing robe with her hair loose about her shoulders.

'Holly!' she cried as she flung her arms about her and almost dragged her over the threshold. 'Oh, I can't believe you're really here. Why didn't you let us know you were coming? We could have come to meet you off the train.'

'I didn't know I was coming myself till a short while ago and with how irregular the post is at the moment I doubted a letter would get here in time.'

'What's all the noise about?' A gruff voice sounded from the stairs and her grandfather appeared, looking stunned and delighted.

'Why, my dear girl, thank God you are safe,' he said in a choked voice.

'He's upset, well we all are. There has been so much bad news in the town and just the other week a German Zeppelin crossed the Norfolk coast during the night and rained bombs on Great Yarmouth and King's Lynn. Over twenty people are dead and ever so many more injured apparently.'

'That's awful,' Holly said as her grandfather gave her a rare hug.

But then Ivy saw the dark shadows beneath her friend's eyes and the droop of her shoulders and she dragged her off towards the kitchen saying, 'It's a cup of tea and bed for you, my girl. You look done in. But how long are you home for?'

'Two weeks.' Holly raised her hand to cover a yawn. 'And I might just spend the whole of it in bed.'

Ivy would have loved nothing more than to sit up all night and catch up on what each of them had been doing but it would have to wait till morning. She could see that Holly was ready to drop and for now just knowing that she was home and under the same roof was enough.

Chapter Forty-Seven

Over the next few days Emma called to see her daily with Katie and Florence and Holly was thrilled to see her mother looking so happy. Walter called in to see her most evenings too after finishing work and gradually Holly began to relax. She had been under so much strain since going overseas and had worked so hard that she hadn't realised how tired she was, but now suddenly she was exhausted.

One morning towards the end of the first week as Holly sat in the kitchen with Cook and Ivy her mother entered looking strained. Holly knew instantly that something was wrong. Emma's eyes were red-rimmed from crying and she was as jumpy as a kitten.

'Hello, we didn't expect to see you until this afternoon.' Ivy too could see that all was not well as she pulled a chair out for her. 'We're just having a tea break, would you like a cup?'

Emma swallowed. What she was about to tell Ivy was not easy but it had to be done.

'Actually, it's you I've come to see, Ivy. I'm afraid we've had rather bad news this morning.'

The colour drained from Ivy's cheeks as she clutched the back of the chair and a terrible sense of foreboding came over her. 'I-it's about Marcus, ain't it?' Her voice came out as a squeak.

Emma nodded, her face grave. 'I'm afraid it is. We had a

telegram just as Walter was about to leave for the factory. It said he was missing in action and is presumed dead.'

Ivy swayed and Holly jumped up to guide her onto the chair before she fell as Ivy's head wagged from side to side. 'He can't be!' She sat as if turned to stone as she fingered his latest letter in her dress pocket, which she had received only days before. She always carried the latest one about with her until the next one arrived. And then finally the dam broke and she began to cry, great tearing sobs that tugged at Holly's heartstrings.

'I'm so sorry, darling.' Emma patted her arm. 'As you can imagine Walter and the girls are in a terrible state so I said I would come and tell you.'

'B-but we were goin' to be wed soon as the war ended,' Ivy said brokenly and now Holly was crying too and so was Cook. Marcus had been such a lovely young man and he and Ivy might have been made for each other. It all seemed so pointless, such a senseless waste of a young life, but then they were all aware that Marcus was only one of thousands who had fallen. Every day countless other families were receiving the same awful telegrams and all across the country people were grieving for their loved ones.

Emma stood there helplessly, fiddling with her gloves. Giving Ivy such terrible news was one of the worst things she had ever had to do but Walter had been in no fit state to do it so the difficult job had fallen to her. Like Ivy, Walter was totally heartbroken, Marcus had been his only son and she feared her husband would never get over his loss. 'I, er . . . ought to be getting back now,' she said apologetically. 'I should be there for Walter and the girls . . .'

'Of course you should. You go,' Holly told her under-standingly. 'We'll look after Ivy.' And so after kissing her daughter on the cheek, Emma hurried back outside to the carriage that was waiting for her.

For the next few days Ivy hid herself away in her room, refusing to eat or drink. Even her little daughter could not lift the cloud of grief she was under, so Holly took care of Alice as she and the rest of them crept around the house like ghosts. On Sunday a memorial service was held for Marcus at Chilvers Coton Church and Ivy attended, standing straight-backed with her eyes looking ahead throughout the service. She hadn't cried once since imme-diately after receiving the dreadful news as far as any of them knew.

It was Cook who expressed her concerns three days before Holly was due to go back to France.

'How am I goin' to cope at my age wi' the little 'un all on my own when you've gone?' she asked worriedly, nodding towards Alice who was sitting at the kitchen table playing with a leftover piece of pastry from the apple pie Cook had just put in the oven. 'I'm already tryin' to do Ivy's jobs as well as my own.'

Holly could understand her point. Up to now they had pussy-footed around Ivy allowing her to grieve but perhaps it was time to rouse her out of her state of inertia, no matter how unkind it might seem in the short-term.

'Leave it with me. I'll see what I can do,' she promised and later that morning she carried a tea tray up to Ivy's room

431

and rapped on the door. 'Ivy, I have some tea and biscuits here for you.'

'I'm not hungry . . . take them away.'

Holly took a deep breath. This had gone on for quite long enough and if Ivy wasn't careful it would be her that was ill next. Drawing herself up to her full height she opened the door and barged into the room to find Ivy lying on her bed staring at the ceiling.

'Ivy . . .' she began. 'We're all heartbroken at Marcus's loss but don't you think it's time you took control of your daughter again? I seem to remember you telling me that Marcus loved her like his own child and that he wanted to legally adopt her when you were wed so that she could have his name. How do you think he would feel if he could see you neglecting her so?'

Ivy leaned up on one elbow. 'I'm not neglecting her!' she denied hotly.

'Oh, but I'm afraid you are.' Holly stood her ground. 'It's been me that has bathed and changed her since we had the awful news. Me that has fed her and played with her. Now I don't mind one bit, I love Alice, you know I do. But what's going to happen to her when I return to the field hospital? Cook isn't up to coping with her full-time. And besides that she misses her mam.'

The angry look slowly disappeared from Ivy's face.

'Last night when I was tucking her into bed she cried and asked for mama,' Holly went on and now for the first time since the day she had heard of Marcus's death there were tears in Ivy's eyes too.

'I . . . I didn't realise . . . I didn't mean to neglect her,' she said falteringly and then she was crying in earnest and, dropping the tray onto a nearby chest of drawers, Holly hurried across and hugged Ivy to her tightly.

'That's it,' she soothed as she rocked her in her arms as she would a child. 'Cry it all out. It's so much better out than in.' And Ivy did just that until Holly was sure she could have no more tears left to cry.

That evening Ivy came down to dine with them in the kitchen and although she didn't eat much, at least she made a brave attempt. And after the meal, she lifted Alice and bore her away for her bath.

Cook smiled with satisfaction. 'I don't know what you said to her, pet, but it seems to have done the job,' she remarked approvingly. 'The poor lass has still got a long way to go but I reckon she's taken the first step in the right direction now, thank God.'

'She'll come through this. Ivy is a tough little nut,' Holly assured her and prayed that she was right.

The day before she was due to go back to France, Emma and her new family all came to dinner to say goodbye but it was a solemn gathering and after news about Marcus, her mother was even more terrified that something would happen to Holly.

'Please promise me that you'll be careful and take no chances,' she implored. 'There are such terrible things happening I almost don't want to let any of my loved ones out of my sight! I feel as if nowhere is safe any more – especially where you are going. It just doesn't bear thinking about.'

'I shall be fine,' Holly answered, wondering how her mother would react if she ever got to know about the mission she had gone on to save Sam. She would probably lock her in her room and throw away the key until the war was over. She hastily changed the subject but when the family finally left, the goodbyes were tearful, even Walter, who seemed to have aged ten years since the news about Marcus had reached them, was concerned about her.

'Do as your mother says and don't take any chances,' he urged. 'This family has enough heartache to deal with at present.'

'I won't,' Holly answered as he gave her an affectionate hug. It was strange to think now that her grandfather had once had Walter earmarked as her husband. She could only imagine what a disastrous union it would have been but he and her mother were perfect for each other so at least that had turned out well. She said her goodbyes to Katie and Florence next and after they had left, Cook retired early and she and Ivy sat in the warm kitchen together sipping cocoa.

'I wish you didn't have to go.'

Holly smiled at her friend. 'I wish I could stay a little longer too, but I'm needed out there.' She chose not to tell Ivy about the horrific injuries she and the rest of the nurses and doctors had to deal with on a daily basis. Losing Marcus was still too raw. 'But I'll come back again just as soon as I can, I promise. Meanwhile I shall expect you to write and tell me what Alice is up to every single week, do you hear me? She's at such a lovely age, she seems to learn a new word every day now.'

'Yes, she does, she's a bright little spark,' Ivy agreed and even managed a small smile.

Holly left early the next morning and Gilbert insisted on carrying her bag and walking her to the station.

'Are you sure you don't need anything? Have you got enough money?'

'I have more than enough,' she assured him. 'There's nothing really to spend it on where I'm stationed.' They could hear the train coming now and he gently squeezed her hand.

'I shall be glad when this damn war is over,' he said. 'You and I have a lot of catching up to do.'

'And we will, that's a promise,' Holly told him before pecking his cheek and hopping onto the train. She hung out of the window and waved until he was out of sight, then sank back in her seat to face the long tiring journey ahead. As always her thoughts turned to Richard. She wondered whether he'd missed her while she'd been away, or perhaps he hadn't even noticed she'd gone. Maybe since she'd left, Angela and he had grown closer and she was taking up all his thoughts. Thinking about this brought her close to tears, but she would just have to put a brave face on it. But oh, how she wished things could have been different.

Holly finally arrived at the port in France in the early hours of the morning and a military vehicle was waiting to take her and some soldiers who had been on leave back to the camp. Thankfully it had been a peaceful Channel crossing and she had managed to sleep for most of the way, which meant she was feeling quite bright-eyed when she arrived at the hospital so she decided to report to the ward to see what shift she would be on that day. As soon as she saw her, Sister Flynn rushed over to greet her.

'Nurse Farthing, I trust you have had a good leave?'

'Yes, thank you, Sister.'

'Good, then might I have a word in my office?'

Holly's stomach flipped. She had an idea where this might be leading when the sister told her without preamble. 'I have another mission behind enemy lines for you. If you feel able to do it a second time, that is? Both Dr Parkin and Dr Phillips are there at present but I desperately need them back here and a nurse to take their place. There is only you I can truly trust and once again the risks are grave. Are you up to it?'

Holly nodded. She had no need to even think about it. 'Yes, Sister, I am. When do you want me to leave?'

'Right now.' Sister Flynn pointed to the clothes that Holly had worn the last time and she was relieved to see that they had at least been washed. 'I knew roughly what time to expect you so Monsieur Le'Fete is waiting for you. I shall tell the other nurses I extended your leave because of a family bereavement.'

How ironic, Holly thought, as a picture of Marcus flashed in front of her eyes. At least she wouldn't have to lie to Angela about that when she got back. If she got back, a little voice whispered, but she pushed it away as the sister turned her back and she hastily got changed. Minutes later the now familiar smell of fruit and vegetables met her as Pierre covered her with sacks in the back of the wagon and then they were on their way, but this time Richard wasn't with her to assure that all would be well and as much as she hated to admit it, she felt sick with fear.

Chapter Forty-Eight

'We have three RFC men here who managed to escape from a prisoner-of-war camp,' Richard told her when she was shown down into the cellar. 'Thankfully Pierre's friend took them in and Pierre fetched them here.'

She glanced towards Harry but he was studiously ignoring her as he packed his bag, just as he had ignored her ever since she had told him they could only be friends.

'The first two are not in too bad a shape,' Richard continued, passing her the notes he had made on each patient. 'This one here has a broken arm, which I've set so he can come back to the hospital with us tonight. The next one is severely malnourished to the point that he can't even stand as yet and he also had a bad stomach infection, diarrhoea and sickness, as does the other one who is by far the worst. I should warn you he's been whipped so be prepared when you change the dressings on his back.' He lowered his voice then and told her, 'Between you and me I don't think much of his chances. He's delirious and doesn't even know where he is half the time. All you can do is get plenty of fluid into him, keep him cool and make him as comfortable as possible.'

She glanced towards the beds. One pilot had his arm in a sling and was dressed in some old clothes of Pierre's, ready to leave. The other two looked very poorly indeed and her heart sank. It would all be up to her now and it seemed a heavy burden to bear, even so she managed a smile.

'Thank you, I shall be fine. But go. It will be light soon and you'll be more at risk if you don't get off now.'

Harry was already helping the pilot up the stairs but after lifting his bag Richard paused to look at Holly. She had the feeling that he wanted to say something but, appearing to think better of it, he merely inclined his head and followed the others up the stairs and then the trapdoor slammed shut and she was in darkness save for the light issuing from the flickering oil lamp. She heard the heavy table and chairs being dragged back into place and for a moment she panicked. But taking a deep breath she looked towards her patients. Their lives depended on her and she would not let them down, she had to be strong for them.

The smell in the room was atrocious and it was all she could do to stop herself from gagging, but if the men had been as ill as Richard had told her she couldn't have expected anything else. There was no window in the cellar so everything that came out of them had to be carted up to the cess pit in buckets. Thankfully Pierre did that job every evening as soon as it got dark.

She immediately began to do what she could for them, sponging them down with cool water and dripping fluid into their mouths, and a day later her efforts seemed to be paying off because one of the men appeared slightly better. He even managed to open his eyes at one point and when he saw Holly hanging over him he started but then relaxed when she smiled at him, before his eyes fluttered shut again. But not before she had seen the terror in them. He must have been imagining himself still in the POW camp.

Francine came down to the cellar whenever she could to take over so that Holly could snatch a few hours' sleep and finally on the third day the stronger of the two men woke properly and even asked for a drink.

'He is improving, yes?' Francine asked with a smile and when Holly nodded she breathed a sigh of relief. Later the same day, James, as he introduced himself, even managed a few sips of some of Claudette's nourishing chicken soup.

'He's still very weak,' Holly explained to Pierre when he popped down to fetch the buckets later that evening. 'But I think he'll make it now. We just have to get him strong enough to get him back to the hospital.'

'And Ben, the other one?' Pierre looked towards the other young man who was still in a very bad way and who as yet had shown no signs of improvement despite Holly's best efforts.

'Still very poorly.' She wiped her weary eyes. 'And the wounds on his back are badly infected, although I think the ointment Claudette sent down for him has helped some of them slightly.' The weals on his back went down almost to the bone in places and Holly had been forced to lie him on his stomach and let the air get to them. The diarrhoea and sickness had stopped but Holly knew that was only because he had nothing left inside him and he remained in a semi-conscious state.

For some reason Pierre did not seem to be his usual cheery self that evening so Holly asked carefully, 'Is everything all right, Pierre?'

He shook his head. 'I am afraid not, mademoiselle. There has been bad news from the hospital.'

'Oh?' Holly raised an eyebrow and removing his cap he began to twist it between his fingers. 'The two doctors who were here when you first came have gone missing.'

'Missing!' Holly suddenly felt sick. 'What do you mean . . . missing?'

'Sister informed me that they went to another safe house in the village to attend to a pilot who had been shot down and while they were there the Germans came.' There were tears in his eyes now and he had to swallow before he could go on. 'The people who took the pilot in were good friends of mine but the Germans took them outside, the whole family, and shot them.'

'A-and the doctors?' Holly felt as if there was an invisible hand inside her twisting her gut.

'One of them tried to stop the Germans and was shot himself. The other was taken prisoner.'

'Which one?'

Pierre shrugged. 'There is no way of knowing because once they had shot them all they set fire to their bodies as a lesson to anyone else who might wish to help the Allies. The bodies were unrecognisable.'

Holly sat down heavily on the end of James's bed, feeling as if all the air had been knocked out of her, her world collapsing before her very eyes.

Was it Harry or Richard who had been taken prisoner? And even if it was Richard who they had taken, could he survive in one of their terrible POW camps? There was evidence right here of how the prisoners were treated.

441

'You are all right, yes?' Pierre gently laid his hand on her arm and she nodded woodenly.

'The fear is now that the Germans may make a search of all the houses in the village,' he continued gravely. 'And so it is imperative that we get these men moved as soon as possible. When do you think they will be strong enough?'

Holly pulled herself together with an enormous effort. 'Possibly the day after tomorrow for James if he continues as he is but this one . . .' She looked at Ben and shrugged.

Pierre nodded. 'Very well, I will go now.'

She watched him climb the ladder before giving way to the tears that had been threatening. Great wracking sobs that never seemed to end. Richard might be dead or languishing in some filthy prison somewhere. And I never told him how I really felt about him, she thought. But I mustn't think about it, Holly scolded herself. And so she got on with her work as best she could although her heart was breaking.

James offered her what little comfort he could and wondered if perhaps one of the doctors had been her lover, but he didn't ask, and Holly didn't enlighten him.

Holly managed to snatch a few hours' sleep that evening from sheer exhaustion but the moment she woke a cold hand clamped itself around her heart as she glanced towards Ben. He had died during the night. She checked his pulse and then gently covered him with a sheet before climbing the stairs and, after listening closely to make sure that the Le'Fetes were alone, she tapped on the trapdoor. It was Francine who opened it. Claudette was standing at the stove stirring a large pan of porridge and Holly quickly told her what had happened.

Claudette crossed herself, then told her daughter. 'Run and fetch your father. We must get his body away from here as soon as possible, God rest his soul.'

She gently ushered Holly back down into the cellar and hastily closed the trapdoor. Sometime later it opened again and Pierre appeared with a neighbour. They silently descended the stairs and wrapped Ben in the sheet he was covered with before carrying him away.

'I let him down,' Holly sobbed when they were gone, as all the heartbreak of losing Richard and then her patient caught up with her. James managed to haul himself out of bed and shakily make his way over to her and she saw that he would be a very nice-looking young man if he wasn't so skeletal.

'Don't you dare say that.' He put his arm about her and tenderly stroked the tears from her cheeks. 'I'd have gone the same way if it wasn't for you. You've worked yourself into the ground for both me and Ben but sadly he had gone too far. No one could have saved him even if we could have got him to the hospital.'

They sat like that for some time, each drawing comfort from the other until suddenly the trapdoor flew open again and Pierre appeared, all of a fluster. 'Come, we must leave straight away,' he urged. 'I have the wagon outside and there is no time to lose. The Germans are searching all the houses in the village and they will be here within the hour. I cannot risk you staying.'

'But James is still very weak . . .'

'I shall be fine if you'll just help me up the stairs,' he told her bravely as he reached for his shirt. And it was then that Pierre dropped his next bombshell.

'I shall take James to the hospital. I know which route the Germans are taking so I can avoid them, all being well. But you must walk there with Francine. No one will think anything of two young girls strolling whereas if they find you in my wagon with James you will be killed, as we surely will be.'

'But I—'

He held up his hand. 'There is no time to argue. Help me to get him upstairs.'

Between them they somehow managed it, although James's legs kept buckling beneath him which slowed them somewhat. Once up in the kitchen Francine slammed the trapdoor behind them and dragged the table into position as Claudette kept guard at the door.

'It is all clear,' she told her husband with a catch in her voice and as he passed her she kissed him tenderly and told him, 'May God go with you, my love!'

They managed to get James into the back of the wagon then Pierre covered him with sacks of vegetables and set off without delay.

Meanwhile, Claudette handed a wicker basket to Holly and told her urgently, 'Follow Francine and if you are stopped speak only in French. Remember, you are Francine's cousin come to visit us.'

On an impulse, Holly threw her arms about the woman and kissed her soundly as Claudette returned her hug. She had come to think a lot of all of them and Claudette had been like a second mother to her during her stay there.

'But what if they find the entrance to the trap door?' Holly fretted. 'They will only have to see the beds and they will know that yo—'

'Go!' Claudette ordered and on legs that suddenly felt as if they had turned to jelly Holly did as she was told.

'We shall go through the woods,' Francine told her. 'It is slightly further but there is less chance of being seen that way, but if we are stopped we must say that we are visiting family.'

Holly nodded numbly as she followed her blindly into a large wood. The branches and brambles snagged at their clothes and when at one stage a small deer suddenly ran out straight in front of them Holly felt as if her heart had stopped. But Francine seemed to know where she was going so she followed her trustingly. Luckily Francine had played in these woods all her life and knew every inch of them so they made good progress, although Holly suddenly realised after an hour's tramping across rough ground that she was physically and emotionally exhausted. Her chest was on fire and her legs ached but she kept going – there was no other choice. Eventually the sound of gunshots and explosions echoed around the barren trees and she knew they were getting closer to the front.

'We shall leave the woods shortly,' Francine told her. 'And then it is but a short distance to the hospital. I will tell you the way but do not worry, you are back on safe ground now.'

'But couldn't you stay here till it's safe for you to go home?' Holly implored.

Francine stopped to drop a light kiss on her cheek as a lane appeared beyond the trees.

'My place is with my family,' she answered and for a moment the two girls stared at each other not knowing if they would ever see each other again.

'I . . . I hope everything goes well for you. You are all very brave,' Holly told her in a choked voice.

Francine shook her head. 'No, it is you and your people who defend our country that are brave,' she told her. 'But now you must go. Walk straight down the lane and you will come to the door at the back of the sister's office. Goodbye, my friend.'

She turned and skipped through the trees as nimbly as a fox and within seconds she was gone as Holly ventured out of the trees and set off down the lane with her heart thudding painfully. Eventually she came to the door that Francine had told her about and tapped on it tentatively. She must make sure that the sister was alone before she entered. It wouldn't do to be seen in the clothes she was wearing.

Sister Flynn herself answered her knock and dragged her inside. 'Oh my dear girl, thank goodness you are safe,' she said. 'Monsieur Le'Fete left a short time ago after delivering the patient and he told me what has happened. Those poor, poor people. But sit down, you're shaking.' She crossed to a filing cabinet and to Holly's amazement produced a bottle of brandy. 'Here, get that down you, it's good for shock,' she ordered after sloshing a large measure into a mug on her desk.

Holly sipped at it, almost choking as the fiery liquid burned its way down her throat but almost instantly she began to feel warm and the trembling eased a little.

When she had finished every last drop as Sister insisted, she hurriedly changed into her own clothes again and the sister told her, 'All of the nurses from your tent are on duty so by the time you get to see them you can say you returned today after extended leave. Meantime go and get some rest.'

Holly nodded and walked away with her head in a whirl. So much had happened in such a very short time that she could hardly get her head around it. Worst of all, though, was the terrible guilt she felt that by wishing so desperately for Richard to be alive, it meant that Harry was dead. Two good men, both of whom had loved her, and neither of whom deserved to die in such a terrible way. And if it was Harry who had been taken prisoner and they were to meet again, how could she ever face him knowing she had, in a round-about way, wished he was dead? Yet as she lay sleepless in bed, it was Richard she prayed for, even though they could never be together.

Chapter Forty-Nine

The following morning, as Holly returned to her duties, heavy-eyed after a sleepless night, Sister Flynn called her into her office. She looked care-worn and exhausted, and with a terrible dread forming in the pit of her stomach, Holly braced herself for news of Richard's death. But it wasn't Richard she wanted to talk about. With tears in her eyes, Sister told her that the Le'Fete family had been shot for harbouring the enemy.

'What? All of them?' Holly gasped

'Yes, I'm afraid so. They entered the farmhouse while Pierre and Francine were bringing you and the patient back here and it seems they discovered the trapdoor into the cellar. They took Pierre's wife out and shot her in cold blood then waited for him and his daughter to get home and shot them too. And they were such good people.'

'Yes they were,' Holly said in a choked voice as pictures of their faces flashed in front of her eyes. Francine would never get to marry the love of her life now or bear his children. A whole family was gone in the blink of an eye and she couldn't forget how dangerously close she had come to being with them when the trapdoor was discovered. If it hadn't been for Pierre insisting they leave, she would have been there too.

'And is there any news of which doctor was killed yet?' she asked. 'Surely they could identify him from his dog tag?'

'Neither doctor was wearing one. It seemed too dangerous while they were working behind enemy lines.'

Holly lowered her eyes. This uncertainty was unbearable, and despite the guilt she harboured about Harry, her thoughts were only of Richard in that moment as she remembered the days when they had thought they would spend their whole lives together.

Somehow she managed to get through the rest of the morning although her face was haggard and she felt quite ill. She was violently sick shortly after lunch and realised with dismay that she must have caught James's sickness bug as she made a dash to get to the rather primitive toilet block.

Sister immediately had her put into a small isolation bay. The last thing they needed was for this infection to sweep through the patients. Most of them were so weak they would never have survived it. One of the doctors who had been shipped in to replace Harry and Richard came in to see Holly shortly after and once he'd examined her he told the sister, 'Her temperature is sky-high and as well as having the sickness bug she is very tight-chested. It could turn to pneumonia if we aren't careful. I think the wisest thing would be to have her shipped back to England as soon as possible. Infections like this can spread like wildfire and we don't want an epidemic on our hands.'

Holly felt as if she had a steel band tightening in her chest and felt so ill and wretched that she listened with only half an ear. She was grieving for Richard, Harry and the Le'Fetes, and didn't much care what they did with her. Suddenly everything was just too much.

Her condition deteriorated over the next two days and

Angela, wearing a face mask and gloves, was allocated to nurse her. 'Come on, please,' she implored Holly as she tried to tempt her to eat. 'You've got to at least try. This is so not like you!'

But Holly just turned her face away, she didn't care any more. A telegram was sent off to her mother who insisted that once she arrived back on British soil she should be returned home and after some consideration the doctor and the sister decided that this might be for the best. She would be shipped back then transported by ambulance to her home when they reached England.

'Bloody hell, gel, I'm really going to miss you,' Angela said tearfully on the morning Holly was due to leave.

Holly gave her a weak smile. 'I'll . . . miss you too.'

But then the stretcher-bearers were there and she was whipped into the back of a waiting ambulance. She vaguely wondered if she would ever see Angela again. She hoped so. Sister Flynn came to say goodbye too, but her eyelids were drooping. She was tired all the time now and before the ambulance had even left the hospital she was sleeping.

'Ah, so you're back in the land of the living again, are you?' a soft voice she recognised said as her eyes wearily blinked open. The light hurt and was so bright that she promptly closed them again.

'I-is that you, Mother?'

'Yes, my darling, it's me. You're at home although you've given us all quite a scare.'

'Home?' Holly was confused. The last thing she vaguely

450

remembered was saying goodbye to Angela and Sister Flynn but after that everything was a blank. 'But how?'

'You've been home for almost a week.' Her mother's voice was gentle and filled with relief. 'And for a time there we thought we were going to lose you. You developed pneumonia and it was touch-and-go.'

Holly was confused. How could she have lost all that time? And then the pain of what had happened back in France stabbed at her afresh and there were tears in her eyes again.

'Oh sweetheart, don't cry.' Emma wiped her forehead tenderly with a tepid cloth. 'With every day that passes you'll start to feel better now.'

As a thought occurred to Holly she asked, 'But what are you doing here? You live at Walter's house now.'

'Yes, I do and I will again when I know you're completely better.' Emma was smoothing the sheets across her, secretly terrified at the amount of weight Holly had lost. 'You didn't really think I would trust anyone else to nurse you, did you?'

'B-but Walter . . .'

'He perfectly understands that I would want to be here with you. In fact, he's been in to see you every single day since you've been home and he's been almost as worried about you as I have.'

Her words reinforced what Holly had thought for some time. Walter was a truly kind and gentle man.

'I . . . I think I want to sleep again now . . .' Holly said drowsily and her mother was only too happy to let her. Sleep was a great healer and now that Holly's fever had broken she would hopefully start to recover.

Over the next two weeks Holly slowly grew stronger,

physically at least, but mentally she was crippled and her eyes looked haunted. Sleep became something she dreaded, for while she was asleep the nightmares came. Terrible nightmares from which she would wake in a tangle of damp sheets with her heart thudding painfully. Sometimes in the dreams she would see Francine and her family being led outside and shot and at other times she would see a German bending down to set light to Richard's body. And then there were the bodies of all the young men she had prepared for the morgue.

'There's something troubling you. Why don't you share it with me?' Ivy pleaded one day. 'You know what they say, a trouble shared is a trouble halved.'

And so finally, after concealing such dark secrets for so long, Holly broke down and told Ivy everything. About discovering that Richard was in fact her brother and of the missions she had gone on behind enemy lines.

'I knew you were sweet on that young doctor,' Ivy said when she had finished. 'How awful it must have been for you to find out he was yer brother. An' as for the French family . . . ' she shuddered as she thought of their fate. 'But my Lord, you were brave.'

'Not really,' Holly said dully. 'I've always thought it isn't the ones that come home that are the heroes. It's the ones who lay down their life fighting for what they believe in.'

'Like my Marcus you mean?' Tears welled in Ivy's eyes but she could also smile as she thought of the happy memories they had made together. 'I still miss him every single day, yer know. An' yet now I realise I'd rather have had the short time we had together than a whole lifetime wi' someone else. It were different for you, o' course. You had to end it an' I understand that but what are the chances o' that happenin', eh? They must be one in a million. Still, a lovely lookin' girl like you is bound to meet someone else someday.'

'I won't.' Holly shook her head. 'I thought for a time that Harry and I might have a future together but as soon as I saw Richard again in France I knew it could never work. My heart will always belong to him. I wish I hadn't finished with him as I did now, though. I think he hated me after that.'

'I'm sure that's not true,' Ivy said kindly. 'But come on now and eat some o' this 'ere soup Cook has made you. She'll be chewin' me ear off again if I take it down untouched an' I'll be in trouble wi' yer mam an' all.'

Content that Holly was now definitely showing signs of recovery, Emma had returned to her husband leaving Ivy in charge of her precious girl with strict instructions that she should contact her immediately if there was anything at all she was concerned about.

Holly sighed and forced a few spoonfuls down and, satisfied that she had at least made an effort, Ivy carried the tray back down to the kitchen leaving Holly sitting in the chair by the window staring vacantly at the grey, overcast sky.

Although she had only gone home the day before, Emma was back mid-afternoon to check on her.

'Walter was saying at lunchtime that they're going to turn Weddington Hall into a hospital for injured servicemen,' she told her daughter. 'And I was thinking that if you insist on going back to work when you're well enough you could perhaps consider working there? At least I wouldn't be fretting about you all the time if I knew you were a little closer. What do you think?'

453

Holly shrugged. She didn't want to think about anything at the moment. It was as if she was trapped inside a little bubble of relentless pain.

And then suddenly, quite out of the blue two weeks later, something happened that gave them all heart again. Emma came bounding in one morning with a smile that lit up the room, waving a telegram.

'Ivy! Where's Ivy? I must speak to her straight away.'

Holly and her grandfather, who was reading the newspaper to her, frowned. 'She was in the kitchen feeding Alice the last time I saw her,' Gilbert told her but before Emma could leave the room Ivy appeared in the doorway with Alice perched on her hip.

'Did I hear my name?'

'Oh my darling, darling girl. The most wonderful, wonderful thing has happened.' Emma was so excited that she could barely get her words out. 'This telegram came this morning. Marcus is alive! He's in a military hospital in Plymouth.'

Ivy stood staring at her, her face impassive, wondering if this was some sort of cruel joke. But then it slowly dawned on her that Emma would never be like that and her face slowly crumpled as tears of joy fell from her eyes. 'Are you quite sure? There can't have been a mistake can there?'

Emma shook her head. 'There's no mistake, I promise you. Apparently he was injured in battle but managed to drag himself to the side of the field where a French family found him and gave him shelter until he could be safely moved to a field hospital. Unfortunately his eye had become very infected by then and the doctors had no option but to remove it and then he was kept there until he was well enough to be shipped home. Walter has already spoken to the matron at the hospital in Plymouth but . . . well, I have to tell you . . . Marcus has suffered a breakdown as well as being blind in one eye.'

'But he's alive!' Ivy cried joyously as she swung Alice into the air. 'When can we go and see him?' she asked next. The fact that he might never be the man she had seen march off to war again didn't seem to bother her at all. He was alive and that was all that mattered and to her it was a miracle.

'Walter thought we might catch the train there this weekend. We could stay in a hotel overnight. That's if Cook and Father think they can look after Holly for us?'

'I don't need looking after, I'm quite capable of looking after myself,' Holly told them flatly.

'Hmm, well just in case Cook and I are here to keep an eye on her,' Gilbert added, grinning broadly. It was lovely to have some good news after all the bad things that had happened.

'Perhaps things are looking up,' he said cheerily and they all nodded, praying he was right.

Chapter Fifty

Walter and Ivy arrived at the military hospital on the outskirts of Plymouth early in the afternoon the following Saturday. Emma had decided to stay behind with the girls at her father's house to care for Holly, for although she was now on the mend Emma was still concerned about her. And the girls would love helping to look after little Alice too.

Ivy had been abnormally quiet throughout the train journey and Walter guessed that she was worrying about how they would find Marcus. He had been through a great deal and they were both painfully aware that many of the young men who were lucky enough to come home from the war were never the same again because of the terrible sights they had seen.

The hospital was actually a large private house set in its own grounds which had been taken over for the duration of the war and the reception area was quite luxurious. Walter approached the desk where a young nurse sat while Ivy stood back, nervously chewing on her lip. She had bought a new dress and bonnet especially for the occasion and now her stomach was in knots.

'I've come to see my son, I believe we are expected,' Walter told the nurse. 'His name is Marcus Dolby.'

She opened a register and smiled. 'Ah yes, here he is. The patients have just had lunch. Would you like me to tell him you are here or would you rather surprise him? He'll probably be in the day room.'

'I think I'll just go in to him,' Walter answered. He and Ivy had already agreed that he should go in first for a few minutes.

The nurse nodded, then beckoned to another nurse who was passing. 'Would you take this gentleman to see Corporal Dolby please?'

'Of course.'

Walter turned to Ivy and after giving her a reassuring smile he advised, 'You wait here, my dear. I promise not to be too long and then you can go in, and perhaps when you've had some time with him I could join you?' He fully intended to spend every minute possible with his son although he appreciated that Walter and Ivy would want a few minutes alone.

He walked away as the nurse at the desk asked Ivy, 'Would you like to sit down over there and perhaps you'd like a cup of tea? I'm sure you've come a long way.'

'Th-thank you that would be nice.' Ivy perched on the edge of a little chair with fancy gilt legs and as she looked about she could hardly believe that this was actually a hospital. There was nothing clinical about the place. In fact it looked like a small stately home. The floor was parquet, highly polished and gleaming softly in the weak sun that shone through the stained-glass windows on the impressive double front doors, and there were beautiful mirrors and paintings hanging on the wall. But even they couldn't hold her attention for long, her thoughts were firmly on Marcus. Would he still want her and be the same young man she had

457

waved off to fight for his king and country? She would know soon enough but the waiting was almost unbearable.

Walter, meanwhile, followed the nurse along the enormous hallway until they came to a door where she paused.

'I just ought to warn you that many of the patients are traumatised,' she told him gently. 'Their physical injuries tend to heal far more quickly than their mental injuries so don't expect too much too soon.'

He removed his hat and after nodding at her began to turn the brim in his hands. She opened the door and he stepped into what had once clearly been a very stately drawing room. There were large sash windows adorned with thick, velvet curtains that overlooked sweeping lawns and he imagined that the grounds would be quite beautiful in the summer. There were sofas and easy chairs set all about the room and as his eyes swept over the men sitting in them they finally found the one he was looking for.

One side of Marcus's face was heavily bandaged and he had lost a frightening amount of weight so his clothes hung loosely off him but Walter would have known that shock of dark hair anywhere. Marcus was sitting in a wing chair by the window and Walter approached him before saying quietly, 'Hello, son.'

Marcus's head swung round and suddenly he was crying as he held his arms out to his father. There had been times over the last months when he had thought he would never see him again but here he was.

Walter knelt down and embraced him as tears ran down his cheeks then he drew a chair close and they joined hands. It was like holding the hands of a skeleton, he could feel every bone, but that was nothing that couldn't be cured with some good, home-cooked meals once they got him home. He was alive and that was all that mattered.

'Did they tell you I'd lost an eye?'

Walter nodded solemnly. 'Yes, they did, but you can live with that, son. And I ought to tell you, Ivy is waiting outside.'

Marcus's breath caught in his throat as he looked away before saying falteringly, 'B-but I don't want her to see me like this. I'm not the same any more. She won't want a man who is half blind!'

'Actually you're very wrong there,' Walter told him firmly. 'It almost killed that girl when you were missing and I happen to know she would still want you if you had no eyesight at all, or arms or legs for that matter, so we'll have no more of that silly talk, if you please. She's come all this way to see you. Doesn't that tell you something?'

'Really?' Marcus had dreaded this moment and had convinced himself that Ivy wouldn't love him any more but if what his father was saying was true then there was hope for him yet.

'Look, I'm going to go outside now and send her in and perhaps when you've had a little time to yourselves I can come back in again, all right?'

Marcus took a deep breath and nodded. This was the moment he had been dreading. The fear that Ivy couldn't deal with the fact that he had lost an eye. But now at least he would know where he stood with her one way or another.

Minutes later he heard the door to the day room open again and he held his breath. But he needn't have worried.

'Marcus!' She spotted him instantly and was across the

459

room like a shot, eager to hold him and kiss him. 'I never thought I was going to see you again,' she sobbed, oblivious to the other patients who would certainly be able to hear her. 'I lost the will to live back there for a time when I thought you were dead and it was only knowing that Alice needed me that kept me going.'

'Oh, sweetheart, I love you so much,' Marcus croaked. 'It was only the thought of coming home to you that kept me going! . . . But you do know that I've lost the sight in one eye . . .'

'Huh! So what, you have another one, don't you?' she replied in her usual forthright way and then they were in each other's arms again and it felt wonderful. 'Right, young man,' she said bossily when they finally drew apart. 'Here's what's going to happen and I don't want any arguing about it! As soon as you come home we're going to be married. You won't be going back to fight again so when you're better you can help your father wi' the business. There's no point in waitin', so what do yer say?'

He grinned. 'Sounds to me like you've got it all planned,' he answered and when his father joined them again a short time later Walter saw a totally different young man to the one he had first seen when he entered the room. It was as if young Ivy had breathed new life into him as they excitedly told him about their wedding plans and he couldn't have been happier for them both.

'Well, you certainly have my approval,' he assured them. 'And I've no doubt Emma and Holly will love helping with the arrangements for the wedding. Katie and Florence will be excited too. In fact, I dare say they'll demand to be bridesmaids.'

'That's all right.' Ivy was hanging on to Marcus's hand as if she would never let it go. 'I reckon we'll make it an early summer wedding. Oh, did I mention that I'd like to be married at Chilvers Coton Church? I'll go and see the Reverend Lockett and set a date as soon as I get home. That will give us a bit of time to get some meat back on your bones,' she told Marcus with a twinkle in her eye. 'I don't want to be marryin' someone's who's lighter than me. There ain't an ounce of fat on yer at the minute but we'll soon remedy that.'

'You make me sound like a pig that needs fattening up,' Marcus laughed.

She smiled lovingly at him. 'Not a pig, but my own dear man. I think I'll have white roses in my bouquet,' she continued with her plans thoughtfully, her head already organising everything. 'Oh, an' of course I'll want a satin dress wi' a train an' a veil. An' I'll have Holly as me matron of honour, she'll like that.'

The next couple of hours passed in the same light-hearted manner and by the time Walter and Ivy left to go to the hotel he had booked them into for the night they were all relaxed and happy.

'Just to think a short time ago I thought I'd never see him again,' Ivy said dreamily. 'An' they say miracles can't happen! Well, one has for me.'

Walter smiled at her indulgently. He had a feeling that his beloved only son and this lovely down-to-earth girl were going to be very happy indeed.

Chapter Fifty-One

Marcus was discharged from the hospital early in May and his homecoming was a joyous one, although he still jumped at any loud noise. The matron at the hospital had assured Walter that this was to be expected after the trauma he had suffered but hoped in time that he would make a full recovery. He was also still very self-conscious of his empty eye socket and had taken to wearing a black eyepatch but Ivy assured him that she quite liked it.

'It makes yer look like a pirate,' she teased him and from then on his sisters nicknamed him Long John Marcus.

Holly was also much improved health-wise, although she was still suffering from dreadful nightmares and her heart still ached like a physical pain every time she thought of Richard. Luckily, having the wedding to organise had helped tremendously, although as yet she'd made no plans to go back to work.

'I might consider going to work at one of the military hospitals on the coast after the wedding,' she told her mother when she asked what her plans were, and Emma was relieved. She didn't think her nerves could bear up under the strain had Holly decided to go back to France. At least this way she would only be a train ride away.

Sadly the war was still raging on and in April the Germans had unleashed a terrible new weapon: poisonous gas, which caused blindness and internal blisters that could result in death. It had been a terrible blow to the British soldiers but they were still battling on with no end in sight.

Even so, nothing could spoil the build-up to the wedding and finally the big day arrived.

On the first Saturday in July, while Marcus got ready at his father's house, all the women congregated in Holly's bedroom, which was slightly larger than Ivy's, to help the bride into her wedding dress. Holly, Katie and Florence were already wearing their bridesmaids' dresses – pretty concoctions in a lovely sea-blue satin that brushed the floor as they walked – and Emma assured them that they all looked beautiful, but now it was the bride's turn.

Ivy had chosen quite a plain style in a heavy ivory satin with a sweetheart neckline, long sleeves, and tiny pearl buttons running from the waist to the neckline at the back. It tucked in tight to the waist then dropped into an A-line skirt that stretched into a train. Below it she wore real silk stockings, a little gift from Emma, and Holly lent her the treasured locket that Richard had bought her as her something borrowed. Once the dress was on they fixed her veil in place and fastened a crown of roses that matched the ones in her bouquet above it and finally, after slipping her feet into dainty silk slippers, she was ready.

'Oh my dear, you look truly beautiful,' Emma breathed as she handed her the bouquet. And she did; her face was glowing with happiness and she couldn't stop smiling.

'Do you think Marcus will think so?' she asked as she peered at herself critically in the mirror. She felt like a princess.

'Marcus would think you looked beautiful if you turned

up in a sack,' Emma laughed. 'But now, come along, girls. The carriage is waiting outside for us and my father is waiting downstairs for you, miss.' She scooped Alice up into her arms. She was wearing a tiny version of the bridesmaids' dresses but they had all thought that she was a little young to be a bridesmaid so it had been decided that she would sit with Emma in the church.

Holly's grandfather had offered to give her away and as she descended the stairs he had a tear in his eye.

'You look absolutely beautiful,' he told her, and she blushed as Emma and the bridesmaids hurried out to get into the first waiting carriage. It wouldn't do at all if they were to arrive after the bride.

'It's very kind of you to do this for me,' Ivy told Gilbert, linking her hand through his arm. It had hurt her deeply when her own parents had refused to even come to the wedding but she supposed she should be used to their rejection by now. And then Mr Mason had saved the day.

'Believe me, the pleasure is all mine,' he told her with a chuckle as he squeezed her hand. 'You're like one of the family now, Ivy. But come along, we can't stand here chatting, we have a wedding to go to!'

They arrived at Chilvers Coton Church in brilliant sunshine. Ivy's heart was pounding with nerves by then but the instant she saw Marcus waiting for her at the end of the aisle, looking ridiculously handsome in his new suit, her nerves fled and there may as well have been no one else present, for they had eyes only for each other. The service was beautiful and as the couple stood at the altar solemnly taking their vows the sun shone down on them through the stained-glass windows as if the good Lord himself were sending his approval. Once it was over they stepped outside to a peal of bells and into a shower of rice and rose petals. The reception was held at Holly's home and even though certain food was becoming hard to obtain now, it was a feast fit for a king.

There were pies and pastries, pickles, salad, a whole leg of pork, a side of beef and ham and bread fresh from the oven, as well as a selection of cakes and trifles. Katie and Alice tucked in the second they arrived and ate as if they hadn't been fed for a month as everyone looked on indulgently. It was a special day after all.

In the evening the chairs and sofas were cleared to the side of the room and Gilbert, who was a surprisingly good pianist, played popular tunes as everyone danced. The cake was duly cut, the speeches were given and the guests drank a champagne toast – a gift from Gilbert – to the happy newly-weds.

'I never in my wildest dreams thought that I could ever be this happy,' Ivy sighed as Holly helped her out of her wedding dress and into her smart new going-away outfit early that evening. 'But I'm going to miss you when you go back to work.'

Holly had decided some weeks before that once the wedding was over she would return to work in a military hospital. She had been offered a post in the same hospital Marcus had been in, as it happened, and she was looking forward to it.

'But you'll still see me every time I come home if you and Marcus are going to be living here till after the war,' she pointed out.

'I know, but I've sort of got used to seeing you every day, like I did when we lived in London. That seems a lifetime ago now, don't it?'

'Yes it does, but at least one of us got to have a happy ending and I couldn't be more pleased for you.' Holly fastened the pin into Ivy's hat. 'There, you look wonderful, Mrs Dolby.'

Ivy giggled. 'Ooh, Mrs Dolby! It sounds grand, don't it? People will be gettin' me an' yer mam mixed up wi' us both havin' the same name.' She lifted Holly's locket from the dressing table and handed it back to her. She knew how much it meant to her and felt honoured that Holly had let her wear it. 'But what about you? When are you goin' to find someone to make you happy?'

Holly shook her head. 'I already found him but it wasn't meant to be and I have no intention of settling for second best. I almost fell into that trap with Harry. I know now it would have been a disaster. But hark at us rattling on. The cab is waiting downstairs to take you to the station and if you don't get a move on you'll miss your train.'

Ivy instantly flew into a panic. 'Oh dear, are you sure you're going to be all right lookin' after Alice? You know she likes—' She wished now that she had agreed to take Alice with them on their short honeymoon to Southend. Marcus had been quite happy for her to come but she had thought they deserved a few days just to themselves. Now she wasn't so sure.

'I know exactly what she likes and doesn't like.' Holly grinned. 'We've been through her whole daily routine at least a dozen times. Now, downstairs with you!'

The family stood on the steps and waved goodbye until the happy couple had disappeared from view.

'I think those two are going to be very happy together,' Emma said contentedly as she leaned back into her husband's chest.

He nodded in agreement. 'I think you're right, almost as happy as us.' He grinned.

Emma blushed as she glanced towards Holly and her father. 'Er . . . as it happens we've got a bit of good news to share with you too. At least we hope you'll think it's good news! We didn't want to take the shine off Ivy and Marcus's day so we thought we'd wait to tell you after they'd left but . . .' She glanced at Walter for reassurance and when he smiled and nodded she rushed on, 'The thing is . . . and I know this is mad because I'm not going to see forty again but . . . well me and Walter have just found out that we're going to have a baby.'

'A baby!' Holly and her grandfather looked shocked then overjoyed.

'Why, how wonderful, when is it due?' Holly screeched excitedly.

'We think it might be a Christmas baby,' Emma told her and somehow the news was the perfect end to a perfect day.

Chapter Fifty-Two

December 1918

'There will be another group of eight patients arriving later this afternoon, Nurse Farthing,' the matron informed Holly.

Holly nodded. 'Yes, Matron, more prisoners of war?'

'I'm afraid so, there should have been eleven of them this time but the captain of the hospital ship has sent word to inform me that three of the poor souls did not survive the journey.'

'Very well, I shall see that their beds are ready for them,' Holly answered efficiently.

The last few years had been busy ones for Holly and she was now a fully qualified nurse and the matron's right hand. It had been extremely hard work fitting in her training and working at the hospital as well but somehow she had managed it, although she'd had to sacrifice a lot of visits home, because any spare time she'd had had been spent studying. But it was done now and she felt that it had all been worth it, although she hadn't decided as yet what she would do when this military hospital was no longer needed and was handed back to its rightful owners. She had toyed with the idea of getting a place in a hospital nearer to home so she could spend more time with her adorable little brother Alfred, or Alfie as he was affectionately known, and with

Ivy's latest addition to the family, a little girl called Lucy. Only months before she had stood as godmother to Lucy in the church where Ivy and Marcus had been married and it had been yet another wonderful day. More good news had come soon after, when the war had finally come to an end. Now the patients they were receiving were mainly prisoners of war who had been rescued from the camps and the terrible condition most of them were in when they arrived was testament to what they had suffered at the hands of the Germans. They were generally lice-ridden and so emaciated and weak that they couldn't even stand. Others were suffering from the effects of poisonous gas, which meant that all the nursing staff could do was make them as comfortable as possible until their inevitable end. Once they had breathed the gas and the lungs had been affected there was little that could be done for them.

They had already dealt with most of the injured from the field hospitals, although a few still found their way to them, but suddenly they were nowhere near as busy as they had been and there were even empty beds dotted here and there. As soon as Matron had gone Holly and a Red Cross nurse began to prepare the rooms and the beds for the next patients and by early afternoon everything was ready for them.

They arrived at teatime and Holly was waiting in the entrance foyer to meet them and tick their names off her list.

They were stretchered in one at a time by the ambulance men and as they gave her the patient's name Holly wrote it down and directed the nurses to which beds they were to have. She would then go and make a report sheet that would hang on the end of each bed for the doctor to look at when he did his round each morning.

The first stretcher appeared.

'Lawson, nurse.'

Holly nodded and swiftly wrote the name down and then the other stretchers began to appear in a line.

Lee, Billingham, Eliot, Lewis, Millward, Parkin . . .

Holly gulped as she felt the colour drain from her face. Parkin! But no, it couldn't be . . . She quickly crossed to the men holding the man called Parkin's stretcher and stared down at him. At first she wasn't at all sure. This poor, wasted human being looked nothing like the handsome doctor she remembered but then just for a second his eyes fluttered open and the clipboard she was holding clattered to the floor. It was him! It was Richard!

'Nurse Farthing . . . are you all right?' Matron had just come from her office and hurried over to her, stooping to retrieve the clipboard.

'I . . . I'm sorry, Matron. It's just that . . . I know this man!'

'I suggest you get yourself off to the staff room and get a nice hot cup of sweet tea,' Matron ordered. It wasn't at all like Nurse Farthing to behave so unprofessionally. 'I can finish up here and direct them to the right rooms.'

'Th-thank you, Matron.' Holly's voice was no more than a squeak as she wheeled about and made her unsteady way to the nurses' room. Thankfully it was empty, and Holly poured herself a cup of tea, but her hand was shaking so badly that she sloshed some over the pristine white table-cloth which would no doubt get her in trouble with the housekeeper. She forgot all about it then as she dropped onto a chair and tried to get her thoughts into some sort of order. Richard was here – he was alive! She had believed him dead for so long that it was hard to take in. But then hard common sense kicked in. What difference could it make to her? They could never be more than friends knowing what she knew so in a way he was still as dead to her as he had been before.

Matron joined Holly after she had seen the men safely into their beds and left the junior nurses washing them, and helping herself to a cup of tea, she asked, 'Is Parkin a relative?'

'No, he's a doctor I used to work with at a field hospital in France.' She daren't tell the woman that she had once believed he was the man she wanted to spend the rest of her of life with until she had discovered that he was actually her brother!

'Oh that's a relief.' The matron smiled as she sipped at her tea. 'It would have been quite difficult for you had he been someone you were close to.'

Holly managed a weak smile as she rose from her seat. It was part of her job to oversee the junior nurses and she didn't want to appear lacking in her duty.

'I'm sorry, it was just a bit of a shock seeing him, because we believed that he had been killed,' she explained.

'I quite understand, nurse. And oh, seeing as he is a doctor you could perhaps make sure that he has a private room. I do like to show respect to the doctors and officers.'

'Yes, Matron.' Holly slipped away with her emotions playing havoc. She was shocked, elated and sad at seeing him all at the same time because it only brought home to her how futile it was to grow too close to him again.

As it happened Richard had already been placed in a private room. She peeped through the door to see a young junior nurse just finishing giving him his wash and waited until she had gone before slipping into the room. As she looked down at his frail form pity flooded through her. He seemed to be half the size he used to be and his lovely hair had been hacked close to his head, no doubt to try and prevent it being infested with lice. His skin was sallow and without even realising she was doing it her hand rose to finger the ring he had given her, still lying close to her heart. She had never taken it off and even though she knew it was useless she still indulged herself from time to time by placing it on her finger and imagining how things might have been.

She crept in to see him again before going off duty but he was still asleep so she tiptoed away again, leaving him in the capable care of the night staff.

She slept very little that night in the nurses' quarters, painfully aware of how close to her he was and she went in early for duty the next morning without even bothering with breakfast.

The doctor had been to examine the new intake of patients the night before and as Holly slipped into Richard's room and quickly read his report she was relieved to see that apart from being severely emaciated and lacking in vitamins there didn't appear to be anything else seriously wrong with him. They had hooked him up to a drip during the night to get some fluids into him and already she thought his skin didn't look quite as yellow as it had the night before. But then she knew that this could well be wishful thinking.

She tried to concentrate on the other patients for the rest of the day. Many of the nurses were off duty that evening as the next day would be New Year's Eve and they were going out to celebrate. Holly had spent Christmas with her family and so had thought it only fair to let the nurses who had worked over Christmas have their turn. Now she was glad that she had.

Late in the afternoon she called into his room to check on him again.

'H-Holly . . . is that you?'

She started and almost dropped his notes which she had unhooked from the end of the bed.

'Yes . . . it's me.' The lump in her throat was threatening to choke her as she moved to the side of his bed and gently took his hand.

'It . . . must have been a bit . . . of a shock to see me.'

She nodded. 'Yes, it was.'

'I'm sorry that it . . . wasn't Harry.'

She frowned. 'What do you mean?'

His head moved restlessly on the pillow. 'The Germans. They burned him and took me prisoner and somehow I survived the camp until our chaps came to set us free. But you must have been heartbroken about Harry.'

'Richard, I think you have this all wrong,' she told him gently. 'There was nothing between Harry and me. Admittedly he wanted there to be and I'm sorry he's dead, but we were just friends.'

'Really?' He looked confused. 'B-but he led me to believe that you and he were . . . that you left me for him.'

'That isn't true,' Holly said staunchly as she felt herself

473

slipping under his spell again. 'I left you because . . . let's just say, I had my reasons. I care about you very much but I don't want to get married . . . to anyone, ever! And anyway you didn't waste much time when we split up. You forget I saw you not long after when I went to London to visit Miss May, walking with a very pretty young woman who was hanging on your every word!'

She was immediately ashamed of lapsing into jealousy and he looked confused but she stood firm. It would be unfair of her for her to give him false hope.

'I'm going to get one of the nurses to fetch you some food while you're awake,' she told him, professional again. 'And does your mother know you're here? I could let her know if you like?'

'How do you know where my mother lives?'

Holly realised that she had made a mistake and grew flustered. 'What I should have said is, you can give me her address and I'll let her know for you.'

'Oh, I see. Well, you don't need to bother. Matron has already done it and my mother is coming to see me tomorrow.'

'Good.' She plastered a smile on her face and hurried away. It was going to be really hard being so close to Richard but she owed it to him to help him get well, and she would.

Chapter Fifty-Three

By midday on New Year's Eve many of the nurses had left to spend time with their families and they were all in high spirits. This was the first New Year celebration since the end of the war and they were all looking forward to it.

Earlier in the morning, Holly had phoned home and spoken to her family, and in the hospital the atmosphere was light. They were expecting a lot of visitors that day as the families of the patients who were not well enough to go home would be coming to see them, so the nurses on duty knew they were going to be busy.

At lunchtime, those that were able to ate in the dining room. The cook had made a special dinner, which was enjoyed by all. When it was over the patients piled into the day room and the visitors started to arrive.

The nurses ran to and fro serving tea and coffee and home-made cakes and biscuits to those that wanted them while the men flirted shamelessly with them and did their best to pinch an early New Year's kiss. No one minded. It was nice to see the patients looking so happy. With the threat of being returned to the front no longer hanging over them, they could relax and enjoy the thought of going home soon.

Richard was looking much better, Holly noted, when she checked on him shortly after lunch. He was even managing to sit up in bed now. After living on a starvation diet in the prisoner-of-war camp for so long he was being fed little and often and it was clearly doing the trick.

'So I suppose you'll be off to a party tonight,' he said as Holly took his temperature. She was relieved to see that it was almost back to normal now and noted it on his chart.

'I should be so lucky,' she quipped with a grin. 'All the nurses on duty will be doing a double shift until the others come back in the morning.'

'That's tough.' She could feel him watching her as she straightened the bedclothes and she felt colour creep into her cheeks, she couldn't help being drawn to him, no matter how hopeless their situation was. There was a tap on the door and a young nurse stuck her head into the room. 'There are two visitors here for you, Dr Parkin. Shall I send them in?'

'Yes, please.'

Holly made for the door to give him some privacy and she was almost there when Richard's mother arrived with an ecstatic smile on her face and holding a large bag full of treats.

'Oh, sweetheart, it's so wonderful to see you. There were times when I never thought I would!' Her eyes settled briefly on Holly and she frowned. She was sure she had seen her somewhere before, but where?

Holly moved on as a second visitor appeared behind her and now it was Holly's turn to be confused. It was Melissa, the young woman she had seen Richard strolling with on the day she had visited Miss May in London. She was so pretty that Holly would have recognised her anywhere. Once out of the room she shook her head. Why should she be surprised

476

to see her there? she asked herself. She was his young lady so obviously she would want to come and visit him. A stab of jealousy shot through her as she pictured them together and she tried to push the image from her mind. It wouldn't do to give in to her feelings today of all days when she and the rest of the staff were so busy.

Because it was a special day the visitors were invited to stay for tea that evening so they could spend a little extra time with their loved ones and the cook had laid on a lovely buffet in the dining room. The whole place rang with laughter as everyone waited to see in the New Year. Although she did her best to keep a smile on her face, Holly felt miserable, but even so, she chatted to the patients and visitors as if she didn't have a care in the world.

She was in the dining room when Richard's mother appeared and spotting Holly she hurried across to her. Richard's young lady was clearly having a few minutes alone with him as there was no sign of her.

'I've been trying to think where I'd seen you before all afternoon,' she said with a smile. 'And it just came to me. You're the young lady that came to see me about my second husband who committed bigamy with your mother.'

Holly's mouth dropped open. What did the woman mean . . . her second husband?

Seeing her confusion, Belle Garratt gently took her arm and led her to two empty window seats. 'I was trying to explain to you when you called but you shot off before I could finish what I was saying.'

'I . . . I don't understand,' Holly answered falteringly.

'Neither did I at the time but then everything clicked into

477

place when Richard kept raving on about the girl he was seeing. Her name was Holly and he was well and truly smitten with her. It was you, wasn't it?'

Holly nodded numbly.

'I thought so. Then shortly after your visit Richard informed me that you had ended your relationship and I put two and two together, although I didn't tell him anything about it. The trouble was I had no way of contacting you and it was awful to see him so heartbroken. You went away thinking that you and Richard had the same father, didn't you?'

Another nod from Holly and the woman sighed, 'What I didn't have time to tell you was that I was married for a very short, precious time before my first husband was killed in an accident on the docks. He was Richard's father, not my second husband who ran off with your mother! That's why Richard's surname is Parkin, that was his father's name, and a more wonderful man you could never have met. Richard was just a small baby at the time and I was still grieving for him when I met my second husband and as your mother will no doubt tell you, he had the gift of the gab and swept me off my feet.'

Holly felt as if the floor was rushing up to meet her. If what Mrs Garrett was telling her was true then she and Richard were not related in any way!

And then she thought of the pretty girl who was even at that moment in his room with him and she shrugged help-lessly. 'If only I'd known that before he met someone else,' she said brokenly and Belle Garrett's eyebrows disappeared up into her hairline.

'Whatever do you mean? Someone else?'

'The girl who came with you. She's very pretty and I can see why Richard loves her,' she said miserably. 'I saw them walking arm in arm in London once.'

Mrs Garrett threw back her head and laughed aloud. 'You mean Melissa? Yes, she is very pretty,' she agreed. 'And yes, Richard does love her very much. She's his sister you see! They've always been close.'

'His sister!' Holly's heart was racing nineteen to the dozen as she thought what a mess she had made of things. All this time she had kept him at arm's length when they could have been together.

Belle Garrett reached out to gently squeeze her arm. 'At least now you know,' she said softly. 'So if you'll excuse me I'm going to load a plate with food and see if I can tempt that son of mine to eat something. He isn't as far through as a line prop, although he tells me you're taking excellent care of him.'

She smiled kindly and headed for the buffet leaving Holly feeling as if the bottom had dropped out of her world once again. All that heartache for nothing and now it was too late because she could never bring herself to try and explain to him. He would never forgive her for what she had put him through and she didn't blame him.

'Nurse Farthing.'

Matron's voice interrupted her thoughts and she looked up to see the woman standing beside her.

'I'd like you to go and grab a few hours rest now seeing as you're doing night duty again. Report back at eleven o'clock.'

'Yes, Matron.' Holly dragged herself out of the chair and back to the nurses' quarters where she slumped onto the bed. She saw at a glance that a letter from Angela had arrived for her. She recognised her handwriting. She was probably going to tell her again all about the handsome young doctor she had married shortly after the war ended and about their lovely new home in America. She was glad Angela had found happiness and normally Holly would have read the letter there and then, but this evening she was too steeped in her own misery to even bother opening it for now.

The minutes ticked slowly by but there was no rest for Holly and by the time she reported back for duty her eyes were red-rimmed from crying. The hospital was quiet, save for a few patients who had elected to stay in the day room and see the New Year in together. Matron had allowed them to have a few bottles of beer and spirits were high, and after checking that all was well with them Holly began her round of the patients confined to bed. It was almost midnight when Matron asked her to check on Dr Parkin and reluctantly she did as she was told. She had expected to find him fast asleep but he was propped up on pillows watching the door avidly.

'Ah, here you are at last,' he greeted her. 'I was beginning to think I was going to have to sit up all night waiting for you.'

'Oh? Why would you do that?' Holly was mildly surprised as she reached for the notes on the end of his bed, studiously avoiding his eyes.

He gave an exasperated sigh as he patted the bed at the side of him. 'Will you please come and sit down for a minute. I need to speak to you.'

480

Reluctantly she moved to the side of the bed and perched on the edge of the mattress like a little bird ready to take flight.

'So what could you want to talk to me about?'

'My mother has told me everything!'

'What!' She stared at him wide-eyed and he nodded.

'Yes, I know everything. You thought I was your brother, didn't you? And that's why you ended our engagement.'

There seemed no point in lying now that he knew about the misunderstanding so she nodded miserably and was shocked when he started to chuckle.

'I hardly find it something to laugh about,' she responded indignantly.

'No, it isn't, not really,' he admitted and when he gently took her small hand in his two large ones she suddenly felt as if her arm was alight.

'So, before I say any more there is one question I have to ask you.'

She peered at him suspiciously.

'Do you still love me, Holly?'

A denial hovered on her lips but eventually she slowly nodded. There was nothing to be gained by lying now.

'Yes, I do . . . I never stopped,' she answered in a small voice.

'In that case, I suggest as soon as I'm well enough we go out and buy you another ring and we'll start all over again because I never stopped loving you either.'

She stared at him incredulously, hardly daring to believe what he was saying. And then he was pulling her towards him and as his lips pressed tenderly on hers she suddenly

481

felt whole again. When they finally broke apart she was laughing as she told him, 'You won't have to buy me a ring though.'

'Oh, why is that?'

Reaching inside the top of her dress she slowly unclipped the chain holding the locket and the ring he had once given her and placed them in his hand.

'I've never taken them off,' she admitted softly as tears started to her eyes.

Sliding the ring from the chain he took her hand and said, 'In that case, Nurse Holly Farthing, I shall ask you again, will you do me the very great honour of becoming my wife?'

'Yes,' she squeaked as he slid the ring onto her finger and this time she knew it would never come off again, or at least only for long enough to place a wedding band beside it. And then they were in each other's arms and totally oblivious to everything as Matron peeped her head around the door and smiled broadly. She was so glad that Mrs Garrett had had a word with her on her way out of the hospital.

The grandfather clock in the hall chimed midnight and while a cheer echoed from the day room, Matron gently closed the door on the newly engaged couple and told the young nurse beside her, 'See that Dr Parkin isn't disturbed for the rest of the night, nurse.'

As she walked away she had the warmest feeling that she had just witnessed the start of something beautiful; a love that would last a lifetime. She thought what a wonderful start to the New Year it had been. Yes indeed, in fact, she doubted there would ever be another to match it!

Epilogue

'Well, I have to say that was some wedding,' Ivy declared as she sat sipping tea one cold and frosty February evening in Holly's kitchen.

Holly nodded as she lifted the teapot and topped up Ivy's cup, but not before Ivy had spotted the tears in her dear friend's eyes. Charlotte, Holly's daughter, had been married the Saturday before in Chilvers Coton Parish Church and as she had drifted down the aisle on her father's arm in a froth of satin and lace, she had looked almost as stunning as her own mother had on her wedding day. She and her husband, James, were now in Weymouth for two weeks for their honeymoon and then they would be living in Nottingham close to James's practice. They had met at veterinary college three years before and had been inseparable ever since and although Holly felt that she couldn't have chosen anyone better for her daughter, now that she was gone, the house suddenly felt empty and time weighed heavily on her.

Gilbert, or Gil as he was affectionately known, Holly's son, had left home the year before to live in London with his wife, Betty. He had followed in his father's footsteps and studied medicine and was now working as a junior doctor at Guy's Hospital.

Sensing her friend's sadness, Ivy reached over to gently pat Holly's hand.

'It makes you wonder where the time goes, don't it?' She smiled sadly. 'It don't seem like two minutes since you an' me set off fer London, green as grass. An' look at all we've been through since, eh? Not that it's all been bad, mind. But it's hard to believe that we've lived through two world wars.'

Holly nodded in agreement. Ivy was right, time seemed to have passed them by in the blink of an eye. It felt like a lifetime ago since she had left home for the first time but she and Ivy were still as close as ever and not a day went by when Holly didn't thank God for their friendship. Ivy had been her rock over the years, as was Richard, who she still adored as much as she had on the day she married him back in 1919. But he worked such long hours at the hospital that now both of her chicks had flown the nest she didn't quite know what to do with herself.

She had counted herself very lucky back then that they had both survived the First World War but during the second war they hadn't fared so well. It had cost the life of their middle child, George, who had been killed at Dunkirk and Holly had never quite got over it. It was still hard to believe that of the four children they had been blessed with only two remained. They had also lost their youngest daughter, Mary, to whooping cough when she was just three years old. Holly's grandfather, Gilbert, had passed away in the same year, and for a time Holly had been weighed down with grief. It had been Ivy who had pleaded and bullied her out of the pit of despair she had sunk into.

'You've still got Charlotte and Gil to think of,' she had

scolded her. 'Pull yourself together, woman. Do yer think yer the only one that's lost someone? I've lost my Paul an' all, yer know?'

Sadly Ivy's son had also been one of the war's casualties but somehow she had managed to stay strong, although his death had left a gaping hole in her heart that no one could ever fill. Even so her optimistic nature had pulled her through, and supporting each other through their losses had brought her and Holly even closer together. 'We still have a lot to be thankful for,' she had pointed out and gradually Holly had come out of her depression and started to live again.

At Charlotte's wedding, Ivy's two daughters, Alice and Lucy had been bridesmaids and Ivy smiled now as she thought back to the special day.

'That weddin' cake were a triumph,' she declared. 'What wi' rationin' still in place I don't know how yer managed to get a three-tier one. An' the dresses . . . Eeh, they were just beautiful. Charlotte looked like a princess. I don't mind tellin' yer she gave me a fair old gliff when I first saw her come into the church wi' your Richard. She's the double o' you at that age.'

Holly grinned at the compliment. 'That's very kind of you but I don't think I was ever as pretty as Charlotte.'

'Oh, but you were, just ask your Richard.' Ivy took another sip of the hot tea as her mind drifted back over the years to when she had gone to be a maid in Holly's grandfather's house. He had been a grumpy old devil back then, but the years had mellowed him and by the time he died he and Holly had been as close as could be and she had taken his death very badly. Thankfully she did still have her mother and Walter, and even though they were now well into their seventies they were still both enjoying good health. She smiled again as she thought of how proud they had been at the wedding.

Her thoughts were interrupted when Holly suddenly told her, 'I've been thinking of going back to work again.'

Ivy spluttered, sending tea spraying all across Holly's snow-white tablecloth.

'You've been thinkin' o' what?' Ivy's eyes were almost popping out of her head as she hastily dabbed ineffectively at the stains with a handkerchief. 'But, pet, yer fifty-three years old now!' she pointed out. 'I think nursin' would 'ave come a long way since you last did it.'

What she said was true, though no one would have guessed it looking at Holly. She was still a very attractive woman and wore her age well. There were streaks of grey in her hair and fine lines were beginning to appear on her face but her skin was still clear and she carried herself upright.

Holly sniffed. 'I dare say it has but there must be something I can do! I don't want to just sit about doing nothing. I'm not entirely useless and Richard works such long hours I shall go mad if I don't do something.' She still lived in the house that had belonged to her grandfather but, as she had pointed out to Richard, now the children were gone it was going to be far too big for them. The old cook who had served the family so loyally for many years had passed away some time ago and so for the last few years Holly had run the house herself. Keen to please her Richard had suggested they could possibly sell it and move to a slightly smaller place but somehow she couldn't bear to leave it.

'I'm sure you'll think of something, then,' Ivy said encouragingly, before gathering up her things and leaving. She and Marcus now lived in a smart house not far away from Holly's so although Ivy still helped out with their millinery business, the two women were able to still see each other regularly.

When she had gone Holly wandered upstairs and into Charlotte's room. It seemed so empty now that all her things were gone and after a cursory glance around to ensure that it was tidy, Holly went downstairs to prepare the vegetables for the evening meal to give herself something to do. She had lived such a full life, first as a nurse and then as a mother and now suddenly she was wondering if the best part of it was over.

That evening as she was waiting for Richard to come home the phone rang and her heart sank as she ran to answer it. It would probably be Richard saying that they had had an emergency brought in to the hospital and that he was going to be working late again, but when she lifted the receiver she was pleasantly surprised to hear her son's voice.

'Hello, Gil, darling.' She hadn't expected to hear from him so soon after the wedding. He and Betty had only left to go back to London two days before.

'Hello, Mum.'

In her eye she could picture him, tall and handsome and the double of his father.

'So is everything all right?' she asked.

'Everything is very all right, as it happens.' She heard him chuckle. 'Actually I'm ringing to tell you some good news. At least we hope you'll think it's good news. We didn't want to tell you at the weekend because we wanted that to be

487

Charlotte's time but the thing is . . . You're going to be a grandma. Betty is having a baby.'

Holly's breath caught in her throat as tears of joy sprang to her eyes. 'A baby!' she gasped in delight. 'Why, that's just wonderful. When?'

'It should be about the end of July,' he told her and she could hear the joy in his voice. 'And if it's a girl we're going to call her Mary. If it's a boy it will be George for . . . Well, you know.'

Tears were openly spilling down her cheeks now. 'Oh, I can't wait to tell your father, he'll be so thrilled,' she gushed excitedly. 'I shall have to start knitting straight away. I shall set Ivy on it too. She's so much better at it than me.' They chatted for another few minutes then and just as she put the phone down Richard walked in and she rushed to tell him.

'How marvellous,' he exclaimed as he hung his hat and coat up and pulled her to him for a kiss. 'But no one will ever believe that you're old enough to be a grandma.'

'Oh, get off with you,' she laughed as she playfully pushed him away and headed for the kitchen to put the kettle on.

He followed her, happy to see her smiling again. He knew how much she was missing Charlotte and how frustrated she was becoming at not having enough to do but now he hoped that he had found the perfect solution for that too.

'So,' he said, smiling at her teasingly, 'I can have a nice long lie-in with my wife tomorrow.'

She turned from the sink, the kettle still in her hand, to raise a questioning eyebrow. 'What do you mean?'

'As of today I am no longer a surgeon. I have done my last shift at the hospital.'

'What? But I thought you said you were far too young to think of retiring when we spoke about it.'

'I didn't say I'd retired, did I?' He grinned as he took the kettle from her hand and led her to the table. 'I've just decided to take another direction that will hopefully involve you and me working together, and I suspect keep you rather busy. The thing is, you see, I thought about what you said about this house being far too big for us now but you not wanting to leave it, so I thought why not put it to good use? And so in two weeks' time builders will be moving in to make the drawing room into a surgery for me. The hallway will become the waiting room. You will become my receptionist and my nurse and I will become the town's new GP. The old one is retiring and we've been planning this between us for weeks.'

The look of pure delight on her face made all the effort of planning this worth every minute. 'And the final surprise is' – he fished in his pocket and withdrew some travel brochures – 'that while all this work is being done you and I are going off on a long, very well-deserved holiday starting next week in London, just the two of us. You can spend some time with Gil and our little mother-to-be and then we're finally going to go on the honeymoon we never got around to having. Better late than never, I suppose. So how does that sound, Mrs Parkin?'

'It sounds absolutely wonderful, Dr Parkin,' she breathed as she nestled against him, her eyes shining. 'But how did you manage to arrange all this on your own without me finding out?'

'Well, I did have a little help from Ivy,' he admitted. 'She'd told me that you'd been feeling rather at a loose end and I thought it was time I did something about it. I know it's not been easy for you with me working all the hours God sends but we'll be spending a lot more time together now our children have gone. Are you happy?'

The kiss she planted on his lips was his answer.

'I'm very happy,' she breathed and suddenly the future that lay ahead of them was shining bright again . . .

Acknowledgements

Once again, many thanks to my lovely team at Bonnier for yet another success in our Days of the Week collection. I am so lucky to have such a wonderful team behind me and feel blessed. Thanks to my editor Sarah, Katie, Kate, Nico and all of you there who work so tirelessly to help me make my books the best they can be. Not forgetting of course my lovely agent Sheila Crowley and my brilliant copyeditor Gillian Holmes and proofreader Jane Howard. And of course thanks to my long suffering husband, who supplies me with support and endless tea breaks, and my wonderful family. I couldn't do it without all your love and support.

Thank you all xxxxx

· MEMORY LANE ·

*Welcome to the world
of Rosie Goodwin!*

Keep reading for more from Rosie Goodwin, to discover
a recipe that features in this novel and to read an
exclusive extract from Rosie Goodwin's next book . . .

We'd also like to introduce you to MEMORY LANE,
our special community for the very best of saga
writing from authors you know and love, and new
ones we simply can't wait for you to meet.
Read on and join our club!

· MEMORY LANE ·

www.MemoryLane.club

Dear friends,

I can hardly believe that Christmas is already a distant memory! Time just seems to whizz past, but I hope you all enjoyed it. It was hectic here as always but in the nicest possible way, with friends and family all spending time together just as it should be.

In this book, number six of my Days of the Week collection, *A Precious Gift*, we meet Holly Farthing and her loyal maid Ivy. Poor girls, I do put them through the wringer as usual but I do hope you all liked it! In this one, we meet the suffragettes and find ourselves in France – but I can't tell you any more because I don't want to spoil it for you if you've skipped ahead.

As you may know, my previous book, *A Maiden's Voyage*, which came out last year, made it into the *Sunday Times* bestsellers and stayed there for some weeks, thanks to you all. Your reviews are always so lovely and I look forward to and enjoy hearing what you all think of my efforts! Each one makes all the time I spend locked away with my characters in my study so worthwhile, so please keep them coming.

And now, here we are fast approaching Mother's Day again and the release of the final Days of the Week book, *Time to Say Goodbye*. Because the series started with Sunday Small in *Mothering Sunday*, I felt that the series should end with her too, and in this one I was able to reintroduce some of the characters from other books in the series too. I laughed and cried whilst writing it and I hope you'll all love it. I certainly enjoyed writing it and have to admit I shed a tear when I wrote 'the end'. It's been such a lovely series to write and I've really grown to love the characters I invented.

My publishers have already come up with some wonderful ideas for competitions to mark the end of the Days of the Week collection, so do join the Memory Lane community for the chance to win some lovely prizes. Just head to the Memory Lane Club on Facebook. On there you'll get to learn all about what myself and all the other lovely Bonnier saga authors are up to.

Finally (for now!) I'm delighted to tell you that I have agreed another contract with my lovely publishers and I'm already working on a brand-new series for them, which we are all very excited about! The first will be out later this year (title to follow!). I can't wait for you all to read it.

And now I suppose I should get back to work, but not before I wish you all a lovely spring and summer, enjoying the sunshine (if we are lucky enough to get any!). Thank you all so much for your continued support. I'll be in touch again very soon and please keep your messages coming.

Much love,
Rosie xxxx

Rhubarb Crumble

Rhubarb crumble is one of the first things Holly cooks for Richard. It is delicious served with cream, ice cream or custard.

You will need:

For the fruit:
16oz rhubarb, chopped into 1–2in chunks
4oz caster sugar
½ tsp of vanilla extract

For the crumble:
6oz self-raising flour
3½oz unsalted butter
2½oz muscovado sugar

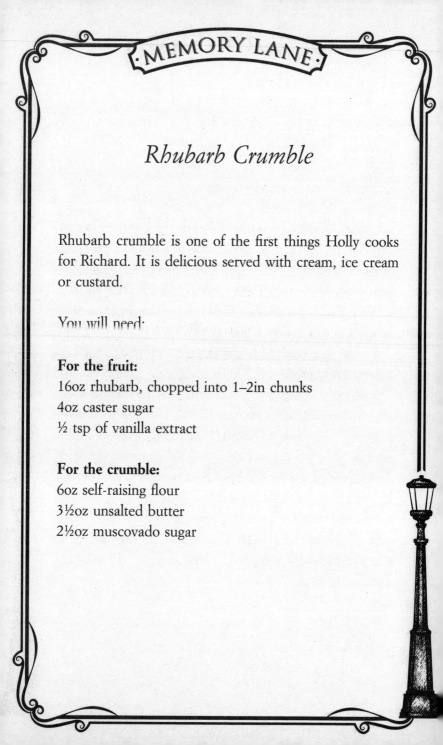

Method:

1. Place the rhubarb, sugar and vanilla extract in a saucepan. Cover and simmer on a low heat for 15–20 minutes.

2. When soft and bubbly, pour the rhubarb into a baking dish.

3. Pre-heat the oven to 200°C/180°C fan/gas 6.

4. Mix the self-raising flour and muscovado sugar together in a mixing bowl, then rub in the butter with your fingers, until the mixture is soft and crumbly.

5. Pour the crumble evenly over the rhubarb and bake for 30–40 minutes, until the top is golden brown.

6. Enjoy!

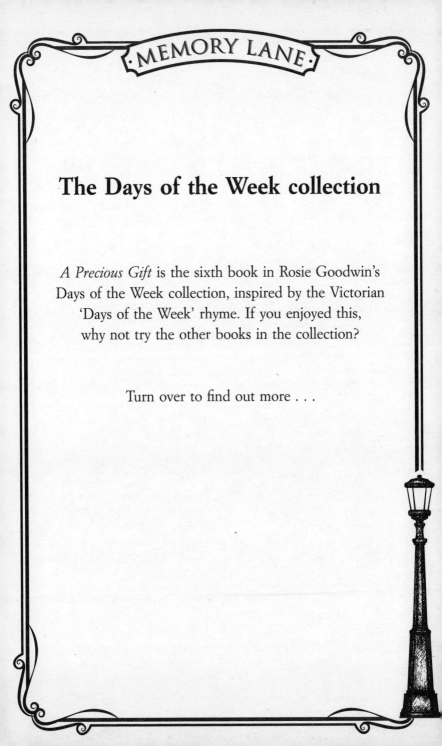

·MEMORY LANE·

The Days of the Week collection

A Precious Gift is the sixth book in Rosie Goodwin's
Days of the Week collection, inspired by the Victorian
'Days of the Week' rhyme. If you enjoyed this,
why not try the other books in the collection?

Turn over to find out more . . .

Mothering Sunday

The child born on the Sabbath Day,
Is bonny and blithe, and good and gay.

1884, Nuneaton.

Fourteen-year-old Sunday has grown up in the cruelty of the Nuneaton workhouse. When she finally strikes out on her own, she is determined to return for those she left behind, and to find the long-lost mother who gave her away. But she's about to discover that the brutal world of the workhouse will not let her go without a fight.

The Little Angel

Monday's child is fair of face.

1896, Nuneaton.

Left on the doorstep of Treetops Children's Home, young Kitty captures the heart of her guardian, Sunday Branning, and grows into a beguiling and favoured young girl – until she is summoned to live with her birth mother. In London, nothing is what it seems, and her old home begins to feel very far away. If Kitty is to have any chance of happiness, this little angel must protect herself from devils in disguise . . . and before it's too late.

A Mother's Grace

Tuesday's child is full of grace.

1910, Nuneaton.

When her father's threatening behaviour grows worse, pious young Grace Kettle escapes her home to train to be a nun. But when she meets the dashing and devout Father Luke, her world is turned upside down. She is driven to make a scandalous choice – one she may well spend the rest of her days seeking forgiveness for.

The Blessed Child

Wednesday's child is full of woe.

1864, Nuneaton.

After Nessie Carson's mother is brutally murdered and her father abandons them, Nessie knows she will do anything to keep her family safe. As her fragile young brother's health deteriorates and she attracts the attention of her lecherous landlord, soon Nessie finds herself in the darkest of times. But there is light and the promise of happiness if only she is brave enough to fight for it.

A Maiden's Voyage

Thursday's child has far to go.

1912, London.

Eighteen-year-old maid Flora Butler has her life turned upside-down when her mistress's father dies in a tragic accident. Her mistress is forced to move to New York to live with her aunt until she comes of age, and begs Flora to go with her. Flora has never left the country before, and now faces a difficult decision – give up her position, or leave her family behind. Soon, Flora and her mistress head for Southampton to board the RMS Titanic.

**And the final book in the collection,
following on from *A Precious Gift* . . .**

Time to Say Goodbye

Saturday's child works hard for their living.

1935, Nuneaton.

Kathy has grown up at Treetops home for children, where Sunday and Tom Branning have always cared for her as one of their own. Surrounded by her beloved horses, and with a future as a nurse ahead of her, she could wish for nothing more. But when Tom dies suddenly in a riding accident, life at Treetops will never be the same again. As their financial difficulties mount, will Kathy and Sunday be forced to leave their home?

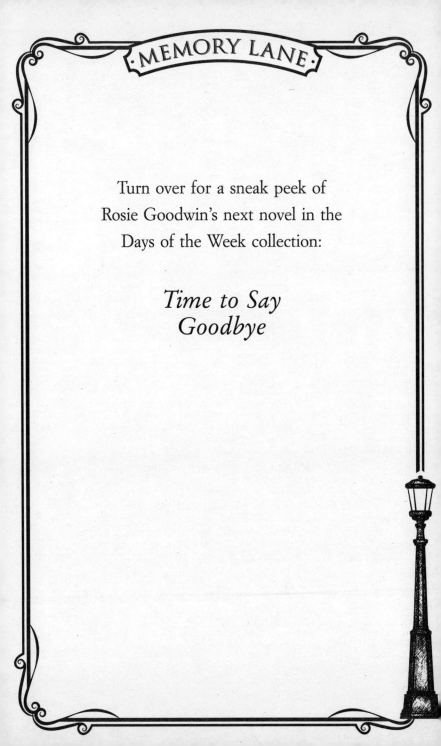

·MEMORY LANE·

Turn over for a sneak peek of
Rosie Goodwin's next novel in the
Days of the Week collection:

*Time to Say
Goodbye*

Prologue

November 1930

Sunday Branning smiled as she stood at the window of Treetops and watched her daughter Lavinia – or Livvy, as she was affectionately known – gallop down the drive on her horse. Livvy adored horses and riding, just like her father, who had once again built up a reputation for being the finest stud breeder in the Midlands. It had taken years to rebuild his stables after the Great War, but somehow, he had managed it, and once again people were coming from far and wide for his horses. Sunday could well remember how heartbroken Tom had been when she had written to tell him that his stock had been taken for war horses, after he had left to fight in the Great War. He had raised many of them from foals and knew that it was unlikely any of them would survive. It was to his credit that through sheer hard work he had got his business up and running profitably again once he had returned.

It was just as well, for following the stock market crash the year before, money was tight for most people and businesses were closing daily. Treetops was an expensive house to run and, now they no longer ran it as a children's home, Sunday was constantly trying to find little ways of saving money.

Once Livvy had disappeared from sight, Sunday returned to her desk, where she had been writing out invitations for her sixtieth birthday party, which she'd be holding in two weeks' time.

Sixty! She sighed as she thought back over her life. It hadn't started so well – she had been left on the steps of the Union Workhouse as a newborn – but things had improved when she had finally been reunited with her birth mother. And then there was Tom, the love of her life. She still adored him as much as she had the day she had married him, if not more. As if thoughts of him had conjured him from thin air, he suddenly stuck his head round the door and gave her a cheeky wink.

'All right, sweetheart? Hope you're not working too hard?'

Sunday laughed as she waved him away. 'Oh, be off with you and let me get this done.'

He grinned and blew her a kiss, and once he was gone, she tried to concentrate on the job in hand again. It was hard to believe she was this old, but then she supposed age caught up with everyone in the end and Tom had always assured her she didn't look it. Glancing towards the mirror, she stroked her fair hair as if to convince herself that he was speaking the truth. It was streaked with grey at the temples now, but her eyes were still a clear, bright blue, and apart from a few lines around them and her mouth, her face was still attractive. Livvy took after her in looks, with her fair colouring, whereas Tom's son, Ben, was dark, and as he had matured had become the double of his father. And then there was their adored Kathy, who at nearly twelve was the double of her mother, Kitty. Sunday and Tom had brought Kitty up from a baby and had loved her as their own, until she left them at sixteen to join her birth mother in London. Once there, Kitty had become the darling of the music halls – but her pretty face and vulnerable nature had made her a target for an unscrupulous man. When she had finally returned to Treetops, she was heartbroken and hiding a secret. She tragically died giving birth to an illegitimate daughter, and it had come as no surprise to anyone when Sunday and Tom had adopted her baby too.

Smiling, Sunday turned her attention back to the invitations – but she had barely started to write again when the door burst open and Cissie Jenkins, her long-term friend, burst unceremoniously into the room, all of aflutter.

'You'd best come straight away, pet,' Cissie gasped, holding her hand to the stitch in her side. 'My George says Tom has had a fall in the paddock. I've sent Ben off for Dr Lewis.'

Whereas time had been kind to Sunday, Cissie looked her age and had grown portly with the years. Their friendship had started when they were both children incarcerated in the Union Workhouse, and had withstood the test of time until now they were more like sisters than friends, and Sunday loved her unconditionally.

The colour drained from Sunday's cheeks, and she stood

up so abruptly that she almost overturned the chair. 'A fall
. . . ? Is it bad?'

Cissie shook her head. 'I've no idea – you'd best come
and see.'

Side by side, the two women rushed through the house
and, once they had emerged into the stableyard, they
turned as one and began to race towards the group at the
back of the stables, where Tom trained the horses.

'Was it Storm he fell from?' Sunday asked breathlessly,
and when Cissie nodded she bit her lip. Hadn't she told
him that she didn't think Storm was ready to be ridden
yet? He was a beautiful young stallion and admittedly
from brilliant stock, but had proved very difficult to
train.

They rounded the corner to see Storm tossing his head,
snorting and pawing the ground at the other side of the
paddock, whilst George leaned over Tom, who was lying
motionless on the ground.

Sunday was glad of the new calf-length skirts that were
fashionable now as she sped towards them.

'Don't try and move him,' George warned, as she
dropped to her knees beside them.

She showed no sign of hearing him as she focused her
attention on her husband and gently lifted his hand.

'Oh Tom, *why* didn't you wait for another couple of
weeks before you tried to ride him?' she whispered.

'He's out cold,' George said unnecessarily. 'Best not
touch him 'til the doctor gets here in case he's broken
anythin'. We might make things worse.' Then, turning to

his wife, he said, 'Run an' fetch a blanket to cover him, would yer, love?'

Cissie set off straight away; the late autumn air was cold. Luckily the cottage she and George lived in was close by and she was back, huffing and puffing, in minutes. George had barely had time to cover Tom with the blanket when they heard the sound of horses' hooves, followed by that of an engine and Ben and the doctor arrived back at the same time.

As Ben leapt nimbly from his horse, the young doctor climbed out of his car and hurried towards them, clutching a large black leather bag.

Dr Lewis was a nice young man, fresh out of medical school, who had recently taken over the practice when Sunday's family doctor retired.

'Is he conscious?' he asked, as he too fell to his knees beside Tom.

Sunday shook her head fearfully, still holding tight to her husband's hand. 'N-no, he isn't.'

The doctor nodded as he hastily took a stethoscope from his bag. 'Could you all stand back please and give me some space?'

His face was grim as he bent to listen to Tom's heart, then very gently he lifted Tom's head. It lolled to one side and Sunday's heart began to pound so loudly she was sure they would hear it.

The doctor sat back on his heels for a moment, then shook his head as he looked at Sunday and told her gravely, 'I'm so sorry, Mrs Branning. I'm afraid he's gone. It looks like he broke his neck in the fall; death would have been instantaneous. He wouldn't have felt anything.'

'*No-ooo!*'

Sunday's head wagged from side to side in denial and Cissie started to cry. George and Ben stood so still they might have been turned to stone.

'B-but he *can't* be dead . . .' Sunday began to shake Tom's hand and Cissie leaned down and gently drew her to her feet.

'Come away, pet,' she muttered through her tears. 'There's no more you can do here. The men will do what needs to be done.'

Sunday suddenly and uncharacteristically lashed out, almost sending Cissie flying. 'So, what *do* I do then?' she cried, in an anguished voice. 'Just leave him lying there?' Then, turning to George and Ben, she ordered in a voice quite unlike hers, 'Get a door from the stables and carry him inside. I refuse to leave him lying out here!'

The men instantly went to do her bidding, and as Sunday turned and staggered back towards the house. At that minute, Livvy appeared on her horse at the end of the drive and she drew her mount to a halt, just as Cissie and her mother were about to go in by the front door.

'What's wrong with you two?' she asked, as she stared at Cissie's tear-stained face.

'Let Cissie take your horse round to the stables and come into the drawing room,' Sunday said. 'I need to tell you something,'

With a deep frown, Livvy dismounted and did as she was told.

'What's happened, Mum?' she asked only a few moments later, as they entered the drawing room. She knew it was something bad. One look at her mother's lint-white face and shaking hands told her that.

'I . . . it's your father . . .' Sunday gulped deep in her throat and forced herself to go on. 'I . . . I'm afraid he had a fall from Storm and he's . . .' She found that she couldn't say the terrible word. But she had said enough and Livvy's pretty face crumpled.

'Y-you mean he's *dead*?'

When Sunday slowly nodded, Livvy broke into sobs and dropped onto the nearest chair as her mother rushed over and gathered her into her arms. Sunday was in deep shock and, somehow, she couldn't take it in. Just a few minutes ago all had been right with her world but now she knew it would never be the same again.

The day of the funeral dawned dark and dismal. Going in search of Sunday, Cissie found her standing by the window in the drawing room, staring out across the lawns. Approaching her quietly, she laid her arm gently across her shoulders. Sunday smiled – a sad smile that didn't reach her eyes. 'I was just picturing Tom and me down there on the lawn on the evening of our wedding day, dancing in the moonlight,' she said huskily. As yet, she hadn't shed a single tear since the terrible day Tom had died, but Cissie knew her well enough to know that when they did finally come, they would be hard to stop.

'It were a grand day, all right,' Cissie said, in a wobbly voice. 'I can still see you both now with all the lanterns that were strung in the trees and the moon shinin' down on you. You looked like a fairy princess in your beautiful gown and Tom looked like the happiest man on earth. It's a precious memory that no one can ever take away from you; you must hang on to that.'

And then they saw the black hearse approaching down the drive, coming to collect Tom, who had been lying in the day room in his coffin. She said sadly, 'Come on, pet, it's almost time to go.'

Without a word, Sunday turned and followed her from the room.

It was with relief some hours later that Cissie escorted the last of the mourners to the front door, leaving only the solicitor who had stayed to read Tom's will to the family.

Sunday was waiting for him in the drawing room along with Ben, Livvy and Kathy.

Cissie turned towards Mr Dixon and, without a word, led him into the room then left, closing the door quietly behind her.

'Before I begin, may I offer my condolences to you all?' Mr Dixon said quietly, as he rummaged in his briefcase and produced Tom's will. 'Mr Branning was a true gentleman and I know he will be sorely missed by all that knew him. I have never seen so many people attend a funeral before. But now, down to business.' He cleared his throat and began. 'This is the last will and testament of Thomas Branning. It is all very straightforward, short and to the point, but should you have any questions, please feel free to interrupt me.'

Ben leaned forward in his seat.

'To Cissie and George Jenkins, my long-term friends, I leave the cottage in the grounds in which they have resided for many years, with my thanks for their friendship, loyalty and support. To my only son, Ben, I leave my gold Hunter pocket watch. To my two beautiful daughters I leave all my love always. Treetops, the business, and all the rest of my worldly goods I leave to my beloved wife, Sunday Branning.'

Ben looked shocked as he leaned even further forward in his chair. 'But surely there's some mistake,' he said, as colour rose in his cheeks. 'Isn't it customary for the eldest son to inherit?'

Mr Dixon shook his head. 'In years gone by it would have been,' he answered. 'But times are changing, and it is quite usual now for the first person in a marriage to pass away to leave what they own to their spouse.'

Ben's lips set in a grim line and, without a word, he rose and marched from the room. No one seemed to notice. Livvy and Kathy were too busy crying, and Sunday seemed trapped in a world of her own.

Tales from Memory Lane

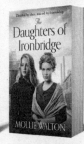

Discover new stories from the best saga authors

Available now

·MEMORY LANE·

Introducing a new place for
story lovers – somewhere to share
memories, photographs, recipes and
reminiscences, and discover the very
best of saga writing from authors you
know and love, and new ones we
simply can't wait for you to meet.

·MEMORY LANE·

A new address for story lovers
www.MemoryLane.club